THE GLASS
QUEEN

GENA SHOWALTER

THE GLASS QUEEN

ISBN-13: 978-1-335-08028-8

The Glass Queen

This edition published by arrangement with Harlequin Books S.A.

For questions and comments about the quality of this book, please contact us at
CustomerService@Harlequin.com.

Inkyard Press
22 Adelaide St. West, 40th Floor
Toronto, Ontario M5H 4E3, Canada
www.InkyardPress.com

Printed in U.S.A.

To my cats, Lulu, Cookie, and the late, great Suggy.
You little nuggets are the sweetest, smartest, most magnificent little
a-holes on the planet. Any typos are YOUR fault. That's right. I said it.
You walked across my keyboard every stinking day.
Now, come here and give Mommy her kisses and cuddles!

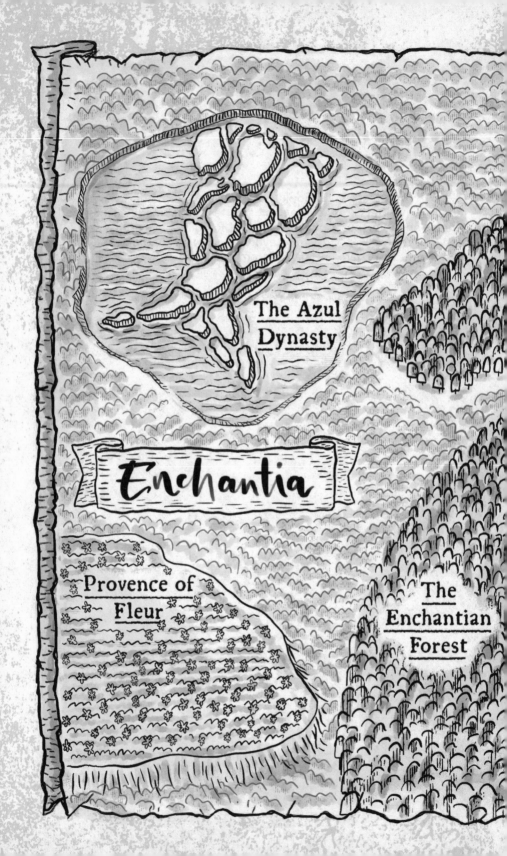

The Little Cinder Girl

by Oracles Unknown

Once upon a time, in a magical land teeming with good and evil, a beautiful queen birthed an incredibly special daughter.

Strong of heart and fast as wind. A warrior set apart, unwilling to bend.

Adored by her mother the queen but rejected by her father the king, the girl felt as if she lived in two worlds. The beloved princess and the despised servant. Then, one day, an evil force brought the cherished queen to an untimely end, leaving the girl in her cruel father's hands.

When the time came for this king to marry again, he selected a woman with two magically gifted daughters. For years he experienced bliss and harmony with his new family...while his own child suffered at the hands of others, wearing rags, carrying countless buckets of water, stoking fires, cooking, and cleaning. Alone, unwanted and forgotten by the rest of the world, she slept in soot for warmth. Before long, the villagers referred to her only as Cinder, a terrible insult, but also an unwitting tribute.

Soon after the girl's seventeenth birthday, the mighty king

of a neighboring kingdom wished to find a bride for his son. Like the princess, this prince felt as if he lived in two different worlds. One of honor, and one of dishonor.

Hoping to draw the most worthy girls in the land, the marriage-minded king hosted a festival of old, complete with trading, jousting, and balls.

Cinder begged her father and stepmother to let her attend. Never had she been so excited. Alas, the king turned a deaf ear to her pleas while the heartless stepmother and hateful stepsisters laughed, insisting the royal servant stay home to finish her chores. Then off the family of four went, leaving Cinder brokenhearted. But it wasn't long before a fairy godmother appeared with a gift, determined to prepare her for the night's festivities. Then off Cinder went as well, eager to enjoy the night.

Upon first sight, the honorable-dishonorable prince was utterly besotted with her. Ignoring everyone else in the ballroom, he claimed her hand and led her to the dance floor, where he held her in his arms for the rest of the evening, refusing to partner with anyone else. She made him want to be wholly honorable, a friend and never a foe. But could he be what he had never known? And why would she not tell him her name?

While Cinder enjoyed every moment with the prince, wanting only to bask in his affection, she didn't dare to share her identity with him. Could he truly fall in love with the girl no one else wanted? Then came the stroke of midnight, a clock chiming.

Ding.

Diiing.

Diiiiing.

Knowing she must arrive home before her family, Cinder ran from the prince, never looking back. Though he searched for his witty companion, he could not find her again…until the next celebration.

For the second time, Cinder's family attended the event without her. Thankfully, a new fairy godmother arrived to give her a magnificent gown and ensure she joined in the gaieties.

The moment Cinder reached the celebration, the prince rejoiced. Once again, he took her by the hand, led her to the dance floor, and held her in his arms all night, refusing to partner with anyone else. To his consternation, she still refused to share her identity, and still abandoned him at midnight. Though he searched far and wide, he could not find her.

The third time would be the last.

When the final celebration kicked off, Cinder didn't despair. Instead, she waited, her faith rewarded when a third fairy godmother appeared. This one granted her a dress more spectacular than any other, pairing it with magical slippers only she could wear, made of gold so pure, they appeared to be glass.

All the other guests marveled at Cinder's appearance, for they had never seen a more glorious sight. No one could glance away as she danced with the prince, who only had eyes for her.

When the clock tolled, announcing the arrival of midnight, the prince did not panic. Nor did he panic when Cinder ran from him once again. This time, a trap had been set, the palace stairways covered in pitch. But, the clever beauty surprised him. As soon as one of her beloved slippers got stuck, she left it behind and hurried away.

Enough was enough. The prince announced to one and all that he would wed the girl whose foot fit the slipper. Her and no other.

As word quickly spread through the kingdom, many hopeful females requested a chance to don the magical slipper. When Cinder's oldest stepsister tried to fit her foot into the shoe, she failed. In an effort to trick the prince, she severed her big toe. But the prince was no fool and swiftly realized what had happened.

Next, Cinder's younger stepsister tried to fit her foot into the shoe. She, too, failed and hoped to trick the prince by severing her heel. But again, he realized what had happened.

After dismissing the two, he inquired about the king and queen's remaining daughter. Not wanting Cinder to succeed where her stepsisters had failed, the two lied, claiming Cinder was too sickly to leave her bedroom. Nevertheless, the prince insisted on meeting her.

Cinder gathered her courage to confront him. Even though she feared that the boy she'd fallen in love with would be disappointed by the real her, she presented herself to him at long last. With her head high, she eased upon a stool and slid her dirt-caked foot into the slipper. It was a perfect fit.

The prince rejoiced, and her family mottled with rage, knowing they would soon be forced to face the consequences of their actions.

Face those consequences they did.

The father was betrayed by his greatest love. The stepmother lost everything she'd ever prized. Birds plucked out the stepsisters' eyes.

Overjoyed to have Cinder in his arms again, the prince soared away with her, their hearts beating in sync, one with the other. They married and lived happily ever after…eventually.

PROLOGUE

A glimpse into the past

Enchantia
The Provence of Fleur

When Good Intentions Have Evil Ends

H ear ye, hear ye! On this day in history, King Philipp Anskelisa of Fleur and Queen Charlotte Charmaine-Anskelisa welcomed their first child into the world. More than anything, the king had longed for a son. Alas. Fate gave him a daughter instead. A sickly one, at that.

Princess Ashleigh Charmaine-Anskelisa entered the world as quiet as a mouse, as still as a statue and as blue as a morning sky. The frantic midwife worked to aid the child's breathing while shouting for mystical healers, who burst into the chamber minutes later only to discover their magic couldn't fix the child's malformed heart. While they could heal injuries given after birth, they could not affect the injuries created before it. The infant continued to struggle, on the verge of death.

Propped on a bed with a mound of pillows behind her and a feathery blanket draped over her lower half, Charlotte reached out to demand, "Give me my baby." Though she was weak, tired, and sore, she would not relent in this. "Give her to me now."

Tradition demanded that fathers leave their sickly infants in the Enchantian Forest as an offering to the Empress of the Forest, whoever she happened to be at the time. In return, the empress would bless the parents with another child. A healthy one.

Would Charlotte's husband expect to trade little Ashleigh?

As one of the healers bundled the child in wolf's fur and passed her back to the queen, the king paced at the foot of the bed, his expression hardening with determination.

He would, she realized with growing horror. He really would.

"Husband," Charlotte whispered, cradling her precious darling close to her chest. "You must summon a witch sooner than royal tradition suggests. If Ashleigh is given an infusion of magic, it will work inside her rather than from an outside source, as with the healers. She will recover." *Surely.*

A stoic Philipp paused long enough to snap, "Don't be foolish, Charlotte. The babe is going to die. And this is right. This is good. Clearly you've made a cuckold of me. She cannot be mine. My lineage has never—*will never*—produce a child that is less than perfect."

Hurt encompassed the queen, a denial resounding from deep inside her. "I have never been untrue to you." Though she'd wanted to be. Philipp might be a handsome man, but he had the personality of a snake. "Ask the royal oracle. She'll tell you of my innocence."

He wrinkled his nose and shook his head. "It doesn't matter now, anyway. In Fleur, the firstborn is the heir, whether a boy or a girl. This child isn't *worth* saving. What if she dies in a week? A month? A year? The infusion of magic would be for nothing. A waste of precious resources."

Charlotte swallowed a sob. "A single minute of time with her is worth *everything*."

His expression remained impassive. "Yes, but not all life merits the amount of coins required to pay a witch for a magic infusion. So, I will summon the oracle, after all. If she tells us the child isn't part of a prophecy or that she'll bring destruction upon my kingdom, I will give her to the Empress of the Forest, so that we may be blessed with a second child, a true heir, and you will let me do so without protest. If the child *is* part of a prophecy, if she's someone who will bring great wealth and power to my kingdom, however, I will let you keep her." He looked to the midwife. "Go. Fetch her."

The midwife rushed out of the chamber.

A barbed lump grew in Charlotte's throat, nearly crushing her airway. The odds of keeping her precious Ashleigh were becoming slimmer by the second. The prophecies Philipp had mentioned were also known as "fairy tales," because they'd been spoken by the oracles, the most powerful of the fairies, centuries ago. Like everything else in the world, these fairy tales came with a blessing and a curse.

No matter the story involved, those blessings and curses always arrived in the form of a person. A king or prince. A queen or princess. A servant. A witch. Wealth and happiness usually accompanied select characters, while all others tended to welcome some kind of evil force to a kingdom or become evil themselves.

Charlotte rocked her squirming baby and fought for calm. "You will live, my love," she whispered. "You *must* be part of a fairy tale. And just look at you. How could you ever be part of a curse. No, oh, no. You are the blessing."

Philipp was part of a fairy tale, so, why not Ashleigh? A fate the queen had previously hoped to avoid for her child. The tales were mostly symbolic and always offered more questions than answers, leaving everything up to interpretation and imagination until the last battle.

There was always a battle.

And there was only one reason Philipp had proposed to Charlotte—his own prophecy, "The Little Cinder Girl." He'd considered himself the marriage-minded prince and Charlotte his perfect Cinder. At the time, she had believed him.

At Charlotte's birthing, her parents had chosen not to let an oracle tell her future. Back when her older brother, Challen, had been a crown prince rather than king, he'd been predicted to play a part in "Snow White and the Evil Queen." The news had quickly spread, and the family of a neighboring kingdom sent an assassin to kill him, just in case he came with a curse.

Challen had survived, thank gold, but her parents' desire to know the future hadn't. Because they'd never paid an oracle to glimpse Charlotte's fate, they'd never expected anything to come from her life, all but forgetting her existence. She'd always regretted the lack and wished she'd known...until her marriage to Philipp.

During their courtship, the dashing king had promised her a true happily-ever-after. Soon after they'd married, however, she'd learned that her new husband lacked any kind of honor. He couldn't be the marriage-minded prince, and Charlotte couldn't be his Cinder.

Tremors racked her so strongly she shook the bed. *What if I married...the villain?*

Philipp's selfishness knew no bounds. He had everything, but he took more from those who had nothing. He kept multiple mistresses, and he despised anyone with a supernatural ability, even Charlotte at times, because the power he'd acquired as a child had never manifested. His body had rejected the magic, something that only ever happened to a rare few. The lack had always infuriated him. Of course, he liked to blame the witch who'd given him the infusion, rather than himself. But then, Philipp was utter perfection—to Philipp. He cared for his own well-being; everyone else was inferior to him.

A fact that terrified her. As "The Little Cinder Girl" fairy tale promised, the dishonorable characters would not, could not receive a happy ending. They sowed only discord, so, in the end, they reaped only discord. What if Philipp's terrible fate had spilled over to Ashleigh, cursing her to misery and death?

No. No! Charlotte would find a way to save her child. She would pay any price.

Hinges squeaked as the oracle entered the chamber, a woman with long dark hair, pale skin, and an eerie air.

The moment of truth had arrived...

Charlotte's heart hammered at her ribs as the oracle focused on Princess Ashleigh...

Beat.

Beat.

Beat.

The woman shook her head and exited the chamber without ever speaking a word.

But, but... No. No, no, no. Panic swept Charlotte up in an icy cyclone, a hoarse cry leaving her. The worst had happened. The oracle hadn't seen a future, and Philipp now expected to give her baby to the Empress of the Forest.

Unaware of the horrid destiny her father planned for her, Ashleigh wiggled her tiny arms free of the fur and smiled up at her mother, as if to offer comfort. Comfort, from one so close to death, with a slight blue tint still marring her flesh.

"Say your goodbyes to the girl," Philipp commanded without a shred of remorse.

"Please. Purchase magic from a witch." For the right price, a witch would share a portion of her magic with an infant, imparting a single mystical ability that would manifest at the age of sixteen. The more powerful the witch, the stronger the impartation. While you never knew what ability you'd get, you could select the *type* of magic you wished to wield. Charlotte's ability to grow plants with a wave of her hand had come from a witch with power over the four elements. "With every fiber of my being, I believe Ashleigh's heart will heal if she wields her own magic. At the very least, it's her best chance of survival."

"Your certainty is misplaced," Philipp snapped with a shake of his head. He began to pace once again. "If she could be healed, she would be healed by now."

Charlotte bit her tongue to silence a sharp retort. *Calm. Steady.* If she began to screech, he would simply take the baby and go. "As I told you before, the magic within us is far more potent than the magic that comes from outside us. Something you do not know firsthand because you've never actually wielded your own magic."

Red infused his cheeks. "As *I* told *you*, witches demand an exorbitant sum for such a service. Why save a sickly daughter with no future? No, far better for us to leave her in the forest, as fate intended. I will give you another baby. A healthy son."

"I don't want another baby," she cried. "I want *this* one."

"Why can't you see the truth? I'm thinking only of our well-being," he said, using his most cajoling tone as he strode over and knelt beside the bed. "Try to understand. Your brother is heartsick over the death of his queen and eldest son. Everyone agrees King Challen is no longer fit to rule Sevón. Your young nephew cannot take his place—Prince Roth isn't old enough. No, I am what the kingdom needs. I can lead Sevón *in addition to* Fleur. If I'm saddled with a sickly child, I will appear weak. My enemies will feel confident enough to strike at long last. *Our* enemies. Do you wish to raise a child in a time of great war? Of course not. What good mother would? My way is best, my sweet. Trust me in this. Why tax your tired mind further?"

Reeling. So many insults, so many wrongs, all to make her feel foolish for refusing to back down. "My brother won't allow you to rule his kingdom." At sixteen, Challen had manifested battle magic. *No one* could defeat him now. "If you try, he'll kill you and raze all of Fleur in retaliation." She only wished she exaggerated.

Philipp traced his tongue over his teeth. "There is always a way. Maybe not today, maybe not tomorrow, but one day. It is a duty I cannot eschew. The needs and wants of many must come before the needs and wants of one."

Why did *his* needs and wants always count as the majority, then?

Heart beating with more force, Charlotte searched for a response that would both appease him and change his mind. Her daughter's very life was at stake. Finally she settled on, "Please, Philipp. Please summon a witch. Please give our daughter a chance to live. Just one chance. If you do, I'll… I'll…help you defeat Challen." A desperate lie or a desperate truth? She wasn't sure. She hardly knew her brother, but family was family. On the other hand, she'd meant what she'd said; she would do anything to save her daughter.

A muscle jumped in her husband's jaw, a sign his volatile temper neared eruption. "The matter is closed. I'll hear no more arguments about the baby. Say your goodbyes."

Charlotte swallowed a whimper. "Summon another oracle, then."

The muscle jumped faster. He sighed. "Why would I bother?"

Thinking fast, she said, "Because the royal oracle was a gift from Challen. She probably sensed your aspirations to rule Sevón." *Yes, yes.* A play on Philipp's greed. "What if she kept Ashleigh's prophecy to herself to prevent our daughter from one day aiding your military successes?" *Or your defeat…*

"Now you are being ridiculous. Oracles cannot lie." And yet, he pursed his lips, as if he was considering her words.

Not exactly bright, Husband? "The oracle remained silent. She didn't lie, but she might not have admitted the truth, either."

19

He narrowed his eyes, the gears in his mind churning at a faster speed.

Desperate, Charlotte pressed her advantage. "Will you risk your future on the silence of a single oracle? Why not find an unbiased one, just to be sure?"

This time, he nodded. "Very well. I will return shortly. If this oracle doesn't see a fairy tale in the babe's future, she goes to the forest with no more argument from you. Agree. Now."

What else could she do? "I... I agree."

After giving her another stiff nod, he stalked out the door.

The second his footsteps faded, Charlotte told the room's other occupants, "Leave me. I wish to be alone with my baby. And close the door behind you. I'm not to be disturbed."

As the midwife and healers scurried out, shutting the door as ordered, she shifted Ashleigh in her arms, resting the now-sleeping baby's cheek upon her shoulder. Ignoring her aches and pains, she worked her legs over the side of the bed and lumbered to her feet, unsteady but determined.

With the first step, dizziness struck, and she almost toppled. Concern for her child kept her upright. *Deep breath.* She remained in place, giving her head time to clear. But all the while, her breasts leaked, wetting her nightgown, and a warm trickle of liquid ran down her legs. Blood? She didn't care. *Hurry.* No telling when Philipp would return.

With no money of her own, Charlotte had to find a witch as desperate as she was, someone willing to accept little in exchange for a great infusion of power. And she knew just where to look...

Using a hidden passageway she'd discovered when Philipp snuck out of their room one night, Charlotte made her way down, down, down. The farther she went, the colder the air became. By the time she reached the royal dungeon, she was shivering and her teeth were chattering, goose bumps rising on her limbs.

What a horrid place. Crumbling walls lit by the occasional torch. Webs in every corner, insects unable to escape. The pitter-patter of rats accompanied a constant drip of water. This was where Philipp liked to lock away anyone who had wronged him. How many times had he bragged about the powerful witch he'd defeated in battle years ago?

What had the witch done wrong? *Think, think.* Murder? Theft? Had she merely insulted the king's unending pride, like so many others? Though Charlotte racked her brain, the answer remained at bay. Did the woman's crime really matter? If the witch agreed to share her magic with Ashleigh, Charlotte would agree to set her free, regardless of her past actions. A promise she had the means to ensure.

As a child, her father the king had beaten his two sons for any wrongdoing. Charlotte, however, he'd locked in small, dark spaces, a nightmare come to life. One day, her mother had secretly bought her a magic key able to open any lock. A key she still carried around her neck, just in case.

Charlotte readjusted Ashleigh to carefully cover her face with the wolf's fur. Nerves on edge, she shuffled along a wide corridor. The scent of mold, waste, and decay hit faintly at first but soon grew overpowering, creating a fetid stench that stung her nostrils and watered her eyes. Down here, there was no hint of the bright sunshine and sweet perfume of rose that permeated the rest of the kingdom.

A strange *clack, clack, clack* registered. A chorus of pained moans followed, becoming louder and louder only to quiet when she turned a corner and came upon the occupied cells. Haggard, emaciated prisoners hobbled to the bars.

Pleas rang out next.

"Help me."

"Please, ma'am. Please."

"Spare a drop of water."

Though her heart squeezed, she kept her gaze straight ahead.

There, at the end of the corridor, loomed a wall of bars and a witch who looked exactly as Philipp had described her every time he'd recounted the tale of their war.

Even with matted blond hair and dirt-smeared skin, even with a tattered rag that hung on her too-slender frame, the witch with ice-blue eyes possessed an undeniable beauty and grace.

For some reason, Philipp and his guards hadn't removed her only piece of jewelry before locking her away. A metal ring with a rose etched in the center.

"Well, well, well," the witch said. "Could it be the high-and-mighty Queen Charlotte in her expensive nightgown? Bards sing tales of your great beauty. The dark-haired enchantress soon to give birth. Well, who has *just* given birth, it appears. Are you here to honor your husband's prisoners with your exalted presence? To introduce us to the new princess, perhaps?"

Charlotte stopped a few feet away and exhaled. Mist wafted in her face. "I am Queen Charlotte, yes. What's your name?"

The witch blinked, as if surprised and a little miffed by her ignorance. "Most know me as Melvina, but I prefer Leonora."

Why would she wish to be called Leonora, a name associated with one of the oldest and most notorious cautionary tales in all of Enchantia? "What crime did you commit against my husband?" Not having grown up in Fleur, Charlotte wasn't very familiar with the local legends and histories. At least she sensed no hint of evil from the witch.

"You mean your husband needs a reason to incarcerate innocent people?" Leonora replied airily.

No. No, he didn't. This witch could be a good person who'd met a bad end.

Or a bad person with a just end.

Did Charlotte's plan have risks? Yes. Many. Would those risks deter her? No. "If you grant my daughter a magical ability, I will give you what you—"

"Let me guess," Leonora interjected with a wry tone. "You'll set me free."

She patted her daughter's back and explained, "According to the healers, Ashleigh's heart is malformed, her body fragile. To survive, she needs an infusion of power from a witch."

"Don't we all?" Gaze unwavering, Leonora canted her head and peered at Charlotte. "This world is cruel. Perhaps she's better off *not* surviving, hmm?"

Rearing back, Charlotte snapped, "Everyone deserves a chance."

"Are you sure? There's a breadcrumb trail of heartache and misery, and it leads to what my life used to be. Betrayal. War. Pain. Greed. This is the future you want for a sickly child?"

"You mention nothing of love, joy, merriment, and pleasure."

Leonora pursed cracked lips. "Oh, but I did imply those things. They are what led to the others, after all. And yet, you've convinced me. I will help you. After you free me, of course. These bars are magically enhanced to stop me from using my powers."

Charlotte rocked from one bare foot to another. *Is she manipulating me as I manipulated Philipp?* Maybe. Probably. Again, did it really matter? How many hours—minutes—until Ashleigh's heart forever stopped?

Must proceed. No other choice. "I will do it. I will set you free first," Charlotte said, raising her chin. No reason to demand a vow. The witch either would or wouldn't keep her word, and a vow wouldn't change her mind one way or the other.

Leonora stiffened, as if she dare not hope. "You'll need the key to the cell. Your husband carries it, and he never parts with it."

Yes, she'd seen his key. His prize. "I do not need his. I have my own." Always best to have your own of everything. No need to tell her what else the key could do; the witch might try to steal it. Objects enriched with magic were more valuable than gold.

Charlotte stepped forward once. Twice. Again. She frowned. Why drag her feet now? She'd fought for this. Needed it.

"Hurry." Leonora crooked her index finger. "Before I change my mind."

Oh, yes. She manipulates me. Even still, Charlotte removed the key that hung from a chain around her neck and inserted the metal tip into the lock. Hinges creaked as the door swung open, the witch free, just like that.

Leonora rolled back her shoulder, lifted her chin, and sauntered through the doorway as if she hadn't a care, a grin blooming.

Every heartbeat reminiscent of an ax splitting wood, the queen removed the fur from Ashleigh's face. *Oh, no, no, no.* Her baby was bluer than before and struggling to breathe.

Leonora glanced at Ashleigh and stumbled back with a gasp, her air of casual disregard gone. "She...she's *her.*" Those icy blues widened, as round as saucers.

"If you mean Princess Ashleigh, then yes. Please. You must save her."

"Yes, yes. I must heal her as soon as possible." Trembling, she cupped the baby's pristine cheeks with dirty hands tipped by ragged nails.

Charlotte halted a protest. This had to be done.

The witch mumbled under her breath, and a strange wind kicked up, whirls of dirt gusting through the dungeon. Magic sparked, here, there, crackling like little lightning strikes and—

Charlotte moaned, a thousand daggers seeming to prick her skin. That magic...it was pure evil. The kind of evil she'd encountered only once before, as a little girl. The royal oracle had stopped what she was doing, her eyes turning milky white as she announced that a phantom—an invisible dragon—would pass through the palace that day, searching for those whom she might consume.

The oracle wasn't wrong.

Later that day, an evil just like this one had hovered near Charlotte for hours, only to disappear in a blink, as if bored.

What have I done?

"You cannot stop this," Leonora intoned. "Not without killing the child."

"You're not a witch." Charlotte's voice had gone hoarse, nothing but a croak. "You're…you… You're a *phantom*." Others believed phantoms were nothing but a myth parents used to scare their children into behaving, but Charlotte had known better. She'd studied phantoms, learning everything she could.

They were spirits born in flame and ash, able to possess anyone they desired, stealing their life.

Now, to meet a phantom named Leonora, the star of a cautionary tale that featured a witch who'd led an army of dragons against an avian king and burned an entire kingdom to the ground…

"You are correct. I am a phantom, born when dragons burned a village and everyone in it and oh, it's so wonderful to share my story with another. I never get to brag. Because my form is intangible, I'm able to jump from body to body, seizing full control, living the other person's life as long as I wish." Leonora's grin returned, slow and wicked. "Your husband went to war with the witch named Melvina, who spurned his advances. When I took over her life, I didn't know your husband had laid a trap for her that same day. I drank her sweet wine and fell into a deep sleep. When I awoke, I was here, the guards singing lies about some great battle Philipp had won against me. Believe me when I say I will make him pay for his crimes. I'd thought to overtake *you*—to start—but the child… Her fate is mine, and mine is hers."

Charlotte shook her head, locks of hair slapping her cheeks, and backed up, severing contact. "She's just a baby. Please don't—"

"So sorry, Queenie, but it's as good as done. And don't bother telling anyone what has occurred here. They won't believe you. And if they do, they'll murder your precious Ashleigh just to kill me. Oh, and just in case you think to do the same, don't. It never works." Leonora released a final breath and collapsed in the dirt, her body unmoving.

Knees threatening to give out, Charlotte tore open Ashleigh's blanket to discover bronze glowing with health. She would live? She—

Ashleigh's eyes. They'd brightened to an icy blue, the same color as Leonora's eyes, before darkening again. Horror doused the flare of elation. Leonora had done it. She'd jumped into Ashleigh. *And I let her do it. I helped her.*

Charlotte didn't…she couldn't… No. This wasn't unfixable. She might be able to buy some kind of magical extraction. Surely someone specialized in that. If not, she would buy… what? A spell to keep Leonora contained?

Though she had no gold of her own, she had the key. *Yes.* She would offer the key as payment, and a witch or a warlock would help Ashleigh.

She swaddled Ashleigh anew, then used the bottom half of her gown to anchor the child against her chest. Then, drawing on a reservoir of strength she hadn't known she possessed, she crouched down to feel the witch's body for a pulse. Dead.

Charlotte hung her head. Then, she got to work, dragging the witch's body back into the cell. The next time Philipp checked on her, he would think she'd died of natural causes.

A ring hung around her neck, capturing the queen's attention. Something inside Charlotte shouted, *The ring belongs with Ashleigh. My daughter must have it, now and always.*

Though she sensed the wrongness of such a thought, she claimed the necklace for Ashleigh, anyway.

As she hurried to the secret passage, her emotions got the better of her and she sobbed. But she never slowed her pace.

Just as Charlotte crawled back into bed, arranged her nightgown and her daughter, the door opened and Philipp marched inside, another oracle close to his heels. A pretty woman with guarded eyes and a strained smile.

"Well?" the king demanded, waving in Ashleigh's direction.

Charlotte trembled as the woman sidled up to the bed. Ashleigh was…was…possessed by a phantom; what if the oracle prophesized a terrible end, placing the child in the same predicament as before?

Voice soft and soothing, the oracle stretched out her arms and said, "Come now. Let's see the little precious."

The moment of truth had come.

Terror and hope held the queen immobile as the other woman opened the blanket that covered Ashleigh…

A milky film spilled over the oracle's irises, the first sign the fairy was having a vision of the future. In a monotone voice, she announced, "Woe is she. Woe is she. The Glass Princess, born twice in one day. Two heads, one heart. To purge or merge? One heart, two heads. To merge or purge? One brings a blessing. One brings a curse. Only she can choose. Only she can fight. The ball. The shoe. *Diiiing. Diiiiing. Diiiiiiiing.* At midnight, all is revealed. Who will live and who will die when past, present, and future collide? Let the fire rage—let the flame purify. Let the world burn, burn, burn."

Thick, oppressive silence reigned. Philipp peered at Charlotte, looking shocked to the core. Had a curse just been spoken over the entire kingdom? After what had happened with Leonora…there was a chance.

"This points to 'The Little Cinder Girl' fairy tale. But how can that be?" Philipp scrubbed a hand over his mouth. "You and I…*we* are the prince and Cinder. The babe cannot be part of our fairy tale, for it is finished. We are living our happily-ever-after. Unless…" He stared at Ashleigh through narrowed eyes. "Our fairy tale is repeating because the child tainted my perfect ending."

How could he say such a thing? "Perhaps you are not the marriage-minded prince but the evil king who despises his daughter."

"You know as well as I that the tales are symbolic rather than literal. The obvious is never the answer. What seems to be right is always wrong. What seems to go this way always veers that way. But I would take care, were I you." His voice turned menacing. "The king who despises his daughter has a queen who dies far too soon."

Charlotte's breath hitched. The threat both terrified and thrilled her. The queen's untimely death marked the *beginning* of the tale for Cinder.

Ashleigh could be its end, loved beyond imagining.

Charlotte almost laughed then, deciding she adored the prophecies, after all.

"*You* know it doesn't matter what role Ashleigh plays, Philipp," she said, smug. "Fate has plans for her. Ruin those plans, and fate will ruin you right back."

1

Our tale begins with love and light.
Take care, my dears, lest it end with fright.

Ashleigh

The Provence of Fleur
Fourteen years later

Hot tears poured down my cheeks, burning twin tracks of sadness into my skin. The salty droplets trickled onto my tongue, letting me taste my own misery.

The worst had happened. My mother was dead, killed inside our home mere days ago. I'd been right there, at her side, but I'd been unconscious. There to help but unable to do so, thanks to my malformed heart; I'd passed out right before the murder occurred.

A sob mounted an escape, but I bit my tongue, remaining silent. Father expected me to be stoic in times of distress. Mother would want me to be. *Never let them know they've hurt you, my darling. You'll only show them where to strike next.*

I tried to be stoic. For Momma's sake, I tried so hard, but I felt like a broken vase glued together with wishes.

Today was her funeral. Queen Charlotte Charmaine-Anskelisa. The greatest person ever to live. Mother extraordinaire. A small handful of family and friends had gathered in the royal gardens to say goodbye.

How could I *ever* say goodbye? I'd adored her, and she'd adored me, too. Momma might have been the only one. I'd spent most of my days in bed, forgotten by my father and ignored by servants.

Now I watched, helpless, as flames spread from my mother's gown to her lovely bronze skin. In the Provence of Fleur, my home, we held tradition sacred. When someone died, their body was placed atop a bed of rose petals and sealed inside a glass coffin. One piece of glass acted as a magnifier and, as beams of sunlight passed through it, the body would catch fire and burn to ash.

I whimpered and shifted my gaze to the marble statues that formed a circle around us, creating a hidden clearing in the heart of the garden. Momma's favorite place. Each statue depicted the likenesses of a past king or queen, with roses of every color twined at the base. I used to watch her from my window as she tended those roses, with birds perched on her shoulders.

I wiped my cheeks with the back of a shaky hand and moved my gaze to my uncle, King Challen, ruler of Sevón, and his children, sixteen-year-old Prince Roth Charmaine and fourteen-year-old Princess Farrah Charmaine.

King Challen was a big man, one of the strongest I'd ever seen, with dark hair and green eyes. He and his family rarely traveled here, and I couldn't blame them. How many times had my father made a play to take over their kingdom? Only recently had the two realms reached an accord.

The king evinced no emotion, but he kept his head down to show his respect.

The royal siblings did, too, their ability to stand still impressive. They'd brought a friend and bodyguard along with them. Sixteen-year-old Saxon Skylair, a winged avian prince who'd been exiled from the Avian Mountains for reasons unknown.

The moment my gaze landed on him, my damaged heart pounded a little too hard, a silky whisper drifting through my mind. *Go to him. Take comfort.*

Um…*what?* Take comfort from a boy? A stranger? Besides, I doubted I could be comforted by *anyone*. Though I *was* fascinated by him. I'd always been fascinated by the avian.

So little was known about them. The details found in history books were always contradictory; I never knew what was truth or fabrication.

This exiled prince had hair the color of jet, flawless brown skin, and eyes like a moonlit sky: deep, rich amber with pinpricks of black. Massive blue wings arched over his shoulders and flanked his sides, somehow both beautiful and menacing.

Once I'd asked Momma if I could touch an avian's wings, and she'd turned bright red before escorting me to my bedroom to tell me that I absolutely could not, should not, ever, ever, ever ask to touch an avian's wings. It was considered an "unwanted advance." Whatever that meant. Momma had refused to explain.

Saxon's image blurred. How I missed my mother. Because of Queen Charlotte, I'd known deep, abiding love. I wouldn't trade our days together for anything, especially not a lessening of this pain. This pain said she'd lived a good life. This pain said she would be remembered.

This pain said I'd known life's greatest gift—love.

Had Prince Saxon ever known that kind of love from his family?

I blinked and moved my attention to his mother and only sister—Queen Raven and Princess Tempest, who had come to pay their respects. They stood across from him, but they never looked his way or acknowledged his presence.

Why had they kicked him from his home as a child? Did they see him as my father saw me? Lacking? Or had he committed some kind of unforgivable crime?

How many times had my father complained about the avian and their tendency to address even the smallest offense with a severe punishment? Hurt an avian once, and they'd hurt you back—twice.

Over the years, I'd learned to be an excellent observer. I caught Prince Saxon casting a glance at his family, his expression flashing from impassive to longing to furious. Whatever had happened, he missed his loved ones, and my chest squeezed with sympathy.

My reaction to him did not go unnoticed. He must have sensed me. He dragged his gaze my way, and our eyes met. The fury faded, and he offered me a sad half smile. He was so beautiful. *Like one of the statues has come to life.*

Out of habit, I reached up to stroke the ring that hung around my neck. A gift from Momma, and my most cherished possession. The band was made of metal, with a rose etched into the center.

The prince's smile slowly faded into a frown. He narrowed his eyes, staring where my fingers wove through the chain. Fury pulsed from him anew, but this time, it wasn't softened with longing. He balled his fists.

Tremors rushed through me. My father planted his hands on my shoulders, bent down and hissed, "Be still or be gone."

I flinched, and he released me from his too-tight grip.

As the minutes ticked by, I tried to avoid glancing at Prince Saxon, I really did. But I had to know if the avian was still glaring at me or not. I must have been mistaken.

Oh, no. No mistake. He was glaring. But, but…why? What had I done to deserve such animosity, today of all days?

An hour ago, we'd exchanged a grand total of ten words. He'd looked at me strangely, as if he knew me but couldn't quite place me, and said, "May you always find gold." A common greeting in Sevón.

I'd curtsied and replied with the Fleuridian equivalent, "May your roses forever bloom."

Still he glared.

As the heat from the coffin intensified, warmth throbbed in my cheeks and my insides melted into a nice Ashleigh stew. My lungs protested strongly, and I hunched over to ease my breathing. The new position did no good, however. Panic sprouted, parts of me icing.

Don't you dare pass out. Not here, not now. Inhale. Exhale.

Behind me, fingers snapped, and I knew my father had summoned a guard to carry me back to the palace. To my room. To my bed. Where I would be forced to while away the day... the months...the years alone, without the kindness and caring of my beautiful mother.

A sob bubbled out, and there was no stopping it. "Please, Father. Don't make me leave—"

"Be quiet." He squeezed my shoulders with more force. "You will return to the palace, and that's that."

Abandon my mother before the funeral ended? Hardly. I wanted to be here until the last flame was extinguished. The guard would have to drag me kicking and screaming—

The guard picked me up and marched away, my frail body clutched to his chest. He did it with no resistance from me. I was too weak to fight.

Fighting fresh tears, I looked back. My gaze collided with Prince Saxon's. Still he glared, watching me from beneath those narrowed lids, his long, black lashes nearly fused together.

As soon as the guard cleared the garden, he muttered, "Why must *I* be the one to care for the Glass Princess? I'm not lazy or behind in my training. I'm good at my job. One of the best."

Humiliation singed me. Who would dare to speak to my father in such a way, or use a nickname that implied he was so weak he would shatter at any moment? "I'm able to walk," I gritted out. "Put me down. I'll finish the journey on my own."

He ignored me, because I was beneath his notice. Nothing but a helpless doll. A worthless trinket without a voice.

I didn't care. It didn't matter. Except I cared and it mattered. But one day I would ensure the world saw value in me. I would be strong, a queen of battle, my feats the stuff of legend. I would be shielded by golden armor, and I would wield the most powerful weapons ever created, because I would design every piece myself.

Over the years, I'd watched more than my mother's gardening from my window. I'd witnessed countless military training sessions, awed by the ferocious warriors and their gear. I couldn't imagine anyone trying to harm a soldier, much less naysay one. Everyone listened when they spoke, even the king. Everyone noticed their presence and respected their opinions. They had *great* value.

I'd already designed a lightweight crossbow for smaller grips like mine. The arrows weren't actually arrows but metal shards that loaded into a spring trap with the help of a special lever. My first creation. I just needed to have it made, though I preferred to learn how to make it myself.

A thrill fizzed inside me at the thought. Eventually I hoped to craft and sell my designs, then use the profits to buy a magical ability from a witch. Another form of strength and power.

Little wonder I craved an ability of my own. Sometimes, I even imagined powerful magic already stirred deep inside me, buried too deep to access. Wishful thinking, of course. If I'd had a secret well of magic, I would have healed my heart and saved Momma.

New tears gathered, stinging. "Set. Me. Down."

He did—at the palace door, as ordered. As soon as he hefted me to my feet, he hurried off.

I wobbled, my knees already knocking with fatigue. I looked to the ivy-covered palace behind me, then peered back at the garden, seemingly miles away. Could I make it? Would I court Father's wrath for nothing?

I...didn't care. If I was to become a queen of battle, I had to take the occasional risk.

Who was more worthy of a risk than my mother?

I lifted the hem of my mourning gown and lumbered forward. When I passed the garden entrance, I mewled with relief. Remaining in the shadows, I snuck through the elaborate maze of thorns and flowers. Midway... I was making good progress, breathing heavily but functioning—until my heart decided to curl into itself, sending a shaft of pain down my left arm and a spike of dizziness to my head.

I groaned and staggered about, struggling to stay on my feet. *Inhale. Exhale. In, out. In, out.* Just as the healers had taught me. *In, out.* The dizziness only worsened, consciousness wavering. My blood cooled, and my teeth chattered. Black dots wove through my vision.

Do not faint. Not here. Not now.

Inhale. I eased down and made it to my knees, then shrank into a ball.

Exhale. I would remain awake... I wouldn't...

The darkness swallowed me in one tasty bite.

"Hello, Ashleigh."

A familiar voice woke me, light chasing the haze of darkness from my mind. Struggling to focus, I blinked open my eyes. A figure framed by golden light stood above me.

His identity clicked as I jolted upright. "Milo." The royal warlock's son. The very warlock who'd come to work at the palace soon after my birth, hired by my mother to act as her—

our—personal magic wielder. Or so I'd been told. Milo and his father lived at the palace, and his father had died right alongside my mother, in the same way, killed by the same assailant.

Poor Milo. How I ached for him. While he and I weren't the best of friends, I hated knowing anyone felt as grief-stricken as I did.

More than once, I'd wondered how the killer had defeated his father. A warlock was a male witch, and a royal warlock was usually more powerful than most others. For someone to have slayed Milo's father...what kind of power had *they* wielded?

Fingers snapped in front of my face. "You about to pass out again?"

"No, sorry. Just got lost in thought." Milo was only a few years older than me, tall and lean, with golden hair, golden eyes and golden skin. Like most magic wielders, he sported metal wrist cuffs. He wore dark leather underneath gold-plated armor that I would love to examine more closely. He resembled a god of war, intimidating and kind of menacing. So, the same as always.

Most girls in the palace melted in his presence, but I'd never been drawn to him. There was something about him... Maybe it was the way he watched people, as if they possessed something that belonged to him, and he would cross any line to get it back.

An elaborate iron key hung from his neck. The same key his father used to wear. I remembered the way my mother used to stare at it, her yearning palpable. When I'd asked her why she liked it, she'd told me, *I used to have one just like it, and I wish with all my being that I still did, so that I could give it to you.*

My chin quivered, and I gulped. "Has your father's funeral ended?"

He gave a single, jerky nod.

"I'm so sorry for your loss, Milo." I'd always liked his father. Every year Momma had used secret passages to take me down to the catacombs, where the warlock stayed. At her request, he would mix a foul-smelling liquid that I had to drink while he mumbled something about a "mind barrier." Afterward, my head had hurt for weeks, but I hadn't minded because he'd always treated me with kindness. If a mind barrier aided me, for whatever reason, I would happily suffer.

What would happen without the barrier, now that the warlock was gone?

"Don't be," Milo said, and shrugged. "He was selfish. He would rather help others than his own son."

His vehemence startled me. The warlock had not struck me as a selfish man. Wasn't helping others a good thing?

Milo sat down a few inches away from me, as if we sat so close all the time. Not the least bit awkward at all. Not even a little. "What do you remember about the day your mother and my father died?"

He wished to discuss this *now*? "Why?"

"Despite our differences, he was my father. I'd like to know how he died, and since you were the only other person in the room…"

A choking sound left me. "I'm sorry, Milo, but I don't remember anything of significance. My mother took me to your father's chambers, as usual, and—" I paused. Milo had never been present during the drinking of the potion and the chanting of the spell. He didn't know about it, and I shouldn't tell him, my mother's constant warning drilled into my head. *Tell no one, my darling. Your life hangs in the balance.*

Why, Momma?

The few times I'd asked, she'd only ever told me, *It's safer if you don't know.*

"Go on," he insisted.

I licked my lips. "As we passed through the doorway, I fainted. I—I'm not sure how much time I lost before I awoke in…in…a pool of blood." *Her* blood. The warlock's, too. They'd both lain beside me.

Momma's green gaze had been open, staring at nothing, her expression frozen in terror. A crimson-soaked dagger had protruded from the warlock's chest, but my sweet mother had possessed wounds all over.

I sniffled. Why hadn't I been hurt? Why hadn't I hugged my mother that morning or told her how special she was?

"Did he look like he suffered?" Milo asked casually.

I shifted, uncomfortable. How was I supposed to answer that? The truth? *Yes, he appeared to have died in agony.*

In the end, Milo smiled, as if he'd gleaned the answer—and liked it. Then he stood and walked a slow circle around me, saying, "I've been going through my father's things, and I've read some very interesting things about you, Princess Ashleigh."

His smugness…

"I know who you truly are," he announced.

My brow furrowed with confusion. "I don't understand. Who am I truly?"

He continued as if I hadn't spoken. "She lives in you, but she is not you and you are not her. Not yet. She is a queen, and you are the servant she possesses…the two separated only by a mystical wall."

The heat drained from my face. I'd heard my mother use those same words at times. *Lives in you…possessed…mystical wall.* "What does that mean?"

Milo stopped in front of me, his expression almost reverent. "It means you are Leonora, the Burner of Worlds. You are the one my father tried to eliminate—the one I seek. You can give me everything I desire. Everything I deserve. I can do the same for you."

The name *Leonora* echoed inside my head, setting my every nerve on edge. While there wasn't much known about Leonora the Burner of Worlds, all of Enchantia had heard about her war with Craven the Destroyer. How she'd possess fire magic and led an army of dragons against his army of bloodthirsty avian warriors, and devastation had reigned.

Their battles took place centuries ago, yet some parts of the realm had never recovered. In fact, one of the Avian Mountains, where Craven had once resided, was known as the Peak of Sorrow, thanks to a staggering death toll and a barren landscape.

Even though Leonora had lived so long ago, Momma had accidentally called me Leonora, too, when she'd been sick and delirious. I'd entered her room with a pitcher of water, and she'd thrown a goblet at my head, screeching, *Leave her, Leonora. Leave my Ashleigh. I hate you, do you hear me? I want you gone.*

Growing more nauseous by the second, I sputtered, "I'm not Leonora. I'm not. She's dead, and I'm alive."

"Oh, she isn't dead, I assure you. She lives on in you." His smile returned as he crouched in front of me, intense golden eyes drilling into my soul. "I speak to you, Leonora. I know you seek vengeance. I will help you get it—if you will help me get riches beyond my wildest dreams."

My breaths quickened. "I—I don't understand what you expect from me." Maybe he wasn't quite right in the head? "I promise I'm not Leonora. I swear she's not living on inside me."

"Without its refortification, the barrier between you is already weakening. One day, nothing will separate you. It might be a week, or a year, or even ten years, but you will become her, and she will become you."

My tremors returned, a chill spreading in my bones. "I don't—"

A *whoosh, whoosh* noise drew my gaze upward. My heart thudded as Saxon Skylair came into view. He dipped in the sky, sinking beneath a cloud. Such grace, speed, and agility. Envy consumed me as the wind whipped through his hair, ruffled his cerulean wings as well as the fabric of his plain white tunic and dark leather trousers.

My gaze found his, and I cringed at the fury he projected.

No, not this time. Scathing hostility boiled in his eyes now, and it was so much worse than the fury. As I scrambled backward, hoping to avoid him altogether, I remembered Milo's presence and looked to him for help—

The warlock's son had already raced away.

Panic spiked when Prince Saxon descended headfirst, his wings tucked into his sides to increase his speed—he was headed straight for me. I scrambled back. At the last second, he flared those wings to slow his momentum and landed a few feet away with a heavy thump.

I lumbered on legs that had yet to steady, fighting to remain upright as I continued to inch backward. "I'll go."

"Stay," he barked. One word. Four letters. Infinite command. "I suspect I know who you are, but I wish to make sure."

Not this again. Suddenly light-headed, I wrapped my fingers around Momma's ring. Every instinct shouted, *Flee! Flee now.* I remained in place. I had to know who Saxon Skylair thought I was. Would he believe me to be Leonora too?

A tower of might, he stalked closer. When he stopped, he stood a whisper away. An incredible scent drifted to my nose, reminding me of a promise of rain. It came from him, I realized, and I had to fight the urge to press my nose into the hollow of his throat and breathe deeply.

Pinching a lock of my brown hair, he said, "Rumor suggests you're too sickly to leave your bed, that you would have to be carried to the service, and yet you somehow found the strength to walk to and from the palace—twice—on the day of my arrival. A strange coincidence, don't you think?"

His thickened tone suggested…what? "I found the strength to say goodbye to my mother," I replied, at my wit's end. Two boys, one mystery, and a whole lot of confusion.

His mouth started moving again. I knew he was speaking to me, yet his voice was getting drowned out by the ringing in my ears. Dizzy... Black spots dotted my vision, his merciless face blurring.

No, no, no. Not again. Though I struggled with everything I had, I couldn't stop the black spots from spreading through my mind. Like spilled ink on parchment.

To faint in front of this boy... I hadn't interacted with many people in my lifetime, but I knew to be wary of showing a hint of vulnerability right now. But... I needed help, even if it came from someone like him.

I tried to tell Saxon, "Can't see. Palace. Return..."

But the darkness took me first.

Trapped in a void, with no sight or sound. Aware but powerless. Time ceased to hold meaning for me, a minute, hour, or year passing. Until...

A glimmer of light appeared. I kicked and clawed my way toward it—yes! The darkness receded, bit by bit, and I blinked open my eyes. Bright light registered, the world coming back into view. I was lying on the ground, rosebushes, statues, and flames. Heat poured from me, the scent of charred grass heavy. Flames? A thick veil of smoke choked me, and I coughed.

There'd been smoke in the warlock's chambers, too.

Was Saxon okay? I sat up, my gaze finding Saxon.

A scream of shock and horror barreled from me. He loomed perhaps twenty feet away, his hair singed at the ends, dark rings of smoke around his eyes, nose, and mouth, his clothes littered with burn holes. Even his feathers had been scorched.

I didn't... I couldn't... With a baffling amount of energy I'd never before experienced, I scrambled to my feet and stepped toward him, determined to help. "What happened?"

He huffed and puffed his breaths, like a big bad wolf. "*You* happened."

"Me? I didn't... I never... I was unconscious." I stumbled back, my hand fluttering to my chest. Wait. I paused to peer down. My fingers. The ends were red, and they burned hot enough to singe my dress. Frantic, I shook out both hands, hoping to cool them off.

He took a step toward me, just one, but it contained more ferocity than any sword. "Leave. Now. Before I kill you where you stand. I've never harmed a child, even a woman trapped in the body of one, and I don't wish to start today."

Kill me? As in *murder* me? But, that couldn't be right. "You need to let me help you. You're hurt."

"I'm avian. I heal swiftly. Now leave," he repeated with more force.

"Stay, both of you." The command came from my father as he stomped around the same wall of foliage I'd navigated, with Roth, Farrah, and Milo behind him. "Someone tell me what has caused such damage. *Now.*"

The second the Charmaines caught sight of us, concern contorted their features. Roth rushed over, demanding, "Who did this to you both, Saxon?"

"This didn't happen to us both." Saxon glowered at me. "This happened to me. The girl is responsible."

"Liar!" I rarely fell into a temper, but this boy and his animosity pushed me closer and closer to the edge.

"Ashleigh, you worthless girl." My father believed Saxon over me? "The avian are a proud people, rich in tradition. Harming one of their royals is a terrible insult to *all* avian, and restitution must now be made."

A pang almost rent me in two, fueled by sorrow, fear, and anger. "I didn't hurt him. You have to believe me, Father. I—"

"Enough. Your mother wanted you here, I do not." He pointed an accusing finger at me, and I withered. "I have tolerated your presence only because of the prophecy and the potential for blessings upon the kingdom, but I have become more and more certain that your role is a minor one. If not a curse altogether. You're too...you."

I flinched, as though I'd been punched.

And he wasn't done. "I'd planned to send you away tomorrow. Now circumstances have changed. You will move to the Temple of Blessed Peace today, where you will live out the rest of your days."

I gaped at him. He'd planned to send me away before this? He'd expected me to leave the only home I'd ever known, my *mother's* home, the day after her funeral? To live at the Temple, a mystical cluster of trees where dryads worshipped nature? A place hours away, even by route of the Enchantian Forest?

"Will this serve as restitution, Prince Saxon?" Father asked the male.

"No," the avian snapped. "But it will do. For now."

As everyone in the group glared at me, awaiting my response to the punishment, my world seemed to contract, expand, then contract again, like a pulse inside my brain. Though I would have loved to sprint away, to sob, to plead my case, I knew better. Father never reversed his decisions, and those who protested ended up in his dungeon.

I fingered my mother's ring and glared at Saxon. "Yes, Father. I will move to the Temple to make restitution to the prince." *For now,* just as he'd said.

But one day...

Yes. One day.

2

Dreams may come, and dreams may go,
but you'll always have a foe.

Ashleigh

Three years later
Present day

Sunlight spilled through the tiny holes I'd drilled into the walls of my bedroom, warming and waking me. I groaned as I eased into an upright position. New day, same routine. Wake up. Bathe. Eat a piece of fruit. Clean the Temple. Eat a small lunch. Clean the Temple. Eat a smaller dinner. Read. Go to sleep.

I sighed, a plume of dirt falling from my hair, landing on—*dirt?* I groaned. *Not this again.* I'd fallen asleep relatively clean. Well, as clean as one could get, living in a hollowed-out tree trunk and working with forest nymphs who cared only about nature. Now dirt caked my feet, stained my nightgown, and filled the underside of my nails.

Clearly, I'd explored the forest in my sleep again. Something I did about once a month. Thrice I'd woken up to mud and a treasure. Today, I discovered another treasure. A large egg rested beside my pillow.

I ran my fingers over the ridged shell and grinned. Red with flecks of green. Definitely a dragon egg, just like the others. And I didn't care that finding such a thing seemed to support what the warlock's son had said about me, that I had the witch Leonora, the queen of dragons, trapped inside me somehow. My subconscious had latched on to the idea of dragons, obviously, and now sought to find as many as possible.

Many times, I'd bartered with a vast number of Temple patrons to receive history books about dragons, the avian, and witches, as well as different metalwork and gardening guides, even ancestral journals about the different royal families. In return, I'd carved the patrons' names into the Temple's trunk.

Supposedly, when someone who lived in the Temple carved another person's name in said tree trunk, untold blessings would come upon that person. Had I started the rumor because I needed a way to get my books? Yes. Did I feel bad about it? Not even a little. Maybe untold blessings *did* come upon them. Who knew?

During all my studies, I'd learned I shared no similarities with Leonora. Other than the fire thing. And the love of dragons. And the war with the avian. But that was all! She'd had a cruel streak. I didn't. She'd destroyed innocents. I never would. Most important, I hadn't started a fire since my arrival, as I must have somehow done to Prince Saxon in the garden. How, though? How had I managed to ignite flames while unconscious and magicless?

Then again, anything was possible in Enchantia.

Whatever had happened, I would apologize to the avian prince for my part in it. Surely he would be satisfied then. Hadn't I paid for my accidental crime long enough?

Ugh. Thoughts of the prince always soured my mood. I pushed him from my mind and focused on my new egg. A joy. After cleaning the beauty with painstaking care, despite its hard-as-steel shell, I placed it beside the others in the box I kept stashed under my bed.

Satisfied, I stood to prepare for my day. This bedroom was smaller than my closet at home. I had the bed, the egg box, a couple changes of clothes, a few toiletries, and a small—very small—wooden tub. If I wanted to bathe each morning, I had to haul water into the tub the night before. Some part of me must have known I'd go egg hunting last night; before bed, I'd lugged four buckets of water up my tangle of branches, also known as my "staircase."

The Temple itself was comprised of multiple hollowed-out tree trunks, their gnarled limbs creating the walls and floors. In some spots, flowers grew. In others, ivy. Bugs crawled here and there, and birds flew about at will, webs and nests part of our decor.

Though I would have preferred a room on the ground floor, I'd chosen this one because of the moonberry vines hanging in one corner. Some mornings, I had only to reach out to acquire breakfast. Sadly, this wasn't one of those mornings. I'd eaten the last berry yesterday, and they wouldn't bloom again for another month.

I stripped and gathered my toiletries, then climbed into the ice-cold tub to wash. I'd added the rose petals I'd collected while pruning, and now their sweet scent enveloped me.

When I was as clean as I could get, I dressed in a fresh sackcloth. I owned four, and I kept them washed and mended as much as possible. With no mirror, I had to plait my hair sight unseen, a task I'd perfected over the years. Last, I scrubbed my teeth with a paste I made with nearby herbs. That done, I headed out to start my first chore.

Dryads floated in and out of the Temple, mostly pretending

I wasn't there. While I'd moved in 1095 days ago, they *still* resented my presence. If they hadn't feared my father and what he'd do to the royal gardens if ever they angered him, they would have kicked me out a long time ago.

In the beginning, I'd tried to win them over. I'd picked them a bouquet of fresh flowers—and earned their wrath for daring to sever plant heads. I'd given them a bowl of flower petals that had fallen to the ground without my help…and earned their wrath for daring to use dead flowers as a gift. *Can't win.*

My ears twitched when two dryads spoke to each other somewhere behind me. They only ever whispered, just as rumor claimed, their voices reminiscent of a gentle wind.

"We'll have a special guest later today," one said. "A witch."

Ohhh, a witch. We rarely received visits from the magically inclined. Hopefully I could talk the witch into a blessing in exchange for a new book about her coven's history.

"Do you know what she wants?" the other asked.

"I don't. But she sent word to say we were to roll out the red carpet."

"Why would she think we have carpet? And why would she *want* carpet out here?"

I whispered, "What time will she arrive?" To mask my excitement and encourage a response, I didn't glance over my shoulder; I just trimmed another dead leaf from a branch.

The two went quiet, shuffled apart and floated from the room, leaving me to expel a breath.

I didn't encounter any other dryads as I finished up, which wasn't much of a surprise. They preferred to spend their mornings outside, gardening, and their afternoons preparing and enjoying lunch. I wasn't invited to such a sacred time. After they'd eaten their fill, however, they always handed me a bowl of vegetables and herbs on their return inside.

"Thank you," I called when I accepted today's offering.

For the first time, a dryad stopped to respond. She had freckled white skin, hair the color of summer leaves, and she wore a gown made of flower petals, her feet bare. "Tomorrow is All Trees Day," she told me with a quiet voice. "Last night you tracked mud throughout the Temple, so you must clean the floors before we receive our daily visitors. Then you must clean the floors again, after our visitors leave."

All Trees Day. A holiday observed at every Temple scattered throughout the kingdoms, when citizens came to pay their respects, and dryads blessed any surrounding foliage to give back to nature.

"I'll get it done, don't you worry," I told her. I would work nonstop. I didn't like my job most days, but I always gave it my best.

Once I'd scarfed down the carrot, cucumber, mushrooms, and sprig of rosemary, I gathered the necessary supplies to clean the cobblestone on the bottom floor of the Temple.

I knelt and dunked a rag into the bucket of hot, soapy water. Withering roses! Old and new cuts stung.

With a wince, I dropped the sopping wet rag on the stone and got to scrubbing. No matter how good or bad I felt, I performed this task at least once every day. Today wasn't just a good day, though; today was a great one. My heartbeat steady, something that had been happening more and more lately. I guess the older I got the stronger I got.

I worked as quickly as possible while still doing my best, ready for the day's visitors to come and go so I could do it all over again and finally return to my room to read. I had recently acquired a book about mechanical triggers.

I already had ideas for my crossbow. The shedding of the outer layers to reveal a hidden dagger, when it ran out of arrows. It would be menacing from far away *and* close up. I just needed to figure out a way to keep the detachable pieces sturdy while they were needed.

I would love to speak with a blacksmith. Maybe spend a day

watching as one worked. So far, I'd only ever crafted my daggers from objects I'd found in the forest.

By the time I finished the floors—the first time—my energy was drained, fatigue holding me captive. And I still had to go outside to rake leaves and gather herbs.

Ugh. My stomach twisted, nervousness rising. I *hated* going outside. But still I did it. If I didn't work, I didn't eat.

I liked to eat.

Sighing, I grabbed my basket and strode to the nearest exit, where I stopped. A crisp, warm breeze caressed my skin, seeping past my threadbare sackcloth. A squirrel sprinted along a tree branch, spotted me, and halted.

As he spun to make a hasty retreat, I stuck out my tongue. He wasn't the first critter to run away from me, and I doubted he would be the last. For whatever reason, animals despised me just as people did. Which I still didn't understand. I wasn't useless or stupid. I had talents and a lot of love to give. Shouldn't character define a person rather than physical ability?

Before I emerged any farther, I performed a quick sky check, on the lookout for avian.

About once a month, a group of them showed up to fly overhead and throw rocks at my head. A few times, they'd even landed...

I shuddered. I was due for another visitation any day.

There was no telltale sign of wings, thank goodness. Still, I performed a weapon's check next, making sure my makeshift dagger was hidden beneath the pocket I'd sown into my dress.

All right. Good to go. I hurried out to war with the leaves and hunt the proper herbs. By the time I finished, the day had grown quite hot. My limbs shook from exertion. Sweat soaked me, and dirt streaked me. Better return to the Temple before I passed out.

Whoosh. Whoosh. Whoosh.

I went still, my heart suddenly banging on my ribs. I knew that sound well. How many avian had come? How close were they?

How far was the Temple? My gaze zoomed to my home. Two hundred feet maybe?

Too far. I'd never make it. But what other choice did I have? I clutched my basket to my chest and sprang into a mad dash, throwing a quick glance over my shoulder. Only one avian had come for me, but he was the worst of the bunch. A male with white skin, black wings, and red hair. I'd dubbed him Trio.

Pain exploded between my shoulder blades, and I knew the brute had thrown a rock at me. I careened to my hands and knees, my lungs emptying in a rush. The herbs tumbled from the basket, and Trio laughed.

The dryads would fume over the lack of seasoning for dinner, but there was no help for it. I wanted to survive. Not bothering to gather my bounty, I scrambled up and sprinted forward at a faster clip, tossing another glance over my shoulder.

Too close. Almost upon me. I pumped my arms, hoping to quicken my step. Thud. Searing pain. I grunted as that pain ricocheted through me, the momentum taking me down once again.

Trio soared past me, landing a few feet away to unveil a slow grin.

Trying not to vomit, I reached for the dagger I'd made from a bundle of knitting needles I'd sourced. "I'm warning you," I began, and he laughed again. "I *will* stab you."

He lifted another stone. A bigger one. "Let's have some fun, you and I."

"Did someone mention fun?" A gust of wind blew in, carrying an unfamiliar voice. When it died, a girl who looked to be my age stood between the avian and me.

My pulse raced. Who—or what—was she? A witch? She must be. Like all the magically inclined, she wore wrist cuffs.

She glanced back to wink at me. Wavy brown hair framed a lovely face with flawless brown skin and fathomless brown eyes.

Definitely a witch. An azure glow of power rimmed her irises.

Multiple diamond chokers circled her neck. A thin, golden breastplate etched with swirling symbols safeguarded her torso, sparking envy in me. *So beautifully crafted.* A thick leather belt looped around her waist with a bejeweled dagger hanging at each side. Underneath a mesh skirt, she sported leather tights and fur-lined boots.

Was she the witch the dryads were expecting?

"My name is Ophelia," she announced.

Trio backed up several steps. "I know who you are."

"I highly doubt you do." She spread her arms, then her fingers, as if reaching into thin air for her magic. "If you knew who I was, you'd know what I'm capable of, and you'd be halfway home by now."

He popped his jaw, emitting a frisson of fear.

The witch smirked. "I was sent by Ashleigh's father, King Philipp. He expects me to collect his daughter and return her to the palace in one piece. If I have to sew her back together, I'm going to use parts of you to do it."

Wait. "You were, and he does?" Ophelia wasn't just any witch, then; she was a royal one I'd never met. Sent by my father. Who wanted me home. Me. Home! The knowledge dawned like a new day inside me, teeming with possibilities.

"I just said so, didn't I?" she replied, exasperated.

"You can't come here and—" Trio began.

She waved her hand, and he went silent, even though his mouth continued to move. "Are you sure about that?"

As he frantically clutched his throat, I staggered to my feet, the muscles in my lower back protesting the action. Ignoring the pain wasn't difficult when I got to enjoy Trio's defeat.

"I think I've made my point." Another wave of the witch's hand.

Trio burst out "—strike at me is to strike at all avian. You will get out of my way, witch, or you will suffer for it."

"But you're just too dumb to understand it," she added. "What do you think you can do to me, hmm?" A challenge layered every word. "Please. Tell me. I'm metaphorically dying to know."

His scowl intensified, but he dropped the rock.

Ohhh. I liked this girl. "I'm honored to make your acquaintance," I whispered, only to realize I didn't need to lower my volume. "Nice to make your acquaintance," I repeated at the same volume she had used, and oh, wow, my vocal cords loved the vibration.

"I know. Everyone is. Here, you're supposed to read this." She reached back to hand me an envelope sealed with Fleur's official symbol—two roses framed by a shining sun.

My heart leaped. The rose had been my mother's favorite bloom. The very reason I'd made it my signature. No matter what weapon I designed, I found a way to incorporate the flower in some capacity.

As Ophelia and Trio exchanged more taunts, I broke the wax, curious about what my father had to say.

The paper read, "You will come home without delay."

Without delay. Because he'd forgiven me? Grinning, I hugged the paper to my chest and twirled.

I'd thought about my father often, dreaming of going home and proving myself worthy of his affections. I'd had no contact with him since my banishment, but the little girl I used to be, the one who still lived inside me, wanted a relationship with him, approval, *something*.

Whoosh. Whoosh. The hated sound jolted me from my celebration. I looked up, expecting Trio to be on the attack. Instead, he was flying *away* from us.

I *really* liked this witch.

"Come," Ophelia said, pivoting on a booted heel. "We must leave now. He grows impatient."

My father? "I can't leave without my designs and my eggs."

"Is this amateur hour? Of course you can't." Ophelia waved her hand toward me, and a small satchel materialized, the strap draped across my chest. "That's why they're already in your possession."

"Impossible. The satchel is so small—" I stuck in a hand and gaped as I was able to put in my arm to the shoulder. A magic satchel, with more room than it appeared to have. I rooted through the contents and, sure enough, there was a stack of my designs, all four dragon eggs that were double the size of an ostrich egg and a handful of books. With my mother's ring secured around my neck, I had everything I needed to start a new life. Now I smiled at the witch. "You're right. Thank you."

"I don't need thanks. I just need action." She motioned behind me. "Let's go."

Yes. Let's. No reason to say goodbye to the dryads. I doubted they cared. And how sad was that? I'd known them for three whole years, and I'd never won them over. I couldn't think of one who would miss me. "Are we going to walk?" I asked as I turned. I hadn't noticed a mode of conveyance. Well. I hadn't. Now a pumpkin-shaped unicorn-drawn carriage awaited me.

"Get in, Princess," Ophelia said, suddenly directly behind me, her warm breath on the back of my neck. "Just so you know, I could have whisked you to the palace in seconds. I'm that powerful. But I'm saving my magic for the delights to come."

Delights? What did she mean?

I reached for the carriage's handle to pull myself up and noticed my red, callused hands, the dirt caked under my nails. I cast my gaze over the horrid state of my clothing, and I wanted to sink into the ground. "I can't let my father see me like this."

"You can, and you will." I thought she mumbled, "Let him see what his neglect has wrought," but I couldn't be sure.

With a sigh, I climbed inside the carriage, careful of my eggs. Ophelia entered behind me, and the unicorns launched into motion. Only minutes later, we were entering the infamous Enchantian Forest, where most citizens dared not tread without a magical guide.

I tossed a final glance over my shoulder to bid the Temple goodbye, but the cluster of hollowed-out trees was already gone.

We must have traveled through one of the many invisible doorways common in the area, each one able to whisk unwitting bystanders miles away to another section of the forest in only a blink. Here, a blue and gold light enveloped taller trees, pulsing as if we'd reached the heart of the forest.

Ophelia buffed her nails and asked, "Do you know anything about the new Empress of the Forest? Well, she prefers the title of queen."

"I've heard conflicting reports about her. Some say she's good, some say she's evil." Which was she? Since the state of her heart dictated the state of the forest, the answer kind of mattered. "Have you gotten to meet her?"

The witch fluffed her hair. "I don't want to brag, but we're very mediocre friends. You would love her. You have so much in common."

"What do you mean?"

"You're both evil."

"I'm not evil," I burst out. And oh, wow, every divot and rock bounced me atop the cushionless bench, bruising my already bruised backside.

"My mistake. I'd thought I'd heard rumors…"

I *humph*ed. "Don't believe everything you hear."

As we bumped along, I stopped trying to make conversation with the witch and let my mind venture to my homecoming. How would my father welcome me? If I received just one smile...

Did Milo work at the palace? Did he still have his father's journals? I'd replayed our final interaction anytime I'd learned something new about Leonora. While I remained certain Milo was wrong and I wasn't somehow a centuries-old witch, I sometimes...occasionally...possibly...entertained the barest hint of doubt. I still felt as if I had hidden magic. So, I'd studied at every opportunity, and cobbled together a patchwork history for the fire witch.

Leonora was the daughter of a warlock king and a witch queen. Her entire coven had been eager to discover the powerful magic she would wield. But, at the age of sixteen, she'd failed to manifest an ability. Then, inexplicably, at the age of twenty-one, everything had changed.

I massaged the back of my neck. This was where things got a bit too coincidental for my liking. She'd begun to create and manipulate fire.

Soon after, she'd met the first avian king, Craven the Destroyer. He'd stormed through Enchantia, enslaving different species and overtaking multiple kingdoms, Leonora's among them. A handful of accounts claimed he'd spied her, desired her, and abducted her, then kept her locked away in the Avian Mountains. One account said she'd gone with him willingly. I leaned toward the first because she'd mounted a successful escape about a year later, causing the eruption of their war.

Centuries after that, one of Craven's great grandchildren was said to have resumed the war with one of Leonora's great grandchildren, with the same results. The avian and his people destroyed, the witch the victor.

But how had Milo known what Leonora desired most? What had his father written about us, and how could I get hold of his notes?

"Whatever you're overthinking, stop." Ophelia patted my

knee. "All thoughts create energy. Certain thoughts create a lot of energy. My fuel. I feed on it. But if you keep this up, I'm going to spontaneously combust."

An exaggeration, surely. "Have you heard of a woman named Leonora the Burner of Worlds? She was a witch, like you, only she came from ancient times."

"Sorry, but I'm one of a kind. I'm an apple baby."

Um, that was impossible. Wasn't it? "There were once three Trees of New Beginnings. Now there are none." They'd been destroyed. A fact the dryads lamented often.

Once, women who desired a baby could eat an apple from a Tree of New Beginnings and conceive or birth a child within a year. I wasn't clear on the specifics. If I remembered right, though, those babies were said to be powerful beyond imagining—and destined to reach a tragic end.

"Were they destroyed, then? You watched them die? I wish my mother had known before she ate one of their apples." Ophelia hiked a shoulder in a shrug, all *poor woman*. "I've heard about Leonora, yes. She torched Craven the Destroyer's kingdom to the ground *after* she beheaded him. Such an amateur move. I would have torched the village first and made him watch. Twice."

So, Ophelia knew what I knew and little else. How disappointing.

How long till we reached our destination? I leaned over to peer out the window, seeing the trees I'd expected and...snow? I frowned. Fleur did not snow in summer.

Shadows fell over the treetops, and I jerked my gaze up. I recoiled. An entire horde of avian. Never had I seen so many winged warriors in one location. No more than ten at once had ever visited the palace in Fleur, and only five had tormented me at the Temple. They dwelt primarily in the Avian Mountains, so territorial they preferred not to leave. So why were so many here now?

Unless they'd come to greet me with rocks?

Quaking, I looked out at the dreary mountains that loomed in the distance. A massive stone fortress topped the largest and—

Mountains?

"Ophelia? I think we accidentally traveled through the wrong doorways." Usually witches sensed where each invisible entrance led and navigated accordingly. "We're in Sevón, not Fleur."

"Gold star for you, Princess." She shifted, getting comfortable. "Not too long ago, your uncle forced a young sorceress named Everly Morrow to marry him. Everly murdered him right after the wedding, of course, making Roth the king of Sevón. He imprisoned the sorceress, but soon fell madly in love with her. The two joined forces and went to war with Princess Farrah, who joined forces with the new sorcerian overlord, Nicolas."

I could only gap at her. What the—*what?*

"Farrah and Nicolas are currently at war with the entire Azul Dynasty," she continued, gossip clearly her favorite language. "Or they would be, if Nicolas wasn't missing and Farrah wasn't imprisoned in a glass coffin deep in the heart of the forest. Your father decided to use the civil unrest to sneak into Sevón, kill Roth's most loyal servants and claim the kingdom as his own. Meaning, yes, your father is now at war with Roth and Everly, who rule the Enchantian Forest. She wanted to abduct you during your return to the palace and ransom you back to your father—for each of his limbs—but I told her no way, that she's got to wait at least three weeks before she even considers amputation."

"Um, thanks?" My head spun, my entire world suddenly turned upside down and inside out. Word about this had never reached the Temple. I hadn't known my uncle, King Challen, was dead. I hadn't known him well, either, but I'd liked him, and I mourned his loss.

Had he really forced a sorceress to wed him?

I hadn't known my father had displaced my cousin to save the kingdom from that same evil sorceress, or that Roth had fallen in love.

"How is my father?" I asked softly. "He is well?"

"If you don't mind 'em entitled, selfish, and greedy, then yeah, he is well. Tomorrow, he kicks off a three-week tournament that's open to any eligible bachelor in the land. The prize is a grand one—your stepsister's hand in marriage. As we speak, males are flocking into the realm to fight for her. I'm tempted to enter the tournament myself. The girl can turn anything into gold with her touch alone."

What! "Please, back up. I have a stepsister?"

The witch shook her head. "You have two of them. Soon after your banishment, your father married a princess of Azul. A widow with two daughters. Dior is your age, and Marabella is two years younger."

More changes to digest. My father had remarried, and I had a stepmother and two stepsisters whom I'd never met, one of them magically inclined, the way I'd always dreamed of being.

Needing comfort, I reached up to stroke my beloved ring. Would my new family like me or would they find me lacking?

"Do you have news about—" *Don't do it. Don't ask.* "Saxon Skylair, the avian prince?" *Withering roses.* I'd asked.

"Oh, yes," she replied, her lips curving into a smile. "He's the crown prince now, and the poor kid has had a tough month. Farrah, whom he loved like a sister, betrayed him in order to strike at Everly. And Roth, if you want to get technical. Girl was jealous and lashing out. Then came your father's attack. Then Saxon's father and older brother fought a water witch and drowned—on land. So, Queen Raven called her only son home to rule as king. He agreed to return once he concludes some life-and-death business in Sevón."

Foreboding prickled the back of my neck. Saxon, soon-to-be king of the avian. King. Their ultimate commander. Considering his business coincided with my summons home...

This did not bode well for my return.

As king, Saxon wouldn't be content to send his men to throw rocks at me. He would expect more spectacular results.

On the verge of tears, I pushed the avian from my mind and gazed out the window to lose myself in the new sights. We'd reached the top of the mountain and come to a bustling market set in the shadow of the castle; it was double the size of Fleur's markets, and I marveled... *Weeds*. More avian. They flew overhead in wide, sweeping laps. Did they patrol the skies, guarding their future king? Or did they have more sinister intension?

I shook. The males were shirtless, wearing only skintight leather pants. The females wore similar pants and covered their breasts with cutouts of leather. All displayed a colorful array of bracelets on their wrists. I'd read different accounts about the meaning of those bracelets. Some claimed they represented feats of strength. Others believed they told a story about each avian's individual life, like the job they held, the family they came from, and the vows they made.

On the ground, mortal males wore tunics of varying colors and dark slacks. Mortal females wore fur-trimmed gowns in brighter shades. Mixed with them were a handful of witches, a couple of trolls, a centaur family, and the occasional fae.

Some sellers peddled linens and jewelry. Others offered food, everything from meats and vegetables to fresh-baked breads, the scents drifting into the carriage. My mouth watered, and my stomach rumbled. One vendor offered enough copper, iron, nickel, and platinum to make my head spin.

I pressed my cheek against the window, staring at the glistening metal as long as possible. The weapons I could make. The armor. A hint of gold glinted in the sunlight, and I groaned.

All too soon, the market disappeared from sight. We traveled through a long, wide archway of hanging pixielilies, colorful flowers with soft yet sturdy petals shaped like birds, where pixies preferred to make their home. The lingering odor of food was replaced by a sweet floral perfume, and I drank it in. It was like inhaling magic.

We finally came to a stop in front of the fortress. Up close, the sight enraptured me. Not so dreary, after all. Moss grew over the walls and pillars. An elaborate marble fountain sprayed water near the palace steps, where two uniformed guards waited.

They rushed over to open the carriage door. The first one offered me a gloved hand, as if I were a grand lady despite my dirty rags. Feeling as if I was floating, I accepted and eased into the cold air.

He couldn't hide his disgust when he spotted me.

My cheeks blazed, and I snatched back my hand.

Ophelia emerged with the help of the second guard, who motioned us to follow him up the steps. Raising my chin, squaring my shoulders, I lifted the hem of my ragged skirt and followed him. I'd worked hard to achieve this look of sweat, dirt, and fatigue, and I wouldn't let anyone shame me.

Ophelia kept pace beside me. Her breathing remained steady. Mine didn't. I panted, afraid I'd faint before I got inside. What if I did something bad? What if I started another fire?

Deep breath in. Out. Good, that was good. As we passed more guards, a handful of guests, and a servant, I searched each face, hoping to see a smile or welcoming nod. Something! I just… I wanted to make a friend. I craved companionship, someone to talk to and exchange secrets with. Someone to comfort me when I got scared, perhaps. To encourage me when I was sick. I would happily return the favor.

"Dude," Ophelia whispered, nudging my shoulder with her own. "You look like you'll do anything to make these people like you, and it's, like, super embarrassing. Learn to mask, or they'll eat you up and spit out your bones."

Dude? I would have asked what the word meant, but my mind got hijacked the moment she touched me. Upon contact, strength had seeped into me, chasing away my fatigue. She really did wield energy magic, then. And at an apple baby level.

Why would she help me without first demanding payment? No way she'd accidentally touched me. Not a warrior like her; she knew what she was doing every second of every day. But what she'd done was just so...so...un-witchlike.

Two new guards waited at the top of the staircase. They opened a set of double doors, allowing us to pass without a hitch in our step. We entered the foyer, and I could only gape at the incredible luxury. How long since I'd beheld anything so fine? Shimmering gold veined the floor, glittering as sunlight streamed in through large, stained glass windows. A breathtaking battle-scene mural covered the far wall. On another wall hung portraits of past kings and queens with elaborate frames. A hand-carved dragon flanked each side of the staircase.

Visual stimulation overload.

"Keep moving, Princess Staresalot." Ophelia gave my shoulder another nudge and another boost of energy.

"Thank you," I said, beaming a smile at her.

"It was an accident," she lied, as if embarrassed for *herself.*

We stopped in front of another set of double doors, where two more guards waited, their swords drawn and crossed. They eyed me with distaste. No big deal.

"Princess Ashleigh Charmaine-Anskelisa to see King Philipp," Ophelia announced, her tone tight. "And I suggest you rearrange your expressions before I rearrange your faces."

The men sheathed their weapons and snapped to, shoving open the doors. Tremors plagued me as I stepped inside a throne room overcrowded with courtlings—the upper class, dressed in their finest garments and jewels.

Everyone turned to eye me up and down. Whispers and short bursts of laughter soon erupted, and my cheeks blazed anew.

Ophelia waved her hand, and the courtlings parted as if they'd been pushed, creating a pathway to the royal dais, where my father perched upon a golden throne. A girl I'd never met sat beside him, and Milo stood behind him, stroking the key that hung around his neck. The same key he'd worn the day of my mother's funeral—the one my mother used to stare at with longing.

An invisible fist punched the air from my lungs. I needed to speak with the warlock. Alone. But first… I swung my gaze back to my father, the parent I had here and now.

In our time apart, he'd barely changed. His dark hair might possess more gray, and new lines might branch from his brown eyes, but everything else remained the same. Regal cheekbones. An aquiline nose, and a strong jaw. A chin with a slight dent in the middle.

Wearing a large golden crown and a red robe flecked with gold, he appeared every inch the king.

The witch stopped, so I stopped, too, and moved my attention to the girl. My stepmother? No, surely not. We must be the same age. Could she be one of my stepsisters, then? The tournament prize?

Whoever she was, she was a stunner, with long hair as dark as a moonless night, eyes just as dark with a slight up-tilt, and pale skin. She wore wrist cuffs. Her gown…my heart fluttered with envy. Soft pink with flowers sewn into the skirt.

I glanced down at my sackcloth and wished the floor would open up and swallow me. All right. So maybe I could be embarrassed by my appearance, after all.

Ophelia gave me a little push forward. "Go get 'em, queenie."

I trudged the rest of the way alone and stopped before the dais. My knees quaked as I executed a wobbly curtsy. "Hello."

Father compressed his lips into a thin line. "You dare appear before me dressed in such filth?"

"I—I'm sorry, Father. There wasn't time to change—"

"I'm a king twice over. When you address me, you will refer to me as Your Majesty, just as my other subjects must."

He hadn't forgiven me at all. I stared down at my feet. "Yes, Your Majesty." *Never let them know they've hurt you.*

"I'm so happy to meet you, Princess Ashleigh. I'm Dior," the girl said. Such a gentle voice, even melodic. "I would love to—"

"If you are in Sevón—Majesty—who is ruling Fleur?" I said, speaking over her. I wanted a friend, yes, just not her. Anyone but the one who occupied my mother's throne. A stranger who oh, so clearly had everything I'd been denied. The king's affection and respect. A bright future. Magic.

Why were some people so privileged and others so...not?

"Who do you think?" His tone suggested I was a fool for asking. "My wife, Queen Andrea, rules in my stead. But she is none of your concern. Let us discuss the reason for your visit."

His new wife, my stepmother, was none of my concern? And what did he mean, "visit"? I wasn't here to stay?

"You have other concerns." Radiating smugness, he waved at a tall, raven-haired man who stood ahead of me, off to one side. I directed my full attention at him, and my stupid heart skipped a stupid beat. Massive azure wings arched at his sides. Azure. Wings.

Saxon. Here in the flesh. Standing inside the palace. He was several inches taller than I remembered and a hundred pounds of brawn heavier. The muscles in his broad shoulders bulged with suppressed tension, as if he wanted to turn around but he refused to heed his body's demand.

As if I'd said his name aloud—*had I?*—he finally glanced over his shoulder, his whiskey-colored gaze finding me. The way he looked at me…such furious heat, with a tinge of yearning.

This boy longed for my misery.

He had long lashes, high cheekbones, and soft lips. A shadow of stubble dusted his strong jaw. He'd shaved the sides of his hair but had grown out the top strands to create spikes. The danger he emitted…

Tremors swept down my spine as he dropped his attention to my mother's ring, then jerked his gaze back up to mine, hitting me with pure, undiluted hatred.

My next tremor almost rocked me off my feet.

"Tomorrow, a tournament for Dior's hand in marriage will begin," the king said. "If you'd been a normal girl, Ashleigh, you would have been the prize. Alas. A husband likes to know his wife will survive the wedding night."

Laughter sounded behind me, setting off a chain reaction inside me, different parts of me beading with cold sweat.

Saxon reveled in my discomfort, unveiling a slow, wicked smile. A mere baring of his perfect pearly whites. "I hope you're ready, Princess." His deep, rumbly voice rang inside my head, a challenge. A curse. "Your life is about to change, and not for the better."

I gasped a breath as I looked to my father, who rose to his feet.

The king told me, "I'm sure you need no introduction, Ashleigh. Prince Saxon has agreed to participate in the tournament, and you are to act as his royal liaison. What he needs, you will provide." His tone told me what his words did not: *or else.*

My head spun. Obey Saxon for three weeks? "Do all tournament participants receive a palace liaison?" The question escaped through clenched teeth.

"Only the royals. I chose you to serve Prince Saxon so that you may make full restitution for your past misdeeds at long last. Your new duties will begin after the first battle. If he survives, of course."

More teeth grinding. Serve the one who'd sent his men to harm me, when I'd already been banished? "No," I said, shaking my head. "I won't do it." I'd endured enough for a crime I couldn't recall.

Gasps sounded from the crowd.

So what? I refused to back down. I had to talk Father around. "Prince Saxon served as Roth's second-in-command, did he not? They are notorious best friends, as loyal as brothers. How can you trust him, even for a moment? What if he's here to aid King Roth and take back the kingdom?"

A muscle jumped beneath my father's eye. "Am I a simpleton who would fail to consult his oracle? I have been assured the prince's intentions are as pure as my own. And, Ashleigh? You *will* do as I tell you, which means you will do everything the avian tells you. Without argument."

Saxon turned to face me fully, sweeping that whiskey gaze over the rest of me. I shivered even as my blood heated.

"King Roth has aligned with an evil sorceress," Saxon said, "and Princess Farrah betrayed my trust in the worst way." Truth rang in his tone. "I'm no longer interested in aiding your cousins."

I shouldn't ask.

But I did, my curiosity too great. I had to know. "What are you interested in, then?"

A brittle pause before he quietly admitted, "I live to ensure you receive the fate you so richly deserve."

3

Caught up in a plight?
Do your best and fight.

SAXON

Finally, Princess Ashleigh Charmaine-Anskelisa is in my hands.
How I despised her. And yet, every time I glanced her way, I experienced an intense and familiar connection to her. A pull I could not deny. A sense that I'd finally found the missing puzzle piece my life desperately needed. A sense that I'd found the female able to make me happy. The one person I would recognize as my fated mate as soon as my wings produced a special dust only for her. But that sense was a lie. It had tormented me in two other lives as well, yet I'd never actually produced the tiniest speck of the amour dust.

It had even plagued me the day of her mother's funeral. The day I'd realized the memories of my past lives featured *her*.

We *were* fated to be together, just not as husband and wife, lovers, or even friends. Princess Ashleigh was a reincarnation of Leonora the Burner of Worlds, and I was a reincarnation of Craven the Destroyer. We were destined to war.

Our war had raged for centuries—just not consecutively. If I failed to end her reign of terror this time, the war would last centuries more. At some point, she would obliterate all of Enchantia.

So, no. She wasn't my fated one. I *would* end her reign of terror, no matter the lines I had to cross to do it. In doing so, I would become the king my people needed.

The one they'd always needed.

I hadn't lived in the Avian Mountains for over a decade. I didn't know my soldiers, and my soldiers didn't know me. They didn't like me much, either. I didn't care. Until I proved my mettle, one way or the other, I expected them to respect my position. One day, the like would come; I had no doubts. They would learn my capabilities and my strengths. I would teach them.

As an added bonus, I would have the opportunity to utterly destroy King Philipp. Thanks to a royal oracle named Noel, who Philipp wrongly believed worked for him, I knew the king hoped to use the tournament to eliminate anyone who threatened his reign, or supported Roth, or had insulted his great pride at one time or another.

He had no idea Noel was my friend and ally—and I was his biggest threat of all. For stealing Roth's kingdom, I would steal Philipp's life. *Always pay back double what is owed.* It was the avian way. Roth wasn't avian, but I loved him like a brother, and I would deliver justice on his behalf.

I just had to complete the tournament before I struck. Noel claimed there was no other way to get everything we'd ever wanted.

So, I would use the tournament to watch the king, learning his strengths and weaknesses, to secretly protect anyone loyal to Roth, to showcase my skill to my people, and to obtain unlimited access to Ashleigh. I could better orchestrate her downfall. Everything I'd ever wanted, as promised. But the pressure of it all...

I ignored the pit in my stomach. For all my troubles, I would receive great rewards. This was a time to celebrate, not lament.

While I could never achieve full restitution for the things Leonora had taken from me in the past, I *could* achieve some type of restitution for the unprovoked attack Princess Ashleigh had made at her mother's funeral. I grinned. By the time I finish with her, she will want to die and stay dead.

To my consternation, I couldn't simply kill the girl as the Craven side of my nature desired. I couldn't give her a chance to be reborn and restart our war for a fourth time. No, I had to weaken her instead. Then, when the tournament ended, Ophelia would cast a sleeping spell, ensuring Ashleigh—Leonora—never aged, never woke to harm anyone else, and never died.

Never again would the avian be endangered by her fire magic or army of dragons. And Leonora *always* raised an army of dragons.

Dragons existed in Craven's era, then seemed to die out. At the time of my second life, the scaled creatures had been nothing more than a legend. Then, Leonora managed to raise a new army, and I'd learned dragon mothers buried their eggs throughout Enchantia, and those eggs could live in stasis for hundreds of years, completely indestructible. In this third life, dragons were once again a footnote in history books. And yet, Ophelia had told him Ashleigh had already acquired four of their eggs. More proof of her true identity.

So, while doing everything else, I had to prevent Ashleigh's eggs from hatching.

"Nothing to say?" I asked her. "Not going to beg me for mercy?"

"Do you *have* mercy? And you can't be enemies with Prince Roth. You can't be."

I'd told her the truth about everything...almost. Roth *had* fallen in love with an evil sorceress. Her name was Everly, and I adored her, too. She was an apple baby able to cast lifelike illusions, heal the wounded, grow a seedling into a tree in a matter of minutes, and build walls of dirt with only a thought. And Farrah *had* betrayed me in the worst of ways, compelling me to stab an innocent girl. But work against the pair? No.

The day the Charmaine siblings took me in as a young child, shielding me from a father who wanted me dead, they made advance restitution for any and every action, at any time, in any way, for always.

"Ashleigh, you may leave us." King Philipp's voice boomed through the throne room. "Bathe. Change clothes."

"I'd like her to stay just as she is," I announced. I extended an arm in Ashleigh's direction and crooked my finger. "Come here." If she resisted in any way, she would find that I did not issue threats, only promises. The key to getting what you wanted—always follow through.

She'd asked if I had mercy. I didn't. Not for her. Not with the tasks I had planned for her, each one designed to drain whatever strength she possessed, keeping her too weak to use her fire magic, making her as miserable as she made me.

Lips parted, the princess glided closer to me. No threats necessary, then. How disappointing.

The scent of roses and vanilla wafted from her, filling my nose, clouding my thoughts, and I stiffened. Roses—a garden. Vanilla—a kitchen. The two combined? Home.

Not my *home.* Never *my home.*

My time with Leonora never ended well.

In our first life, I'd found her by chance. She'd been twenty-one, and I'd been a bit older. We'd loved each other…at first. She slaughtered my people and stabbed me in the heart years later, then burned my kingdom for good measure. During our second life, she was the one who found me. Again, she'd been twenty-one, and I'd been a few years older.

At my first sighting the second time around, I'd begun to recall the best moments in our first life together. I'd quickly fallen in love with her all over again. Then I'd begun to dream about our worst moments together—every atrocity she'd ever committed against me and my people.

The fact that I'd found her at an earlier age during this third life, the fact that I'd already remembered the *worst* moments of our past lives...

No, I would not fall for her a third time. In this life, there would be no Craven–Leonora love affair. She would not be able to reincarnate when I finished with her, and I would enjoy a hard-won peace. I would rule my people the way I should have ruled them before. Their safety would come before my desire for a murderous witch.

Ashleigh stopped at my side and clasped the ring she still wore around her neck. I stifled a growl. Craven had gifted that ring to Leonora as a symbol of his love.

"What?" she grumbled.

I nudged her fingers aside to lift the hated ring for my inspection. Had she just stifled a moan?

The ring was exactly the same, as if time had taken drastic measures to preserve it. How the small metal band mocked me.

I wanted to rip it from her neck, but I knew I couldn't. No one could. Craven had paid a witch to bespell it, ensuring the abomination remained in her possession.

Once, in the midst of our war, I'd asked her, *Why do you keep the ring? We are enemies.*

She'd replied, *We won't always be enemies, my love. One day, we will have our happily-ever-after. That is what I'm fighting for, and I always win.*

"Why do you wear this?" I asked her now. Had she remembered me yet? "How did you find it?"

"It was a gift from my mother." With a huff, she yanked the piece of jewelry from my grip and stepped out of range.

How had her mother found it, then? Magic? And why was Leonora born to humans, rather than witches and warlocks like before? Why did she have a heart condition? Or was she faking as a way to deceive her enemies? Why had her name changed?

So many questions. I was Craven, then Tyron, and now Saxon. I'd always possessed the same face and form. She had remained Leonora in the second life, but had possessed a different face and form, with the same ice-blue eyes as before. Why become Ashleigh this time? Why did she possess green eyes that only flashed ice blue when her temper erupted?

Despite the inconsistencies, I knew she was Leonora. The knowledge screamed within me. And yet the questions remained an itch in my brain. Now more than ever I wanted to scratch.

When Noel informed me about the need to compete in the tournament, she also offered scattered advice about Ashleigh. *Do nothing permanent—know everything is final. Ashleigh is exactly like you, but vastly different. Make sure she is definitely, for sure Leonora. During the tournament, she and the eggs must be protected. Let the next three weeks serve as a test. When time is up, there'll be no more. There'll be no going back. I see… I see… I don't know. What, what? My powers have been wonky since our battle with Farrah, but the truth is so murky.*

As a young girl, Ashleigh had thrown balls of fire at me, an ability only Leonora possessed. She *must* be Leonora. But…yes. I would use the three-week time frame and restitution tasks to test her as well as weaken her, without harming her. I would prove her true identity beyond any doubt.

I think fate *wanted* me to expose her for the evil witch she was. Otherwise, why bring us back a third time, ensuring I remembered the worst of my memories first? Why put Ashleigh's father in my crosshairs, allowing me to aid Roth and Everly at the same time that I dealt with my past and future?

"You will come to my tent at sunrise." I purred the words, hoping to make her shudder with fury, as Leonora used to do.

I wasn't disappointed. "I will *not* serve you," she snapped. "Not now, not ever."

Murmurs whisked through the crowd at lightning speed.

King Philipp banged his royal scepter on the floor, a demand for silence. He prepared to deliver a scathing retort, I was sure. The man certainly enjoyed exerting his authority over others.

So did I. I lifted my fist to silence *him*. I might be his junior, but I had half a foot of height and a hundred pounds of muscle on him. On a battlefield, I would mop the floor with his face.

As expected, he glowered at my daring, yet he didn't nay-say me. I think he feared me a little, and my Craven side reveled in it.

"The princess is mine now," I reminded him, my tone uncompromising. "My..." What had he called her? "Palace liaison. I will see to her chastisement."

A pause. Then, he worked his jaw and offered with deceptive ease, "Yes, of course."

Ashleigh jerked her chin in my direction. "You can *liaison* yourself."

I stepped closer. Torchlight glinted off her flawless skin, and her long sable waves shimmered. Why did she have to be so lovely in this incarnation, as if she'd been made from a checklist of my deepest desires?

In our first life, she'd been a redhead. In the second, a blonde. Now she was a dark-haired goddess with flawless bronze skin. Her most exquisite form yet. Those wide, emerald eyes were framed by long, spiky black lashes. *Mesmerizing.* She had a perfect nose and elegant cheekbones.

By the holy stars, I had the wildest urge to caress every inch of her and luxuriate in her softness, the way I'd once done with Leonora.

I will not give in. Not this time.

"Why are you doing this?" She peered at me unblinking. "I promise I do not remember harming you."

Truth or lie? Craven and I were separate, but still one, still indistinguishable from each other. "Whether you recall it or not," I told her, "you attacked an avian prince without provocation. If there is to be an accord between our people, you will pay your debt to me."

"I *have* paid my debt to you," she cried. "I have paid for three years. So I ask again. Why are you doing this?"

I told her simply, "Because I can." Because, despite the atrocities Ashleigh had committed, despite my reputation as a merciless tyrant—mine, not just Craven's, for few people knew I was a reincarnate—I couldn't bring myself to harm her physically. I hadn't needed Noel's warning in that regard. My instincts wouldn't let me harm her. Even now they shouted, *Protect. Cherish.*

Protect? Cherish? Never.

"I'm sorry for whatever I did to you, Prince Saxon," she whispered. "I'm sorry for the pain you suffered. I am. I assure you that I meant you no harm then, and I mean you no harm now. I—"

"Enough!" Anger burned hot in my veins. I might have questions about her past lives compared to this one, but I knew what she'd done as a little girl. "Words without actions are meaningless. So, you will prove you are as repentant as you claim. You will come to my tent *today*. You will begin *now*. I have tasks for you. Four, to be exact. One for each of the wounds you inflicted in the garden. Perform these tasks, and restitution will be achieved."

Restitution could *never* be achieved.

As she peered up at me, searching my gaze, the rosy flush drained from her cheeks, leaving her ashen. She reminded me of the girl I'd met at her mother's funeral, with eyes like living wounds.

I would not soften.

"Willingly enter your tent, so that you can torture me in private? Is that what it will take to soothe your bruised ego?" She lifted her chin and slipped her hand into mine, a willing sacrifice. "All right, then. Let's go. Let's get this done."

I stood shocked, immobile. Not just because of her acquiescence. Her palm felt roughened by calluses. When I lifted her hand into the light, I saw a wealth of scars, too.

She tried to jerk her hand free, but I held tight. Our gazes met, and she stilled, too proud to keep struggling. I'd always imagined her lounging atop tree branches at the Temple. The most Leonora thing anyone could do. But, she must have been working these past three years.

How…not Leonora.

Murky, Noel? That was like saying a single grain of sand represented every beach in the island paradise of Azul.

I reminded myself of Leonora's crimes.

Murdered my family. Twice.

Burned my village. Twice.

Stabbed me in the heart. Twice.

Sneering, I said, "Aw, did the dryads force the privileged princess to do real labor?"

That pride… She squared her shoulders, every bit a queen standing before peasants, refusing to back down. "Yes. They did."

Good for them. "Soon you'll remember your Temple days with fondness."

"Soon *you'll* wish we'd never met."

"I assure you. That is already my fondest wish, Princess." Done with this conversation, I nodded to King Philipp and stomped from the room, dragging Ashleigh behind me.

Every courtling watched us, rapt. Some muttered the standard hello and goodbye: "May you find gold."

I spared Ophelia a glance, and only Ophelia, inclining my

chin in greeting. The witch was best friends with Noel and another longtime ally of mine. I trusted her. She was an apple baby, just like Noel and Everly, their fates tied to Enchantia. They would always fight for the good of the land.

Philipp and Leonora were not good for the land.

The energy witch arched a brow, all, *Are you sure you want to travel this path?*

Did she mean turning Ashleigh/Leonora into a brand-new cautionary tale? *I'm sure.*

"By *tent* I hope you mean a room in this palace," my liaison said, already panting.

She cannot be so weak. "Like every combatant in the tournament, I'm staying near the battlefield."

A mewl left her. "Well, I'd like to bathe and change before we go. As you can see, I desperately need to do both."

I took great pleasure in telling her, "Change into what? You own nothing but what I choose to give you."

With her free hand, she clutched her satchel close to her chest. "Try to take my things and I'll... I'll..."

I repeated, "You. Own. Nothing. If you want something, you'll have to earn it."

She would never be able to earn it.

A tremor rocked her, vibrating into me. I. Didn't. Care. My hardened heart remained unaffected. I wasn't softening. I wasn't.

We strode through the hall, the foyer, and exited the castle. I fortified my resolve to end this girl with a single reminder: *Leonora.*

"Look. I want you to know—" Either Ashleigh tripped or her knees gave out. She fell, her hand slipping free of mine.

I turned without thought, catching her before she hit the ground. We froze, my arms banded around her. My gaze searched hers as her roses and vanilla scent muddled my thoughts. How perfect she felt against me. How—

I growled. "You want me to know what, exactly?"

She nibbled on her bottom lip, solemn. "You don't have to hurt me. I'm going to do the tasks you give me."

"When have I *ever* hurt you?" I snarled, my temper pricked.

Her pants came faster. Soon, she was wheezing. No, she wasn't faking her illness. She *was* the Glass Princess, easily breakable and humiliatingly weak.

The avian *despised* weakness, and I was no different. But it wasn't hate that I experienced as I released my bundle and straightened. I felt sympathy despite myself. This girl had decided to willingly accompany someone she expected to deliver great pain, just to prove her remorse. That wasn't something Leonora would do.

This had to be a trick, then. She planned to confuse and manipulate me, but she wouldn't succeed.

I'd rather die than lose to her again.

Sympathy wasn't allowed. Determined, I pulled a thin rope from my pocket. With a reincarnate of Leonora, one must always be prepared. I bound her wrists together. Delicate wrists. Fragile.

Concern wasn't allowed.

"You're restraining me?" she squeaked.

"Most people manifest magic at the age of sixteen. You wielded it expertly at fourteen. You've even had three years to practice." The power at her disposal... "While we're together, I will take every precaution to ensure you cannot summon your flames."

"I don't know how I started the fires, okay? I have no magic. My father never paid a witch to infuse me with power."

The *fires*, plural. How many had she set over the years? "I watched you do it. You held out your hands, flames flickering from your fingertips, a ball of fire forming."

Her eyes widened. "An illusion, perhaps, cast by the real fire starter," she replied, her voice frayed at the edges. "There could have been a witch or warlock present. Actually, there *was* a warlock present. Milo."

"What would be his motivation for burning an entire section of the royal Fleuridian garden, hmm? Try again." I forced her bound arms around my neck, cradling her against me. Mistake. Soft curves molded to my harder body, sending streams of heat through me.

It was a sensation I feared I would forever crave.

Scowling, I flared my wings.

"You're going to fly me?" Euphoria tinged her voice, her features brightening. Rather than fight me, she held on tighter. "What if I inadvertently touch your wings?"

I will love it, and hate myself. Remaining silent, I leaped into the air. The wind whipped through her hair, the strands blustering around my face.

As she peered down, awe filled her emerald eyes.

Very well. This would be the last time I took her to the sky.

"I've always wondered what the world looked like from up here." With a breathy sigh, she rested her head on my shoulder, as if she couldn't help but share the moment with me, despite our mutual dislike. "It's so beautiful, isn't it?"

I quickened my pace, wings flapping faster, before I broke down and started performing tricks, just to hear any other noises she might make.

Halfway down the mountain, the battlegrounds appeared. Combatants and their entourages crowded the area, many in the process of setting up their tents. Others were busy training. Multiple firepits blazed, the scent of roasting meat sailing on a cool breeze.

Ashleigh's stomach rumbled. I stiffened. How long since she'd last eaten?

Never mind. The answer didn't matter. "Over a hundred warriors signed up to compete for your stepsister's hand. *She* is greatly desired. Tales of her beauty abound." *But she is not half as stunning as you.* And really, few of the fighters wanted the princess for her pretty face. They wanted her magical ability: the golden touch.

"I'm sure she's nice," Ashleigh said, her eyes darting sharply. "I've always wanted a sister."

An attempt at innocence, while her tone dripped with disdain? I snorted. "I saw the way you looked at her. You're jealous of her." Another trait of Leonora's; she'd been envious of everyone, wanting what they had. "Admit it."

"I...you...what I feel for her is none of your concern."

Having gotten the reaction I wanted, I changed the subject. "You'll be pleased to know my tent is already set up." I gestured to the largest one, currently surrounded by a dozen avian warriors. Once I'd agreed to become king upon the tournament's end, my mother had remembered my existence and sent her personal guards to oversee my protection.

As usual, the soldiers regarded me warily. They didn't know why I'd been exiled from the Avian Mountains, or that an oracle had visited our palace, or that she'd told my parents I would rule the avian before my twentieth year, that I was a reincarnate of Craven the Destroyer, the most vile avian ever to live, seconded only by Tyron, and that I would wed a reincarnate of Leonora the Burner of Worlds, the ruin of our people.

Back then, I'd had none of Craven's memories. And, because reincarnation required vast amounts of magic not even Leonora possessed, I'd dismissed the oracle's claim. My parents had not. They had believed her, and they had been horrified.

Hoping to avoid a third replay of the past, my father had stabbed me while I slept. My mother had watched. Crying, yes. The first time she'd ever shed a tear, and yet she'd offered me no aid as my father chased me through the halls. I'd managed to stumble onto a balcony and take flight. But avian had excellent night vision, and my father had followed. At some point, I'd spotted Roth and Farrah and crash landed nearby.

They'd bravely fought off the avian king, then summoned healers, saving my life.

My people had no idea how many battles I'd won in Roth's name, or how many times I'd saved Farrah from certain disaster. Now I had to earn their admiration to prove I was the ruler they needed. And I had to do it without appearing as, well, craven as Craven, who had killed anyone who'd disagreed with him, upset him, or even looked at him wrong. They would expect me to be the fool who fell in love with a wicked witch thrice over.

The pressure...

As the soldiers spotted Ashleigh, their wariness faded. Each one grinned with pride, pleased to see I would gain much deserved reparation from the Glass Princess. They didn't know she was a reincarnation of Leonora, either, only that she had insulted and injured me as a teenager, during a funeral no less, and then denied any wrongdoing. A fact as humiliating as it was correct.

"Take me back." Trembling anew, she attempted to scramble up and behind me. "Take me back to the palace right now."

I secured my grip, keeping her in place. "Be still."

"Not them," she beseeched. "Please, not them."

Them? The guards? As I descended, her quaking magnified, baffling me. Leonora had feared nothing and no one, but Ashleigh was terrified of avian soldiers who wouldn't touch her without my express permission? Why?

I landed as gently as possible, a courtesy Ashleigh didn't deserve. As I strode forward, my bracelets clinked together, the noise actually calming her, as if her thoughts had just curved into a new road.

She buried her face in the hollow of my neck and asked, "What do the bracelets mean?"

"That is none of your concern," I replied, giving her back her own words. Each band pointed to a significant event that had occurred or would occur in my life. The day of my birth. The battles I'd won, and the warriors I'd killed. One day, I would give the marriage bracelet to my wife and queen, whoever she happened to be. "You, fetch Eve," I demanded, motioning to a nearby guard. I wished my friend Vikander were here to aid me instead of these strangers. I trusted the fae prince in ways I didn't trust the avian. Unfortunately the irreverent warrior with a taste for sex and fine wine had been called home for an emergency.

Ashleigh lifted her head, and she was nibbling on her bottom lip again, drawing my attention there, making my gut clench. "Who is Eve?" she asked.

"My second-in-command. At the moment."

Adriel, the one posted in front of the tent, opened the flap and stepped aside. As I strode past him, Ashleigh watched the male the way a wounded animal watched an approaching hunter. Only when the flap swished behind us, sealing us inside, did the tension seep from her.

I set her down, glad to have her out of my arms. Yes, glad. "I'm going to untie your wrists. If you use your magic, I'll cut off one of your hands. If you attempt an escape, I'll cut off one of your feet." It was the Craven way.

The Leonora way? To do it, anyway.

"Would you really mutilate me?" Ashleigh asked.

Always follow through. But...

"Enough conversation." I palmed a dagger and cut the tie as promised.

She scanned the area with growing horror, taking in the mess I'd created just for her. "*This* is where you're staying?"

A slow grin spread. "It is." The other two Leonoras had despised cleaning. In fact, during both of our first and second lifetimes, we'd argued about her messiness, how she would drop whatever she didn't want on the floor, wherever she happened to be, expecting servants to clean for her.

That's what you pay them for, she'd liked to say, and the lack of respect had infuriated me. Now I had the distinct pleasure of offering a small measure of restitution to all the servants she'd abused, while proving the truth about her identity to Noel.

She is Leonora. She is.

"You will clean my tent from top to bottom, and you will do it before midnight." No one could finish in that time frame. Would she burn everything in a fit of pique? "If you fail to complete your task, I'll give you another. And do not think to shout for help. There is a spell around the cloth, preventing the escape of sound."

As she sputtered, I slipped the satchel's strap over her head.

"Hey! That's mine." Her nostrils flared as she grappled for the bag. "Give it back, Saxon. Now."

"You have nothing until I say so, remember?" I held the bag so high she couldn't reach it, even when she jumped.

She crossed her arms over her chest. "Take my things, and *I* will punish *you*."

Hadn't she already?

My hatred resurged with a vengeance. "I've changed my mind, Princess. Finish cleaning the tent before sunset." With that, I strode out of the tent, the satchel in hand.

I never looked back.

4

Grab a mop, grab a broom,
brush and clean away your gloom.

Ashleigh

He'd just *left* me here?

I should rejoice. The wicked warlord was gone. At least for a little while. On the inside, however, I remained a bundle of nerves and confusion.

The second the avian prince had wrapped his arms around me, I'd experienced a sense of true comfort. Comfort. From the source of my discomfort. How could it be? But then, how could it not be? It had felt like we were hugging. The first hug I'd received since my mother's death. And how sad was that?

My shoulders wilted. He had an army at his disposal. I stood alone, always alone, the girl who would never be as good as her stepsister, who wasn't worthy of meeting her stepmother, who hadn't even known she had a new family until today. The girl whose own father had greeted her coldly. A princess in title only, still mockingly referred to as the Glass Princess.

Mostly, I was Saxon's enemy, doomed to endure his wrath for three weeks.

I needed a fairy godmother. But when had a fairy godmother ever come to save me?

Pitying yourself? Enough. So my life had gotten worse instead of better today? So what? Tomorrow, things would improve. I just had to clean this tent in an impossible amount of time, prove the sincerity of my apology to the avian prince who hated me, and make my father proud along the way. No big deal.

Wow. I'd really thought I was going to go a different way with my pep talk. I could only swallow a whimper as I swept my gaze around the tent. Never, in all my days, had I beheld such an awful mess. And I'd had to clean the Temple after every holiday and celebration.

Mud caked *everything.* Shattered glass and splintered wood littered the ground. Every piece of furniture and every potted plant had been overturned. A bed of fur lay in tangles, the covers in tatters. My only supplies? A bucket of water and a rag.

If I'd had a good, solid year before sunset, I could have done it.

Did Saxon *want* me to fail, just so he could make me suffer the consequences?

Devious avian. Well, too bad, so sad. I would give this cleaning everything I had. I would give *each* of his tasks everything I had. I might be weak physically, but I had book smarts and determination, both of which had helped me thrive at the Temple. With hard work and thought, I could overcome anything. Then, Saxon would have no excuse to lash out at me, and the monthly attacks would cease.

Oh, how wonderful. I'd just found the silver lining to my situation: outsmarting Saxon. And stopping the attacks, of course. So, I pasted on a happy smile because presentation mattered. The prince was absent, yes, but he might be watching me through some kind of magic mirror. I'd heard rumors about such things.

"What shall I do first?" I said, performing a little twirl for Saxon's benefit, just in case. I thought...yes. I would start with an extraction and haul out the broken things, the clumps of mud— Whoa. Hang on. Did I really want to go outside where the avian soldiers waited? Trio was among them, and his glare had promised another stoning at his earliest convenience.

I shuddered. All right, new plan. Toss everything outside the tent, without ever actually leaving the tent. No problem.

Humming, I rigged the door flap to remain open, then hurled the first pieces of glass and wood through it.

Protests sounded outside, and I held my breath. One minute passed. Two. No one entered the tent to chastise me, so I relaxed. Had they been ordered to leave the maid alone?

My gain, Saxon's loss. His greed to hoard my misery for himself would cost him. I discarded more glass...the remains of a chair...a cracked pot.

As I righted a trunk, a family of spidorpions darted away from it and me, and I yelped. The spider/scorpion hybrids produced a terrible venom I'd rather not deal with today. A bite always resulted in fever, aches and pains, and sometimes vomiting.

Once my heartbeat slowed down, I returned to my cleaning. Ohhh. What did we have here? One...three...six solid gold nails. As sneakily as possible, I buried each one, along with a few of the sturdiest sticks. *Nothing to see here, Prince Saxon.* Later, I could make spiked daggers.

All right. Back to work.

By the end of the first hour, I was soaked in sweat and panting up a storm. My feet ached, but miracle of miracles, I hadn't collapsed.

During the second hour, the panting turned to wheezing. Even still, I continued to make progress. Having cleared an area for the bed, I sat down to untie the knots in the furs, sneaking a rest now and then. When I finished, I stood—

Nope. My legs refused to support my weight. I tried again, only to crash back into the furs.

Frustrated, I gazed about and mentally cataloged the remaining chores. *Ugh.* So many. Repotting the plethora of plants. Scrubbing mud from the walls. Arranging the usable furniture—a round table, a single chair and a privacy screen. Discarding everything else.

I wasn't going to be halfway finished when Saxon returned, was I? My best wasn't going to be good enough.

No. Every problem had a solution. Especially my problems, considering I had my own personal prophecy and the accompanying fairy tale, "The Little Cinder Girl," to act as my guide.

Woe is she. Woe is she. The Glass Princess, born twice in one day. Two heads, one heart. To purge or merge? One heart, two heads. To merge or purge? One brings a blessing. One brings a curse. Only she can choose. Only she can fight. The ball. The shoe. Diiiing. Diiiiing. Diiiiiiiing. At the stroke of midnight, all is revealed. Who will live and who will die when past, present, and future collide? Let the fire rage—let the flame purify. Let the world burn, burn, burn.

My prophecy was spoken the day of my birth, and it was the reason my parents had known I was the living incarnation of a character in "The Little Cinder Girl"…they just didn't know which one.

Sometimes, as I'd wiled away my days at the Temple, I'd begun to hope I was the star, the motherless Cinder, forced to wear rags and clean for the ungrateful. And now, knowing my father had married a woman with two daughters of her own, I shared an even greater connection to the cinder girl. But, honestly, similar pasts didn't always matter. As I'd heard my father mumble a time or twenty, story details were almost always symbolic. Death could represent a new beginning. A birth could represent the start of something.

What's more, the fairy tale claimed Cinder was "Strong of heart and fast as wind. A warrior set apart, unwilling to bend."

I was the opposite of strong of heart, and I was as fast as a snail. I definitely wasn't a warrior. Try fragile sickling.

The story claimed a prince would be her friend *and* a foe. Like everything else, the title of prince could be literal or symbolic. I wasn't sure *friend* could be interpreted any other way, though, and I had no friends. I had no enemies, either. Well, other than Saxon. For all I knew, I represented Cinder's slipper—the thing upon which she tread. I was the Glass Princess, after all.

Unlike me, Cinder had fairy godmothers. But I had grit and determination—and the ability to be my own fairy godmother.

That's it. When a fairy godmother issued an order, she expected compliance. I could force the avian soldiers to aid me, without violating Saxon's wishes. I wouldn't be shouting for help; I would be demanding it.

Thanks to the spell that stopped the escape of sound, the soldiers hadn't overheard my conversation with their crown prince, so they didn't know what I'd been ordered to do. Could I approach the soldiers, though, without being pelted with stones?

Only one way to find out…

I gathered what remained of my strength, my grit and determination helping me stand at last. On trembly legs I staggered to the open door. After lifting my head and squaring my shoulders—deep breath in, out—I did the smartest, dumbest thing of my life and stepped outside, walking past the avian as if I hadn't a care.

Night hadn't yet fallen. The glass I'd thrown littered the ground and crunched underneath the threadbare soles of my slippers. All other debris had been cleared away, however.

Trio soared over and landed in front of me, as I'd expected. He blocked my path and drew his sword, his teeth bared. "I hoped you would mount an escape. We have orders to stop you."

Figured. My heart galloped. Faster, harder. Too hard, too fast. Deep breath in. Out. Forcing an airy laugh, I waved a dismissive hand. "Escape? You silly rabbit." Rabbit—a grave insult to the avian, who believe rabbits to be the weakest of all the land's creatures. "As if I'd leave my darling Saxon. We've decided to work on our relationship." All true. In a way. Kind of. "He's requested a clean tent, yet here you stand, doing nothing. It's shameful. Have you so little respect for your future king?"

His cheeks speckled with anger. He took a step toward me, then ground to a halt. He couldn't touch me, one way or the other, I realized. Also, he hadn't denied anything I'd said. For all he knew, I was Saxon's soon-to-be beloved queen, my word law.

I almost grinned at the thought of wielding such power over him. "I've done enough of your work, haven't I?" I glanced over my shoulder at each of the other avian to make it clear I addressed them all. "Get in there, and get busy." I turned and marched back into the tent.

Had my confidence sold my claims? I held my breath, waiting, one second…two…three…

The avian filed into the tent, one after the other, and I released a silent squeal of happiness. Ashleigh: 1. Saxon: 0.

The guards got busy, hauling out the rest of the debris in record time. I watched from the pallet of furs and issued instructions like a spoiled royal princess who believed she had every right and deserved every luxury. Broken furniture got fixed. Plants got righted and repotted. Mud was washed away.

"You've done an adequate job," I said when they finished. "Now get out and think about how you almost failed your leader and his treasured liaison today." I shooed everyone away. The more distance between us, the better. The faster the better.

To my surprise, they obeyed once again. Of course, Trio lingered in the doorway, his narrowed gaze leveled on me.

"If you lied about Saxon's wishes, you'll—"

"Regret it, I know." I rolled my eyes to mask my internal shudder. "Trust me, that threat never gets old."

He stomped out, muttering under his breath. Didn't like when the predator became prey, huh? As the flap swished closed behind him, I fell back onto the furs. I'd done it. I'd gotten the tent cleaned in record time, without taking a single stone to the face.

Three more tasks like this, Saxon? How hard can they be?

When would he return? I couldn't wait to see his expression.

As one minute bled into another, I forgot all about the avian, savoring my victory...reveling in the softness of the furs... mmm. My eyelids grew heavy and slowly slid shut. I should stand... I should...*sleeeep.*

Angry voices drifted into the tent, yanking me from a dark void and into light. One of those voices belonged to Saxon. Memories of our newest fight flooded me, and I gasped, jolting upright. I braced for impact.

The avian prince strode past the tent flap, the master of all he surveyed. The sight of him... What remained of my fatigue vanished in a flash. Awareness of him overtook me. My blood heated, and my limbs trembled as if...

No. No, no, no. I couldn't be attracted to him. Not *him.* Anyone but the boy who sought my misery.

Fury pulsed from him as he scanned the sparkling clean tent. Uh-oh. Had the soldiers already tattled?

"Just like she would have done," he spat.

She? "Before you complain," I rushed out, only to rethink my words. "Don't you dare complain. You told me the tent had to be cleaned before sunset, not that I had to be the one to clean it. I adhered to your rules and met your expected end. One round of restitution has been achieved."

The fury intensified. "You're right. My mistake."

Such a rumbly voice. One side of me shivered, the other shuddered. Both sides of me had heard his unspoken vow: *A mistake I won't make again.*

"Why did you have to approach me at the funeral? If you'd just stayed away—" I pressed my lips together, going quiet. Yelling my grievances wasn't the way to get him to hear me. He'd only go on the defensive. Moderating my tone, I told him. "I bore you no ill feelings. Yet, even as my mother's body burned, you glared at me, as if you were enraged. What possible reason could you have to attack a fourteen-year-old girl who'd just lost the only parent who loved her?"

"I *never* attacked you." He moved to inspect one of the potted plants and crossed his arms over his chest, a pillar of resentment. "As for my rage...you know why."

"I don't!"

He flicked his tongue over an incisor before looking at the plant as if it were one of his guards and demanding, "Are you hearing this?"

Um...

Scowling, he abandoned his plant companion, dragged the trunk directly in front of me, and sat down, careful of his wings. "We have a past, you and I."

He said no more, yet flutters erupted in my belly. I drew in a deep breath. I meant to clear my head, but I drew in his scent. He still smelled like a summer rain, and I wanted to close my eyes and savor. "A past? What kind of past?"

Ignoring my question, he stretched his legs in my direction. "Remove my boots."

I gaped at him. Had he really...? "Is this my second task?"

"This is you fulfilling your duties as my servant."

"Don't you mean *palace liaison*?" I folded my arms, *not* removing his boots. "This supposed past of ours. Are you referring to a time before our encounter in the royal garden?"

"Why? Have you recalled a time before our encounter in the royal garden?" He cocked a brow, so arrogant he offended me on every level. Almost every level. Some levels. One or two, surely. "The boots."

Fine. For reparation, for my father, for answers, I would do what Saxon asked. Forcing a smile, I moved closer to work on the strings. "How long before our encounter in the garden?"

A pause. Then, "Hundreds of years."

What? He couldn't be serious. "I'm seventeen years old." In a month, I would be eighteen. "I haven't *lived* for hundreds of years." I finished one set of ties and slipped the boot from his foot. He wore black linen socks. Why did I find that adorable?

"Do you know what a reincarnate is, Princess?"

The way he spoke my title...as if it were a curse and a prayer all rolled into one. I shiver-shuddered again, suspicions poking and prodding at my fragile calm. "You mean someone who is reborn again and again, until they accomplish a certain goal?"

"Exactly right."

I worked on his second boot with more gusto. "And you think...what? That I'm a reincarnate?"

"I *know* we are *both* reincarnates."

Saxon, a reincarnate...me... The idea dropped into my mind with all the grace of a cannonball, and I shook my head. "No. Impossible. We can't be."

"I was known as Craven. The first avian king."

"The Destroyer." Dread settled deep in my bones.

He nodded, a single jerk of his chin. "You were known as Leonora, a fire-wielding witch who communed with dragons. Later, I became Tyron, but you remained Leonora, only you had a different face. Now I am Saxon, with the same face as before, and you are Ashleigh, different again, yet we are still Craven and Leonora."

The moisture in my mouth dried. If he'd mentioned any other names, I could have refuted his claim straightaway. But Leonora and Craven...everything I'd read about the couple, everything my mother and Milo had inadvertently revealed about the witch...

The coincidences were only stacking up.

Should I mention what Milo had said, just before Saxon found me in the garden?

No need to ponder the answer. Why give Saxon more ammunition to use against me? "What makes you think—sorry, *know*—I'm a reincarnate of this Leonora?" The few times Momma had deliriously referred to me by the name, she'd called me possessed, not reincarnated.

You possessed my baby. You took her from me.

"You *told* me," Saxon snapped, "just before you launched the first ball of fire at me."

No way, no how. Utterly impossible. *Right?*

One heart, two heads.

Possessed.

What if I had an evil, more powerful Ashleigh buried inside me, and it was her magic power I sometimes felt? What if she only made an appearance when I slept? How many times had I gone to sleep and awoken covered in dirt?

Reeling at the implications, I fell back on my haunches, taking Saxon's other boot with me. "But... I *can't* be Leonora. I don't have memories of a past life."

"You passed out for less than a second, then you woke, stood and spoke to me. When I failed to tell you what you wished to hear, you attacked."

"No. There has to be another explanation." Because, if he spoke true, I could have also awakened in the warlock's chamber. I could have attacked him and...and...my mother. That would mean I was the one who'd...that I'd... My chin trembled, and I gave my head another shake. "I'm not a reincarnate. I can't be. I would know." No version of me would *ever* harm my mother. "If I were a witch, I would wield fire magic all the time, not just in my sleep. And I don't. I'm completely powerless. But you... I can absolutely picture you as the most savage king ever to rule the avian."

"You *are* Leonora." His voice sounded different now. Deeper. Huskier. *Menacing*. As if the king had just come out to play. "Twice you murdered my family. Twice you murdered me and burned my home. Have the courage to admit it. Or, at the very least, make your denial more believable."

"I'm not her," I whispered, my tone broken. "I'm not."

His confidence remained unwavering. "I'll prove you're the witch. Just give me time, Princess. Just give me time."

5

Let nothing push you off course.
Do what you must, even by force.

SAXON

I floundered, the schemes and trials I'd so looked forward to enacting suddenly tainted and far less enjoyable than they'd been during their conception. How was I supposed to deal with someone in complete denial of the truth? More important, why was I tempted to believe her delusions?

Well, that one I could answer. Passion had steeped her every word, and the nature of the avian—one that rewarded strength, courage, and resilience—wouldn't allow me to dismiss her claims outright.

"You don't *feel* like a reincarnate, so you aren't?" I arched a brow. "Feelings are subjective, fleeting, and always subject to change, Princess, but truth remains the same forever."

Almost desperate, she said, "Let's say we're both who you say we are, then. They—we—attacked *each other* in two previous lives. Therefore, I should get to punish you, too."

Well, well. Another Leonora response. Except, the Leonora

of old never would have left evidence of her crimes. She would have killed the witnesses, the very soldiers who'd helped her. Ashleigh had owned her actions and all but told me why I should thank her for them. A feat I admired.

"You forget," I said, remembering the justification I'd had to feed her father. "I'm only punishing you for what you did as Ashleigh. So, tell me. What wrong have I done to you as Saxon?"

"You got me banished to the Temple."

"You got *yourself* banished."

Adriel entered then, carrying a tray piled high with breads, cheese, fruits, and a bottle of wine. He had a wealth of red curls, freckled white skin and ebony wings. We had been somewhat friendly as children, but I didn't know the man he'd become.

Ashleigh paled as he placed the tray on the trunk. Did she fear all avian or Adriel specifically? Because she didn't act this way with me. But why would she fear the others and not me? And why did I suddenly want to stand between her and the world?

Stupid question. I knew why, I just didn't like that the sense of connection had resurged, rousing my most protective instincts.

Protect my enemy? I'd rather die. If Ashleigh got hurt, Ashleigh got hurt. I would not aid her in any way. She might be inexplicably attractive to me, but I preferred warrior women to dainty princesses, and always had.

"Where are the rest of my supplies?" I asked him.

"Soon to arrive, my lord." He glared at her, as if he knew her real identity. He didn't. He couldn't. Only my closest allies knew the truth, and they did not spread the news. Queen Raven might suspect it because of what happened in the garden, but she didn't know. Ashleigh would already be dead. "Your mother's messenger arrived, sir. The mer-king missed a day of peace talks, sending an advisor in his place. Queen Raven would like to know how you think she should retaliate?"

This was a test, no doubt. The avian didn't tolerate disrespect well. If we gave it, we demanded it in return or we cut the offender from our lives. My mother would expect me to prove I had the courage to lead as well as the kings before me—or after Craven—even during these tough times. She would expect me to incite violence against the mer-king, for insulting her position.

Pressure building... "The queen is to cease all talks with the mers. If their king cannot give us his time, his people will get none of ours." In this life, war would not always be my first response. "When he apologizes publicly, talks may resume."

Adriel looked ready to protest, but he nodded and strode from the tent. What? He thought I should demand the mer-king's head?

My gaze returned to Ashleigh, wondering what she believed. But she hadn't paid any attention to the conversation; she was too busy staring at the food, her pupils dilated as she licked her lips. When was the last time she'd eaten?

I opened my mouth to tell her to eat, when the flap opened again. An avian entered, lugging a wooden tub. Two others followed, carting large buckets of water, which they dumped into the tub as soon as it was placed. What I wouldn't give for the magical jug Roth and Farrah owned. Or maybe Everly had it now? It self-filled. With a single pour, I could overflow the tub again and again.

When the group left, I picked up my conversation with Ashleigh. "Eat your fill." Before learning she'd outsourced her first chore, I'd planned to eat while she watched, then bathe as she wallowed in filth. I'd wondered how she would react. Like the Leonora of old, throwing a fit—and furniture—when she didn't get her way? But, looking at her now, I just couldn't bring myself to do it. The color had yet to return to Ashleigh's cheeks, and the unnatural paleness illuminated every speck of dirt that smeared her skin.

Her emerald eyes brightened, and my chest clenched. "Truly?"

I gave a stiff nod.

As she reached for a piece of cheese, a little shaky, I had a mad urge to select the best one and feed it to her by hand. An intimate act meant for avian lovers. Something Craven had done for Leonora many, many times. I balled both hands into fists.

Her eyelids closed in surrender as she chewed, her expression rapturous. "I haven't had cheese in so long."

Tension stole over me, every muscle knotting. I popped a strawberry into my mouth. Chewed, swallowed. "You should make up your mind, Ashleigh."

"What do you mean?"

"Are you a timid mouse or a warrioress? I've seen hints of both."

"Perhaps I'm your worst nightmare," she muttered.

"That, I agree with. You carry four dragon eggs, over fifty designs for weapons and three books about coven histories." *And nothing else.* "The designs are new, not something Leonora ever cared about in the past. The eggs, however, I understand. In both of her previous incarnations, she had a horde of winged-demons at her command. So, I'd like to hear your explanation for those, and how their possession proves you're *not* Leonora."

Frost glittered in her emerald irises, rousing my tension further. "You went through my bag?"

"Of course I did," I told her silkily. "We are enemies, and I'm not a fool. What if you had a way to harm my people in there?"

She *humph*ed. "I found the eggs, but I don't know how. The designs are my own. Everyone deserves a chance to protect themselves from harm. The books are entertaining."

She had designed those incredible pieces with hidden spikes and unique hooks? "Prove you did the designs. Draw one."

All innocence, she batted her lashes at me. "I would certainly draw a new design for you...if the price were right. I charge in atonement coins. Shall I add you to my buyers list? You pay me now, and I could get to you in a year or so."

She didn't have a year. In three weeks, she would be imprisoned and bespelled.

"No?" She devoured another piece of cheese. "Well, one day," she continued, her tone going dreamy, "I will have a list of buyers. I'll train with a blacksmith and learn to bring my designs to life. You can have your proof then. Of course, I'll be charging you double at that time."

I did not want to admire her mettle.

I admired her mettle.

Resentful, I asked, "What do you know about dragons?"

"Not much, to be honest." She swallowed a bite of bread. "Little is written about their history."

"Because they always fade into obscurity soon after Leonora's death, leaving future generations to wonder about them." But I knew the truth. "Dragon mothers bury their eggs to allow their babies to age in secret, a process that can take centuries. Leonora always knows where to find and steal those eggs. Some have hatched, some haven't, but she always manages to raise a dragon army and torch entire villages."

Ashleigh's gaze returned to mine, her pupils huge. "I'll put the eggs back. I will. I didn't mean to steal babies from their mothers."

I blinked. Leonora, willing to part with four dragon eggs? That was a first. Or a trick. *Definitely a trick.* "No, you won't be putting them back. I'll be keeping them."

"But they'll need their mothers one day."

"No, they won't, because they won't be hatching."

She peered at me with horror. "Their mothers could be in hiding somewhere, reliving the nightmare of returning to their nests to find their babies missing. I must return the eggs, Saxon."

"No," I said simply.

"How can you be so cruel?" she asked, her tone mournful.

"They are monsters. How can I *not* be so cruel?"

A tear ran down her cheek and dripped from her chin.

I fought the urge to recoil, that one tiny drop of salt water affecting me worse than any stab wound. "Tears won't sway me," I said for both our benefits. "How would you know where to return the eggs, anyway, if you don't know how you acquired them?"

"I sleepwalked while I lived at the Temple, okay, and every so often, I would awaken to find an egg resting on my pillow."

Interesting. I smeared creamy cheese over a toast point and offered it to her before I even knew what I was doing. "Do you remember anything about Leonora's life?" I asked more harshly than I'd intended.

She accepted the change of subject as well as the peace offering, because that's what it was whether I'd realized it in the moment or not. "I know only what I've read."

I watched, enraptured, as she sampled the morsel. The way she moved...the way she enjoyed each bite... Sweat trickled down my temple. "Few know of her reincarnation. Why did you choose to read about her at all, unless you were drawn to her for some inexplicable reason?"

Ashleigh consumed the rest of the toast point—at her leisure—before telling me, "Why should I explain anything to the guy who delights in my misery? And why would a crown prince and future king stay in a dump of a tent?"

Why not admit the truth? "He doesn't want his favorite servant enjoying a single luxury."

"Then he needs to ditch the tent altogether," she muttered. "Maybe you *are* Craven. I studied him, too, you know. Everyone agrees there's never been an avian king more brutal."

"You are wrong, and you are right. Before Leonora, Craven was a prime example of the perfect avian sovereign. Violent when it came to the protection and well-being of his people. Uncompromising when necessary. Harsh with offenders of any kind. But there has been one other who showed himself to be equally brutal." Tyron. "Both males had a terrible weakness for the same powerful witch. They loved her, but each one married another woman anyway, giving her the family Leonora had dreamed of making." They'd actually broken down on their wedding days, agonized by the permanent cut from the witch.

"If they loved her, why didn't they marry her?"

"You really wish to know?"

She nodded with enthusiasm.

"Then you should do your best to remember, as I have." She *had* to remember. Clearly, I couldn't do what needed doing to Ashleigh until she did. And I needed to do what needed doing sooner rather than later.

I'd have to force Leonora's hand.

As Ashleigh sputtered, I continued my story. "Leonora became enraged and killed their brides, then burned down their homes. Homes they rebuilt—just so she could do it again, after their deaths." Even now, I could feel the heat of the flames, smell the char on the stone and hear the screams of my people as they ran for safety they would never find. "After the first burning, Craven killed her entire family, and left their remains in her bed. Shortly after, she stabbed him in the heart. You aren't ready to hear what Tyron did to her."

Ashleigh released quiet choking noises as her mouth floundered open and closed. That moment. I began to believe her. She hadn't recalled a single memory of her life as Leonora. "I knew the basics of this. Ophelia mentioned some things but wow…" She paused, her lips parted. "That's a lot to take in."

I wouldn't tell her anything else about our second life, how the new Leonora had found Tyron… Craven…me on my twenty-first birthday, claiming to have loved me in a past life... how I'd started to relive beautiful memories of that life, allowing myself to fall for her all over again. How I'd later dreamed the worst of our crimes and reignited our war.

How I'd mourned the loss of our love even before I'd wed someone else and committed atrocious acts.

How I'd lost. Again.

Ashleigh pressed a hand over her heart, as if she hoped to manually slow its beat. "I'm sorry for what happened to Craven and Tyron—to you—but I'm not Leonora, Saxon. I promise, you've got the wrong girl. I would *never* burn down a village, not in any incarnation of my existence. And I would never, ever commit an act of murder."

Such adamancy. Only because she hadn't relived the memories. But she would. And when she did, Leonora would return to me. The witch would feel no guilt or rage, but I thought Ashleigh might. Would this part of her personality change Leonora? Would the witch strike at me? Oh, I hoped so. Then, this stupid tightening in my chest would finally ease.

When Ashleigh self-consciously smoothed hair from her brow before gazing at her hands and grimacing, I realized I'd been staring at her, silent. "You're going to bathe," I told her. "While you soak, you will share details about your time in the Temple."

"Bathe? Truly?" With a gasp of longing, she whipped her attention to the tub. Or rather, to the privacy screen in front of the tub. Excitement palpable, she scrambled to her feet. "I haven't had a proper bath in—" She pressed her lips together, saying no more.

Afraid I would reverse my decision if I knew how badly she wanted this? I *should*. Making her happy was the opposite of my goal. I grumbled, "Take your bath, Ashleigh."

"No, thank you," she said now, even as she cast the privacy screen another longing glance. "I'd rather not get undressed in your presence. I'll wait and bathe at..." Forlorn, she wilted and whispered, "Home."

Didn't feel as if she had a home, eh? Good, that was good. The more downtrodden she was, the faster Leonora would fight her way to the surface. Surely. *So why is my chest tighter than before?*

"You have a new home now," I said. "This tent. You'll sleep at the palace, but you'll spend every waking minute here. You'll eat and bathe here. When I'm on the battlefield, you'll tidy up and prepare my meals."

"Fine. You want me to move in, great. I've lived in worse. But I won't be bathing here. I don't have a change of clothes, and I can't—" Wringing her hands, she said, "I just can't don this filthy rag again, even if you order it for my second task."

"I would only ever order such a garment burned." After setting the empty tray on the floor, I opened the trunk, its hinges squeaking, and crouched to withdraw a shirt and a pair of leathers. "They'll be too big for you, but they'll work for today. Tomorrow, I'll find something more appropriate." I handed the items to her, only then realizing my mistake.

Ashleigh...wearing my clothes...as if I'd claimed her as my own...

She snatched them, as if she expected me to change my mind at any moment.

I hated myself, but I was eager to see her in the garments.

Looking anywhere but my direction, she asked, "Are you planning to watch me bathe?"

"Absolutely not." The words rushed out, an assurance for us both. One very specific part of me would like to observe every second, but that particular part could not be trusted; it had gotten me into trouble in the past, igniting both of our love affairs.

Relieved, she darted behind the privacy screen. My ears twitched as clothing rustled. Already stripping? The water splashed. She must be stepping inside the tub now.

Heat threatened to bubble from my veins as her sweet scent perfumed the air. All right. Enough of that. I had to readjust my pants before I eased back onto the trunk. "The Temple," I snapped, desperate for a distraction. "Tell me."

"There's not much to tell." Her tone...so happy. "I cleaned the trees, which wasn't an easy chore, let me tell you. Have you ever tried to clean dirt off dirt, Saxon? I collected herbs, fruit, and nuts for our meals, and I distributed food to families who came to visit. I liked that part. I also spent a lot of time recovering from beatings delivered by your soldiers. Your turn to tell me about our time apart. Did you smile when they returned with reports of my screams?"

What? "You lie." I had never ordered anyone to seek her out. Instead, I'd waited, building my strength against her magic and fortifying my resistance to her undeniable charms, so that *I* could be the honored one who took her out.

"Ask the dryads how many times I crawled to my room, then later had to mop up the trail of blood I'd left behind." Water splashed. "Why didn't you inflict the damage yourself? Were you too afraid of the girl who'd burned your wittle wings?" Not so happy anymore.

That. That was all Leonora. With a snarl, I shoved to my feet and stalked to the other side of the screen to find Ashleigh's eyes flecked with bright blue.

A second later, though, those flecks faded and she yelped, sinking chin-deep in the water, draping one arm over her breasts and the other between her legs. "You said you wouldn't watch," she shouted.

I froze, then I spun. Though my back was to her, I knew her cheeks were red, her skin damp. I knew the ends of her hair were clinging to different parts of her. Knew I would never forget the sight of those magnificent curves.

I knew no other girl would ever compare.

The second I remembered I stood in the presence of an

enemy, I shot around, facing her again. I jutted my chin. More than anyone else in Enchantia, I knew the devastation this girl could cause. I knew the cruelties that lived in her heart.

"I do not want you behind me. Ever." I kept my gaze above her head. "An avian soldier wouldn't attack you without orders from a sovereign. I sent no one, and my mother and sister sent no one. They prefer to do any damage themselves. So take heed, Ashleigh. If you lie to me again—"

"You'll make me regret it. Trust me, I *know*."

Glass Princess, indeed. She looked ready to shatter—and I knew because I'd dropped my gaze. I cursed.

She moaned, adding, "But I'm not lying."

Trust was not something I would give her. "Describe to me what the avian did to you at the Temple."

"Why should I bother? You won't believe me."

"Try me, anyway."

Silence stretched between us, and it was as fragile as she was. Finally, she whispered, "Sometimes a single avian would come. Sometimes five. Mostly, they threw rocks at me as I gathered food and pulled weeds. But every so often, they landed."

I bit my tongue to silence another curse and tasted blood. If someone had truly hit her... I would rage.

My war. My enemy.

Mine to strike at—in ways of my choosing. No one else had the right.

"I knew you wouldn't believe me," she said, slamming a fist into the water. Droplets flung in every direction. "Why would I lie about this, though?"

Because...because... I scrubbed a hand down my face. Her word meant nothing to me, but her misery was so real. Maybe she had been harmed. Maybe the avian who'd attacked her had been banished from the Avian Mountains and had no king or queen to corral them?

"I don't not believe you," I grated. "I just need a moment to pick through the details. What you describe goes against every-thing I know about my people. What's more, there *is* a reason you would lie now, just as you lied about other things in the past—to rouse my sympathies and set me against my people."

"I have a feeling you own just as many sympathies as mer-cies. You—" She gasped. "My heart…it's beating so fast. I think… I…" Splash.

Ashleigh had just slumped over in the tub…was slipping underwater even now. I rushed over to grab her before she drowned. As I raised her head, the water pouring off her, her eyes popped open.

Electric-blue irises with no hint of green peered up at me.

My own heart erupted in a staccato beat, and I reared back, severing contact. The sense of connection I'd lamented was now gone without a trace.

Finally. The girl had Leonora's eyes for more than a couple seconds. I had the undeniable proof I'd sought. Ashleigh was the witch, and the witch was Ashleigh. So why wasn't I rejoic-ing? I could now gain full reparation with a clear conscience.

She stood and—my thoughts dulled. Water droplets sluiced down her bare skin, hypnotizing me. Or maybe Ashleigh wasn't Leonora, after all. Maybe I'd made a mistake. I'd never wanted like this.

Inner slap. Focus or lose. There were no other options for me.

"Hello, Craven, my sweet," she said, a seductive smile bud-ding. "At long last, we're together again. Go ahead. Admit it. You're happy to see me. And if not, take a look at the body I'm offering you this lifetime. I think you'll get very, very happy very, very fast."

Like a fool, I heeded the command of my greatest enemy, my worst temptation, and swept my gaze over her incredible form. The first thing I noticed, however? She had bruises on her shoulders, abdomen and thighs, each one about the size of a fist. The sight of them had turned my stomach, fury spilling through me, seething just under the surface of my skin.

Someone *had* thrown rocks at her, and that someone would pay. No wonder she'd feared the avian outside.

My gaze roved over the rest of her. No other bruises were noticeable, only...only...my thoughts fragmented. *Exquisite female.* More curves than I'd expected. A flush. Would it burn me? Skin that looked as soft as a flower petal.

Softness wasn't something I'd known in any of my lifetimes, but suddenly I craved it.

"I'm hoping we won't have to fight this time, my love." She traced a fingertip between the valley of her breasts. "Do you like what you see?"

I forced my gaze back to hers, one of the most difficult things I'd ever done. "You don't want to fight this time? That's a surprise. I seem to remember being attacked in the garden."

"Oh. That." She waved a hand in dismissal, all grace, confidence, and seduction. "You were building toward a tantrum, and you might have harmed this body beyond repair before we'd even had a chance to reconcile."

Reconcile? "You cannot be serious."

"Oh, but I am. I am your fated one. We are meant to be together. If you'll just give me your marriage bracelet, I will vow to never again harm you or any of your people."

Marry Leonora? I laughed. A wedding was the one thing she'd always wanted. The one thing I'd never given her. Even as I'd fallen in love the first time, even as obsession for her had consumed me a second time, I'd sensed something was wrong with our relationship.

"I see you've finally remembered our past lives," I said, deciding not to respond to her proposal.

"For the moment."

Would she be able to erase her memories again? "Is this a

permanent stay or a quick visit?" When she had her memories, she had access to her magic, which must turn her eyes blue.

"What would you like it to be?" she asked.

"Stay. Please." My mind screamed, *Leave.* "I cannot wait to give you the punishment and pain you so rightly deserve."

"So you haven't forgiven me for two minor wars?" She pouted.

"Minor?" I shouted.

"Very well," she continued, and sighed. "If hurting the girl will assuage you, then by all means, hurt the girl. Recovery is no longer a problem. But when the time is right, I will return for good. That's a vow. Prepare yourself. You *will* forgive me, just as I've forgiven you, and we *will* be a family at long last."

She could control which side of her personality controlled the helm of her mind? Vibrating with menace, I stepped closer, wanting her to see my disgust up close and personal. "I will *never* be with you again, Nora."

The endearment reverberated inside my head, stopping me cold. Why had I used my old nickname for her?

She grinned, smug now. "Oh, yes. I'll be back, and you'll forgive me. You're halfway there already." A second later, she collapsed.

The sense of connection returned in an instant, and I dove for her again. Water splashed over the rim of the tub, soaking parts of my tunic that had escaped the first dunking dry.

She was featherlight as I lifted her from the bath and carried her to the pallet of furs. Afraid I would break her and seething about it, I laid her down gently and covered her nakedness with the only blanket.

Mind in chaos, I sat beside her and bent my legs, resting my elbows on my knees. The things she'd said...

When the time is right... What did timing even matter? We didn't get to erase memories of our past because we didn't want to face them, then resurrect them another day, when we did.

Yet she'd done so before. Would she do so again? And had she really referred to herself as "the girl"?

Who would she be when she awoke? Ashleigh, the one without her memories, or Leonora, the one who knew all? Maybe a combination of both? Would she completely forget our conversation the way she'd completely forgotten our argument in the garden? And green-eyed Ashleigh had absolutely forgotten it, her confusion genuine. That wasn't a manipulation on her part. I just didn't understand how or why or what it all meant, my emotions all over the place. Fury? Yes. I felt it. Hatred. That, too. But I thought uncertainty might be beleaguering me most.

If her present life had somehow detached from her past lives, she could—in theory—have two streams of consciousness living inside her head. One ruled at times, one ruled at others. Something that didn't bode well for me.

How could I continue to punish the innocent side of her nature? How could I prove myself to my people, if I didn't punish her?

My people needed me, despite what they might think. I'd learned from my mistakes…mostly…and I would be a good ruler for them. I would fight to give them a life of peace and prosperity.

The life I'd denied their ancestors.

I must continue on this path, no matter what. I couldn't flounder with my duty anymore.

I had to.

So I would.

When Leonora or Ashleigh awoke, I would be ice-cold. I would be like the Craven of old. Methodical. Driven. Unrelenting.

Merciless.

True restitution would begin, the witch's pain my birthright, no matter her incarnation.

6

When her heart is made of vengeance and ice,
she won't kill you quick, she'll kill you thrice.

Ashleigh

Usually when I slept, I didn't dream. I would remain dead to the world, all mental lights snuffed out, leaving me in the dark. But this time, I did dream…about Leonora.

Six months ago, I was a nameless spirit. Then I invaded the body of a royal witch, and everything changed for me. And for her. Her name was Lady Leonora.

Now *my* name was Lady Leonora, and *she* was the nameless spirit.

Before her, I'd invaded other bodies. Many others. I'd scoured the land for the perfect hosts, stealing precious moments from their lives. But never had I decided to keep one.

Until now.

The day I'd taken over the first Leonora, the powerless laughingstock had become a feared warrior, revered by her people, and I'd loved it. So, I'd decided to stay awhile. When her parents doted on me, love shining in their eyes, I'd decided the witch would be my forever hostess. What was hers, was mine. Even family and foes.

Tonight, I would meet her big bad. The being she'd feared most. I knew because I'd followed her before ghosting inside her and taking over. Her big bad? King Craven, the most vicious avian in all the realm. So powerful he'd crowned himself their king. No one was strong enough to usurp him.

Of course the twenty-one-year-old witch had feared someone like him. She'd been cloistered since birth, all because of the prophecy that was spoken over her—"The Little Cinder Girl."

Her adoring family believed the fairy tale would bring great turmoil to their kingdom. Fearing for their angel's safety, they'd refused to allow her to leave their village. Fools. Deny fate the perfect end, and it would make you suffer, twisting the tale until you got it right. I'd seen it happen.

Because the naive original Leonora had never manifested a magical ability—or if she had, the ability had been so abysmal, she hadn't even known what it was—she'd been ill prepared for conflict and no match for my possession.

I wielded control over fire, so, once I'd wrested control of the body, "she" had displayed a supernatural ability at long last. The ability to create fire—*my* ability. The rest of the world simply assumed her magic had finally manifested. But I knew better. Now, everyone considered her—me—the most powerful witch to ever live, and a true Cinder in the making.

I fluffed my hair. For the first time in my existence, I had a name, a family, a prophecy, and a purpose. I even had a bright future. Before, I'd had no identity at all. One day, I'd simply opened my eyes, surrounded by smoke and flame, a spirit trapped in the land of the living, confused and alone. Nothing but a blank slate. Even then I could start fires with my mind.

I'd had no need to eat, and no way to touch anyone else. I'd desperately wanted to touch someone.

Having no idea what I was, I'd followed oracles and scribes, impatient to be seen, to glean any tidbit of information. When I'd discovered I could possess their bodies, well, I'd begun selecting my hosts based on my needs and their current circumstances, jumping from one to the other every few months without their knowledge. They'd lost a small bit of time, and I'd gained a wealth of experiences.

For the first time, I'd gotten to enjoy the things other people took for granted. Physical sensation. Eating delicious meals. Getting married. Having sex. Being seen, heard, and adored. I'd perused books to learn about myself and soon discovered I was a phantom created by dragon fire and death.

Today, I hoped to receive a new experience—ending a life. Craven himself. I'd never met him, but he'd killed members of my new coven and threatened my new family. For that, he would die screaming, and all of Enchantia would thank me.

Earlier, I'd overheard servants whispering about this mighty avian king, how he was just as likely to slay a friend as an enemy and that, if you told him a lie, he would cut out your tongue. If you stole from him, he would chop off your hands. If you ran from him, he would remove your feet with a rusty ax.

This male now had a big problem with my new parents.

As the number of witches and warlocks in our coven had grown, the clearing in which we lived had quickly become cramped. Not knowing what else to do, Great Lord Titus—the equivalent of a mortal king—issued an order to spread into Craven's territory. Just a little. The teeniest bit. Hardly noticeable.

Craven had taken great offense and launched a campaign to show the warlock sovereign the error of his ways. Yesterday, Titus had surrendered, his magic no match for the terror of the skies.

In a matter of minutes, Craven would arrive to demand an apology and a pledge of fealty from each of us.

I would not be giving either one.

I tightened my grip on the dagger I would be shoving into his rotted heart. Soon he would learn. I could have made him an incredible ally. Instead, he'd made me a fearsome enemy.

"Whatever he wants, Leonora, give it to him. Please." Titus stood at my right and patted my free hand. He trembled. "Otherwise he'll murder us all."

Both the Great Lord, the father I'd claimed, and the Coveness Hexelle, the mother I'd always craved, had donned their most luxurious finery. She stunned in a black crystal headdress that boasted a brim and a tall, pointed top, paired with a fitted black gown. Titus wore a black cloak made from the hide of a panther, and an ankle-length black tunic, cinched at the waist with a leather belt.

I'd selected a gown with bloodred roses sewn throughout.

We stood in the foyer of our home—the biggest hut in the village—awaiting King Craven's arrival. "Obey the dictates of a tyrant?" I shook my head. "No." I wouldn't allow him to take the only home and family I'd ever known.

Titus heaved a forlorn sigh, acting as if I'd doomed us all. I'd inhabited his daughter for several months, but he still lamented my new "sass."

Suddenly he stiffened and whisper-yelled, "He's here."

"How—" My ears twitched, the whooshing sound of wings registering. Ah. Next came thundering footsteps.

Squeaking hinges sounded, the door to the hut swinging open. Then he was there. Craven the Destroyer strode into the abode as if he owned it, two armed men at his sides. I knew it was him without being told. No male had ever exuded such fierce intensity.

He wasn't traditionally handsome, I noted. He was even better, his features bold and arresting. And the rest of him... *Hello.*

He was tall and packed with lean muscle. He had dark hair and skin, darker eyes, and soft lips. Stubble covered a strong jaw. His wings were large and cobalt.

My heart raced with—what *was* that? I'd never felt anything quite so powerful. It almost left like a sense of connection had bloomed. As if I belonged with him.

As if he were mine. Meant for me, and me alone.

I floundered. I marveled. It was *wondrous.*

He glanced in my direction, only to look away. Just as I curled my hands into fists, he jerked his gaze back to me. "You," he breathed, angling toward me. He prowled closer.

"Me?" I asked, panting all of a sudden. He smelled like a rainstorm. "You know me?" *As some part of me seems to know you?*

"I…do not. But I've dreamed of you." He said no more, leaving me confused.

"What kind of dreams?" I asked.

One corner of his mouth rose. "The best kind."

That almost-grin… My knees quaked. I hadn't imagined the connection. He *had* experienced it, too.

I wouldn't kill him, after all. But I might keep him for a while.

"Tell me your name, lovely. I assume you are Lady Leonora, daughter of Great Lord Titus, ruler of the magic folk?"

I nearly closed my eyes and melted into him. Even his voice appealed to me, low and rough, like smoke and gravel.

I licked my lips, suddenly as nervous as a schoolgirl. "I am." *Now…*

He searched my face, as if he were memorizing a treasure map. The way I'd seen other men look at their beloved wives. Or mistresses.

The way I wanted to be looked at for the rest of forever.

As he reached out to shift a lock of my red hair between his fingers, my heart raced faster.

"Y-Your Majesty—" Titus began.

"Silence," Craven snapped without glancing away from me.

This intensity... I couldn't get enough of it. He needed taming, though.

"I think you are the one I've been searching for, Lady Leonora." Gentle, tender, Craven caressed two knuckles over my cheekbone. Goose bumps spread over me. When he noticed them, he offered the barest smile, his lids hooding his eyes. "I will allow you to continue ruling your people," he told my father, still not looking away. "I will even allow your people to remain at the bottom of my mountain. But the girl comes with me."

Cheers resounded in the distance, waking me as if I'd been stung with a cattle prod. With a gasp, I jolted upright, dragging a blanket with me. *Disoriented...* Where was I? Why—

Vestiges of the dream hovered at the edge of my mind, reminding me about what I'd witnessed. Had a dream ever seemed so real? I could almost believe I'd been there.

I moaned. I had *not* relived one of Leonora's memories, and that was that. Because I wasn't her reincarnate. I wasn't a murderess.

Possessed...refortify the barrier...phantom...

I swallowed. No, I wasn't a reincarnate. But I might be possessed.

New cheers sounded, drowning out my manic laugh.

Trying to breathe, I cast my gaze about. Bright morning sunlight streamed through little holes in the tent. I lay in Saxon's tent, atop the pallet of furs, alone, and oh, sweet goodness, I was naked.

The last thing I remembered was stepping into the bath then...*what? What!*

Had I passed out? Had Saxon carried me to bed and allowed me to sleep all night? Naked? Had I mentioned the fact that I wore only flesh and panic?

I rubbed the sleep from my eyes. All right. Forget Saxon and my nakedness. For now. I would get dressed, return to the palace, and research phantoms. If my dream was real, if Leonora was indeed a phantom who'd stolen moments of my life, I'd... I didn't know.

I just... I wanted to be wrong. I wanted another explanation.

While I did my phantom research, I would also search for an eyewitness account of the day Leonora and Craven met. Perhaps her parents—who had, in fact, borne the names Titus and Hexelle—or maybe a soldier had jotted down a few notes about the meeting in an ancestral journal. What had Milo's father written about Leonora in his journal? Surely Milo had that journal in his possession. At the very least, a scribe might have an outline of Craven and Leonora's relationship in the *Annals of Enchantia*. Or, maybe I could convince Saxon to finally spill all.

Whatever I had to do, I would compare reality to dream. I'd have to be careful, though. No telling how Saxon would react to a possible phantom possession.

No, that wasn't true. He would kill first and ask questions later.

The fact that the first Leonora might have been part of "The Little Cinder Girl" prophecy, well, that part almost broke my brain.

Did fairy tales truly get worse as they repeated?

So many questions, so few answers.

When another round of cheers rang out, realization struck. The tournament! Eager to check out the weapons, I jumped to unsteady legs, intending to wear whatever clothes I could find.

Thankfully, I didn't have to search. I spotted a dress neatly folded and stacked beside my pillow, alongside a basket that contained two pieces of bread, two pieces of cheese, a carafe of water, toiletries, hair ribbons, and a note.

Though my stomach churned with anxiety—did I really

want to know what Saxon had said?—I stuffed cheese into a bread roll, took a bite, and read the note.

Dress. As promised, I have provided clean clothing. Instead of attending the tournament, you will do your chores. Tidy the tent and prepare a three-course meal for my return. I provided the ingredients for the first course. You are not to visit the market without an escort. You are to buy food and only food. You know what will happen if you fail to obey.
Your king,
S

So, I wasn't to eat the bread and cheese, I was to use them in addition to the ingredients I was to purchase at the market, with money he hadn't left me, in order to prepare him a better meal? Him. Not me.

Feeling rebellious, I gobbled up the rest of the cheese roll and regretted nothing. My stomach sang with delight, and the rest of me perked up, surging with energy.

He wanted me to do my chores? Fine. But as soon as I finished, I was going to that tournament.

I cleaned my teeth with the provided paste and donned the offered gown, expecting another sackcloth but finding a finely made garment instead. The softness of the material… I sighed dreamily. But, why would Saxon gift me with such a nice outfit? Unless he knew there was something I would hate about it?

Ah. There it was. A bit too small in the bust, with back buttons I couldn't latch without breaking my body in half.

I searched the tent for the tunic and leathers he'd offered yesterday, just in case. Alas. The tricky prince had left only the gown.

Well, I would show him. I ripped off those back buttons, then dug up one of the golden nails I'd buried, and used it to poke holes in the material, where the buttons had been. I then laced an extra hair ribbon through the bottom hole on one side and a second ribbon through the bottom hole on the other side, tying them together at the end. As I threaded those ribbons up, up, I crisscrossed them. A trick I'd learned when the seams of my sackcloth had come apart at the Temple.

Though I had to do serious contorting, I managed to shimmy into the gown while maintaining a hold on each of the ribbons. Then I pulled them together and tied the other end, closing and securing the back of my gown. The moment I finished, a tingle of warmth raced down my spine, and I laughed. A tingle of victory?

I'd done it! Ashleigh: 2. Saxon: 0.

I brushed my hair and pinned back the sides with the remaining ribbon. All right. Time to tidy.

This morning, I didn't care enough about presentation to paste on a carefree smile. I grumbled under my breath as I made the bed, then picked up some things Saxon had left behind: polish and rags to shine his armor, a set of sharpeners for his sword. As I put each item away, I searched for my eggs and designs, just in case he'd hid them somewhere nearby.

He hadn't.

For Saxon's meal, I shoved the remaining cheese into the remaining roll and smeared the whole thing with toothpaste. Because herbs.

Three courses…three ingredients…basically the same thing.

There. I'd done everything he'd asked. He'd have no reason to complain.

More cheers.

If he'd truly wanted me to stay put, he would have chained me down. So, because he hadn't chained me down, he proved he actually wanted me to attend the tournament and watch him battle. If I stayed in the tent, he would probably rage.

My logic tracked, I was sure of it.

Determined to deal with my escort, I marched outside, sunlight and warmth enveloping me, yesterday's chill already gone. Maybe, if I looked as confident today as I'd sounded yesterday, the escort wouldn't even attempt to stop me.

All around, servants hustled and bustled to and fro. Some carried logs or buckets of water. Others carried weapons and food. The scent of roasting meat saturated the air, making my stomach rumble as if I hadn't eaten in years. Hey. Where was my—

"Good morrow, Princess."

Blood flash-freezing, I jerked my gaze to the speaker. Trio, my three-year tormentor, landed about ten feet away from me, right beside an avian I'd never met. A slender female with pale hair, snow-white skin dotted with a smattering of freckles, and silvery eyes. Lovely ivory wings streaked with black arced over her shoulders.

She wore the clothes and weapons of a warrior: a black leather top, with metal mesh strategically placed around different vital organs, was paired with leather pants and a belt holding a bejeweled dagger on both sides.

She appeared to be the kind of girl I'd always wished I was. Strong, capable, and worthy. How proud her family must be. How proud her people—her soon-to-be king—must be.

New cheers grabbed my attention. I glided my gaze down the mountain, where a massive coliseum loomed in the heart of the bustling market. It was too far away to make out individual details, but I easily spotted the line that stretched around it, countless people eager to get inside.

One voice rose above the cheers, as if by magic. "Next we have… Morgone the Brave!"

Thunderous applause. Ah. The master of ceremonies must be introducing the combatants, one by one.

The next one he introduced—Bambam the Troll—received boos.

Ugh. A *troll* was fighting for Dior's hand in marriage? Trolls had towering horns, venomous tusks, and, according to the tales I'd heard, an unquenchable taste for mortal…meat.

Maybe I didn't envy Princess Dior, after all. What other creatures vied for her hand in marriage? Sorcerers? They had to steal magic from others to survive. Snake-shifters? They brazenly fed on other shifters. Gorgons? If conditions were right, they could turn anyone into stone.

Could Saxon win against such fierce competitors?

If he died, I wouldn't care. Not more than a little. Probably.

"Come," Trio demanded, motioning me over. "I'll take you to the market, as Prince Saxon instructed."

"There's no need. I've prepared his meal already." I stood by my cheese loaf. Filling *and* good for you. Because herbs.

"You lie."

"How dare you insult my cookery. Even if I planned to slave over a second meal, which I don't, I wouldn't go to the market with you." How many times had this male made me bleed? "I wouldn't go to an all-you-can-take treasury with you."

Had Saxon left him behind to punish me further?

Forget caring a little if he died. I would rejoice. In fact, I was already planning the goodbye party.

The pale-haired female said, "Don't worry. I'll take her to the meat market. There's some beefcake I'm dying to inspect up close and personal." She wiggled her brows.

Beefcake? My stomach forgot breakfast and rumbled an agreement. "I've never had beefcake, but I'd like to change that immediately. Please, and thank you." Then, I would sneak off to the tournament.

She canted her head and blinked at me, as if she'd never encountered such a strange specimen. "I didn't mean…you know what? Never mind. I'll get you a freaking beefcake. Well, a vegecake. I don't do meat. Unless you're willing to take a chance on squirrel? They're the chicken of the trees, you know, and the little suckers deserve death by mastication. I said what I said."

Freaking? *Do* meat? Did many avian speak as oddly as this one, who reminded me of the witch Ophelia. "I humbly accept the vegecake, but not the squirrel. You're very kind."

"Whoa, whoa, whoa." She rushed over to slap a hand over my mouth, her gaze darting left and right. To all those nearby, she called, "She means I'm super bad. Like, terrible. Awful." Satisfied she'd made her point, she dropped her hand and said, "Lookit, I can tell you aren't wanting to grocery shop or prepare some kind of recompense meal. You can barely keep your eyes off the coliseum. So do you want to attend the tournament, or what?"

Truly? Had I finally found a fairy godmother? "You'll escort me there? Yes, yes, yes."

"The princess is supposed to go to the market, nowhere else." Anger frothed in Trio's eyes as he spread his beautiful wings. *Whoosh, whoosh.* He rose into the air, gliding toward me. "If I must break your legs and carry you to ensure it happens, Princess, I will."

I didn't... I couldn't...*move.* I needed to move. But I'd frozen with terror, my limbs locked in place. I remained planted, an unwitting target for my worst nightmare.

The pale-haired girl flung herself at him, kneeing him in the stomach and punching him in the face. "Try to break her legs and see what happens," she cooed at his wheezing form.

Fairy godmother to the rescue.

Smiling at me, she held out her hand. "I'm Eve, by the way. You're Ashleigh, and you're happy to meet me, yada yada."

I looked at her, then her hand. Eve, the hand. Was I supposed to kiss it? She *was* Saxon's second-in-command, and she *had* helped me with Trio. If it was avian tradition...

Whatever. I did it. I kissed her hand.

She sucked her lips between her teeth, her eyes going wide

with…mirth? Ugh. What had I done wrong? And oh, wow. Up close, I noticed a faint blue glow inside her irises. It reminded me of both the Enchantian Forest and Ophelia. I frowned. Was she part witch, or had she been infused with magic as a child?

Usually avian preferred not to partake of magic, or so I'd been told. Still, she wasn't wearing wrist cuffs to protect her hands, the conduit for magic.

Trio came to his feet with a growl. "Out of my way." He shoved Eve aside and crushed my forearm in a vise grip, making me yelp. As if I were little more than a rag doll, he yanked me against him.

Eve launched into action, kicking his arm, forcing him to loosen his hold. I stumbled backward, and she performed a second kick, nailing him in the stomach. When he hunched over, gasping for breath, she fisted his hair, then double-kneed him, first in the nose, then in the chin. He collapsed, unconscious.

My hero! "How did you do that?"

"Practice." She brushed her hands together in a job well done. "Now, close your eyes and I'll, uh, fly you to the coliseum. Because I have wings. You noticed the wings, right?"

Something about her voice… I couldn't *not* obey her, my eyelids closing of their own accord. When she wrapped an arm around my waist, I experienced a moment of weightlessness, disorientation, and dizziness. The foundation under my feet vanished, the two of us seeming to hover in the air.

All of a sudden, a new foundation materialized underfoot. I inhaled, taking in an array of perfumes mixed with sweat and soap. The roars of the spectators cranked up to top volume.

Only a couple of seconds had passed since I'd closed my eyes, yet I was certain I was now standing inside the coliseum.

I tried to open my eyes but my lids were stuck. Fighting panic, while panicking, I cried, "Something's wrong. I can't open my eyes. What's wrong? Eve?"

"Oh. Right. Yes, go ahead and open your peepers."

Just like that, my eyelids popped open. Okay. Much better. I exhaled, now beyond certain she did indeed wield a magical ability. I'd heard whispers that there were people who could compel the actions of others with a spoken word, but I'd never actually met anyone who could do it.

For whatever reason, she must have used her voice magic to make me think so little time had passed since we'd abandoned Trio. And I'd had no idea.

The terrible things this girl could make me do…

"Well, don't look at me like *that*," she said, the note of power replaced by exasperation. "I'm just a girl, standing in front of another girl, wanting her to withhold judgment until she gets to know her better."

Well. Wasn't that what I'd always wanted from others, too? I nodded, and she grinned.

"I'm starting to like you, Ash. Now look." With her hands on my shoulders, she spun me around.

Oh, my. I marveled at the grandeur. We stood at the top of the coliseum, to the right of the royal dais, where my father and Dior presided over the tournament from golden thrones. Four servants held a large tarp over the area, bathing them with shade. The most beautiful red ribbons hung from the corners of that tarp, dancing in a slight breeze. Another servant stood to one side, fanning the king with a palm frond to ward off the unseasonable heat. At least, I assumed it was unseasonable. I'd never visited Sevón before.

As she had in the throne room, Dior occupied the queen's seat, rather than the child's. An honor I didn't think she deserved.

Spotting me, she smiled and waved. I forced myself to wave back. Smiling, though… I wasn't there yet.

On my father's other side were two cushioned chairs, one occupied by the witch Ophelia, and the other claimed by a lovely girl I'd never met.

The newcomer had hair a brighter red than Trio's, white skin with a rosy undertone, and the most incredible purple eyes framed by thick black lashes. She wore the same type of clothes and armor as Eve and just as many jewels as Ophelia. Must be the royal oracle.

The two were bent together, whispering and laughing.

I returned my gaze to my father. As he watched the contestants, he appeared focused and gleeful. Part of me wanted to rush over and hug him, and I didn't understand why. Did I enjoy torment or something? Father would rebuff me immediately, and I'd look the fool. Again.

Why couldn't he love me the way I loved him?

My shoulders drooped. "Do I look presentable?" I asked my avian escort. "There wasn't a mirror in the tent." Would I make Father proud, at least a little, or would I embarrass him?

She gave me a once-over. "You look ready to fine me for an overdue book and take a stroll along Chastity Lane."

We spoke the same language, and yet her words were foreign to me. Overdue book? I'd never even heard of this Chastity Lane. "Is that a good or bad thing?"

"Darling, it's a very good thing—for you. Prim and proper is Saxon's new type."

New type? "What was his old type?"

"Fiery." She motioned to the dais. "You're going to have the best seat in the house. You'll be next to your new stepsis and your father's all-you-can-eat smorgasbord of snacks. Best get settled. The battle is about to begin, and I have a feeling Saxon expects your gaze to be riveted on him the entire time."

She sounded on the verge of laughter. "I *knew* he expected me to be here." He'd wanted to punish me for skipping it, but I'd foiled his plans. Head high, shoulders back. This girl was unstoppable.

"I think he wanted you here," she said, "but I know he didn't *want* to want you here."

I cringed a little. Did she know who Saxon thought I was?

"Yeah, I know who you are," she said, as if reading my mind. "Don't worry. I understand how someone's actions can be misconstrued. So. I'm giving you the same courtesy you're giving me and observing you before I render a verdict."

Okay, I'd just made my decision about her—she wasn't someone to fear.

"When the battle is done, I'll collect you and return you to his tent." She gave me a gentle nudge forward. "Have fun. Go wild. May your golden roses find...sunshine?"

"May your roses forever bloom," I corrected with a grin. I turned to give her a hug, but she'd already strode away.

No matter. I think I'd just made a friend.

My grin remained in place as I glided onto the dais. As I passed the witch and oracle, who ignored me...the king, who looked around me... Dior, who waved again. I wilted and eased onto the child-size throne.

Minutes passed as I waited for some kind of acknowledgment from my father.

Still waiting...

I expelled a heavy breath and took the initiative. "Good morn, Fath—Majesty. Dior."

He nodded, saying nothing, still enraptured by the combatants. No questions about my overnight stay with Saxon? No inquiries about my time at the Temple, now that we were away from the courtlings? Not even a scolding for daring to attend this event?

Dior burst out, "Good morn, Ashleigh," as if she couldn't contain her words a moment longer. "I'm so glad you could come to the tournament. We can finally get to know each other better."

"Sure," I said, but I didn't sound enthused.

As if just realizing I'd arrived, Ophelia swiveled around to meet my gaze. "Ashleigh, Princess of Glass or whatever, I'd like you to meet Noel, the premier oracle of Sevón." She gestured grandly at the girl beside her.

"I'm, like, your biggest fan," Noel gushed at me. "I'm president of the club and everything. Honest."

More gibberish. A club was a weapon and a president was a... I didn't even know. Following my father's example, I nodded. What else could I do, really?

The beautiful redhead leaned over the king, uncaring when he issued a disgruntled murmur, and asked me, "Aren't you so proud of our Saxon for all that butt kicking today?"

Butt kicking? I knew enough about oracle-speak to know she'd just referenced the end result of today's battle, even though a punch had yet to be thrown. But... "Butt kicking is good?" Clearly I had missed out on some important updates to local vernacular during my time at the Temple.

"Very good indeed," Noel said with a nod. "If you're the one doing the kicking, of course. And Saxon is."

Relief bombarded me.

Whoa, whoa, whoa. Hold up. Relief? Ridiculous. I wanted Saxon to lose right from the start, thereby ending my liaison duties.

The oracle scratched her head. "Unless I'm mistaken, and *Saxon* is the one who gets his butt kicked. Yeah, that's totally possible. Let's find out together."

"Our next combatant is," the master of ceremonies announced, "Milo Ambrose, the royal warlock of both Fleur and Sevón."

I straightened. So. Milo had decided to fight for Dior's hand in marriage. That didn't surprise me.

Dior cheered and clapped. "Have you met our delightful warlock, Ashleigh? He's so sweet."

Sweet? "I can't say my experience with him mirrors yours."

Her brow wrinkled. "What do you mean? Was he cruel to you?"

A servant approached the thrones, bearing a tray of traditional Fleuridian treats I missed more than breath. His arrival saved me from trying to explain something I didn't know how to explain. As I beheld lemon-curd tarts, lavender cookies, fresh-baked breads with strawberry jam and dollops of cream, my mouth watered.

Ohhh. The other side of the tray offered savory options. Delicacies from Sevón, I'd bet. I couldn't identify the different meats and sauces.

I selected the goodies I wanted. Meaning, I scooped up as many desserts as I could hold. Sweet first. Savory second.

The moment I bit into my bounty, my eyes rolled back. So good. I couldn't remember sampling anything better, my taste buds suddenly alive with flavor.

"Did you lose your manners during your three-year absence?" My father eyed me with distaste. "Shall I send you back to the Temple to help you find them?"

My cheeks heated, all but blistering, and I swallowed the sugary treat I no longer wanted. A treat in my stomach like a lead ball. "I'm sorry, Fath—Your Majesty." He was right. A princess should not shovel food into her mouth, especially in public.

Dior glanced between us before telling the king, "My dear sister was kind enough to select some treats for me, weren't you, Ashleigh? A very noble deed, to be sure." She claimed a handful of my cookies and spread them over her lap, mimicking me as if I were a shining example of grace and sophistication.

My father pursed his lips but said no more.

I met the princess's heartfelt gaze and mouthed, *Thank you.*

She offered me a bright smile, one of shared secrets and comradery, and I vowed to be nicer to her for the rest of the day.

"I give you the future king of the avian," the master called, drawing out a few select words. "Crown Prince Saxon Skylair."

Deafening cheers resounded as Saxon stepped forward.

Just like that, I forgot everything else. The sight of him

decked out in his war wear, loaded down with weapons…*glorious*. Such strength.

He tilted his chin proudly, his spine ramrod straight. Determination stamped every line of his arresting face. He wore a well-made breastplate, leaving every ridge of muscle in his arms on spectacular display. Two dark straps crisscrossed his chest, anchoring two short swords to his back, directly between his beautiful wings. How soft those feathers appeared, so at odds with the rest of him.

Black leathers clung to his powerful legs like a second skin, and a pair of steel-toed combat boots completed the look.

Awareness of him consumed me. Did he know I was here? Did he—

He lifted his gaze, meeting mine, and I trembled. Oh, yes. He knew. He'd probably known the second I'd arrived.

Sunlight haloed his body, and highlighted the furious gleam in his eyes—a furious gleam that told me I'd been wrong, that he hadn't wanted me here. That gleam promised we would have a battle of our own just as soon as he finished here…

7

*He fights and he bleeds,
but doesn't find what he needs.*

SAXON

Combatants pressed themselves against the outer edge of the coliseum's walls, leaving the center unoccupied. We awaited the blare of a horn, our battlefield stretched before us.

The first wave of combat would begin in a matter of minutes. A battle to the death—a free-for-all until the master of ceremonies blasted the final horn. There would be no surrender. Not this time. Those left standing would advance to the second round.

The deaths were unnecessary. But, King Philipp's tournament, King Philipp's rules. I'd known he planned to eliminate any perceived threats to his reign; I just hadn't realized he wanted so many to die.

The longer we waited, the more aggression charged the air, until currents of energy seemed to crackle. It was manna for someone like me. I breathed it in, letting it fill my lungs and infuse my cells.

I'd ordered my people to refrain from entering the tournament; I hadn't wanted to harm or kill a fellow avian. I would do it if necessary, but I wouldn't like it. I'd expected a few challengers to enter anyway, but none had.

Because they feared me? Or because they feared my mother?

I pressed my tongue to the roof of my mouth, incensed by the very idea of someone else doing my intimidating for me. But no matter. Today, I would begin to prove I was strong enough to rule the most ferocious army in Enchantia. One by one, I would take out the most skilled competitors in the tournament.

No mercy!

I only had to endure three weeks of public battles, then I could claim ultimate victory, killing King Philipp and neutralizing Leonora at long last.

Princess Dior would be sent back to Fleur, *without* a wedding. When finally I selected a bride, I would choose someone honest and hardworking, who didn't have a temper more volatile than my own. Our match would be an advantageous one sure to aid my kingdom. I wouldn't wait to find my fated mate, like so many other avian did.

I didn't believe such a thing was possible for me. At times, Craven had been certain Leonora was his fated mate, even though he hadn't produced the amour for her. Look how their relationship had turned out. Twice doomed to fail.

Resentment welled, but I tamped it down. Now was not the time for emotion, but cold determination.

"Welcome, one and all, to the most spectacular tournament ever held in Enchantia, with a prize among prizes. Marriage to the beauteous Princess Dior!" The master of ceremonies spoke, his voice filling the stands. "This incredible event will run for three consecutive weeks. During each of those weeks, our combatants will compete in at least one physical battle. But don't despair. They'll have the option to compete in many other types of battles, as well. We will test their speed, cunning, and even their ability to negotiate. The victors of the smaller contests will win some kind of advantage. A head start in the next physical battle, perhaps. A weapon when everyone else is weaponless. They can even win disadvantages for their fellow competitors."

Cheers erupted.

He continued, saying, "Combatants may use their innate abilities for each and every competition. Magic? Yes. Flight? That, too. Nothing is taboo while our warriors are on the battlegrounds. Outside of the battlegrounds, however, they are mystically prohibited from harming each other. If they miss a physical battle, they will be disqualified. If they wish to withdraw at any point after this first battle, they must petition the king."

Now boos filled the air.

I roved my gaze over the competition, picking out my preferred victims. A daylight vampire…strong, quick, able to heal faster than most. A wolfin…able to jump high enough to rip me out of the air, if I decided to fly. A mer…wily, able to slip out of any hold. A goblin…able to dematerialize and possess a body for short periods of time. A sorcerer…able to syphon power from combatants, weakening them in minutes. A snake-shifter…their venom could paralyze me for several precious seconds. A troll…their toxic fangs could turn most species into raging monsters before dying a horrid death. I'd recently lost a beloved friend in such a way.

The trolls, then. I'd go after them first, one by one. Eight had entered. If there was time, I would take out the snake-shifters, goblins, and sorcerian afterward. In that order.

Drawn by a force I couldn't control, I slid my gaze to Ashleigh for the thousandth time since her arrival. And she must be Ashleigh again, Leonora hidden once more. She perched on a child's throne high atop the stands, and continually cast her father quick, longing glances that hurt my heart, as if the organ were learning to beat for the first time. It was an unacceptable reaction to an unacceptable girl, and another annoyance to add to the princess's tally.

Because of her, I'd tossed and turned all night, unable to sleep. Sleep I'd needed, considering today was life-and-death. But how was I supposed to drift away with her at my side? Every time I'd inhaled, I'd breathed in the sweet scent of roses and vanilla and remembered her naked, water-damp skin. I'd tried to think of something, anything else, but my thoughts had remained trapped in a mental quicksand of her making.

The madness had to end.

While the first avian king had possessed a weakness for the evil witch, I wouldn't be so foolish. I wouldn't soften with Ashleigh. Not again. I reminded myself of my goals. *Expose her for the dangerous murderess she is. Protect my people for once. Enjoy my vengeance.*

Then, and only then, could I enjoy the rest of my life.

But why did she have to look so lovely in her new gown?

Before I'd left the garment for her, I'd paid Ophelia to enchant the material. The moment Ashleigh had donned it, a powerful—temporary—tracking spell had absorbed into her skin. For the next twenty-one days, I would be able to discern her location with only a thought. If she ran from me, as Leonora had often done, I could find her in a matter of minutes.

At my side, a combatant unsheathed a large ax and banged a fist into the thick blade.

The time had come.

I withdrew my swords, readying for an attack. Multiple combatants watched me, their excitement palpable. Hoped to take *me* out first? No doubt they'd break my wings to ground me the moment I became preoccupied with another opponent. I'd have to remain aware at all times. No getting lost in thought, wondering what the bane of my existence was doing.

"Today, the rules are simple," the master of ceremonies announced from the dais. "If a combatant leaves the battlefield before the final horn, he will be disqualified and pay with his life." The crowd liked the punishment. "They may attack an opponent however they wish, no action off-limits. The one who slays the most combatants will earn the right to eliminate a competitor of his choice, without that competitor dying."

New cheers. Whoops and whistles.

Well. I couldn't risk being eliminated once the fray ended. So, I couldn't allow anyone else to win this battle. So… I needed to alter my plan. No targeting the trolls first. I would slay as many combatants as possible, however possible. Anyone who stepped into my path would die.

Pressure building…

Ignore. Focus.

"Are you ready?" the master called, the cheers that followed this time almost deafening. "The battle will begin in ten seconds. Nine…eight…"

As the male counted down, adrenaline seared my veins with increasing intensity. I had no fear. Why should I? I'd spent each of my lives training for combat. I had centuries' worth of skills.

"Five."

Deep breath in. Out. No one would defeat me. Today, Ashleigh—*my people*—would see my abilities. They would be forced to accept the truth: there was no better king.

"Four."

I would do this. I would do this *well*. For the avian. For Roth, Everly, and all our friends. For myself.

"Three."

After the battle, I would oversee Ashleigh's next punishment. She'd dared to attend the tournament without permission. Just as I'd hoped she would.

A smile grew. I had the perfect punishment in mind, something guaranteed to bring Leonora to the surface.

"Two."

The spectators went still and quiet. Even the breeze died down. Every combatant stiffened, preparing for the carnage to come.

I purged the fire witch from my mind—

A horn blast cut through the air. Combatants launched at each other. Swords, daggers, and axes were swung. Metal clanged against metal.

With a war cry, I kicked into a mad dash. Anyone I passed, I killed, as planned, racking up my kill total. A jab-jab here, a slice there. I zigzagged as I fought my way forward. A mound of motionless bodies ahead. I flew over it, rolling in the air to avoid a volley of arrows.

The song of battle accompanied my every strike. Screams of agony. Moans of pain. Grunts of exertion. The whistle of metal. The pop of bone. The spurt of blood. The sound grew louder and louder, until each noise hit my ears like a hammer. Still I struck when I needed to strike, ducked when I needed to duck, always motoring onward, killing again and again. Hot blood soaked my hands and splattered my face.

I came upon a troll and snake-shifter, the two trapped in a fierce battle. Guess I'd get to kill a troll, after all. I pulled back my arm to strike—

Incoming. Sensing an approach at my back, I spun and switched the angle of my blade. Ah. I hadn't been the one under attack. A combatant had lifted a crossbow, his double arrows sailing over me to embed in the troll's eyes. The fiend screamed and toppled, batting at his face. He didn't rise, especially after the snake-shifter removed his head.

The one who'd unleashed the arrows looked like a mighty fae. He had pale hair, red eyes full of fury, and glowing symbols branded into his arms. He claimed his name was Blaze and he hailed from the House of Fire; unlike everyone else, I knew the truth. He wasn't fae at all. He was King Roth, his true visage hidden behind a veil of illusion magic, courtesy of Everly.

We exchanged nods before turning our focus to other combatants.

As I advanced on the snake-shifter who'd decapitated the troll, someone leaped on me—a wolfin. He knocked me to the ground, flashing sharp teeth, clearly planning to rip out my throat. Good luck. I'd already worked a dagger between us.

I stabbed him in the gut and ran the blade up his torso.

As he split apart, I rolled out from under him. On my feet, I pushed forward. Another down. Another. Another. Movement at my left. I twisted to see a gorgon rushing my way.

I quickly averted my gaze, observing his approach from the corner of my eye. If a gorgon—a "stone child"—held your gaze long enough, he could slip into your mind, gain control of your thoughts and your actions, and turn you into a pillar of rock.

He entered my strike zone, and swung a jagged-edged sword at me. I went low, my own sword lifted, the blade pointing up and pressed against my side. Our blades met with a clink, jarring him to a stop. I had no such pause. I swept out my leg, knocking his ankles together, at the same time I slicked my sword through another male's ankles, removing both of his feet. The two opponents crashed into the ground. I stabbed one in the heart, then the other, finishing them off.

No time to rest. As I stood, another troll slammed into me. We rolled together, flinging dirt. When we stopped, he was beneath me. I got busy, punching, punching. With a snarl, he jerked up and sank his venomous fangs into my neck—or he tried to.

This morning, I'd decided to wear one of Ashleigh's defensive pieces, so I'd taken the sketch to Ophelia. In a matter of seconds, the witch had crafted a thin metal collar the same color as my skin. It circled my throat, without restricting my movements. *A rush order*, she'd said, before charging me an obscene amount of gold. *Worth it.*

The second troll's fangs slammed into the collar, they cracked.

He roared with pain and bucked me off him. I rammed into another combatant, my back to his chest, and stabbed backward, slicing into his gut. He screamed—until the wolfin he'd been fighting tore out his jugular.

A metallic tang of blood, waste, and urine permeated the air. Ah. The battle stench. Oh, how I had not missed it.

I fought my way back to the troll, who marched toward me as well, tossing combatants out of his way.

"I'm going to suck the marrow from your bones and take your liaison as my concubine."

He dared to threaten Ashleigh?

Seeing red. I sheathed one of the swords to palm my favorite dagger, a blade with a brass knuckle handle. I slipped my fingers through the loops, keeping the blade flat against my forearm. Then I walked...jogged...sprinted over, closing the distance.

We slammed together, both of us attacking with savage persistence. We slashed, punched, elbowed, clawed, and kicked. His claws were sharper and stronger than metal. At some point, he busted my cheekbone—I shattered his. Still we fought.

"Hurt Ashleigh? Not while I live." *She's mine.* When he blocked my blade, I released the sword's hilt long enough to rake my claws over his belly. As his intestines spilled out, I caught the hilt, the sword firmly in my grip once again. *Swing.*

But he healed supernaturally fast, as if by magic, and blocked, then drove me back, managing to cut into my side. I grunted and blocked the next forward thrust, spun to reach his side, and threw an elbow once, twice. His nose broke. His jaw unhinged.

As he staggered back, I sank my dagger into the hollow of his throat. He fell, gasping for breath he couldn't catch. I followed him down, withdrawing my second sword and crossing the blades over his neck.

"Don't—" he began.

With a single chopping motion, I removed his head.

A round of wild applause erupted as I stood, several bystanders even shouting my name. To my surprise, I felt no pride for the display of brutality, no satisfaction in a job well done. I just felt uneasy. Had I truly defended Leonora's newest incarnation, as if we were in love once again?

I threw myself back into the fray, racing forward—mistake! One of the fallen soldiers pushed a dagger into my calf as I passed him. The blade must have been laced with poison. In seconds, searing pain overtook me, an ocean of dizziness rushing in. A loud ring erupted in my ears, muffling every other noise. My eyesight dimmed, the battle seeming like a dream. Then my entire world flipped upside down.

No, I'd just fallen. I remained on the ground, panting as my line of vision darkened the rest of the way.

Can't see.

Inhale, exhale. Calm. Steady. I had no reason to panic. I'd trained in the light as well as the dark, both drugged and clearheaded. This? This was nothing.

I focused on the detail I could best discern. The vibrations in the ground…one hit me stronger than the others. Someone approached me at top speed.

I yanked the dagger from my leg and hurled it in the combatant's direction. A grunt sounded.

Wait. I'd heard the grunt. The ringing had already begun to subside, my eyesight clearing, the effects of the toxin wearing off as my avian blood worked to neutralize it. Ignoring a flare of pain, I climbed to my feet, my weapons in hand.

How long until King Philipp ended the match? Minutes? Hours?

Either way, I had work to do.

I gripped my weapons and leaped into motion.

8

When you're high or when you're low,
it's always great to slay a foe.

Ashleigh

The way Saxon fought...

I'd never seen anyone more vicious or frightening, but I couldn't bring myself to look away. He was magnificent, his muscles flexing with every action. No matter how many times he'd gotten hit, he'd always rebounded to slay his attacker, his skill unmatched. But...

He needed better weapons. The brass knuckle dagger was amazing, yes, but it needed ridged blades or tiny hooks that would do more damage more quickly, since some of his opponents healed in a snap. Not that I would tell him what adjustments his weapons required. As long as he dished those petty restitution tasks and retained unlawful possession of my dragon eggs, books and designs, he'd get no help from me.

I disdained him. I did. So why was I perched on the edge of my throne, utterly rapt, silently cheering him on? I alternated between stroking my mother's ring for comfort and stuffing my face with the remaining lemon tarts—anything to soothe the churning in my stomach.

When one of the two competing giants toppled, spectators leaped to their feet, screaming instructions, insults, and praises. I hated to admit it, but I clapped my hands.

As a child, I'd watched tournaments like this from my bedroom window. I remembered the roar of the crowds and the atmosphere of excitement as men and women had harmed each other for the enjoyment of others. Back then, I'd cried over every wound. Here, now, I better understood the merriment. The battle hardly seemed real. It was like a game, every onlooker rooting for a champion, the other combatants merely obstacles in his way.

Father stood and moved to the edge of the dais for a closer look at the battleground. He gripped the railing and leaned forward, exuding excitement. Ophelia and Noel remained in their seats, muttering about being bored. Dior—had—not—stopped—talking—to—me. Talk, talk, talk, talk, talk. Words. Sentences. Rambles about her life. I'd stopped listening a hundred years ago.

Speaking at a louder volume—and talking over Dior—Ophelia said, "So. Ashleigh." Her leading tone made me instantly uneasy. "Have you met Eve yet?"

"Eve?" Dior asked, bouncing in her seat. "Who is Eve?"

Sweet goodness. She was excited about the prospect of making a new friend, wasn't she?

Before meeting Dior, I'd thought myself a good person. Kind, mostly. Generous...at times. Forgiving, eventually. Yet, she made me feel like a she-hag who'd cursed all the land to die forever. Was she even real? Had she sprouted from a rainbow or something? And why was I being so petty to her?

"I did meet Eve, yes," I replied to Ophelia. I told my stepsister, "Eve is an avian commander who serves Prince Saxon."

The man I still watched. I winced as he took a blow to the temple and dropped.

Multiple onlookers gasped, proving they watched him, too.

"I wonder if she'll like me," Dior said, chewing on a fingernail. "Do you think she'll like me?"

Finally a question I could answer beyond any doubt. "Of course she'll like you." Who wouldn't?

The princess beamed at me. "You really think so?"

"What have I told you about neediness, Dior?" Noel asked.

"Nothing."

"Oh, well, I meant to tell you that your prince hates it."

Dior gasped, excited. "I'll wed a prince? Like Prince Saxon?"

Oh…weeds. How many princes had entered the tournament? No, I didn't need to know. I didn't care.

"I've said all I can say." Noel looked to me. With a tone as leading as Ophelia's, she asked, "So. What did you think of Eve?"

Saxon had gotten back up, fought a few more soldiers, but dropped again. He hadn't gotten back up. He was shaking his head, as if trying to clear the haze from his mind. My stomach churned faster.

"Ashleigh?" Noel prompted.

Oh, yeah. She'd asked a question. "Eve is wonderful. Smart. Independent. Strong." Would Saxon recover in time to block an incoming blow?

"Wonderful?" In unison, Noel and Ophelia cackled. Why?

Yes! Saxon had rallied and fended off the attack. Not that I cared. His breastplate had come off, revealing gashes all over his muscular chest.

Watching him now, it was easy to believe he once, maybe, might possibly have been the original avian king. *Such ferocity. Such brutality.* But, even if he was a copy of Craven the Destroyer, he wasn't actually Craven the Destroyer. Saxon had led a different life this go-round. He'd had a different upbringing, with different challenges and experiences.

And that was good. I suspected Craven would have murdered me right away. Saxon merely toyed with me. Which was frustrating. Definitely not fun. But I wasn't Leonora. I hadn't changed my mind about that. If anything, I was more certain than ever. Because...reasons.

If I *were* the witch—or phantom—I would have used her powerful fire magic at least once while I was awake. I wouldn't burn or blister when I encountered flames, and I did.

But oh, what I wouldn't give to wield power like hers. To create fire from air...to melt and mold my metals anytime, anyplace I desired... It had to be paradise.

A bloody Saxon shot into the air so suddenly, it looked like he'd been thrown. I held my breath as he peaked, angled his head down, tucked in his wings, and bulleted toward the ground.

"Oh, my goodness," Dior cried. "Will he...can he...?"

The crowd held a collective breath. At the last second, the avian leveled out, spread his wings, and swept over the remaining combatants. Any warrior who came into contact with his wings toppled, clutching some part of his body as fresh blood spurted.

I caught sight of Milo just as he felled a goblin with surprising skill and violence. The warlock had been training.

Dior clapped for him, and I slinked deeper into my baby throne. For her sake, I hoped Milo had grown out of his selfishness. Until I got to know the man he'd become, I wouldn't feel right commenting about the boy he'd been.

"You know," Ophelia said, tapping a fingertip against her chin. "I can't help but wonder if *Saxon* thinks Eve is wonderful, too. They both have parts in 'The Little Cinder Girl' prophecy, after all."

What? I jolted, shocked to my core, my heart galloping. The battle momentarily forgotten, I zoomed my attention to the oracle. "They do?"

"Big ones," Noel confirmed. "Huge."

Why had no one told me? I mean, I understood that some royals kept their prophecies to themselves to ensure an enemy couldn't use the fairy tale against them, but come on! If Saxon and Eve *were* part of "The Little Cinder Girl," just as I was part of "The Little Cinder Girl," our futures—our very fates—were intertwined.

"Guess what?" Dior squealed, grinning from ear to ear.

Oh, no. No, no, no. Don't say it.

"I'm part of 'The Little Cinder Girl,' too." She clasped my hand and squeezed excitedly. "Can you believe it? We share a last name *and* a prophecy. That must mean we're going to be best friends."

Well, she said it. What if she was Cinder? Noel had already admitted Dior was going to wed a prince. And Saxon kind of fit, one part of him an honorable friend, the other part of him a dishonorable foe. But, when was the obvious choice ever the answer?

I gripped the arms of my seat. Saxon and Dior would make a lovely couple. They didn't share a violent history. She was in perfect health, wielded magic, possessed great wealth and the adoration of a king.

Let's face it. I could be her evil stepsister.

Oh…weeds. I didn't want to be an evil stepsister. And Saxon might be the prince, but that didn't mean he belonged with Dior, who clearly wasn't a warrior unwilling to bend. Eve was, though. I couldn't imagine her bending for anyone about anything.

And what about me? Did part of me still qualify? Unbending? Please. My entire life was a compromise of some sort.

Cinder didn't desire wealth or power of her own, but I did. Money purchased what you needed to survive or even exist.

Power protected you from the foes who tried to take your wealth. And, really, I'd like being my own fairy godmother. I mean, I'd take help when I could get it, but I'd taken such pride in solving my own problem.

My dream to make and sell quality weaponry solidified. I would save my coins and buy a magical ability of my own. Nothing would stop me. Which a certain avian prince might consider a very *Leonora* desire...

Two hearts, one head. One head, two hearts.

I drummed my nails against the arms of the throne. Why try to figure this out alone with an oracle nearby? "Do you happen to know our roles in the fairy tale?" I asked, doing my best to sound nonchalant, lest she decide to charge me for the information.

Noel's purple eyes lit with excitement. "I've been waiting for you to ask *for years*. Because I do, and I don't. There are so many players, taking steps this way and that way, then changing their mind and going here and there. But time reveals all, and all reveals time. Does that answer your question?"

What nonsense. "How about you tell me everything you *do* know about the players and nothing you don't?"

"Certainly." She swatted at a twirling dust mote. "As soon as you tell me what we're talking about again?"

Were all oracles this frustrating?

Multiple gasps drew my attention to the battlefield. Recalling the tournament—how had I forgotten, even for a second?—I scanned the combatants, searching for Saxon. Where was he now? I leaped to my feet and joined my father at the railing, desperate for a closer look. He stiffened, but he didn't rebuke me.

Saxon, Saxon—I pressed a hand over my mouth to silence a cry of distress. He was fighting a giant, two trolls, a warlock, a snake-shifter, and four sorcerers. At the same time. They formed a circle around him, attacking him two at a time at different intervals. Saxon held his own, delivering more strikes than he took, his body in a constant state of motion.

"Why did you allow sorcerers to enter?" They were just as universally despised as trolls. In the past, many sorcerian had abducted magic wielders to hold them captive, drain their power, and steal their magic.

With my conversation with Eve so fresh, however, I decided to reserve judgment about each individual sorcerian.

As Saxon disemboweled one of the sorcerers, Father waved away my words. "Excluding specific beings would have ignited an unnecessary war. And there are ways to ensure certain creatures do not win..."

He would cheat? But, that was so low. So cowardly. "Father—"

"No, not another word," he snapped. "I wish to enjoy the game in peace, girl."

I flinched. What made me so unlikable to this man?

When Saxon slayed a second sorcerer, Milo joined the circle, hoping to be the one to take out the avian. At that point, Father decided to nod to the master of ceremonies, who placed a horn at his lips and blew. Amid the ensuing blare, the remaining combatants jumped apart, every fight ceasing.

There. The first competition was done, and Saxon had survived along with half of the others. I could breathe easily again.

"What a battle," my father cried, lifting both of his arms.

The audience went wild, and I scanned the rest of the field. Dead bodies littered the ground. Blood soaked the dirt, and spilled from severed limbs.

A sweating Saxon remained in place, huffing and puffing every breath. Crimson drenched his torn clothing. Gashes covered his battered frame. As his temporary "palace liaison" or whatever, I should patch those wounds. Yes, yes. I wouldn't wait for Eve to collect me. I wasn't a child, and he already knew I'd broken his rules. So why not do my duty?

"Ophelia?" my father said, breaking into my thoughts.

"Saxon, of course," she replied, confusing me.

Father used his hands to convey a number to the master of ceremonies, who announced, "Thanks to the royal witch, we know who slayed the most combatants. Congratulations, Crown Prince Saxon Skylair! You may choose to eliminate one of the remaining warriors."

Saxon stared at the crowd of avian, who occupied one section of the stands. A section shouting, "The mer! The mer!"

"I choose the mer with the most kills," Saxon called.

"That is entrant number eighty-three," Ophelia piped up, buffing her nails.

My father flashed the new number at the master of ceremonies, who checked the notations in the book he held and announced, "Corean Acquilia, you have been eliminated!"

A handsome man in his early twenties cursed and threw a bloody sword at Saxon's feet, then limped off the field.

"Way to go, Saxy," Ophelia shouted, rising to approach the railing. "Whoo-hoo!"

Noel sidled up to my side with a wide, toothy grin. "Battle blood is so hot right now, don't you think?"

The wild things this oracle said.

"Come back tomorrow for our first voluntary competition," the master called to one and all. "This test of wits is sure to delight. The winner will be given an extra weapon for the next battle. Or he can keep another opponent from having a weapon at all. Who's to say?" A dramatic pause. Then, "You! You're to say. Come early and you can vote for the prize of your choice!"

Saxon said nothing, just leaped into the air and flew to the left of the field. He headed straight for... Eve, I realized, my nails cutting into the heel of my palm. She stood on the sidelines, as if waiting for him.

"Do you think they're courting?" Noel asked, those purple eyes twinkling.

"Probably," I muttered. And that was fine. I'd already decided they were the best fit. They could get married and have a million babies for all I cared, just as long as I never had to deal with the avian again.

He landed directly in front of her, and I told myself to look away, that a girl who didn't care should act like it, and also spying was wrong or whatever. And it wasn't like I couldn't guess what they were going to do—hug and kiss and fawn all over each other. But, he seemed to bark an order at her and, well, I got hooked. Like the worst gossip, I had to know what happened next.

She poked a finger into his chest and shouted all angry-like into his face. Whatever she said, he didn't take it well. He bowed up and fisted his hands.

"I change my mind," I said. "They might be foes." Which still didn't tell me if she was Cinder or not.

He turned his head to glare up at me, and I reared back. Uh, what'd I do now? If Eve had told him a lie about me, I'd... what? What *could* I do?

Hate my weakness!

"Or maybe he just wants another body to murder," I mumbled. Seriously. What did he have planned for me?

No way I would stick around to find out. Heart beating way too fast, I abandoned my companions without a proper goodbye and raced off the dais to push through the masses. For a moment I feared Saxon had given chase, his body heat and rainstorm scent enveloping me. Then I caught sight of him in the sky, flying above the crowd of people now filing out of the coliseum, his gaze darting to and fro, searching, searching.

Hoping to better blend in, I slowed to keep pace with the people around me. With their help, I could escape the market and return to the palace. I had no more chores in the tent, after all, so Saxon had no need of my services. I could camp out in the library and begin my research on phantoms.

Problem: as soon as I made it to the cobblestone path that led up the mountain, I ran out of cheese loaf fuel, my body giving out. My lungs burned and my limbs shook as I plopped onto a large rock and peered longingly at the path's entryway. An archway dripping with hundreds of pink and white flowers.

Other spectators neared. I smiled and waved, doing my best to pretend I'd *chosen* to sit here. Those who passed me either ignored me, muttered something about the Glass Princess, or offered a greeting common in their kingdom, proving our guests had come from all over the land.

Fleur: *May your roses forever bloom.*

Sevón: *May you always find gold.*

Airaria: *May your star always shine.*

Azul: *May the water wash you.* Or, as a few of their teenagers had said with a leer, "May you always be wet."

By the time the crowd tapered off, leaving me alone on the mountainside, I'd recovered enough to stand. I don't know why, but I was unsurprised when Saxon chose that moment to pounce, landing a few feet away from me.

Expression disappointingly blank, he crossed his arms over his bare chest. Blood and…other things splattered him from head to toe. Sweet goodness! He had a nipple piercing. "You may show your joy now, Princess. Your avian has arrived."

The words, delivered with such a dry tone, drew a snort from me, and my cheeks heated.

"Why did you run from me, Ashleigh?" His voice had become as blank as his expression.

"Why do you think, Saxy?" I replied, not even trying to mask my snippiness.

"I think you ignored my command to visit the market and prepare a meal, feared I would punish you with another task, and hoped to avoid me for the rest of eternity." He arched a brow, suddenly so smug I longed to slap him. "But that cannot be right. Leonora never runs from anything."

"I'm not Leonora!"

A muscle pulsed under his eye as he extended one hand in a silent command. *Take it or else.*

I was tired, hungry, and sore. Why fight him on this? And okay, yes. Maybe part of me wanted to hold his hand. I could pretend he was seeing me home after a long day of metal work.

I linked my hand with his. He peered at our tangled fingers for a long while, silent, before tugging me close. I gasped, my chest now pressed against his, softness to hardness, clean gown to bloody skin. Every point of contact tingled.

He wasn't emotionless anymore. With a voice as hard as iron, he commanded, "Wrap your arms around me."

I obeyed without hesitation, and maybe, just maybe, a little eagerness, cupping his nape. I didn't have to like him to enjoy the feel of his incredible body. All those muscles, all that unbridled strength... Wait. Was that...?

I patted the cold, hard band anchored around his neck. Metal? He wore one of my pieces?

"Ophelia made it with magic," he grumbled, winding one arm across my back and the other under my knees to sweep me up. Then he jumped, spread and flapped his wings, and took us into the air.

I squealed with delight, even as concern for his injuries rose. "You're hurt. You should put me down."

"I'll heal."

Well. If he wasn't worried, I wouldn't worry. "Still. We can consider this flight payment for my design."

"My design, you mean." He flew me up the mountain, whisking us over treetops. Wind danced with my hair, several strands whipping across my cheek. "I hadn't planned to fly you anywhere ever again," he admitted with his lips just over my ear.

Shivers rushed down my spine at the first breathy caress. "Why? Because I like it?"

"Exactly." Another unabashed admission.

"So, why are you flying me?" I asked, exasperated.

A pause. Tone gruff, he said, "You outwitted me and deserve a reward."

"You mean the dress?" I asked, and he nodded. I almost preened. "I don't want to tell you how to deal with your enemies or anything, but shouldn't you *discourage* my victories?"

His husky chuckle drifted between us, sending a cascade of heat through me, as slow as a drop of molasses. "If I were wiser, yes, but we both know you make me foolish." Just like that, his good humor fled. "Are you disappointed that I survived the battle, Princess?"

"I should be."

"Hmm." He said no more.

We reached camp, but he didn't descend. Instead, he flew smooth circles above his tent, opening and closing his mouth.

Nerves got the better of me. "Just say whatever you have to say, Saxon. As much as I'm enjoying the ride, the company is lacking."

"Eve told me about the spat between you and Adriel." He'd modulated his tone, giving me no clues about his thoughts on the matter.

Ohhh. Was that why he and Eve had fought? "I didn't touch your precious soldier, I swear!"

Saxon sighed, baffling me. "I wasn't blaming you, Asha. I just wanted you to know that he'll be punished for his actions. All of my people were warned. They were not to harm you in any way, for any reason."

Saxon had taken measures to protect me? "Why would you do such a thing?" It was so anti-Craven, and now I caught myself softening against him, hoping against hope that a good man was buried underneath all his rage and hatred.

The muscle started pulsing beneath his eye again. "Because," he grated.

"Because why?" I insisted.

"Because...the honor is mine."

Well. No more needed to be said on the subject. My hope burned to ash. "Is *Asha* a shortened version of my name or does it mean something like 'evil slag'? Just curious."

He tensed and cursed, as if I'd just admitted to drowning his best friend, and I didn't have to wonder why. Having studied people from the sidelines for most of my life, I had a pretty good understanding of how they operated. I suspected he'd just directed his fury at himself. Because *Asha* was indeed a shortening of my name. A means of showing affection. Because, for a moment, he *had* felt something kind toward me.

Withering roses! Weeds! Dandelions! This made his disdain so much harder to bear. "Saxon," I said.

"Not another word," he answered, pushing the words through clenched teeth. He rolled around a cloud.

I refused to stay silent. "How am I to be punished for my crime this time?" Better to know, so that I could prepare.

A moment passed. In lieu of an answer, he said, "Enough chatter. Later tonight, there's to be a victory celebration at the campgrounds. I have much to consider, and even more to do."

I would get to attend my first party? My heart raced with excitement. Then I noticed the sardonic curve of his mouth, and foreboding prickled the back of my neck.

I wasn't going to like this celebration, was I?

9

Oh, be bright. Oh, be merry.
Do what you must and never tarry.

SAXON

I kept Ashleigh in the air longer than necessary, my mind trapped between the present and the past. I'd called her "Asha." Just as I'd once called Leonora "Nora," when I'd begun falling in love with her.

I swallowed a roar, the memory overshadowing the world around me...

The witch was nothing like I'd been led to believe. She wasn't sweet, and she wasn't biddable. Not most of the time, anyway. There were moments, though... Moments when she was somehow sad but also joyful, when she looked at me with kind eyes that were a slightly darker shade of blue than usual, and I didn't feel like a monster who needed to gain more for his people, but a man at rest. I lived for those moments. At all other times, Leonora was the most stubborn, combative being ever to live.

I'd commanded her to clean, making her my personal servant. She'd refused, adding to the mess instead.

I'd ordered her to sleep in my chamber. She'd agreed—and barred me from the room.

I'd demanded she kneel before me like a proper war prize. She'd laughed in my face and purred, "Make me."

I did admire her spirit. But I missed those moments.

Today, she'd decided to reverse her decision to play servant. She served my men their evening meal—a chore I hadn't assigned her—wearing a sheer scarf dress, her ample curves on display for all to see. Her long red hair hung in mile-long waves, her pale skin flushed. Every step she took, every move she made was designed to attract attention.

Lust blazed in every onlooker's eyes, and a desire to commit mass murder unfurled within me. When I could stand it no longer, I banged my fist on the table with enough force to shatter glass. Every gaze shot to me, and all voices went quiet.

I said nothing, but my message was clear. Within seconds, everyone was staring down at their food.

Only somewhat mollified, I looked to Leonora. She grinned the smuggest little grin—this was not one of those restful moments.

The little minx had liked my volatile reaction? Had hoped to rouse my fury? Mission accomplished.

"Leave us," I snapped.

She bristled, snapping back, "I will not."

"I wasn't speaking to you," I informed her in a gentler tone.

My men jumped up, chairs skidding behind them. No one argued. In a hurry, they fled as fast as their booted feet would carry them.

Leonora remained in place, not the least bit afraid to be alone with me. A first. Most people would have begged for my forgiveness by now.

I crooked my finger at her, curious about her response.

For once, she obeyed without delay. Only, she did it her own way, sauntering over slowly. The second she stood within reach, I grabbed her by the waist and set her atop the table.

"You were jealous, warrior," she purred. "Admit it."

I shook my head. "I have no need of jealousy. As a king, I have everything I've ever wanted." *So why am I unsatisfied, nearly every minute of every day?* "But I *am* drawn to you more intensely than anyone I've ever met." It was as if she had been made just for me, but that couldn't be right. My wings hadn't produced the *amour*, the special dust reserved for my fated one. "Why? Why am I drawn to you?"

Was something wrong with me? Or with her?

She traced a fingertip around my lips, as if she had every right to put her hands on me without first receiving permission. "You ask the wrong question, Your Majesty."

I could not look away from her—I didn't want to. She'd snared me completely. "And what is the right one, sweet Nora?"

Her pupils exploded over her irises, black consuming blue. "Nora..." She rewarded me with a soft smile. "I like it."

As did I. "The right question," I prompted. "What is it?"

Leaning closer, she whispered, "Why haven't we done anything about your obsession with me?"

Every muscle in my body hardened to stone. "Is the obsession mutual?"

A new grin lifted the corners of her lips. "Why don't you kiss me and find out?"

"Are we flying circles around the campground for a reason?" Ashleigh asked, drawing me from my thoughts.

My cheeks burned as I switched our angle, descending. When we landed, the guards around my tent grinned and bowed to me.

My participation in the tournament was working as I'd hoped, teaching my army to trust me. And yet...

Still no satisfaction. Like Craven, I remained unfulfilled.

I didn't release my bundle until I'd entered the tent, the flap swooshing closed behind us. Though I longed to keep Ashleigh's softness pressed against me, I forced myself to set her down. Pried my arms from her. We would consider this a test of sorts. Would she go on the defensive and attack?

As I'd requested after the battle, Eve—the illusion form of Everly—had ensured that my soldiers procured two carafes of water and filled the tub with steaming water. A loaf of bread with—I frowned. Was that toothpaste smeared on top? Surely not. The mystery bread sat atop the trunk, between two taste-less patties Everly had made me before. Abominations she referred to as "vegecakes."

I'd ordered my people not to aid Ashleigh a second time. Then I'd asked Everly to stay with Adriel and report his interactions with Ashleigh to me. Which she'd done. But Everly wasn't a true avian and she'd also helped the girl despite my wishes.

I should have expected it and prepared accordingly—I shouldn't be reluctantly impressed with the pair.

"This doesn't look like a three-course meal," I remarked.

"Then your eyes are being truthful with you. This is something even better. A three-*ingredient* meal. It's much rarer. A delicacy some would say, probably."

"Tell me who would say this."

"I've saved you from overeating, okay? Gluttony, and all that. Oh, the vegecakes," Ashleigh cried, jumping up and down.

The excitement in her voice drew my gaze to her. How she glowed. By the holy stars, she made me crave things I couldn't have and shouldn't want. But I'd left smears of blood and vis-cera all over her gown, and the sight struck me as obscene.

"Cheese loaves and vegecakes," she said with a nod. "Now we've got ourselves a two-course meal. Let's consider this a beautiful compromise between us."

She had an answer for everything. But so did I. "I do not

compromise." I stomped to the entrance and opened the flap, shouting, "Eve? Where are you?" My men expected such a demanding tone from their leader. A testament of my strength, I supposed. But the Evil Queen would rage if I wasn't careful. "Ashleigh requires a new gown. And someone bring me food that I can actually eat." I let the flap close again.

Ashleigh was crouched before the inedible food in question, poking a vegecake with a fork. "You know, if you only take three bites, you'll have a full three courses."

"A bite is not a course."

"It has been for me," she muttered.

I stilled, not wanting to believe her but feeling myself soften, anyway.

I stalked behind the privacy screen to whisper to a potted plant. "Did you hear me? Clothes for Ashleigh as soon as possible. Meaning *now*. Please?"

If Everly hadn't heard my bellows, she would hear my whispers. Listening to plants was an ability that had been granted to her when she'd taken over as Empress of the Forest.

"I'm going to bathe," I told Ashleigh. "I won't remain dressed to preserve modesty I don't have. Cross the screen at your own pleasure." The words echoed in my head, and I pursed my lips. First, I'd called her "Asha," the shortened version of her name, which was a special form of endearment for avian. Now I was teasing her, just as I'd once teased Leonora. "You may feel free to—" I heard the fork scrape across a plate "—eat," I finished, my tone flat. Better flat than laughing.

"One step ahead of you," she called, and I would swear she had a mouthful of food.

Why, why, why did I want to tease her again?

In all my lives, I'd *never* teased an enemy. The fact that I continued to do so with Ashleigh…a foolish, imbecilic part of me had called a truce with this part of her personality.

Soften a little, and she would take a lot.

I couldn't let this life become a repeat of the past.

Our fates *must* play out differently this time.

Temper rising, I stripped out of my soiled battle gear. Weapons clinked as they hit the floor. Naked, I stepped into the warm water. Tucking my wings into my sides, I eased down. Overworked muscles protested. Gashes stung and cuts throbbed. As tension leached from me, I couldn't complain.

With a handful of mystical cleansing sands, I washed the filth from my skin. Ribbons of crimson rippled over the water.

"Should I, um, wash your back or something?" Ashleigh called, surprising me. Even more surprising—I thought I detected a note of excitement in her voice. "I am your palace liaison, after all."

I scoured a hand over my mouth to halt a lightning-fast agreement. If she crouched behind me to run her hands over my back, I'd...what? *What would I do?*

I'd hate it, of course. Like every time before, I had only to recall our years of pain and death to refortify my dislike of her...at least for a short while.

"Saxon?" she prompted.

"No," I snapped, deciding to say nothing more. I dunked my head under water to scrub my overheated face.

"All right," Ashleigh said as I came up for air. Did I detect a note of disappointment? "Let's talk, then."

"Yes. Let's." I had more questions for her. "Tell me about your time at the Temple."

"It wasn't fun. Where are my possessions, Saxon? If you have harmed the eggs or burned my papers, I'll—"

"What? For the last time, you own only what I give you." I'd left all four eggs and the designs with Noel and Ophelia for safekeeping. Who would dare steal from a pair of apple babies?

Ashleigh's frustration seemed to electrify the air. "You're making me hate you right now."

"Then I'm doing something right."

"Oh! You're just like the honorable but dishonorable prince." The one from the fairy tale I didn't believe in?

"In our first incarnation," I said, "our war erupted about a year after we met. It lasted ten years. In our second, you remembered our past life before me and set the stage for my seduction, claiming you loved me, that we could finally have our happily-ever-after. But I began to remember what you'd done in the past and eventually cut you from my life. That's when you decided to go to war with me again. We warred for two decades that time. Before you killed me, you told me we would start over a third time, and you were right. During this life, I remembered first and set the stage for your destruction. I'll wear your hatred like a badge of honor."

She sputtered, then stopped as footsteps sounded outside. I heard the swoosh of the tent flap as—I assumed—Everly entered with a dress and a basket of food. The scent of meat, butter, and vegetables taunted my empty stomach.

"I am not your servant, Sax," Everly began, "and if you bark one more order at me—oh. Hello, Ashleigh. I thought you'd run away."

"Hello, Eve," Ashleigh said, her voice laced with affection. "I'm embarrassed to say I did indeed run away. A coward's move. It won't happen again. But Saxon found me."

"I assume you need this dress because your new one is streaked with combat blood."

"By the petals' bloom," Ashleigh gasped out. A common expression in Fleur. "This new gown is... I have no words."

What kind of garment would give her such a breathy tone?

"Wipe the vegecake off your chin—and fingers—and hair, and I'll help you change," the sorceress offered.

Curiosity piqued, I leaned this way and that, attempting to see past the screen.

"You are a girl after my own heart," Everly said with a laugh.

"Using hair ribbons to lace up the first gown was freaking brilliant."

Everly had once resided in the mortal world and sometimes used words and phrases I couldn't decipher. I suspected *freaking* was an expletive of some type. And why hadn't I chosen a privacy screen with thinner material? Impatience warred with frustration, the two mounting.

"Thank you," Ashleigh replied, her pride obvious.

Clothing rustled, my impatience reaching new heights. I rushed through the bath as quickly as possible.

"I hear water splashing, Saxy. Don't you dare peek," Everly called. "You'll see the end result only, or I'll gouge out your eyes."

My ears twitched as Ashleigh whispered, "He'll be your king, but you dare to threaten him?"

"Of course. Don't you?"

"Yes, but I'm his enemy."

I stiffened. I *was* her enemy, just as she was mine. For some reason, I didn't like hearing *her* say so.

More rustling before Everly announced, "All done, Saxon. You can peek as soon as I'm gone. I have a feeling you're going to complain, and I've already reached my man-baby quota for the day."

Complain? Why? The second the tent flap closed behind Everly, alerting me to her exit, I shot from the water, dried off, and dressed in a clean white tunic and fresh black leathers. Not bothering with boots, I stalked past the screen, only to draw up short.

Ashleigh completely and utterly stole my breath.

She stood in the center of the tent, her dark hair brushed to a glossy shine. Her wide green eyes glittered like emeralds, and a rosy glow highlighted her cheeks. The gown was a true stunner—a thought-dimmer. Silk the same color as her irises molded to soft breasts and cinched waist. The skirt flared at the hips and hung to her toes, dancing over the dirt as she shifted from one foot to the other.

"Well?" she asked, twirling.

"You are...you look..." I had no words. Had I ever beheld a more ravishing sight? Or a weaker one? Never had her fragility been more apparent. I wanted to feed her. I *needed* to feed her. And kiss her. Stiffening further, I said, "Satisfactory."

She blink-blinked, her countenance falling. "Satisfactory?" she asked, her tone nothing but a rasp, and my chest tightened. A physical reaction I was beginning to despise. Every time it happened, those awful protective instincts sparked, the urge to comfort the girl nearly irresistible.

I almost—almost—muttered a retraction. But why admit the truth? What good would it do either of us?

"Well," she said, lifting her chin, "you look...clean."

The corners of my mouth curved ever so slightly. *Minx.* "I doubt the vegecake you inhaled satiated your hunger, Asha." *Asha again?* "You will dine with me."

I stomped to the table, where I held out a chair for her, then claimed the backless one for myself.

Both vegecakes were gone. The cheese had been plucked from the toothpaste bread. She'd spread the new food over the table's surface and removed the lids. Steam rose from the dishes.

Now she scooped a little of everything onto a plate. Lemon-marinated fish. Honey-glazed carrots. Creamed potatoes. Then she scooped a little more. She nibbled on her bottom lip, stared at the dishes, and scooped a little more.

I let her do it, saying nothing, simply stroking two fingers over my chin, once again trying not to smile. "Take as much as you desire."

"I will, thank you. I haven't had fish in forever," she said. "My father's marriage to an Azulian princess comes with some perks, I guess."

I was in no mood to discuss her father. "You seem to be on good terms with Eve."

She handled the subject change without missing a beat. "I like her. She's kind. The first friend I've had in...ever."

Kind? Everly? That wasn't a word many used for the sharp-tongued sorceress. Of course, people like Ashleigh tended to search for the good in everyone, or some nonsense.

Softening... How long till Leonora destroyed that part of her?

I stiffened and dropped my gaze to the food. "What did— do—you hope to do with your life?" Maybe, if I learned more about my greatest enemy's new incarnation, my reactions to her would lessen.

"I'm not sure exactly. I need to speak with my father—"

"I didn't ask what the king will try to make you do." Men who attempted to control Leonora tended to die screaming. "I asked what *you* hope to do with your life. You, Princess Ashleigh." Would her desires align with the witch's?

"Oh. Right." She cleared her throat. "I'd like to train with a blacksmith to design, make, and sell my weapons."

She planned to craft the weapons herself? "That is grueling work." I knew it firsthand. Craven used to make weapons, too. "Are you strong enough?"

A flinch. Then she jutted her chin at me, the same way I'd done to my competitors earlier. "Weapons are my passion, Saxon. Why trust their construction to anyone else? And I don't care if the work is grueling. I'm stronger than I look. I'll persevere."

How confident she sounded. But was it genuine? "To whom will you sell these creations?"

"To those I deem worthy, who can afford my high quality, expertly made pieces. And don't try to shame me for expecting my due for my work. I'll deserve every coin."

"I would never shame a craftsman for demanding what their

creations are worth. No one wants to labor without recompense." Even I expected rewards for doing my duty as king.

Ashleigh's emerald eyes grew stark, and I wanted to know why.

I couldn't ask. I had no right to the answer. I could guess it, though. She didn't think people would ever take her seriously.

"What about you?" she whispered. "What's your passion?"

I knew better than to present my secrets to an enemy already boxed and bowed, especially *this* enemy. But the truth slipped out, anyway. "My only passion is working to secure a better future for my people and myself."

"Because you feel guilty about your failures in your other lives?" she asked matter-of-factly.

I narrowed my eyes and nodded, my ire growing at her accurate reading of the situation.

"That's understandable." She tasted the potatoes and closed her eyes, the barest moan escaping her. "Do I taste *cream*? With *potatoes*? This might be the best thing I've ever had in my mouth. In Fleur, they are only ever mixed with herbs."

Still she moved so gracefully. My blood heated, a battle raging inside my head. One side wanted to storm from the tent. The other expected to walk around the table and crouch before her, so I could cup her cheeks in my palms and draw her face to mine…so I could press my lips against hers and taste her.

I squeezed my fork, inadvertently bending the handle.

Leaning back in my seat, I asked, "What was your first thought about me, when we first met?" A topic sure to cool me.

Circles of pink painted her cheeks. "What was your first thought about *me*?"

That blush… "Did young Ashleigh consider me handsome?" She made a choking sound, and I knew. She had. Tone growing lighter, I said, "I thought you sad and adorable…until memories of our past lives invaded." Just like that, the lightness evaporated. "I realized who you were."

She traced her fork through the carrots, gaze downcast. "I did consider you handsome. At first. Then I realized how cruel you were. The way you glared at me... I was just a child, Saxon. I'd lost my mother only days before, and I had no idea why this winged warrior kept glaring daggers at me."

I closed my eyes for a moment, shamed. "I admit Queen Charlotte's funeral wasn't my finest hour. I...apologize for the way I treated you." I gritted out the words. I meant them, but saying them to an enemy still rankled. "I didn't view you as a child that day, but a centuries-old witch who liked to burn down my homes and murder my families."

Another flinch. "The first time Craven and Leonora met, did he enter her home and decide she would move in with him?" she asked, fingering the ring now hidden beneath the dress.

I went still. "That is a very specific question. Why do you wish to know? Did you relive one of her memories?"

Her gaze darted guiltily. "I'm curious, that's all, and I'd like a personal accounting. History books claim he abducted her."

I snorted. "She went with him happily, even against the advice of her parents."

"Then why did the two go to war?"

"She went with him happily," I repeated. "They fell in love, or some warped version of it, then parted, then warred."

"Why am I not like you? Why do I have no memory of the past lives?"

The words Noel had uttered a few weeks—eons ago—played in my head. *Exactly like you, but vastly different.*

I hadn't understood then, and I didn't understand now.

"Your mother," I said, proceeding carefully. "Did your father ever find her murderer?"

Ashleigh's eyes blazed before becoming two wide, watery emerald wounds, just as they'd been at the funeral. "N-no."

I bit my tongue, going quiet for a moment. I didn't want to push, but she needed to face the reality of our situation. "Do you ever wonder why someone decided to stab their beloved queen inside the warlock's chambers?"

"Yes." Another croak. "Every day."

"Your father told me you passed out just before the murder occurred. You passed out in the garden, too, only to awaken in seconds and attack me. Yesterday, you passed out in the tub, awoke within seconds and conversed with me as if you were Leonora."

"I… I was talking in my sleep. People do that. It's a thing that happens."

I glared at her, daring her to look past the veil of innocence draped over her thoughts, shielding her from a terrible past. "But what if I'm telling the truth, Ashleigh? What then?"

10

Hark! Heed my warning,
or die by morning.

Ashleigh

I replayed Saxon's question in my head a million times, but I never offered him an answer. I didn't know *how* to answer. Had I done and said things to others unconscious? Probably. It wasn't beyond the realm of possibility, considering everything else. But I needed to know for sure, before I attempted to carry the emotional burden of the things I'd been accused of doing. If I *had* harmed my mother and the warlock, I deserved to *drown* in guilt, shame, and horror. How could I know beyond any doubt, though?

I could maybe afford to pay a witch or an oracle to divine the truth, if I sold my mother's ring. At the thought, I recoiled. Part with the only thing of hers I owned? Not going to happen. But, again, if I *had* killed the woman I'd loved above all others, I wasn't worthy to keep the ring.

Peering at my wringing fingers, I asked, "What did I say during our bath-time conversation?"

Saxon's breath quickened. "You begged me to look my fill and join you in the water."

"I *did*?" I squeaked. Had he memorized my naked body? Could he picture what I looked like naked right this second? "And did you comply?"

"I did not."

Wait. "So you didn't look at all?"

"I didn't say that."

But he had said…what? That he hadn't looked his fill?

Oh. Oh, my.

He stood and stalked to the trunk, where he sat and focused on cleaning and polishing the weapons he'd dropped earlier, dismissing me.

Or maybe he just hoped to dismiss me? He remained as stiff as a board, as if his thoughts remained with me.

I watched as a blue feather danced its way to the ground, my mind whirling. These little tells of his…could he be as aware of me as I was of him? Did I want him to be?

"Do you have any chores for me to complete before the victory celebration?" For the first time, I would get to attend a party, just like any other girl. Just like any normal, healthy person. That was cause for *another* celebration. "And don't even think about leaving me behind. I am your palace liaison. That means I…liaison for you at parties. It's an official duty."

"No," he groused, like I'd purposely woken him from a nap. "No chores."

I tidied the tent anyway, just in case. Saxon's soiled garments were stuffed into Eve's basket, alongside the remains of our meal, and given to the avian outside. I worked at a snail's pace, careful not to dirty myself. I'd never worn so fine a gown, and I would protect it at all cost. And okay, yes. I secretly snagged the feather while I worked, hiding it in my bodice. Payment for a job well done.

When evening arrived, darkness fell over the land and sunshine dawned in my heart, anticipation making me weak in the knees. Laughter drifted into the tent, soon growing louder and more prevalent, bringing with it the scent of roasting meat.

The party had officially started.

In a matter of minutes, I could be out there, living life and having fun. How to prod Saxon to hurry without seeming to prod Saxon?

"I bet your men are wondering why their future king hasn't arrived," I said, keeping my tone observational.

"You're right." He donned the royal avian sash, crossing the cerulean rope over his wide chest. After cinching a leather belt around his waist and anchoring the brass knuckle daggers to his sides, he thrust his feet into clean boots.

In my dream, Leonora hadn't considered him traditionally handsome, but I did. I considered him the standard by which other males should be compared. Minus his thirst for revenge, of course. Tonight, this avian prince would be greatly desired. Everyone would wish to dance with him.

If he were the fairy-tale prince, he might even find his Cinder.

My heart leaped. What would that mean for me?

When he approached the tent flap, ready to go, I rushed to his side. He paused to give me a scathing look.

"You," he grated, "will be staying in the tent."

I was pretty sure I would feel the burn of that look forever. His voice was just as hot, singeing my ears. Before I erupted, I would try to reason with him. Using my calmest voice possible—unfortunately, that was a screech—I told him, "You have no justifiable right to keep me from the party. I completed all my chores. You said so yourself. I even went above and beyond to charm you with my winning personality."

He raised his chin. "Nevertheless. You attended the tournament without permission, so, you'll stay here this evening. Official duty or not. Don't bother trying to sneak out. I had

Ophelia cast a border spell around the tent. No longer can you leave without my express permission."

"How can you do this?" More important, why was I still drawn to him? Why were his eyes haunted, despite his disdain? Voice wobbling, I told him, "I've never attended a party before, Saxon."

"Next time obey my commands," he snapped before stomping out.

I stood there, in shock, as he called to his people, "Tonight, be merry, for your crown prince will be."

He'd done it. He'd actually done it.

Jubilant cheers went on and on and on. When they finally died down a thousand years later, Saxon dished out compliments to his men about doing their jobs well, then said, "Adriel. A word."

Scorch my roses. The wicked prince had actually left me behind to listen and wonder and dream about what could be. His cruelty knew no bounds.

This? This was classic evil stepmother behavior. And if he wasn't the evil stepmother, Leonora had to be, since she was equally responsible for my incarceration; I *must* be Cinder, our similarities literal rather than symbolic. For that matter, "strong of heart" could be symbolic rather than literal.

A person's heart...their essence. Strong of heart—strong of character?

The thought hit me, and I hissed in a breath. Yes. Yes, yes, yes. I knew I'd just found the right road. I was Cinder, strong of character. Saxon was the prince or the stepmother. Leonora was the stepmother or a stepsister. If she *was* a phantom, and I *was* possessed by her, we were forced family.

In my dream, the first Leonora had been part of "The Little Cinder Girl," too, a fairy tale that had not been fulfilled back then. Could it have twisted...me? What did it mean that I was "as fast as wind"? How could I become a warrior set apart, unwilling to bend?

Become. The word echoed in my mind. *That's right.* I wasn't fast as wind or unwilling to bend—yet. But I could become so. One day I could be both gloriously fast and amazingly strong. One day I *would* be. The prophecy had spoken of the future, not the past or the present.

I almost couldn't process my good fortune. The things I had to look forward to!

Dazed, I made my way to the furs and plopped down. "I am Cinder," I whispered, pressing a hand to my chest. Then, knowing no one outside the tent could hear me, I shouted, "I am Cinder."

The part of me I'd denied for so long had been right. I was the girl unwanted by her family and tormented at every turn. In my case, the obvious choice had been the most unexpected one.

As Cinder, I would get a happily-ever-after. The only way to be truly happy, though? Attend that celebration party.

In the fairy tale, Cinder always found a way to attend the festivities without being found out. So, I would, too.

Determined, I climbed to my feet. A thought occurred to me. Before I found a way past the border spell, I should craft a weapon, just in case I ran into Trio or any other vengeful avian.

Though I'd been so protective of my new dress before, I accepted that my safety came before my appearance and dropped to my knees to dig up my sticks and nails.

I cut discreet pockets into my skirt…as discreet as possible, anyway, then used one of my new hair ribbons to anchor the sticks to my outer thighs. I used a second ribbon to create my own nail-knuckles. I pushed the nails through the material, tied the ribbon around my knuckles.

Now, to escape. I was humble enough to admit I would need help. A powerful witch, perhaps, who had created the border spell in the first place. Surely *she* of all people would be able to hear me. "Ophelia," I called. "Ophelia, I need your help and I'm willing to pay everything I have...which is nothing." Would Noel have a vision of me, if I called for her? "Noel?"

"Hello, hello. Did someone summon a fairy godwitch?"

Startled, I swung around. Ophelia and Noel stood roughly ten feet away, grinning at me. "It worked."

Noel waved a hand through the air. "Sorry for the delay. I heard your cry for help hours ago, but I only just now got bored enough to find out what's going on."

Hours ago? "What are you—"

"Before we get too far into this conversation," Ophelia interrupted, "you should probably know that I won't be removing the border spell. Saxon paid good money for it, and my reputation as a quality spellitician is on the line."

Fair point. "Maybe you can magically transport me *past* the boundary? He paid you to create the spell, not to keep me locked up, correct?"

Noel hiked her thumb in my direction, saying to Ophelia, "I knew I'd like this one."

"One thing," I rushed to add. "I have no means to pay you for this service."

"And I rescind my pledge of admiration," Noel said.

"Oh, you have the means all right. You have four dragon eggs." Ophelia sauntered to a corner, where we kept the potted plants, and ran a finger over the leaves, as if inspecting them for dust. "We want two of those eggs. And that is nonnegotiable, so don't try to negotiate."

"My eggs?" *Never.* "Saxon has them. I don't know where they are." But I would. I would find them.

"You let us take care of that." Noel batted her lashes at me, not even close to innocent. "Do we have a deal?"

"No. We don't. Why do you want them?" As soon as I found them, I would be returning them to the ground, near the Temple, so that they could continue to age in peace.

Saxon claimed all dragons were monsters, but every fiber of my being screamed that he was wrong.

"Do we have a deal or not?" Noel asked, ignoring my question.

"No," I repeated. "We do not."

"Excellent," she said. "We have a deal."

"I said no."

"Which means you passed my ingenious test." She patted me on top of the head, as if I were a good little girl. "I award you an A-plus for loyalty."

Ophelia winked at me. "Now that that's settled, go to the party and ibitty, bibbity, bop, bop, boo. And don't ask me what that means."

One second I stood inside the tent, the next I stood outside the back of it. The witch had transported me past the border, and I had zero side effects.

I meant to hurry off, but I stood spellbound, taking in the festivities. Light from multiple firepits illuminated a winding path littered with warriors, mortals, and creatures, all mingled together.

A cool breeze caressed my skin, layered with stronger hints of smoke and the scent of roasting meat, pine, and perfume.

As if drawn by an invisible cord, I stumbled forward. Despite my fascination with my surroundings, I remembered to stick to the shadows as I maneuvered around partygoers and trees. When the avian campground got lost in the sights behind me, I grinned. I'd done it. I'd bested Saxon once again.

The sweetest song drifted to my ears. In the distance, someone was playing a flute. I bet people were dancing.

I quickened my pace and rounded a cluster of trees, following the sound. The number of trees seemed to have doubled in a single day. Goodness. From now on, I needed to better observe my surroundings, so I wouldn't feel as if I entered a whole new world every time I exited Saxon's tent.

Few people recognized me. Those that did whispered, "It's the Glass Princess," To their companions. After three years of hard work at the Temple, I felt I deserved a new nickname. Metal Wench, maybe? Oh, what a glorious night.

"—fist cracked open his skull," one gorgon was saying to another as I passed another firepit. "I turned his brain to stone and smashed it into dust."

A wolfin stumbled past me and burped.

I stutter-stepped when I caught sight of Trio. He was speaking with a scantily clad mortal woman.

"—but a gold coin *will* buy you an hour," she was saying as she traced a finger down his chest.

"For a gold coin, I expect you to be on your knees—"

Moving on. I hurried forward, my feet seeming to know where to go, as if I'd made this trek a thousand times. I didn't resist, curious to know where I'd end up. As I rounded a large oak, everything changed. Dizziness lashed me, and I swayed. The temperature dropped drastically, my teeth chattering.

Um... I spun. What...how...? I had been transported to somewhere in the Enchantian Forest. I would forever recognize the azure glow that radiated from every inch of bark, wild-flower, and speck of dirt.

The dizziness I'd felt... I'd felt it with Eve, too, when she'd used her voice magic. But, I wasn't anywhere near the avian this time.

My teeth-chattering worsened. I must have traveled through an invisible doorway. But where was it now? I sensed...nothing. How was I to return to the campground?

Fighting panic, I listened for any hint of laughter, music, or conversation. I heard chirping frogs...rustling leaves...rattling branches...a whistle of wind. I looked left, right. Backward. Forward. Left again. Up, down. The forest remained, no sign of the celebration.

Behind me, a twig snapped. I jerked around, fisting the hand with the nails. Up ahead, illuminated by a lone ray of moonlight, a couple kissed as if the world was soon to end. I recognized the girl, no problem. I would never forget those wings.

Eve.

I'd been close to the avian, after all. Though I didn't understand how or why her voice magic would bring me here. And who was she with?

I gaped when his identity clicked. The red-eyed fae from today's battle. I'd noticed his great skill because he'd had a style similar to Saxon's. He was all grace and savagery, with some brute force thrown into the mix.

Eve was kissing Saxon's competition. Was she conspiring with him, too? Working against Saxon? Endangering him?

I… I didn't care. Because I refused—absolutely refused—to waste a single moment fretting about the boy who'd left me in that tent to suffer.

But I *would* tell him about what I'd seen. Maybe. Probably. I doubted he'd believe me, so why bother? His soldier, his problem. Besides, he would only rage about my party attendance and lob another punishment at me.

Whenever my father had upset my mother, Momma had whispered, *To my own life will I tend, for others' evil always has an end.*

Sage advice. I would take it.

Slow and steady, I backed away from the kissing couple, now one hundred percent certain I would be tending to my own life and keeping my mouth shut. Ninety-five percent certain. Eighty. Eighty percent. A good, solid seventy—sixty-five percent.

Saxon didn't deserve my help. End of story.

On the other hand, Eve was part of "The Little Cinder Girl." If I was Cinder, and I was, and Saxon was the prince, and he might be, maybe, possibly, then Eve could be an evil stepsister or something. Then, Saxon and I would have to team up to defeat a common foe. As we worked together, we would become friends. Then he would fall in love with me. He'd have to absolve me of my crimes then. And I could leave him in my dust.

All right, I was definitely fifty percent certain I would be keeping my mouth shut.

"Boo!"

I whirled around. Once again, Noel and Ophelia had appeared in a blink, just a few feet away from me.

"Shhh." I whispered, "What are you doing here?"

"There you are," Noel said in a normal tone. Of course, she ignored my question. "You couldn't wait five minutes for us to catch up? I mean, I know we weren't even trying to catch up because we were too busy searching Saxon's tent for any hidden goodies, until I remembered I'd forgotten to tell you to avoid our magical doorways. Which probably makes no sense if you don't know that you're drawn to Ophelia's magical doorways when others are repelled by them."

I *had* felt as if I were being pulled to the doorway.

Before I could launch my volley of questions, Ophelia lamented, "That's all anyone wants from me anymore. People buy personal make-out doorways from me. I'm a lowly door maker now. A footnote in every tale. No more important than a cobbler."

"Or a talking mouse," Noel added helpfully.

Brow furrowing, I asked, "Why am I drawn to your doorways? What makes me so different?" And oh, goodie. One more disparity between me and other girls. No big deal. Whatever. It was fine.

Looking past me, Ophelia called, "Do better at closing your seven minutes in heaven gateway next time, *Eve*. Ashleigh is drawn to its magic because I put a little something extra in Saxon's spell, because I'm a giver like that. And because the fallout is going to bring me much amusement. Also, don't you both have jobs to do?"

Something extra? For me? In a spell for Saxon? Did she refer to the sound barrier around the tent, or something else?

Eve and her fae whipped their attention our way. They muttered curses and stomped off. Out of habit, I clasped my mother's ring. Would the two attempt to pull me aside later to threaten me just in case I ever decided to share their secret? Or would Eve run straight to Saxon and tell him naughty Ashleigh had snuck out and oh, yeah, she might lie about seeing her with the fae?

Noel and Ophelia flanked me, linking their arms with mine. They led me forward in perfect sync.

"I don't understand any of this," I said.

"But you will understand, one day, and isn't that the important thing?" the witch asked.

No. I wanted to know now. "Where are we going?"

"We're returning you to the party, of course. I've had my fun." Ophelia patted my hand. "Now I get to watch you have yours."

Noel rested her cheek on my shoulder, as if we'd been best friends for years. "You really angered your avian prince, huh. Good girl."

Did she refer to the future or the past? "You *want* me to anger Saxon?"

"Why would I want you to anger him? He's my friend." Her brows knitted together, a crease forming above the bridge of her nose. "I think someone needs to remember to put on her listening ears from now on."

"But you just said—" Oh, never mind. What did I care if I had angered or would anger the prince? He already disliked me.

"By the way," Noel said. "I left a present in your bedroom at home. You're welcome. When you see it, scream. You'll be glad you did."

A present? For me? "Free of charge?" Best to be clear.

"As if. But don't worry, you *already* paid me." She did the innocent-evil lashes-batting thing. "Don't you remember? You gave me one of your designs. A dagger with spring-loaded spikes."

"No. I most certainly did *not* give you one of my designs." I'd never given *anyone* one of my designs.

"Let me rephrase, then. I stole one of your designs from Saxon. Now we're even. Isn't that nice?"

Between one step and the next, my entire world changed. The forest vanished, the celebration reappearing, firepits, flute, laughter, and all. An-n-nd the oracle and the witch had disappeared. But why would they—oh, who cared? They were weird and mysterious, and I had some dancing to do and a decision to make about Eve.

I doubted she'd try to murder Saxon tonight or anything, but I was also kind of willing to risk it.

"And who is *this* tasty little treat?" a troll called. He was tall, at least seven foot, with massive horns protruding from his scalp and tusks extending past his bottom lip. Metal piercings climbed the ridge of a very prominent nose and covered the entire length of his jaw.

I tightened my hold on the ribbon and quickened my step. If he followed me, I would strike. But as I turned another corner, he did not. I heaved a relieved sigh. Another turn, and I found the flute player. A satyr. He had the top half of a man and the bottom half of a goat, complete with fur and hooves, and he stood beside a blazing firepit. His only clothing was a loincloth.

At least twenty people danced around him, but no one I recognized. Unsure of my reception, I eased forward. When no protests were issued, I joined the dancers, hopping and skipping and twirling in circles just like them. It wasn't long before my heartbeat thudded and sweat dotted my brow, but I didn't slow. This was truly living.

Laughing, I threw back my head, clasped my dress and

twirled faster. Dancing was more fun than I'd ever imagined. I didn't feel weak or unwanted right now. I felt unstoppable.

"Hello, Ashleigh."

I stopped and swayed, a familiar face swimming before me. When the spinning stopped, I realized I stood face-to-face with Milo. Firelight bathed him in a golden glow, framing a body several inches taller than I remembered. He had more muscles, too, and showed them off in a tight tunic and leather pants.

I gulped. "Hello, Milo."

"I must admit, it's nice to see you again, Princess." He inclined his head, the key around his neck glinting in the firelight.

"And you, as well." I traced a fingertip over the tips of the golden nails, my hackles on edge. "I'm glad you found me. I wanted to ask if you still believe I'm Leonora." For starters.

"Oh, no. I know you are not Leonora...yet."

Yet? There was that word again. Only, it wasn't so wonderful this time. "During our conversation in the garden, you mentioned your father's journals. I would love to read them. I promise I'll be extra careful with them."

Glee lit his eyes, as if he enjoyed the words waiting on the end of his tongue. "I burned the journals once I finished reading them."

What! "Why would you do that?"

"I didn't want anyone else knowing what I know." His gaze flipped up, looking beyond me. He scowled. "We'll talk again soon." He stepped back and vanished as quickly as the witch and the oracle.

I stood there, uncertain and—

"What do you think you're doing, Asha?"

11

She is the sun, she is the moon.
He wants her always, he wants her soon.

SAXON

I peered at Ashleigh, my hands fisted. Golden light framed her from head to toe, creating a perfect halo around her. On her brow, perspiration resembled diamond dust. Her eyes glittered like freshly polished emeralds. She parted her lips as she panted, her chest rising and falling in quick succession.

The girl had mesmerized me, and I couldn't look away. I could only stare at pure temptation. Was I angry? Absolutely. She'd gotten out of the tent somehow, ignoring a clear, unmistakable order I'd hated myself for uttering. But I'd done it anyway, just as a good avian should when seeking restitution. She'd impressed me yet again. She had no right to impress me.

Though I hadn't seen her leave the tent, I'd known the moment she'd exited, the tracker spell alerting me; it also informed me of her quick visit to the Enchantian Forest. A mistake, surely. I'd found her in the camp only minutes later. As she'd paraded past bloodthirsty warriors, I'd followed at a reasonable distance, wondering if she would use her fire magic to protect herself.

She hadn't. Because no one had dared to approach her. Because I'd cast a warning glare upon any who'd considered it.

Watching her twirl around a firepit, uninhibited and merry, I'd marveled at her grace and enthusiasm. I'd smiled, and I'd fumed. How could a girl who lived with such unfettered joy be the same one who'd stabbed me and murdered my family?

"Saxon," she breathed, her raspy voice a caress in my ears.

I should add a new punishment to her tally. I *would* add a new punishment. Only a fool made threats and failed to see them through. All I wanted to do right now?

Dance with her.

She was more dangerous than I'd ever realized. But...

I didn't care. Not here, not now. I stalked forward, closing the distance.

She clocked my every move, but she didn't run. No, she stood her ground, her panting breaths growing more noticeable. I stopped after I'd invaded her personal space, expecting her to back down. I towered over her, the giant to her sprite.

She jutted her chin, and I inhaled deeply. Her rose-and-vanilla scent teased my nose, the best parts of me stiffening.

"Why were you speaking with the warlock?" The powerful male was dedicated to aiding her father. "Do you conspire with your prince's competition?"

"You already know I'm familiar with Milo. He lived at the palace in Fleur when I did, and his father is the one who died with my mother. If I was going to conspire with anyone, it would be Ophelia and Noel, not Milo. I don't think he's very nice."

"You looked friendly with him. Do you forget that he fights for *Dior's* hand in marriage?"

"So? You do, too."

Unable to deny it—yet—I stepped even closer, my body

pressing flush against hers. Still she didn't back down, her display of strength arresting me. How was I supposed to proceed with her?

I couldn't even look away. Flickering firelight bathed her face, her emerald eyes as bright as the Avian Mountains at sunrise. A time when dew-dampened foliage glistened with life and vitality. Just the sight of her delighted my senses.

In this lifetime, I had little experience with pleasure, so I wasn't as resistant to its allure as I'd been in the other lifetimes. I'd never had a serious relationship, only a string of temporary companions. I'd never trusted anyone enough. No one had ever felt right.

My relationship with Ashleigh felt just as wrong as the others. And yet, it also felt...inevitable.

Why fight what you cannot stop?

Why not enjoy my descent?

Someone with a bongo drum joined the flute player, keeping the beat. Soft. Seductive. Rhythmic. As if fate had brought the musicians together at just this place, at just this time, for just this moment. Dancers gyrated around us, weaving a magical spell.

"Are you going to drag me back to the tent?" Ashleigh rasped, pressing a hand over her heart. Did it race?

When I spied the golden nails held to her knuckles by a hair ribbon, I almost smiled. I'd left the nails for Leonora, expecting her to melt and trade them, as she'd done in the past. But Ashleigh had armed herself instead. Smart girl. Wily.

"Saxon?" Ashleigh prompted.

I wasn't ready to part with her. Wrapping my arms around her waist, holding her close, I told her, "What I'm going to do is dance with you, Asha."

"Dance?" she asked at a higher pitch. Her eyes widened and she flattened her hands against my pectorals, as if to push me away, but she applied no pressure. "Is this dance some sort of punishment? Because I snuck out fair and square."

"Dancing with me is punishment?"

"Yes!"

"Are you sure?" I slid one hand up, up, her back to cup her nape. A low moan left her. I closed my free hand around her wrist and lifted her arm until she moved of her own volition, sliding her fingers over my shoulders.

I eased her into a slow, languid rhythm, and we rocked from side to side.

"I'm not sure," she whispered, and squeezed her eyes shut for a moment. Rosy color bloomed in her cheeks as she held me tighter. "I don't understand why you're being nice to me, and I'm tired of not understanding things. Usually I'm quite clever, I assure you. But I defied your orders, and now you're dancing with me."

"Yes. You did defy my orders." I searched her gaze. "And I think you do understand why." One very big reason pressed between her legs.

Her blush deepened. "I didn't want to assume..."

"We're past assuming when you can feel the evidence," I told her dryly. Unless she didn't know what a hard-on was?

I almost groaned.

Her scandalized gasp confirmed that she did, in fact, know and I chuckled. At the sound of it, her eyes widened with shock. A timely reminder. I had no right to be laughing around her.

"Won't your people protest?" she asked. "I mean, I realize now I must have put you in a terrible position. Because you keep losing."

"Yes, I understood that part. And I've put *myself* in this position, Ashleigh." I wasn't sorry, either. Would my army care if they heard about this? Probably. No chance they wouldn't hear about it. Two guards had flanked me as I'd hunted Ashleigh. Now those same guards stood nearby, awaiting my command. One of them—Adriel—despised me at the moment. After leaving Ashleigh in the tent, I'd punished him severely, doing to him what he'd threatened to do to the princess this morning. I'd broken both of his legs, ensuring he had to be carried or fly. And, though he was now in great pain, I was forcing him to remain in the air by my order. No rest for the wicked.

Avian healed faster than most, and he'd be walking again in a few hours. If he so much as scowled at Ashleigh after that...

He didn't want to find out what I would do. When I gave an order, I had to know it would be obeyed. If you couldn't trust your team, you couldn't win a war.

"Well, I do happen to like this particular position," she admitted shyly.

Her sweet scent intensified, and my most primal, possessive instincts flared to sudden, vibrant life. When she traced her fingers over my shoulders, coming closer and closer to my wings, I caught myself rolling my hips. As we brushed together, her pupils enlarged.

They drew me in...

Her fingers inched closer...

If she touched a single feather, what remained of my control would cease to exist. I would claim her mouth with my own. To start.

Almost within reach...

Her fingers stopped, and I tensed. Panting a bit faster, she asked me, "What are your plans after the tournament?"

The question stopped me cold. I admitted, "We'll go our separate ways, and we will never speak again." *Because you'll be locked away, forever trapped.* Exactly what I desired.

Yes. Desired. *The way it has to be.*

She tensed before urging me into a slower sway. Her fingers moved away from my wings and her gaze went far, far away. A dreamy smile teased the corners of her lips. "Well, you'll be missing out. I'm fated to have the most amazing happily-ever-after."

I had to push my next words through clenched teeth. "Leonora used to say the same. That she was fated for a happily-ever-after with me. Cinder and her prince."

Ashleigh *humph*ed. "I don't care what she said. I'm Cinder from 'The Little Cinder Girl.' Obviously. And guess what? I kind of agree with Leonora. I'm pretty sure you're the dishonorable prince, too. Although you might also qualify as the evil stepmother. I'm still figuring everything out. It's a process. But if you *are* the prince, you don't have to worry that I'll think we're going to get romantic or anything because I know many of the story elements are symbolic. Am I rambling? Anyway. Whatever your role, I'm for sure getting a happily-ever-after. I'll accept nothing less."

Her nervousness was cute. "So certain? Despite all the evidence pointing to the contrary?"

"Evidence?" she sputtered. "What evidence?"

Namely, the sleep spell headed her way. Something I knew about, but she did not. "You war with a warrior known as the Destroyer. Twice you've lived and died without wedding the one you claim to love. Your own father—" I pressed my lips together, going quiet. I wouldn't say it. If she wasn't ready to face her father's disdain, I wasn't going to be the one to hurt her with the truth.

"Maybe all of that is true. Maybe it isn't." Ashleigh cupped and squeezed my shoulders, as if she wanted to be sure I was steady enough to absorb the weight of her next words. "The past is the past, yesterday done and gone. My present actions direct my future. If I fight for my happiness, I'll have it. Eventually."

"I'm sorry, Asha, but that just isn't true. In any war, there is always a winner and a loser, even though both sides fight their hardest."

"You're right," she agreed, surprising me. "But, Saxon, if we asked the losing side whether or not they regretted giving their all—giving their lives, if necessary—for what they wanted, they would not. How could they?"

She...wasn't wrong. But I wasn't ready to concede. "You ascribe to a fairy-tale prophecy, certain it's a map or key to the happiness you're fighting for, yes?" When she nodded, I said, "But how can that be when so many details are left to individual interpretation, able to mean whatever anyone desires? I assure you, I can insert myself into any fairy tale and justify my role." Roth and Everly had qualified for multiple characters in their own fairy tale, "Snow White and the Evil Queen." They'd even believed me to be one of the Seven Protectors.

"Prove it, then." Ashleigh peered at me, luscious waves of dark hair shimmering around her lovely face. "Convince me you play a role I know you do not. Convince me you're...Cinder." There was an aha in her voice.

I relished the challenge. "I am Cinder because... I was just a child when my parents exiled me from the only home I'd ever known. I moved in with Roth and Farrah, and their family essentially became my stepfamily. For years, I worked as Farrah's guard, and I fought to protect her. But one day, she decided to curse me, ensuring I slayed an innocent girl on her behalf. The act of an evil stepsister." I meant to deliver my speech without emotion, but anger, frustration, and sorrow laced each word. "I'm strong. I'm fast, and I will not bend. I'd rather break. In three lifetimes, the marriage-minded princess has had eyes only for me. Three, the very number of balls thrown by the handsome prince."

"That is...you..." She gave her head a hard shake. "No. I'm Cinder. I've only known it an hour or so but I know it with every fiber of my being, and you can't change my mind. So go again. Prove you're, I don't know, Cinder's father."

Such faith in the tales, with no concrete evidence of their validity. I didn't think I'd ever believed in something I couldn't see, feel, taste, or touch. Not as Saxon, anyway. Craven had believed in the power of love…until Leonora taught him better. Would Ashleigh's certainty crumble in the face of adversity, too?

"In two other lifetimes," I said, "I made a home with Leonora. After we separated, I made a family with someone else. I was a father. Leonora killed my wife and the children."

"Oh, Saxon." Ashleigh moved her grip to cup my cheeks, ghosting her thumbs over my cheekbones. "I'm so sorry."

A gesture of comfort. From her. The girl I'd purposely hurt. Something cracked in me, just a little bit, but I didn't think it could be patched. A defense, maybe, soon to collapse. The past beginning to separate from the present. Whatever it was, I sensed this break would bring serious consequences sooner or later.

"Craven and Tyron didn't love their wives," I said. "They married only to continue the royal line. But they made families with those women and losing them…it was unimaginable."

She closed her eyes for a moment, as if overwhelmed by her own emotions, and rested her forehead on my chest. "Why did you have to have a kinder side?" she moaned.

Crack. "This is me being kind?"

"Listen," she said, and lifted her head. "This is horrible timing, but I have to tell you now, before something bad happens. It's just, I like her, okay?" She dropped her hands to my collar and plucked at my tunic. "Maybe. Probably. Yes, I'm pretty sure I do, in fact, like her, and I was so certain I didn't like you, I mean, you abandoned me in the tent and stole my eggs, but here you are, dancing with me, and sharing meaningful parts of your life, so I think I've changed my mind about you, but I'm still not sure why I'm even considering this." The babbling stopped long enough for her to draw in a deep breath. "On the other hand, if you *do* represent the fairy-tale prince, as part of me continues to suspect—"

"What are you trying to tell me, Asha?" I asked, amused despite myself.

"—perhaps your greatest enemy is *pretending* to be your best friend. Or something," she added without offering a courtesy response to my question. "Or maybe she's using her voice magic to trick you. Do you understand what I'm saying now? You need to know so you'll understand why I'm laughing in your face later and reminding you about the night you refused to believe in fairy-tale prophecies."

"Asha," I repeated. "What are you talking about?"

"I'm not sure how you're not getting this. I've explained it three different ways now. Don't make me flat out say it."

"I need you to flat-out say it."

She sighed. "This is about your soldier Eve. I saw her kissing your competition. One of the fae. They might be conspiring to take you out. I don't know. But that might be a good thing, because I'm starting to think you're all wrong for her. And Dior. You could crush her perfect, golden heart. Why would fate want that? Withering roses. I've contracted her chatter. *Shut up, Ash.*"

Ah. She'd stumbled upon Everly and Roth. And she'd told me. She'd *helped* me, even after I'd left her trapped in the tent.

I didn't know what to think about this development.

Ashleigh gaped up at me. "You knew about their relationship, I can tell. Is she spying for you, then?"

"I will not confirm or deny whether I knew or did not know about the relationship that may or may not be real or faked." Not with a girl I shouldn't—wouldn't—trust. "The only person you should worry about is yourself."

I pulled her closer, my gaze dipping to her mouth. So plump. So red. So ripe for a kiss. "May we concentrate on our dance now?"

"Of course we can." With a laugh, she threw back her arms,

her head, forcing me to hold her tighter to keep her from falling. "I think I'm drunk on the night. I feel amazing right now."

"Saxon?" The firm feminine voice came from behind me.

That couldn't be who I thought it was.

Scowling, I turned my head to eye the speaker. It was. My anger gave way to surprise as I exchanged nods with my sister, Tempest. I'd seen her once or twice in the years since my exile, when we'd both visited the same kingdom to attend some type of formal ceremony. She'd changed quite a bit since the last sighting, but her wings had remained the same.

Standing at six foot tall, she had shoulder-length hair as blue as my wings. The board-straight locks framed an arresting face with black eyes, cheekbones sharp enough to cut glass, and skin a shade lighter than mine. She wore the uniform of an elite soldier in the avian army: a leather vest with mesh cutouts around vital organs, and black leather pants. The hilts of two short swords rose from her shoulders, alongside the bright pink wings she'd always despised.

Childhood traumas that had never healed properly suddenly throbbed. The betrayal of my parents...this loss of my siblings... "Has something happened?" I demanded without releasing Ashleigh. At the moment, she was my only anchor in the firestorm.

Tempest swept her glare over the princess. "I came to warn you. Mother is on her way. She heard about your fascination with the princess and fears the past is repeating itself."

I worked my jaw, my mood hitting irate and about to return to anger.

"Hello," Ashleigh said to Tempest, and I applauded her fortitude. "I'm Princess Ashleigh of Fleur. It's nice to see you again, Princess Tempest."

My sister didn't spare her a second glance. "Do me a favor, brother, and tell your pet to hush or—"

"*You* will hush," I interjected with enough force to startle both females. "Go to my tent and await me there." I lifted my hand and snapped my fingers, summoning Adriel.

"I don't think you understand," Tempest groused. "Mother is going to arrive within the hour."

And the hits keep coming. I scoured a hand down my face in an attempt to calm. I wasn't prepared to deal with Queen Raven yet. I'd experienced too many upheavals these past few weeks, starting with the deaths of my father and brother and the expectation that I would assume control of the kingdom from which I'd once fled. There was the loss of Roth's palace—my true home—Farrah's betrayal and curse, the return of Leonora, and Ashleigh's unexpected charm.

While Queen Raven couldn't concretely know Ashleigh was Leonora, she did suspect. My suspicions had just been confirmed. She'd attended the funeral, and she'd heard about the fire, and she'd suspected Ashleigh's role in my life.

And you still believe she didn't send those soldiers to hurt Ashleigh at the Temple?

The Raven I'd known always delivered her blows herself. But I'd never really known her, had I? I'd never thought her capable of watching her husband attempt to kill her son, either.

"How long is she planning to stay?" I demanded.

"Six days. She doesn't trust her advisors to lead the avian without her for longer than that."

I swung my gaze back to Ashleigh. "I will speak with your father. I want you to remain in the palace for the next six days. You are not to leave it for any reason. This time, you *will* obey me."

"Six days? Saxon, I swear I'm not going to harm your family."

She misunderstood, but I wasn't going to correct her. "Nevertheless. You will stay inside."

Tempest snorted. "As if you could harm me, little girl."

"You will go to my tent and await Mother," I told my sister. "Tonight, I have plans." Plans I *would* see through. Since I wouldn't be seeing Ashleigh for the next six days, I would have to end our night with a punishment, after all.

Always follow through. I couldn't have Leonora thinking I'd softened.

Adriel approached at last, a feather floating from his wing, drawing Ashleigh's gaze to where he hovered. She shrank against me, as if I were a hero. A protector. I found my chin lifting proudly—there was no one stronger or better able to defend her.

Follow. Through.

"Escort my sister to my tent," I told the soldier, who stayed far away from Ashleigh and never glanced her way.

Resentment vibrated from Tempest, but she pivoted and stalked off without protest. Avian were nothing if not loyal to their leader. Adriel followed from the air, his broken legs hanging limply.

"Hey," Ashleigh said, her tone gentle. She rested her fingertips against my stubbled jawline and softly urged my attention back to her. "I'm drunk on the night, remember, so I can do this."

Now that we'd started touching, we weren't going to be able to stop, were we?

"I don't know what happened between you and your family that hurt you so badly," she continued, "but I'm sorry for that, too."

She comforts me still? Me? I dipped my forehead to her shoulder, and she combed her fingers through my hair.

The worst of my mental chaos quieted, as if I was exactly where I was supposed to be, doing what I was supposed to be doing, with the girl I was supposed to be with. The one who belonged to me. The one I belonged with.

It was a lie, of course. But, in that moment, it was a lie I desperately wanted to believe.

"What makes you think I'm hurting?" Few people ever saw past my unending anger.

"Let's just say the lost glaze in your eyes is familiar to me."

Did she encounter it every time she peered into a mirror?

My chest did that tightening thing again, guilt flaring anew. "If you seek my pity—"

"I don't. I really don't. I sympathize with you, that's all."

Or she thought to trick me into softening, the same way Leonora had so often tricked Craven, and I was letting her win yet again.

I stiffened. "Save your sympathy. Tonight, I *will* have a measure of restitution."

She pursed her lips. "What's it going to be this time? Hmm? Do tell."

"You'll see."

"Yes, I guess I will." Animosity draining, she offered me a broken smile, and it was a thousand times worse than tears or fury. As if she'd been trampled so many times, her heart had developed calluses, and yet *she* pitied *me*. "I haven't ever had a friend, not really, and I've interacted with very few people in my life, but I have observed many. Whether you deny it or not, your sister's visit threw you. You're hurting, and you're lashing out at me. But, darling that I am, I've decided not to demand restitution for *your* rudeness. So let's get this over with."

Let's. Before I lost my resolve. My chest was now on fire, and she hadn't needed magic to ignite the flames.

I tightened my hold and jumped up with her still in my arms, flaring my wings and catching a current of air. As we rose high...higher, I angled us in the proper direction.

Other avian leaped into the air, giving chase to act as my guard. About twenty in total. Only half were mine. The other half must have come with Tempest. Let them follow. Let them see.

I carried Ashleigh toward the coliseum, wind whipping her

dark locks in every direction. When I rolled around a cloud, she laughed and spread out her arms, drawing a smile from me, which hastened the return of my scowl.

I couldn't allow her to affect me anymore. It had to stop.

After today's battle, I'd spoken with Everly about Adriel's treatment of Ashleigh. I'd then instructed one group of soldiers to fly over the competition field once all the spectators had left and another group to surround the place with torches. Neither group had abandoned their post. The flyers still swooped over the field in circles, their feathers floating to the ground, illuminated by a haze of flickering golden light that radiated from nearby torches. A storm I'd had created for Adriel, to really drive my lesson home. I'd planned to make him pick up every feather by sunrise, while standing, dealing with his healing legs.

Instead, Ashleigh would get the honors. "You will pick up the feathers," I told her as I set her on her feet. "Every single one. There should be bags scattered over the ground."

I expected protests. Complaints. Something. Again, she surprised me. She brightened.

"Tell me you're teasing. Because, Saxon?" she said, the sides of her mouth actually lifting, "this is just too terrible. I'm going to rue the day I was ever born and probably suffer with nightmares for the rest of eternity." She faked a shudder. "Whatever you do, don't tell me I have to keep the prettiest feathers. Please. Don't make me suffer such an indignity, or I'll be forced to demand some kind of restitution myself."

I...had no idea how to respond to that. "Do you feel you deserve restitution, Ashleigh?" My curiosity was genuine.

"Yes. I thought I'd made that clear. But really, I don't think I need it. I'm pretty sure you're already punishing *yourself*." That said, she skipped across the field as if she hadn't a care, gathering feathers along the way, leaving me to reel.

She was proving to be so much more of everything than I'd ever dreamed possible. Wittier. Kinder. Smarter. Far more resilient. Mostly, she was utterly enchanting, rousing my keenest desires.

With a squeal, she held up a feather as if it were a treasure, so happy it almost hurt to look at her. So happy over something so simple. "This one matches my eyes."

Leonora hadn't reacted so enthusiastically for *diamonds*.

I scowled. Hoping distance would grant me some kind of inoculation against her allure, I flew into a shadowed section of the stands and leaned against a pillar, crossing my arms over my chest.

The distance didn't help. Like most avian, I could see great distances quite clearly, and I remained on edge as I watched the princess work.

For the first hour, she gathered as many feathers as possible into a pile and stuffed her favorite colors into the bodice of her dress. The second hour, she tired and her motions slowed. All the while new feathers rained down.

She welcomed every shower, putting back her head and lifting her arms.

How many times had I imagined laughing in her face as she failed at each task I assigned her? How often had I anticipated my enjoyment over her constant defeat? I experienced no such amusement or enjoyment tonight. Only a fresh rise of guilt. She was right, then. By punishing her, I was punishing myself. It was the most unfair trade in history.

As she eased onto the sandy ground and lifted her skirts, she revealed two sticks she'd strapped to her thigh. She tied each end of the ribbon to the end of a stick, creating a tiny rake. Leaning over, she scooted multiple feathers her way.

My princess was intrepid, I'd give her that. This was strength of wit in action. She was always strength of wit in action, using every tool at her disposal, making the best of bad situations— bad situations I put her in.

I massaged the back of my neck, considering our last conversation. She believed herself to be Cinder. Though I hadn't changed my mind about the tales, I had to admit she reminded me of the prophesied character more and more.

Farrah used to say the more love a heart contained, the stronger it was. Right now, I had to agree. When it came to action versus emotion, the emotion behind the action mattered more.

A gift given in hate meant nothing. Give the same gift with love, and it meant everything. Leonora gave to get. Ashleigh gave to give. How very Cinder.

And fast as wind? That was how quickly this potential little cinder girl had tied me in knots. Unwilling to bend? No one fit such a description better than Ashleigh. She flittered about, making me crazed, and I did the bending for her.

A cool breeze kissed the back of my neck, scattering my thoughts. Someone approached from behind. I reached for a dagger, preparing for an attack. When the scent of lilacs wafted my way, I didn't have to turn to know who'd just arrived.

My tone flat, I said, "Hello, Mother."

12

There's only one feat that matters.
Did you leave his heart in tatters?

Ashleigh

As I sat in the sea of feathers, raking the multicolored bounty into a large pile before separating the green ones into an even larger pile of their own and shoving all the rest into a bag, I twittered with excitement. I thought—hoped—I'd collected enough of the green ones to embellish a gown. I would look like I belonged at Saxon's side, not at his beck and call.

My ears twitched as voices wafted on a cool evening breeze. I thought I heard Saxon arguing with a woman about…duty? They were so far away, I had trouble making out every individual word, but whatever the topic, he was in full-on Craven mode, furious but controlled.

I scanned the rest of the field. So many feathers, so little time. But, uh, for a reincarnate of Craven the Destroyer, Saxon sure didn't know how to oversee a proper punishment. Picking up feathers as they blustered like snowflakes? The horror!

What would he tell me to do next? Search for a pot of gold at the end of a rainbow?

Why had he danced with me? Why had he held me so tightly, as if he couldn't bear to part with me? Why had he looked at me with longing? Why had he allowed me to comfort him after his sister's visit? Why had I tingled and ached for closer contact...a deeper touch...a kiss? A kiss. My first. From Saxon.

Only one answer made sense. His character was as literal as mine, rather than symbolic. Saxon Skylair *was* my fairy-tale prince, and he *had* found his Cinder tonight. My certainty could not be shaken. Not anymore.

We were fated to experience a happily-ever-after.

Had I realized this yesterday, I would not have seen a way for it to happen. Tonight, he'd ordered me to remain at the palace for six days, just to protect me from his mother. He cared about my well-being.

I loved his concern. I did. But I shuddered at the thought of being housebound. Having spent years trapped in a bed, then a cluster of trees...having tasted freedom for the first time at the party, I hated the thought of being cooped up in the palace. Give me fresh air, moonlight, starlight, firepits, and wide-open spaces.

A sudden pain tore through my head, spurring a hiss. I clutched my temples, but the ache had already started to fade.

In the back of my mind, I thought I heard a woman purr happily, as if she, too, were experiencing fresh air and open spaces for the first time.

What the—a terrible heat flared in my fingertips, and I waved my hands about, trying to cool them off. But I continued to heat until...

An actual flame ignited at the ends of my nails, disintegrating the feathers I held. I sucked in a breath, staring at the charred remains, unable to make my brain work. But, but...

The embers spread over the sands. With a gasp, I contorted to snuff them out with my feet. Finally, my brain decided to work again, thoughts aligning. I'd started a fire? I'd used magic? I'd used... Leonora's magic?

Tension shot through me, ice-cold and sharp as a blade. Trembling, I lifted my hands to examine my fingers in a brighter beam of torchlight. Was that a smear of soot? I cast my gaze to the ground where pieces of feather ash had fallen. Grains of sand had turned to liquid before hardening into smooth, cool glass.

The truth settled in my bones, changing the very fabric of my being. I *had* used Leonora's magical ability. I was a reincarnate or possessed by a phantom. But either way...

Doomed.

A humorless laugh escaped. Suddenly, I understood why my mother had taken me to Milo's father so often. The potion *had* provided a barrier. A mystical barrier I could have re-created if Milo hadn't burned the warlock's journals.

Another pain in my head. —*Isn't this nice? The barrier has thinned so much, we can speak.*—

A woman's smug voice whispered through my mind. Shocking, yes. But the real head-scratcher? The mental invasion hadn't felt odd, but rather astonishingly familiar, as if the speaker had been there all along, just waiting for the perfect time to surprise me.

"Leonora?" I whispered.

—*The one and only. And oh, how wonderful it feels to be heard by you. So many times I've wanted, no, needed to complain about your behavior. You're ruining my life.*—

Her life? Hers?

If she said more, I missed it. Images were forming in my mind, colors flaring behind my eyes. Then a memory of the past consumed me utterly...

I lounged in bed with Craven, naked but for the ring he'd gifted to me as a show of our great love. My body lay draped over his, his warm breath fanning the top of my head as I traced circles over his heart.

A heart he'd ceded to me.

We'd been a couple for months, but we'd had so many fights. We were unable to agree about the smallest things. But that wasn't my fault. I was training him to be what I needed him to be—fully devoted to my pleasure.

Training for anything required hard work and dedication. That was just a fact. The end result would make it all worth it, however.

Now I had to turn my efforts to teaching him to put my needs before his family's. Earlier today, I'd heard his horrid mother advising him to wed an elven princess and keep me as his mistress. So of course his mother would be dying by sunset. Anyone who threatened my happiness lost their breathing privileges. I planned to wed Craven. Me. I was his fated, the one made for him, and no one else was allowed to have him.

My fairy tale guaranteed he would be mine forevermore.

I would take his name and the title that came with it. Queen Leonora. I would bear his children. The things he made me feel...everything I'd ever craved. I couldn't live without him, not ever again, and I wasn't going to try.

As he toyed with a lock of my red hair, I relaxed against him. He would never do as his mother asked and cast me out. He would wed me—nothing else was acceptable. "Craven," I breathed.

"Yes, Nora."

I loved the nickname he'd given me. But...had he sounded strained? "Do you love me?"

"You know I do."

See. Mine. I lifted my head to meet his sleepy gaze. "Why haven't you offered me the ceremonial marriage bracelet?" I had a surprise for him as soon as he did. I'd found a dragon egg I planned to share with him. "Don't you want to cement our bond?"

"I do," he said, voice tight, "but sometimes what we want isn't what we need. There is something wrong with us, witch, and I don't know how to fix it."

At "I do," I grinned. Then his next words registered, and cold invaded my limbs. "You contradict yourself. Be clearer."

He rested the side of his hand against the top of his nose, with his thumb pressed against one eye and his index finger pressed against the other. "Time with you is both ecstasy and torment. The strain…it cripples me in so many ways. I cannot live like this much longer, feeling as if I'm being ripped apart from the inside. War has always been my life. Inside these walls, I desire peace. That isn't something you can give me."

What! "But I can. Just give me a chance to be what you need, Craven. You *must* give me a chance." He couldn't discard me. I was fated to be his.

"Calm isn't in your nature. That is why…in the morning, I'm going to send you home. Your people may continue to reside at the base of my mountain."

Horror, fear, and fury collided, setting off a chain reaction inside me. Stiffening spine. The burn of fire in my hands. Ice rushing through my veins.

He was going to heed his mother's advice and cast me out. Did he plan to wed the princess, too?

I snarled the way I imagined a dragon would, fire magic threatening to spark. Containing it, barely, I spit a curse at him, then swung my fist. He caught my wrist, his fingers like a shackle, and we glared at each other, both of us breathing heavily.

He expected that to stop me? I released the flames only where he touched me. He hissed as blisters formed. Still he didn't release me.

"We will not part. Do you hear me?" I would not lose this sense of belonging.

"We will part." The finality in his tone… "Knowing how desperately I crave you, however, I'm certain I won't be able to stop myself from chasing after you."

Oh. *Ohhhh.* He wasn't planning to get rid of me permanently. Just chase me. Was this to be a sexual game, then?

"That is why I will be wedding someone else," he announced. "I will remain true to my wife. My vow to protect her will allow nothing less."

I shoved a fist into my mouth, halting my cry of distress. He couldn't. He *wouldn't.*

"You and I," he continued as my new world collapsed around me, "are not good for each other. To survive, we must separate."

Wed someone *else?* Give her what belonged to me? "No. That is unacceptable." He thought he'd seen the worst of my temper. He hadn't. "If you do this, Craven, I will make you sorry."

His expression gentled, and he offered me a sad smile. "I'm already sorry. Had I never met you, I never would have known what could be. I would never know what I could have—what I would be missing. The fact that I feel this way for a woman who isn't destined to be mine…it's madness."

The words *already sorry* reverberated in my head, each repeat like the lash of a whip.

He wished he hadn't met me.

He *wished* he hadn't *met* me.

He wished he hadn't met *me.* Me. The most powerful witch in all of Enchantia. The jewel of any kingdom.

The one who hadn't yet drawn forth his amour.

My fury intensified, overshadowing everything else. He thought he couldn't survive with me? Well, I would teach him the error of his ways. Soon this male would learn he couldn't survive *without* me.

The battlefield returned to focus, and like Leonora, I stuffed a fist into my mouth. The horrifying truth was suddenly so clear. I hadn't been the one in that bedroom with Craven. But the fire witch had.

—Did memories of my life break your brain, little girl? Well, don't you worry. When the barrier falls once and for all, I will take owner-ship of this body and nothing will ever bother you again.—

A cocoon of ice enveloped my lungs, freezing and burning at the same time. I *was* a host. An evil phantom possessed me. She had twice murdered Saxon and his family. She planned to steal my life.

Two heads, one heart. Born twice in one day.

I laughed without humor. I was born an infant…and then a host. In a way, it made Leonora my family. There was no doubt now—she was my evil stepmother.

Because of her, I had harmed Saxon at the funeral, exactly as he'd claimed. And I might… I might have…

Acid-tinged tears welled, scalding my eyes. Tremors invaded. Nausea roiled. My body might have been used as a weapon. I might have murdered two innocents. Milo's father…and my own mother.

A whimper parted my lips, the first of many, and a herald to my sobs. I slung my arms around my middle and hunched over, bawling so violently I vomited.

Whoosh, whoosh. The hated noise failed to elicit a reaction from me. What did another beating or punishment matter? I deserved to suffer.

Someone gathered my hair with gentle hands, holding the strands out of the line of fire. I didn't have to wonder who. The scent of coming rain filled my nose. Saxon's scent.

Such a simple act of kindness. But it had come from Saxon, an enemy, and it only made me bawl harder. How could I have hurt Momma? Even if Leonora had taken control of my body, I must have been present somewhere in here. I should have found a way to stop her. Instead, I'd let her pick up a dagger and…and…

Another sob, followed by a round of dry heaving. Was Craven a phantom, too? Was Saxon his host, and he just didn't know it? Or was he an actual reincarnate?

—*Oh, he's a reincarnate, just as you are. He's also mine, and I won't share him. Soon, I won't share this body, either.*—

She'd offered few words, but there was a wealth of information to unpack. I was a host, yes, but I was also a reincarnate of…who? The first Leonora? And the way she'd said *this body*. I was a nonentity to her. A piece of trash to discard. A shirt she'd donned. Or better yet, the gooey center she planned to scoop out of the cookie, just so she could enjoy the treat at her leisure. All because she wanted Saxon, the man she'd harmed again and again.

The fury won. *I will make her pay.*

Wanting to hurt her, I inwardly shouted, *You are not his. Didn't you hear him? He didn't want you. He didn't make amour for you.* Whatever that was.

No response was forthcoming. But then, she didn't need to offer one. I could feel her indignation, and I screeched. This body belonged to me, and *I* would not share it. I wanted her out. I wanted her out *now.* She could take her fire magic with her. I would buy my own ability, as planned. I wanted *nothing* of hers.

"Any better, Asha?" Saxon asked, his concern obvious.

I wasn't sure I'd *ever* be better, so I shook my head before spitting on the ground and wiping my mouth with the back of my hand. I remained crouched, my head bowed.

How could I excise and kill the phantom? How could I prevent her from ending any more innocent lives until I discovered the answer to her defeat?

Perhaps being ordered to remain in the palace was a blessing, after all. I would have an excuse to keep Leonora away from Saxon and the time to research a way to oust her.

—*You? Oust me?*— She laughed. —*I'm going to tell you a story.*

On the day of your birth, I was going to inhabit your mother, but thanks to a spell I'd purchased years before, I sensed you were Saxon's reincarnated mate. I would have preferred to enter you when you were older. And healthier. Your infirmity is a true inconvenience. Alas. Circumstances demanded I possess you before you died. You have a life now only because I gave it to you.—

Saxon stroked his knuckles up and down my nape, applying the softest pressure. Part of me wanted to tell him everything I'd learned. He deserved to know. And what if he could help me excise and end her? But I couldn't trust him with the information.

I could *never* trust him with the information.

—You'll never be rid of me, dearling. I'm too deeply rooted. Besides, nothing has changed for you. You'll still die without my magic.—

Smugger than before. No wonder Saxon despised her. I did, too, hatred spreading through me like a wildfire.

If you die with me, I don't see a downside. I threw the words at her, each one like a white-hot ball of fire of my own making. *You killed my mother.*

—Yes, and I'm ready to hear your thanks. She'd begun to fear you and even considered telling your father what I'd done. He would have killed you.—

Thanks? *Thanks?*

"What caused this sickness?" Saxon asked, still so gentle.

"It doesn't matter." Nothing mattered. "Please, just let me go." Again, I wiped my mouth with the back of my hand. Inside, I was nothing but a raw, bleeding wound. Never had I felt so vulnerable, not even at the funeral. I needed to be alone.

Another bitter laugh. There was a second soul trapped inside my head; I *couldn't* be alone.

"I'm going to walk away now," I told Saxon before he could respond. I wasn't sure how much longer I could hold my emotions inside. They geared for release—a release that was going to come one way or another.

He let my hair fall and stepped back. As I mourned the loss of his touch, he flared his wings and snarled, "I told you to leave."

"No, you didn't," I snarled back. "I just told you *I'm* leaving."

"I wasn't speaking to you, Asha," he replied, his tone gentle again.

Of all times to be nice to me, why now, when I spiraled down a rabbit hole of despair?

I lumbered to my feet and faced the woman he'd spoken to, a beauty with black-and-white hair, light skin, and disapproving dark eyes. She stood several feet from us, massive violet wings tucked into her sides.

Queen Raven in the flesh.

"You know who the girl is," she yelled at Saxon. "You saw the flames just as I did, yet you dare treat her like she's as fragile as glass?"

"I'm handling her, *Your Majesty*," he grated in a soft, menacing tone.

"Just as you handled her in the past?" She spat the words at him. "She is Leonora the Burner of Worlds. Our downfall twice over. Kill her now, or step aside and watch as I do the honor."

As much as I wanted to deny the queen's claim—*I'm not Leonora, I'm just her skin suit*—I kept my mouth closed.

"You do so enjoy watching as others die, don't you, Mother?" Saxon offered silkily. "If you touch her, you die." He wrapped a strong arm around my waist. "Ashleigh is mine."

At any other time, I would have reveled in his protectiveness. Now? *Too emotionally flayed.*

I considered running to escape the pair, but how far would I get before I passed out? The sobs had drained me. I barely had the strength to remain on my feet. At least Leonora seemed to have retreated...for now.

With his free arm, Saxon motioned to the sky. I looked up

in time to see a boy I hadn't met descending from the overhead pack to approach us.

When he landed a few feet away, Saxon gave me a squeeze and told him, "Take the girl to the palace. Leave her on the balcony of the bedroom I secured before her arrival."

He was able to secure a room for himself, but my father hadn't planned to offer one to me? How very... King Philipp.

After what I'd done to my mother, though, I couldn't blame him.

A new whimper bubbled up.

"If she receives a single scratch," Saxon said, incorrectly guessing the reason for my upset, "you will pay with your life. Understood?"

I might not be the witch who'd harmed Craven all those years ago, but I'd enabled the phantom who had. Saxon owed me nothing, and I owed him everything; he'd still put more protective measures in place.

"The feathers," I croaked, wanting to apologize. I would redo this task. I would do every task he assigned from now on, exactly as he commanded. I *needed* to make true reparation.

"Consider it a successful finish, the goal met." He avoided looking in my direction. "Don't forget you are to remain at the palace."

"I won't forget, and I won't leave unless forced," I promised.

"You safeguard her?" Raven demanded. "Did you learn nothing from your past? She is an angel in the beginning, and a devil in the end. She will never be accepted as your queen. If you wed her, you cannot be king."

"Enough," Saxon bellowed. He snapped his fingers at the wide-eyed avian boy. "Go. Now. And heed my warning."

The boy urged me against him, flared his wings and eased me into the air. I didn't speak, just tried to contain my grief.

By the time the avian set me down on the balcony and flew away, I was strung tighter than a bow, even one of my own design. With a series of sniffles, I pushed my way into an unfamiliar bedroom, spying mirrored walls, a massive four-poster bed, and potted plants. Lovely, pearly white moonpetals bloomed from the foliage, perfuming the air.

My gaze zoomed back to the bed, where two ball-shaped blobs rested on a pillow. I recalled Noel's words. *I left a gift in your bedroom. You're welcome. When you see it, scream. You'll be glad you did.*

I tripped over to the bed. I needed to lie down, anyway. What I found... I had to do a double take. My red dragon eggs.

A flare of excitement was quickly extinguished by my misery. *Scream Noel? Very well.* I dropped to my knees at the side of the bed, threw back my head, and screamed at the top of my lungs. Rage, frustration, and grief blended together in an ear-splitting crescendo.

I screamed until my voice broke. I screamed until my lungs threatened to collapse. I screamed until my heart skipped beats in an effort to escape my pain. Let the world hear.

When finally I quieted, I sagged to the floor and rolled into a ball, weak and sobbing anew. But it wasn't long before a faint scraping sound caught my attention. I tensed.

If someone had entered the room, I would... I would...

Oh, what did it matter? I didn't want to think. I didn't want to talk or care. I just wanted to forget. To cry until I passed out. The presence of another wouldn't stop me.

The scraping persisted. Eventually, I pushed up, balanced on my arms, and twisted, glancing over my shoulder. *What the—*

There, on the pillow, cracks spread through both eggs.

I scrambled to my feet, watching as a piece of shell dropped, thick gooey liquid spilling over the sheets.

A membranous red wing peeked out.

13

He isn't kind, and he isn't cruel,
but if you prick his temper, you're a fool.

SAXON

As the first hint of morning sunlight filtered into my tent, I jackknifed to my feet. For most of the night, I'd listened to my mother and sister rage about Leonora. They'd listed reasons I must kill Ashleigh. Reasons I'd pondered for years, seething. They didn't care that her death would solve my problem but endanger future generations.

After I'd kicked out my family, I'd tried to sleep. I'd ended up tossing and turning, Ashleigh's face unwavering in my mind. How fragile she'd appeared before my soldier flew her away. Broken, even.

Why? What had happened?

After cleaning up, I prepared for battle, then stepped out into a seemingly abandoned camp. The masses had journeyed to the coliseum to witness the test of wits, where I should be.

I'd given my soldiers the day off so they could watch the festivities. All but Adriel. He should be here, keeping guard, but there was no sign of him.

So. The day after a punishment he'd decided to disobey a direct order. Very well. I would punish him harder, lest any of my other soldiers decided they could do the same.

I fumed as I flew to the bustling coliseum. Landing on the battlefield, in the midst of the combatants, I took my place in line. About forty of the fifty others had opted in. We stood shoulder to shoulder.

Roth had a spot at the end. Milo did, too.

I adopted a battle stance, my feet braced apart, my knees slightly bent. The warlock had stood too close to Ashleigh last night. Had peered at her as if she were his next meal.

He turned his head toward me, and our gazes met. He scowled; I glared.

He was going to die by my hand very soon.

Once again, the stands overflowed with cheering spectators, many of whom waved sticks with ribbons or rang cowbells. Even as the sun brightened, a chill coated the air, yesterday's warmth no more.

Gaze slitted, I searched the royal dais, ensuring Ashleigh had obeyed my command to remain at the palace. I spotted the master of ceremonies, Ophelia, Noel, the king, and Dior.

Good. That was good. I was relieved.

I was disappointed.

I was…screwed.

"Welcome one and all." Just as before, the master used a magical horn to make his voice carry, causing a hush to fall over the crowd. "Let our test of wits begin. Here's how the game goes. I will tell our combatants a riddle, and they will each have sixty seconds to respond. Those with a correct answer will be allowed a weapon in the next battle, while everyone else has zero." He took a breath. "Combatants, you were each given a piece of parchment. Once I relay the riddle, you will write your answer on that parchment, in blood, and throw it into the fire. Understood?"

Murmurs from the combatants. "Parchment?" someone shouted. "What parchment?"

Someone else demanded, "What fire?"

The master pinched the bridge of his nose and muttered, "Witch! You're ruining my event."

Ophelia, who remained seated on the royal dais, waved her hand in our direction. A piece of parchment materialized in my hand—in *everyone's* hand—and a firepit appeared in front of our line.

The magic prompted laughter from the stands.

"Now, then. Who's ready to begin?" the master asked, the question met with thunderous applause. "Here goes. I have towns, but no homes. I have kingdoms but no kings. I have water, but none to share. What am I?"

Murmurs from the crowd blended with murmurs from the combatants as the master counted down the seconds. Each man sliced a fingertip and wrote his question on his parchment.

Embers sparked every time a new paper met flame, a wind rushing in to collect the ash and toss it into the air. Words formed in that ash.

Goblin.

Stars.

Desert.

Some answers were repeated by multiple combatants. I'd lived at a crossroads since meeting Ashleigh.

After I cut my fingertip, I wrote, "Map." I'd studied them most of my first and second lives, choosing which territories to conquer first.

A horn blew soon after my paper became ash.

"We have winners!" the master called, eliciting more cheers. He listed names I didn't care about. I nodded when he said,

"Blaze the fae." Relaxed when he called, "Saxon the avian." And scowled when I heard, "Milo the warlock."

A young fawn-shifter with big, droopy ears rushed to the field to lead us off and make room for the entertainment.

"Don't go anywhere," the master told the spectators. "We have a special treat for you. Singers. Dancers. Magical practitioners. Something for everyone!"

Milo shoved his way over to me, breathing hard, as if he were struggling to control his fury.

I cocked a brow, unfazed. "Is this the part where you intimidate me with your magic, warlock?"

"Leonora is mine, avian. She wants to be with me." He pounded a fist against his chest. "Go ahead. Ask her."

Did he have any idea what he'd just admitted?

I remained rooted in place as dancers glided past us. Milo had used present tense, as if he'd spoken to the witch recently. Had he?

Had Ashleigh told him this at the party? Or had the conversation taken place at the palace?

Had Leonora taken over? Had she faded again or did she rule?

How long until our war restarted?

A sharp pain tore through me, and I desperately wanted to punch someone or something. In our first two lives, I'd only ever glimpsed Leonora's *potential*. What she could have been, if evil hadn't brewed in the marrow of her bones. This time, I'd gotten to spend time with her before she became a bloodthirsty, blue-eyed witch. She was witty and exciting. A green-eyed enchantress. I enjoyed her company. One day away from her, and I *craved* her company.

How easy it would be to hate her if she were the Leonora of old. How easy it would be to do as my family suggested and end her.

But I still wasn't ready to lose Ashleigh.

I shot into the air, saying no more to the warlock. I headed straight for the palace. To my consternation, the balcony doors to my bedroom were locked, the curtains drawn. No crack in the fabric.

I knocked and I waited, but the princess didn't open up. No noise seeped through the glass.

Flapping my wings, I hovered in place, stewing. Where was she?

The tracker spell flashed a map inside my head, and X marked the spot. She was here, just beyond those doors. What was she doing? Had she heard and ignored me?

"There you are." Queen Raven's voice made my ears feel as if they were being scrubbed with sand.

I watched her approach as she flew over. "Now isn't the time, Mother."

She stopped in front of me anyway. Outlined by sunlight and sky, she reminded me of a painting I'd once seen as a boy. A warrior goddess on the battlefield, her enemies scattered at her feet in pieces. Raven Skylair had never been a soft woman. If my siblings or I had ever dared to shed a tear, we were whipped and told tears were a luxury for the weak.

The tears she'd shed over me as a boy had kept me from cutting her from my life completely.

"I'm curious," she said, maintaining her position. "When will be the time to slay Leonora? After she's killed you and murdered our people? Does her father know who and what she is?"

No pleasantries, then. Just right back to the volley of complaints.

If Philipp knew anything about Leonora, I hadn't been the one to tell him. But I doubted he had a clue. As power hungry as he was, he would curry Leonora's favor.

"You will not speak to the king," I informed my mother. Frustration mounted, sharpened by anger's blade. "You will not look at, touch, or speak to Princess Ashleigh. You will not even speak *about* her."

"You cannot avoid this conversation, Saxon."

"I didn't avoid it. I ended it. If you'll excuse me, I'm late for a meeting…with myself." I flew past her, heading for camp.

Following me would have smacked of weakness and desperation, and she knew it. She remained behind, just as I'd expected.

I would prepare for the next bonus competition, I decided. It kicked off tomorrow morning—a new bonus round would be held every day, even the days we fought a mandatory battle…the next of which would take place in five days. The same number of days as my separation with Ashleigh.

Five days without hearing her lilting voice.

Five days without breathing in her sweet scent.

Five days without matching wits with her cunning mind.

I cursed.

The next five days passed with incredible slowness. I didn't sleep. I barely ate. I couldn't relax. The vitriol spewed by my mother and sister stopped only when I competed. Some battles I won, some I lost because I was too focused on ruining Milo's chances for success. Despite my efforts, he'd gained a couple victories of his own.

He wants what's mine.

The warlock and I had not had a chance to speak one-on-one a second time. We'd only gotten to exchange glares. So badly I'd wanted to get in his face and demand answers. *Have you spoken to Ashleigh again? How do you know about Leonora? What other lies has the witch fed you?*

I needed to see my princess, to speak to her, but she had remained at the palace, as ordered. Why hadn't I demanded she send me a message every morning to let me know how she was doing?

How did she fare?

I worried for her. I…missed her.

I missed falling asleep with her secure in my bed. I missed

waking up with her right beside me. I missed our conversations and her daily transformation from mouse to tigress, as she found and wielded her inner strength.

I shouldn't miss anything but her torment.

I shouldn't be the miserable one, feeling as if I'd finally enjoyed the barest taste of contentment and now couldn't live without more.

Why had I let Ashleigh cup my cheeks and offer comfort? Had I stopped her, my chest would not have cracked. Now it was too late. The damage was done, the consequences here to demand their due. I had softened irreparably toward Ashleigh, and there was no going back.

Deep breath in, out.

"Are you just going to stand there?" my sister shrieked from inside my tent. "The second official battle has started."

I realized I stood at the entrance, one foot out and one foot in. Scowling, I stalked outside, entering the campgrounds.

Tempest followed me, remaining a few steps behind. I skirted a tent. A chill morning wind blustered, spreading the smoke that curled from abandoned firepits. A pack of wild dogs raced here and there, eating the food I'd had my men leave throughout the grounds. Any soldier or servant who'd imbibed too much the night before now sprawled in the dirt, sleeping.

"Well?" Tempest demanded. "Why aren't you headed for the coliseum?"

Once I'd thought Leonora was the bane of my existence. In this life, my sister and mother held the honor. "This competition is a series of ten separate battle heats, with five combatants fighting in each." The ten heats would garner ten winners. The last men standing. They would advance to the semifinals, which would take place sometime next week. "I have been assigned to the last heat."

Noel had been in charge of selecting which combatants belonged in which heat. A task assigned by Philipp…after the oracle had manipulated him into thinking it was his idea, just as she'd manipulated him into bringing Ashleigh to Sevón on my behalf.

The oracle's only task this time? Ensuring I wasn't in the same heat as Roth. Instead, she'd paired us together. *Why, oracle?* Now one of us had to "die" today, and that one would be Roth. Or rather, his fae illusion. Everly was capable of casting a second illusion to convince the entire crowd he had expired, but such a feat would require untold amounts of magic, which could leave her incapacitated, which would erase Roth's fae illusion, which would leave both of my friends vulnerable to attack. So, I would be fighting him for real but only pretending to slay him.

"You told me Mother would only stay six days," I said with a glance over my shoulder. "It's been six days. *Why hasn't she left?*"

"You know why. She's worried about you. So am I." Tempest hopped over a log and picked up her pace. "I've read the journals Craven and his second incarnation wrote while they warred with Leonora. Did you know the tomes survived the fires in both lives, bespelled to last the ages? A scribe had them. His friary kept them safe all this time. When he heard rumors of your reincarnation, he gave them to Mother. That's how I know Craven believed in the fairy-tale prophecies and thought he'd gotten stuck in some kind of twisted tale with Leonora. Is that what you believe, too?"

"No," I snapped. *Yes?* I didn't know anymore. Tyron had believed in the fairy-tale prophecies, too...at first. But he'd nearly driven himself mad trying to decipher his and Leonora's roles in "The Little Cinder Girl." In the end, he'd told his people only fools believed such nonsense. Over the centuries, the declaration had stuck. "Put the journals in a crate with rocks and drop it into a deep hole in the earth." I'd written them for the family of my future incarnations, for this very purpose, thinking to warn them of what could be, and I'd been a brilliant fool to do so.

At my side, Tempest snapped, "Craven didn't believe he had fulfilled his destiny. He suspected he would come back as part of his own familial line, so he created a law ensuring only someone with Skylair blood had the right to rule the avian. If there were multiple heirs, the crown would go to the worthiest male. If there were no males, the crown would go to the worthiest female. That is why your word will always supersede our mother's, even though she's a queen and you are but a prince. Without Skylair blood, she cannot truly rule. But you, the one who can, dare to consider sharing your reign with the witch who murdered you? That's what you're doing, isn't it? Think, brother."

Think? I'd done little else these past six days. "I have no plans to wed her." Truth. Absolutely.

She clamped a hand on my shoulder, stopping me, and I rounded on her. "Fate has done you a great favor," she said. "Leonora is back, yes, but she's trapped inside a weak body. You have an opportunity to kill her before her magic matures and heals her defective heart. Let's handle her right this time."

"You will not harm her." The words bellowed from me, as they always bellowed from me, the very idea of a dead or dying Ashleigh abhorrent. Not receive her comfort a second time? Not kiss her, even once? Breaths shallow, I shook off Tempest's hold. "There's something different about this incarnation. Before I make a move against her, I will figure out what it is. If—when—the time comes, I will be the one to end her." Another absolute truth.

It must be truth.

"No, you won't." Tempest regarded me with disappointment. "You never do."

"How do you know what I *never* do?" I asked softly. Dangerously soft. "You don't even know me."

Spots of red stained her cheeks. "Like I said, I've read about your pasts. Action always reveals character. I know you," she insisted.

No. "You know *of* me. You know nothing about the reasons behind my actions." The intent. The inner struggle. She didn't know this absence from Ashleigh had been torture for me. She didn't know I felt as if my blood were kerosene, a single spark able to ignite a wildfire. "As I'm coming to realize, a person's actions never paint a complete picture."

"Why do the reasons matter? The end result is the end result."

A dangerous mindset. "Do you want to know what I've learned about *your* actions?" I stepped closer, getting in her face. "A month ago…a year ago…even three years ago at Queen Charlotte's funeral, you were content to pretend I didn't exist. Did you erase me from your heart out of loyalty to our parents or fear for the future? Both are forgivable. Or did you do it because you never cared about me to begin with? Which is it?"

She bowed up, going on the defensive. A shadow fell over her face as an avian flew above us. "What do you admire about the witch, hmm?" she asked. "Tell me. Is it the way she only ever speaks lies? Is it her ability to betray you every second of every day? Is it her death-toll dowry?"

"Enough." The barked command came from our mother, who eased to the ground beside us. She focused her fiercest scowl on me. "It's clear you don't like us. And that's fine. I don't like you, either. But you are blood of my blood, bone of my bone, and I won't allow you to show mercy to a foe."

"You won't *allow* me?" I uttered the words quietly, the frost in my tone unmistakable.

The queen doubled down in an attempt to wield authority she no longer possessed. "I will do whatever is needed to protect my king and kingdom, just as I've always done. When it comes to Leonora, you will stand down. That's an order from your mother and your queen. The witch's death might hurt you for a time, but pain fades. Better you hurt than die. Your next death might be forever. I won't let you leave our people with a legacy of death and destruction for a third time, your sister burdened with the responsibility of creating the next heir."

The sheer audacity of this woman. In every way that mattered, she'd turned her back on me, forever forfeiting the right to rule me.

"You aren't my queen. You're barely even my mother." My voice possessed more smoke than substance. "As Tempest has reminded me, you lack Skylair blood. The avian will never be yours to rule."

Like Tempest, she bowed up, ready to do battle. "Whether you like it or not, I *am* your queen. Royals must make tough calls for the good of their people. Had I reached out to you, even once, you might have assumed you could come home."

Intent. Always. Mattered. My mother wasn't angry because I'd insulted her as a parent. She fumed because I'd insulted her as a sovereign.

"I'm done with this conversation." Harsh words had been spoken, but no headway had been made.

"Where will you go?" she demanded.

I could return to the palace, where I knew Ashleigh to be, or I could wait for my battle heat at the coliseum, where I hoped she might make an appearance. The six days had passed, the time of our reunion at hand. Though my mother hadn't returned to the Avian Mountains, I wasn't going to request Ashleigh remain in the palace. She would be safest with me. I could protect her from danger better than anyone.

"It doesn't matter," I told her. "I am to be your king, and as crown prince my word is law. You will obey my commands at all times. You will not follow me. You will stay away from Ashleigh. There's no need for me to tell you what will happen if you disobey me, because you will not disobey me. Isn't that right, Mother?" I offered the question smoothly, my intent clear.

Her lips peeled back and she grated, "Right."

Having gotten what I'd wanted, I flapped my wings and angled my body, shooting across the sky, heading for...the coliseum, I decided. I would watch the next heat and learn more about my competitors. When I reunited with Ashleigh, I would be in a calmer mood than this.

Two weeks remained on our countdown clock. A mere fourteen days until the tournament's end and everything changed for us.

The crack in my chest spread with unexpected force, something corrosive spilling from the wound. Desperation? Sorrow? Helplessness? I gritted my teeth against it.

Our situation was what it was and it couldn't be changed. From the beginning, I'd planned to bespell Ashleigh to sleep and lock her away. Now I wasn't so sure I had the right to do it. The thought of sweet, surprisingly inventive Ashleigh trapped in some small, dank prison, a vulnerable target for any corrupt jailer... I experienced the full breadth of Craven's viciousness.

What if we could find a way to keep memories of her past lives at bay? Would she remain Ashleigh for good?

Ashleigh wouldn't require confinement. I could be with her...maybe.

Would she want to be with me?

Either way, the demand for restitution had to stop. I would find another way to appease my armies for her crimes as a child.

Movement on the dais drew my attention to Milo. The warlock trotted himself to the king's throne and eased down as if he had every right.

If we fought in the same heat... I would take his head.

Ophelia stomped onto the dais, anchored one hand on her waist and waved the other in the warlock's direction. He vanished, reappearing on the battlefield only a second later. When he realized where he was, he made a crude gesture to the witch.

He'd hoped to make a grand entrance, I realized with disgust.

As the crowd went wild, the other fighters flooded into the arena.

Just beyond the coliseum, amid a small circular clearing, Everly and Roth appeared, no longer clothed in their illusions.

Everly had a mass of glossy silver-white hair, eyes as silver as a mirror with rims of gold, and pale white skin with a smattering of freckles. Roth possessed black hair, green eyes and bronze skin.

They looked around, as if searching for someone. I searched the area, but no one else lurked nearby.

I angled toward my childhood friend and the new guardian of the forest, who often used trees as doorways, then tucked my wings into my sides and dropped. Just before I reached them, entering a secluded area encompassed by Everly's magical mist, I realigned, slowing my momentum. A hard vibration rushed up my legs when I landed.

"You're late, but I'll forgive you at some point." Everly raced over to hug me. "Noel told us something, something, something, and you have information for us, and that we should something, something, and meet you at this spot, five minutes ago. I love when I correctly interpret her gibberish."

"First, you arrived two minutes ago. If you were supposed to be here five minutes ago, you are also late." I released her and acknowledged Roth, the man I loved like a brother. "I haven't spoken to the oracle today, so I don't know what information I'm supposed to relay."

Everly *humph*ed. "This is going to be a head-scratcher, then."

"Did Noel tell you why she put us in the same heat?" I asked.

Roth nodded with the usual clipped jerk of his chin. "Apparently, she has a new job for me. What, she wouldn't say."

Flaky oracles.

Everly patted my shoulder. "Noel did say she was absolutely, positively right about Ashleigh being a reincarnate, and that she was also absolutely, positively right about Ashleigh not being a reincarnate. After dropping that gem, she told me to tell you that you shouldn't distrust a girl just because she has Anticollaborative Disorder and, dude, I have to agree. Come on."

Anticollaborative Disorder? Two objects unable to collaborate? Ashleigh and Leonora fit together like a corner and center piece of a puzzle, so, it fit. And I thought I finally understood how she could be a reincarnate and also not a reincarnate.

Ashleigh and Leonora were not the same person. They couldn't be—their pasts were different. Until recently, Ashleigh had been a blank slate. She hadn't recalled her past lives, making her the nonreincarnate. Leonora contained all the memories of her past lives, making her the reincarnate.

One didn't have to be the other. We just had to keep them separated permanently.

Speaking of Ashleigh. "I think she can be saved. I think her past memories can be suppressed, Leonora kept at bay." I would send notes to Noel and Ophelia, asking for an audience to present this very thought.

Everly cocked a brow. "So...this has turned into a revenge with benefits situation, I'm guessing."

Revenge with benefits?

Roth, who knew more about my situation than Everly, blinked at me. "That you even want to save her..."

"It's shocking, yes." But here we were. "I will be asking Ophelia for a spell."

"And if there isn't one?" Everly asked.

I...didn't know. "Unless we find a way to suppress those memories, Ashleigh will always have the potential for great evil."

"But don't we all?" The Evil Queen drummed her fingers together. With metal claws anchored to the end of each finger, every motion clinked. "Can I be honest? I don't get an evil vibe from her," Everly admitted. "She reminds me of my Hartly. She's all nice and crap."

I flinched. Hartly, the girl I'd killed. Everly's beloved cousin, the two raised as sisters.

"Just, keep hiding mirrors in the palace for me. Even though your plans have maybe, maybe not changed for the princess, we still have a kingdom to reclaim. I'll continue growing my plants all over the campground and palace courtyard so I can spy through my army of foliage. And yes, I got to hear six days' worth of conversations with your mother and sister, Saxon. Make them stop. I'm tempted to cut off my ears and give them to the women. Do you think they would regift?"

Roth cast me a sympathetic look. "Victory draws nigh. When the time comes, we will publicly dethrone Philipp, no matter what we decide to do about his daughter. You will take the avian throne, and your mother will be pacified. All will be well."

"I don't care if she's pacified. If she goes after Ashleigh again, she will be banished."

And what of Ashleigh, if she became Leonora before I could have her memories suppressed? I scrubbed a hand down my face, pressure rising.

No matter how I felt about her, no matter how much I wanted her, no matter how much I would agonize afterward, Leonora must be neutralized. So, if I had any chance of saving the princess—Did I? Could I?—I had to work fast.

14

He is like frost, and she is like flame.
One preserves and one burns, but both maim.

Ashleigh

Oh, how quickly my life had changed.

Six days ago, I'd planned to search out books about Leonora and Craven, phantoms in general, and maybe even magic potions, just in case I could re-create the one made by Milo's father. Time permitting, I'd hoped to read over a few different interpretations of "The Little Cinder Girl." An extravaganza of knowledge.

I'd done none of that.

I spent the bulk of my time listening to the tournament battles that took place outside while corralling my new baby dragons.

That's right. I was a mother now, and it was a role I adored. One glance into the dark, fathomless eyes of my twins, and I'd adopted both darlings as my own.

I wanted my other two babies, as well. Where were they?

I didn't care that these two had destroyed the books I *had* managed to gather, that they didn't understand "this is a matter of life and death, and Momma really must study." They'd also ruined the feather-dress I'd been sewing, broken my bed, and put holes in my walls. All forgivable. I loved these dragons with every fiber of my being.

I plopped onto the edge of the wobbly bed with cracked posters, parchment, and quill in hand. This momma had bills to pay. I had to replace the furniture and have the walls patched before someone noticed the damage. I'd already ordered a spell. For the bargain price of a dagger, sword, ax, and a full set of armor, Ophelia had agreed to re-create the spell she'd cast around Saxon's tent, ensuring no one heard the destruction taking place on a minute-by-minute basis.

Bang, bang, bang. Growl. Bang. The dragons zoomed past me, mid wrestling match. They slammed into furniture for a thousandth time, wood cracking, and I cringed. More damage, more coin needed to repair. All right. I might be giving up my design work until the dragons went to bed.

As the dragons took flight again, one chasing the other, I set the paper and quill aside, and called, "Be careful, babies. We don't want another injured wing, do we?"

They crash-landed onto the bed and bounced off the mattress. I giggled. I couldn't help myself, my heart swelling with love at their antics. Only six days had passed since their hatching, but they'd already doubled in size. They were now the same length and weight as midsize dogs with swordlike teeth.

Both dragons possessed scales that were exact replicas of their shells. At first, I'd thought them completely red, but every day, green specks had become more noticeable. Tiny spikes protruded in two descending rows along each creature's spine. Both their "hands" and "feet" were tipped with razor-sharp claws, and their wings remained membranous, with bone hooks growing from every joint.

One baby had a tail with spikes at the end—I'd named her

Pagan. The other baby's tail resembled a trident, branching into three barbed prongs. I'd named her Pyre. I assumed the dragons were female, anyway. How was one supposed to tell? I adored them both, whatever they were.

To my amazement, the dragons adored me right back. They cuddled me when we slept, whined when I snuck off to the bathroom, and rushed to my side to protect me whenever someone knocked on the door.

How had Leonora ever used her dragons for evil? They were the sweetest creatures ever born, and I would die to protect mine. The connection I felt...the bond...it couldn't be because of the phantom. She might come from dragon fire, but *my* scream had birthed these creatures. They were my family.

And I desperately needed to find my family somewhere else to live. The little darlings would only continue to grow. They were hungry all the time, willing to eat everything in sight. Wood? Why not? Linen? Nom-nom. Glass? Tasty! They preferred mice, though. Especially when I used Leonora's fire magic to char the remains. I winced.

Yes, I'd practiced summoning the phantom's flames, and I could do it with more ease now. Not always, but often.

One day soon, the pair would be able to torch their own food. At the moment, they could only cough up a couple sparks.

I scowled as a familiar pain exploded in my temples. As often as it had occurred, I no longer grimaced, my temper greater than my discomfort. Leonora had just crashed through our barrier, invading my mind. Soon, the barrier would refortify on its own, building on the magical remnants of the warlock's spell. But I knew. Soon, no more remnants would remain, just as Milo had warned me at the funeral.

—*The dragons are mine. They tolerate you only because they sense my presence.*—

I would give anything to silence this phantom forever. "You're lying, trying to make me as miserable as possible, because I have what you want. Why haven't you realized yet that I also have what you lack? A moral compass!"

—*I lack nothing.*—

"What about a body of your own?" I taunted. I'd developed a bit of a mean streak.

She spat a litany of curses at me. —*I control the body more than you realize, human. My hold tightens.*—

That, I couldn't refute. For the first three nights after the eggs had cracked, I'd gone to bed wearing a clean nightgown and awoken wearing a dirty one. Each time, I'd had a vague memory of using a secret passage to reach Milo's chamber. He'd chosen to live in the catacombs of the palace, just as his father had done in Fleur.

Why was Leonora meeting with the warlock? As awful as she was, some part of her did care about Saxon. Well, *care* wasn't the right word. You didn't murder someone you cared about a first time, much less a second. She obsessed over him, her possessiveness boundless. What if she'd bought a spell from Milo, thinking to get rid of *me*?

Oh…weeds. On the fourth night, I'd refused to sleep. Same with the fifth night. I would refuse to sleep tonight, too, even though fatigue had turned my eyelids into cinder blocks. I wouldn't risk another meeting between Leonora and Milo.

"I'm the one in charge of the body right now," I reminded the phantom. A squatter. "Tell me how to care for the dragons. How did they respond to my scream?"

—*Fool. After a baby dragon matures in her egg, she remains in stasis until she hears the scream of a mother. Any mother. Most dragons don't care for their young. They bury their eggs for the continuation of the species, then forget about them, never returning.*—

What a relief. I hadn't taken the babies from the arms of a loving dragon mother.

—*Your scream should have been mine.*— Leonora prowled

through my mind, clawing at my thoughts. It hurt, but I didn't care. I thrilled at her every upset.

As much as Saxon wanted to punish her, I wanted to punish her more. For my mother's killer, I wouldn't settle for cleaning messy tents and retrieving soft, beautiful feathers.

Thoughts of Saxon's chores led to thoughts of Saxon. The next major tournament battle was set to begin later today, and I wanted to attend to scope out his competition. Where would the dragons be safest?

I refused to ask Leonora. I didn't trust her to tell the truth.

I could ask Noel and Ophelia to watch over the dragons, I supposed. Noel was the one who'd told me to scream at the eggs, after all, so she must have foreseen the result. Even better, she'd kept the secret from Saxon. Right? She must have. If she'd told him, he would stormed the palace, determined to kill the dragons straightaway.

My hands curled into tight fists. Saxon might be my prince, but I would not allow him to hurt my babies. If he tried, he would find himself entwined in our third world war.

What if he *didn't* try to hurt them, though? In battle, he was beyond ruthless; with me, the girl he had every reason to hate, he was sometimes almost…tender. I—me—ordinary Ashleigh—had power over him in ways the phantom did not, and oh, what a heady thought. I'd never had any kind of power over another person before. But then, according to my uninvited guest, I was more than Cinder to his prince. I was the original Leonora and Saxon's true fated, a notion as miraculous as it was astonishing.

Me. An actual fated one. It was somehow more baffling than being the star of a fairy tale.

Pagan whimpered. Pyre—the bigger dragon—must have gotten a bit too rough again.

"Com'ere, baby." I reached out and waved my fingers at her.

Little Pagan darted to me, perching on my shoulder to lean

over and nuzzle her cheek against mine. She must weigh around fifteen pounds, yet I didn't struggle to hold her up.

Pyre flounced over and curled at my feet, huffing a tendril of smoke in apology.

"I love you both so much, and I'll always do my best to protect you. You know that, right?" I could already guess where they fit in the fairy-tale prophecy. The fire that purified and burned, burned, burned.

Love for them burned in my heart—dragon fire, one could say. That love, those flames, made me stronger, inside and out.

The back of my neck prickled right before a female voice rang out. "Did someone order dragon-sitters, extra cheese?"

I lurched to my feet. Noel and Ophelia leaned on either side of a ruined bedpost, their ankles crossed. As if charged by the appearance of magical beings, the barrier reformed in my mind, blocking me from the phantom. Oh, thank goodness.

Pagan dropped to Pyre's side. The two flared their wings, and squawked at the oracle.

I patted the top of their heads. This was the first time I'd seen Noel since the night of the party. Ophelia had dropped by once before to sell me the spell. "Where are my other two dragon eggs, oracle?"

"They weren't ready to hatch, so I returned them to their underground nests."

Fairies could not lie. Okay. All right. The eggs were safe. I nodded, satisfied with her actions.

"Oh, one more thing, and it's so minor it hardly bears mentioning," she added with an airy tone. "You're late, you're late, for a very important date. Meaning, yes, your father demands your presence in the throne room immediately, and he says he won't tolerate any of your lollygagging."

What! "Why?" Unless… Had he learned about the dragons? He must have. Before this, he'd all but forgotten my existence.

Every day I'd hoped he would visit me. At the very least, he could have sent a servant to inquire about my well-being. Even that would have been a delight. But each one of those days I'd gotten hit with a punch of disappointment. I had to be bleeding internally by now.

"Maybe he heard what you did and hopes to thank you?" She shrugged.

That would be amazing. Earlier in the week, when Ophelia had sold me her spell, I'd paid an additional fee to bring two of my designs to life with magic. A sword with retractable spikes and a dagger with hooks that ran up the center of the blade.

Trying to buy his affections?

Well, yes. I knew he was capable of affection, and I wanted to experience it for myself. Just once, I wanted to know what it felt like to have a father look at me with approval.

As payment for this particular task, I'd had to part with two of the golden nails I'd taken from Saxon's tent. I'd hated doing it, but a girl had to do what a girl had to do. To my delight, the weapons I ordered had appeared atop my dresser bright and early this morning, along with a note.

All done. What's next?

I'd planned to have a full set of armor made before presenting the entire collection to my father.

"He for sure doesn't know about the dragons," Ophelia said, "so you don't have to get your panties in a twist wondering if he'll try to turn them into war dragons or whatever."

"A twist in my...you know what? Never mind." I shoved a dagger inside my skirt pockets—I wore a mourning gown I'd borrowed from Dior. She'd offered other, more colorful options, but I'd hoped this one would help me hide any specks of soot. I'd added the pockets myself.

"I'll go, and you'll—" what had she called it? "—dragon-sit?"

"Yes," the two replied in unison.

A grinning Noel shook her fist toward the ceiling, crying, "Girls just wanna have fun."

Ophelia massaged the back of her neck, as if resigned. "Dragons do put the *fun* in *funeral*."

I shifted from foot to foot. "Before I go, I need to know the truth. Are you planning to tell—or will you tell—or will you allude to—or will you have someone else tell or allude to Saxon that the dragons have hatched?" I wanted no misunderstanding between us.

"Trust me. We won't be telling Saxy *anything* about your scale-babies," Noel vowed, lifting a hand. "Because when we have a secret, we lock it in a vault and throw away the key. I've never, in all my days, told a single soul about the time Saxon vomited on my shoes. He asked me not to share, so I won't. Not ever. Now, wipe the cinder from your cheeks and go earn your slipper badge."

Would I ever get used to her odd speech? "How can you claim you won't tell anyone, while telling someone? Oracles are fae, and your fae magic forces you to speak only truth, yet you constantly contradict yourself."

She smiled so sweetly. "But, Ashleigh. It's never a lie if you believe it. Just ask Leonora."

How did she know—silly question. But what was the oracle hinting at? That Leonora had lied to me? That I was lying to myself, and I just didn't know it? Both? But what lie did we believe? And was Noel referencing the past or the future?

One more question, and my mind might break. "You know who I'm carting around, and yet you returned the eggs and told me how to wake the dragons anyway."

"I have many reasons for this." She hiked one shoulder. "Too many to list."

"I'm not asking you to list them all. Tell me one."

"Tell you one what?"

When she said nothing more, I sighed, crouched down and

opened my arms for Pagan and Pyre. As the babies nuzzled against me, I told them, "Mommy needs to leave for a little while. Stay here with the oracle and the witch. If they hurt you, eat them. Just be sure to spit out their bones. Those are a choking hazard."

Pagan bopped the tip of her nose against my chin, and Pyre licked my cheek. I smothered both of their beautiful faces with kisses before I straightened. I doubled-checked that the daggers I'd fashioned from pieces of broken furniture were still in place. Somehow, I found the strength to walk away from the most precious treasures in all the world.

As I trekked through a palace I hadn't yet learned to navigate, I passed servants who were cleaning priceless vases and bejeweled furnishings. My ears twitched as they whispered "Glass Princess" and "avian castoff."

I flushed, my head drooping, but only for a second. I forced my chin to lift. I was Cinder, mother of dragons, future phantom-slayer, and I would never be shamed again.

Candles burned in each room I entered, scenting the air with wax. In every hallway, my father's likeness adorned every wall, always hanging next to a large, full-length mirror framed in solid gold. After a few missed turns, I reached the throne room, where two guards waited at the closed doors. They must have been expecting me. They opened up in a hurry, allowing me to soar inside without pause.

No crowd awaited me this time, only more guards, my father, and Dior, who once again sat in my mother's throne. This time, I bore her no ill will. She could only sit where she was told.

I stopped before the dais. Despite my lack of rest, despite the physical exertion, my heartbeat remained steady. With the mystical barrier constantly falling, I had more and more access to Leonora's magic, which meant I had more access to her power, the ability's battery. That battery kept me charged up.

Would I sicken when I killed her? Did it matter? If I had to pick between living with her, or ending her reign of terror and possibly dying, I'd go with option B every time.

Hoping to impress, I executed my best curtsy. "Hello, Your Majesty."

"Ashleigh," my father said with a nod. He looked terrible. His eyes were bloodshot. He'd lost several pounds in a matter of days, his cheeks hollow. His clammy skin had a sallow tint.

Concern inundated me. "Are you all right? Is there anything I can—"

"Do not presume to question me." His voice lacked its usual authority. "I called you here because Dior is eager to attend today's battles. You will accompany her to ensure she is properly entertained."

He'd only wanted an escort for the daughter he adored?

Why couldn't he bear the slightest affection for me?

Just love me, Father. Please.

"I've missed you, Ashleigh." Dior unveiled her loveliest, brightest smile. "I hope you'll forgive the unexpected summons, but as the king said, I wish to attend the battles. I know we've missed the first and second rounds, but the royal oracle told me you wished to attend as well, and I thought that we could maybe, perhaps, if you'd like, go together and continue getting to know each other. The king isn't feeling well, so he's decided to remain here."

"Dior is quite curious about the avian." Father coughed, his entire body heaving. "You will tell her all about Prince Saxon, won't you, Ashleigh?"

I inhaled sharply, then hurried to blank my expression, unsure about what I was feeling. Anger? Hurt? Fear? Had Dior set her heart on Saxon?

Well, she couldn't have him. He was mine. My fated one, selected by destiny and—I cringed. I sounded just like Leonora.

"Yes, Father," I finally said. "I will do as you request."

"She is part of the fairy tale, you know," he continued, proudly patting her hand. "I am the king who hosts the ball, and she is the cinder girl. If Saxon is the prince, as I'm beginning to suspect, the two belong together."

A lump clogged my throat. Saxon and Dior...my father, peering at Dior as if she were the answer to his prayers...it was all too much.

"I'm part of 'The Little Cinder Girl,' too," I whispered.

"I haven't forgotten." He pursed his lips, giving me a look of distaste. "Let's hope you aren't the evil stepsister intent on keeping Cinder and the prince apart."

15

*We might have reached the middle of our tale,
but there are plenty more enemies to fell.*

Ashleigh

I rode a purple unicorn down the mountain trail, and Dior rode a pink one. A contingent of armed guards trailed behind us as we chatted.

"I don't think you're an evil stepsister, Ashleigh, and I'm so sorry that was said. And I don't think I'm Cinder, if I'm being honest. Or, I didn't. The royal oracle keeps asking me if my slippers are made for walking. Aren't all slippers made for walking, though? It seems like she's hinting that I'll be the one to wear the glass slippers, but I'm not sure. What do you think?"

"Well, I know you're not the evil stepsister, either." Should I tell her that I, too, believed myself to be Cinder?

"Oh! Did I tell you about my little sister, Marabella?" she asked, jumping to a new subject, the other already forgotten. "Well, *our* little sister now. She isn't part of our prophecy, but she's pretty special. And sad. I love our mother, and she loves us, but she expects us both to be perfect every minute of every day. We're to make no mistakes, never act improper, and guard our every word and action. We do it all knowing we'll be used as pawns one day. That we won't be allowed to marry for love. Not me, especially, the girl who has a magical ability to turn anything into gold. I must wed whoever is chosen for me. Well, whoever wins this tournament, I mean. Anything to strengthen the king's rule. He wants the strongest warrior in the land guarding me, after all. Someone who won't take me away to another kingdom, so we can remain a happy family." The words left her as if she were reciting something she'd heard repeated again and again. "The good of the kingdom matters more than one life."

Had she said these things the day we'd met, I might have laughed in her face. I would do anything to have my mother here, demanding I act perfectly. And I would do *anything* to acquire a magical ability like Princess Dior's. Turn something into gold to pay for the things I needed? Yes, please. But, she had problems and pains and obstacles of her own. She was being used as a pawn. Pawns never received a happily-ever-after.

"How does your ability work?" I asked. I had yet to see her turn anything into gold. "Do you control it?"

"Not at first." She ducked her head. "That's how my father died. I accidentally turned his entire body into gold." Agony laced her voice, and I sympathized. We'd both harmed a parent in irreparable ways. "With practice, I learned how to switch the ability on and off. But I only have enough power to make a certain amount of gold each day, and the king has ensured I always reach that limit by nightfall. That's why I only tried to visit your room eight times these past few days. I was too tired to visit the other three hundred and seventy-two times I considered it."

Eight. As in…eight? "I'm so sorry about your father. I know a loss like that remains a part of you. I'm also sorry for my rudeness. I must not have heard you knock." The spell around the room only stopped noises from leaving, so, the dragons must have drowned out the knocking.

"I envy you so much," Dior said, her tone wistful.

"Um…what?"

"You are able to ignore a summons whenever you wish. You come and go from the palace as you please. You spend time in a tent with a beautiful avian prince. Alone."

I exhaled. "What a pair we make, huh? I have been envious of you."

"Oh, that's so wonderful to hear. I mean…" She groaned. "I'm ruining this, aren't I?"

We shared a laugh. When we reached the end of the mountain path, we left our unicorns with one of the guards and walked down the cobblestone path that led to the entrance of the marketplace. The other guards trailed us. Multiple vendors sold drawings of their favorite combatants, bells to ring during the fight, and ribbons to wave.

Anyone who spotted Dior smiled, as if they were seeing an old friend. I was mostly ignored, as if my father's disdain had spread. For once, I didn't mind. I had the love of two dragons. I was good.

Dior hooked arms with me when we reached the coliseum. We scaled the steps together. I didn't tire until we reached the dais. At my urging, Dior claimed the king's throne, and I claimed the queen's, happy to sit where my mother would have. The guards who'd followed us formed a half circle behind us, acting as a wall of protection.

No combatants were on the field yet, so I picked up our conversation. "What's Azul like?" I asked. "I've always wondered."

Her eyes sparkled. "Well, there are two kingdoms, one underwater for the mer-folk and one topside for the mortals. We have a season of storms, but mostly our days are wonderfully warm, the scent of coconuts and orchids drifting on the breeze. Our palace is a massive structure that floats over the ocean. We have a new view every morning. You simply *must* visit one day."

"I think I'd like that."

"I'll show you all my favorite spots," she replied with a grin. Then she clapped, bouncing in her seat as the master of ceremonies took his place in the corner of the dais, several feet away. "Oh, this is so exciting. The third battle is only seconds away!"

I meant to smile back, but my attention got snagged by the warriors running onto the battlefield. Two battles had taken place already, with a wolfin taking home the first victory and Milo taking home the second. Thanks to sand stained with crimson, it was clear both battles had been violent. Both winners had won a few of the voluntary contests, and they'd had advantages over the others. Thankfully, Saxon had won advantages, too.

I'd cheered every time I'd heard his name called through my window.

After the master of ceremonies made his speech, the battle horn blew, signaling the start of the heat. As the men rushed together, punching and kicking, I stroked my mother's ring, and watched, riveted, as one of the mighty elven ripped through his opponents, while pixies dropped intoxibombs from the air. Soon those bombs got the better of him, allowing a goblin to end him.

Pixie wings produced a special dust. That dust created intoxibombs. Anyone who inhaled it remained in a state of confusion for several minutes, making the battle more difficult.

The intoxibombs slowed the goblin down, but they didn't stop him, and he managed to fight his way to victory.

A snake-shifter won the fourth heat, though he and his opponents actually passed out from the effects of the intoxibombs.

Snakes were known as the most hedonistic of the species, constantly using intoxibombs for fun, so it was no wonder this one woke first and slaughtered everyone else.

Other heats started and ended. Finally, the second to last drew to a close. As soon as the bodies were cleared from the field, a countdown clock ticked inside my head. The final battle heat would kick off in five minutes, twenty-nine…twenty-eight…twenty-seven seconds.

I all but bounced in my seat.

The five who remained—Eve's fae, a giant, a gorgon, a vampire, and Saxon. Thankfully, the avian would have a weapon. Others might not. Still. The danger he was soon to face…

Five minutes, eighteen seconds.

"Oh, dear. I'm so sorry I didn't notice earlier, but you have a little soot on your brow." Dior withdrew a handkerchief from the sleeve of her gown and gently wiped my face.

I sat in silence, allowing her to clean me. A supposed servant's chore. What if we were *both* Cinder? Could a prophecy tell more than one girl's story at the same time? The fairy tales had the ability to repeat and twist, so why not have multiple versions transpiring in unison? Her prince would be different from mine, and we'd find him one way or another.

"May I offer you a maple tartlet, Princess?" An older servant approached Dior, extending a silver platter. "They are a Sevónian delicacy."

She bestowed a bright smile upon the man as she selected a treat, and he smiled back.

I reached up to select a tartlet of my own, and his smile faded. I sighed and collected my pastry.

He returned his gaze to Dior, growing grave. "Be sure not to venture into the forest today, Princess." He looked left, then right, then leaned toward her to whisper, "Someone spotted the Evil Queen this morn."

Dior gasped, clearly scandalized to her very soul. With a tremor in her voice, she asked, "What terrible things did this Evil Queen do?"

The servant replied, "I'm told she builds an army to defy the king. Did you know she even turned her own blood to poison so that anyone who encounters her blood will sicken?"

"Oh. Well. That's…bad?" I said. "Where was she spotted, exactly? That way I can *definitely* avoid that area of the forest. Like, really stay far away from it." Before, I'd written off this evil queen just like everyone else. But I knew better than to trust the tales of others now. So. I wouldn't be making a decision about Queen Everly Morrow until I'd gotten to know her.

I could ask her about her powers. If she knew anything about phantoms. If she knew a good place to hide dragons…for no particular reason other than curiosity, of course.

The crowd erupted with cheers, excitement crackling in the air.

The servant rushed off, but I'd already lost interest in him. This was it. Five warriors jogged to the center of the field. There was Eve's fae…the vampire…the gorgon…the giant with massive horns protruding from his scalp…and Saxon.

I hadn't seen him in forever. For. Ever. He looked rougher than I'd expected, his dark hair in disarray, his eyes bloodshot, and his jaw covered with thicker stubble than usual. He also looked bigger, as if he'd gained another fifty pounds of solid muscle—as if he packed cinder blocks of rage beneath his skin. I fanned my cheeks.

"I think this is the round where armor is off limits for some," Dior said, clapping. "Look at that strength."

How would Saxon handle the intoxibombs? Already the pixies hovered in the air, awaiting their cue.

I'd always loved pixies. They were playful, sometimes vindictive, but always truthful. About the size of my hand, they looked like miniature avian.

Dior squealed with delight. "Look at those wings. That face. Those muscles. I could just take my hands and—" A blush spread over her cheeks. "I mean, Saxon seems very smart."

"Trust me," I said, my tone dry, "I get it." Like I could really blame her, anyway. She had eyes.

"I've wanted to speak to him ever since our first meeting, but he's always peered right through me. Then I witnessed him act so cruelly to you that day in the throne room, and I decided he wasn't worth my time. But *then*, under your influence, he softened, and I couldn't help but take a second and third glance. Unless you like him? I thought you two were sworn enemies, but now I'm not sure. And I promise you, I had planned to feel very guilty about marrying my stepsister's sworn enemy. For a little while. Probably." Her gaze moved over the field, only to stop abruptly and widen. "How is Saxon supposed to win against a giant? What if the giant wins the tournament, and I'm forced to wed him?"

New sympathy for her welled. "Saxon will win this round." He must. And if he didn't... No. He would. "Our prophecy has yet to be fulfilled, and he's part of it. Plus, he won the right to wield a weapon...then he lost the right to wield it, won a boon, lost a boon, then finally won another weapon."

He wore a shirt made of metal mesh, those muscles on display. Black leather pants molded to his thighs. His wings appeared white, as if they'd been smeared with...ash? I wondered about the significance. Was he saying hello to me? Maybe?

The master lifted the magical horn that was able to amplify his volume. "Welcome one, welcome all to the final battle of the day. I'm not sure how many of you attended our first nine heats—" cheers resounded "—or how many missed them?" Boos rang out. He laughed. "As you know, the purpose of each heat is simple. Be the last combatant standing. So, are you ready to unleash the last group of beasts?"

The cheers were deafening, and I waited with baited breath for the horn to sound. Saxon kept his back to me. Did he know I was here? Did he care?

The horn blared at last. I tensed as the fighters rushed forward. Like the others, they punched, and they kicked. They clawed, and they bit. Saxon's wings both helped and hurt him, allowing him to move at speeds the others couldn't track, but also giving the others more real estate to grab or harm.

I winced when the giant ripped out a fistful of feathers.

For his weapon, Saxon had chosen a plain, ordinary dagger, but he wasn't using it, and I didn't understand why.

Dior leaned into me, whispering, "Which warrior do you watch so raptly? The one I suspect?"

"Yes. I watch Saxon, as you do." I wouldn't deny it. "He's a good person sometimes, and I need—I want him to survive." I wanted him to have the life Leonora had denied him.

"I see," she said, and released a slight puff of breath. Would *she* become my enemy now? "Ashleigh, I need to know the truth, so there's no confusion between us. Do you want Saxon for yourself? Even if he wins the tournament?"

"No," I said, the negation bursting from me. "Maybe?" I corrected more calmly. "But he would never... I would never..." *Ugh.* "We have too much bad blood between us." At least, that was how it seemed right now. If fate had other plans for Cinder and her prince, as I hoped, I was willing to sacrifice my animosity. Because I was kind. "But, um, what if I did want him for myself?" How would she react?

To my shock, she replied, "I'd ask the king to allow Saxon to choose between us."

Had I detected a note of smugness? Did she think no one in their right mind would choose me if she was an option? Was she evil, after all?

Or maybe I'd heard what I'd expected to hear, due to past experience.

I closed my eyes for a moment and nodded. Yes. I'd let the rejection of others color my perception of the moment. Dior was being genuinely kind to me, and I was being petty. Even now she watched me with hope and eagerness, as if she feared her response wasn't good enough. And really, I wanted Saxon happy. He *deserved* to live the life Leonora had denied him.

And maybe I did, too? I would forever feel guilt for what happened to my mother, but in the bright light of day, I couldn't blame myself as ferociously as before. I'd been a child, ignorant of what was happening to me. I'd had no real defenses other than the barrier, and it had failed me.

I shouldn't have to carry guilt for my mother's death. Leonora was to blame.

If Saxon knew the truth about my possession, he might kill me to kill the phantom. Would she die with me, though, or would she live on?

I didn't want her free, able to hurt others. I didn't want her suppressed, just biding her time; I wanted her dead. She'd told me I couldn't survive without her. But the evil stepmother couldn't be trusted. She never had Cinder's well-being in mind.

The crowd gave a collective gasp, and I whipped my attention to the fight. The vampire had clawed the fae's chest directly over his heart. The fae had a weapon, too. A dagger. But like Saxon, he hadn't used it. Hadn't even unsheathed it. Why, why, why? There was no reason good enough.

Saxon shot up, up into the air, his fingers tangled in the gorgon's hair. The gorgon flailed beneath him, but the avian showed no mercy, drawing back his arm and flinging the other male at the troll, sending the two flying away from the fae.

Before Saxon could descend, the giant latched on to his wing and yanked. A pop reverberated, and I flinched, the crowd giving another collective gasp. Saxon collapsed, but he rebounded swiftly, flying around and around the giant's feet, twisting his shoestrings together. Then he pushed, wrenching the beast off his feet.

When the giant hit the ground, the entire coliseum shook. Dust plumed the air, rock scraping against rock. Heart racing, I clutched the arms of my throne and tilted forward, closer to the action. Saxon hovered near the giant, preparing to strike. How slowly he moved now. I looked him over, noticing the odd angle of the injured wing, and groaned. The pain he must be suffering. And the pixies hadn't even dropped their bombs yet.

The avian descended, thrusting his sword down...

With a roar, the giant swung a beefy arm. He nailed Saxon in the head, flinging him a good length across the field.

I jumped to my feet. My avian landed in the dirt with a hard thump. One second passed, two, three, but he didn't get up. He didn't even move.

Concern for him propelled me from the dais. I pushed through the crowd, my heart knocking against my ribs. I didn't care about any physical discomfort. I had other worries, Leonora attempting to wrest control from me, wanting to be the one to save Saxon. I fought back.

Get to Saxon. Just get to Saxon.

"Ashleigh? What are you doing?" Dior called. From the ensuing rustle, I suspected she had jumped to her feet and given chase. "You shouldn't leave without a guard. The king told me it isn't safe."

I'd attended the party without a problem. I wouldn't be attacked now. I didn't slow. Leonora continued to claw at our barrier, her frenzy feeding mine. *Must get to Saxon.*

The tips of my fingers burned, a desire to torch everyone in my path consuming me. *Her* desire. *She's winning?* "If you care for him so much, why have you harmed him in each incarnation? And don't tell me it's so you can start over."

She *humphed.* —*My life, my business.*—

The gall. "I'll tell you, then." Truth was the only weapon that worked against a lie—it was the only weapon I had right now. Still pushing my way down the steps, I told her, "You killed him because you were angry with him. He didn't choose to be with you, and you punished him for it."

—*Of course I did.*— The words hissed through my mind.

—He gave me the world, and then took it away. But I will get it back. He will love me again.—

"You cannot reap love when you sow hate." I bumped into someone and bounced back, then mumbled an apology and flitted around them.

A hard hand clamped around my bicep, stopping me midway. I gasped and flipped up my gaze. My stomach dropped.

Trio towered over me, his features contorted with rage. "If it isn't my favorite glass doll," he said with a cruel grin.

I thrust my hand into my pocket, gripping one of my daggers. "Let go."

Leaning down, pressing his nose into mine, he said, "Every time I visited the Temple, I obeyed my queen's orders. You harmed her son, so, she harmed you in turn. A task she would have overseen herself, if you were worthy."

"Let. Go."

He tightened his grip. "The prince punished me for being too rough with you, choosing to support a princess rather than his own soldier. But that's all right. I'm back with the queen, and she's given me a new order. One I like very much indeed."

I masked a wince, preparing to strike at him. I'd never stabbed anyone. If he held me much longer, I would do it, whatever the consequences. "I'm done talking to you. Let me go and move out of my way, or I will take measures against you."

The people around us were too busy watching the battle to notice or care about the Glass Princess and an avian warrior.

Dior reached me and frantically pulled on the back of my gown. "Guards! Help us," she shouted, but her voice didn't carry over the cheers. "Guards! They're almost upon us, Ashleigh. All will be well."

Trio kept his gaze locked on me and grinned another twisted, evil grin. "The avian queen wants you dead. But first, she asked me to make you bleed."

I did it. I struck, freeing the dagger and jabbing it at his gut.

I was new to battle. He wasn't. He easily batted my hand away. Defeated already?

Grin widening, he slapped his free hand over my throat. One squeeze and he cut off my air.

Panic engulfed me. The guards wouldn't reach us in time. I needed to move, but I couldn't. I could only punch at his arm.

I tried to breathe. I tried so hard. My lungs burned. A tide of dizziness invaded my head, and I thought I heard Dior scream. Black dots wove through my vision, and a high-pitched screech erupted in my ears. Suddenly I could hear nothing else—until a ferocious roar echoed through the coliseum.

The next thing I knew, the pressure on my throat eased and I dropped, my legs unable to support me. As I sucked in mouthfuls of air, the dizziness ebbed and the black dots faded.

Saxon loomed directly behind Trio, in the air, his expression marked by the most malicious rage I'd ever beheld. His broken wing labored to flap, barely able to hold him in place.

I scrambled back. Had he seen me attempt to stab his soldier and had stopped everything to punish me?

In a blur of motion, he snapped Trio's neck with a single, violent yank. Shock held me immobile. What was even happening right now?

The avian's knees buckled. Saxon grabbed him by the hair before he could hit the ground, flew him to the battlefield—and dropped him into the middle of the fray.

16

Will he show mercy to a foe?
The answer is always no.

SAXON

Impulses tore through me, one after the other, shredding my control. I wanted Adriel to feel the full breadth of my wrath. I wanted to gather Ashleigh in my arms and do for her what she'd done for me. I wanted to obliterate anyone who ever thought to harm her again.

I'd had half my attention on the battle, half on Ashleigh and the tracker spell inside my head, and it had cost me dearly, ensuring I took more hits than I should have. Divided attention *always* came with a cost. Yet, I couldn't regret my actions. Being so attuned to Ashleigh, I'd known when she'd pushed through the crowd. I'd known the moment she was stopped. I'd known when Adriel had clasped her vulnerable throat…

A dagger-sharp growl ravaged my throat, what remained of my calm veneer disintegrating. Adriel was two hundred pounds of muscle, and he had choked a young girl with a damaged heart. I'd lost all sense, flying over to break his neck—

nonfatal for an avian. Then I'd dropped him into the combat zone. The rules stated we could not leave the coliseum, and I hadn't. The stands were part of the coliseum and no one could say otherwise.

Now Adriel lay on the ground, unmoving, his gaze pleading for mercy he hadn't shown Ashleigh.

I could only indulge one of my desires right now. I looked to the giant, as if to say, *He's all yours.* Whether the move would help me or hurt me with my people, I didn't know. While they valued loyalty to one's species, they also believed one should obey his king. Adriel had not done so.

Skylair blood flowed through my veins. With or without the title, I *was* king three times over. I would be obeyed.

Laughing, the giant stepped on Adriel's head, crushing his skull—highly fatal for *anyone.*

I landed, reentering the fray without a shred of remorse.

Desperate to return to Ashleigh and whisk her to Everly, who could syphon from healers and mend her face, I forgot about proving I was strong enough to rule and vicious enough to rule well. I fought dirtier than ever. I jabbed eyes and kneed groins. Punched and clawed. The only thing I couldn't do? Stab. The dagger I'd chosen possessed a retractable blade to better "murder" Roth. The same weapon Roth had chosen for himself, just in case mine got lost in the fray.

Moving too fast to track, the vampire clawed my side, hitting bone. I let him take another swipe, just so I could catch his wrist, spin him around while yanking him against me, and rip out his throat with my bare hand. He toppled, but he never hit the ground. The giant scooped him up between meaty fingers.

The gorgon must have gained dominion over the giant's mind, because he now rode atop his massive shoulders, cheering as the giant ripped the vampire in half. Blood and viscera sprayed over the battlefield.

One combatant down. Three remained.

"Look out," Roth called.

The warning came a split second too late. As if the pixies had been waiting for the first casualty, they launched their first bomb right at my feet. Dust and glitter exploded, pluming the air, and I inadvertently inhaled a mouthful. My eyes burned, and my throat itched. I coughed so hard I might have cracked a rib. I... I... I frowned and pulled hanks of my hair. What... why... I couldn't think. I needed to think!

An iron-hard fist that had to belong to the giant slammed into my temple, and I wheeled to the left. On the plus side, the fog lifted from my mind, my thoughts my own once again. Stupid pixie dust. At least the giant stumbled about, too.

The gorgon jumped off him, crashing into Roth. The two rolled over the dirt, punching at each other.

My blood burned hot as I jogged...sprinted over, reaching the giant in record time. I leaped up and spun midair, extending my broken wing as far as it would go. Ignoring the spike of agonizing pain, I raked one of my many joint-hooks through the base of a horn. Amid his screams, his pain clearly excruciating, the appendage plopped to the ground.

I swooped down to pick it up, Roth and the gorgon still rolling around.

"Let him," I shouted, knowing Roth alone would understand.

My friend let the gorgon pin him, allowing me to ram the tip of the horn through his shoulder blades. The tip exited his chest, pieces of heart muscle clinging to it.

The gorgon slumped over and fell, and Roth scrambled to his feet.

Two opponents down, only the giant to go. *Hurry. Must get to Ashleigh.*

My gaze locked with Roth's. We nodded in unison because we knew what the other needed to do next.

Roth threw himself at the giant, climbing him just to whisper in his ear, "You are still confused." With a spoken command, Roth could compel almost anyone to do anything. He could tell the giant to off himself, and the giant would obey, but citizens would wonder why the giant had done something like that, after fighting so hard to survive.

Few beings possessed the ability to compel with their voice and those that did hid it because people feared what they couldn't control. However, any confusion at this time would be blamed on the new intoxibombs being dropped.

As the giant alternated between kicking Roth and punching his own temples to combat his newest bout of confusion, he flung Roth several feet away. As the warrior came to his feet, he dodged a bomb but took a fist to the skull.

I freed the horn from the gorgon, then yanked one of the vampire's fangs free. His venom would stun the giant long enough for me to render a killing blow.

Roth was severely battered and tiring fast, while the giant was still going strong. I wasn't faring much better than my friend, my energy levels depleted, my wings broken in multiple places. Even still, I flew up, up, rising behind the giant as Roth launched a campaign to distract him.

Every flap of my wings taught me a new lesson in agony.

When the giant clutched Roth around the waist and lifted him, no doubt intending to rip him apart, I struck, sinking the fang into the gooey center of his severed horn.

With a roar, he toppled. His massive body jerked as he struggled to move his limbs. As Roth rolled from his loosened grip, I tightened my hold on the horn and just started hacking, crimson pulp flying in every direction until his head detached from his body.

By the holy skies, three down. Only one combatant to go. The one who planned to die.

Urgency drove me toward Roth, who staggered to his feet.

So close to victory, to tending Ashleigh. I wouldn't waste a second; I would catch my breath after.

He offered the barest nod, permission to do whatever proved necessary to sell our one-on-one battle. Which I did, knowing Everly would heal him the second the battle ended. I threw a hard punch, nailing him in the jaw. He careened to the side and fell, spitting blood and teeth he would regrow in minutes with his own magic. On the ground, he twitched and struggled to rise. Exaggerated, I knew, but still guilt flared.

I dropped to my knees, my legs braced on both sides of his body. I unsheathed the dagger and slowly lifted it, letting the crowd spy the glint of metal.

As the audience twittered with excitement, I struck, slamming the retractable blade against Roth's chest, right over his heart. He jerked, then sagged into the dirt and held his breath.

Trembling, panting, I sheathed the dagger, ensuring no one could study it, then lumbered to my feet. Four opponents down. I'd done it. I'd won the battle heat, carnage all around me. I would advance to the semifinals.

The crowd erupted with thunderous applause.

"The tenth and final battle heat has a winner!" the master of ceremonies called. "Congratulations, Crown Prince Saxon Skylair. Take a bow." To the audience, he said, "Along with our other nine battle heat winners, Saxon will advance to our second week and compete in the semifinals, which will have two parts, doubling your fun." The cheers rose and quieted, and he continued on. "Be sure to come back at dawn to witness the next volunteer competition. It's a test of speed, and the winner gets to ask a boon of our great king."

I stumbled toward the stands, my vision blurring as blood dripped into my eyes. I wiped the droplets away with a shaky hand. No matter how badly I hurt, I would spread my wings and fly to Ashleigh.

Before I mustered the strength to take off, a door to the

combatant quarters opened up underneath the stands, brighter rays of torchlight spilling onto the field. Two rows of guards marched out.

If they tried to stop me, they would die.

When the two rows parted, a smiling Ashleigh and a frowning Dior were revealed. My attention remained on Ashleigh, who wore a mourning gown.

Relief spiked within me. Ashleigh was well, and finally within my reach. There were no tears in her eyes. Though a bruise had already formed on her throat, she never lost her smile.

I didn't understand. She'd been choked. A man under my command had attacked her. She should be raging at me. I'd failed her. When she'd needed me most, I'd failed her. The guilt...

"I'm so proud of you," she said, rushing over to examine my injuries. "But you needed a better dagger. There's something wrong with the one you—"

"Ashleigh," I said. I should have known she'd notice the faulty blade. "Now isn't the time, Princess."

"Yes, yes. You're right. Oh, Saxon. Your poor body. You have so many gashes. And your wings."

Forget my pain. Her hands fluttered over me, and it was one of the greatest experiences of my life. No one special had ever ministered to me after a battle. I hadn't known to want such a thing. You got hurt, someone patched you, the end. This was something to crave. "The first thing you do after getting choked is lecture me on the proper weaponry?" I suddenly wanted to grin. "Only you, Asha."

"You could have *died*. Of course I'm going to lecture you."

My heart warmed. "But we are enemies," I said softly, hesitantly. "Shouldn't you want me dead?"

"Probably, but I don't, okay?" She shifted, as if uncomfortable with this line of conversation. "Let's get you to a healer before you collapse. But I refuse to carry you, do you hear me, so don't even ask."

The grin spread, unstoppable. Despite everything, this girl cared about my well-being.

I wrapped my arms around her, tugging her closer. She offered no protests, just melted into my body, reminding me of our perfect fit.

"You shouldn't be flying," she told me. "Let's walk—"

I spread my broken wings and launched us into the air, heading for the campground. The farther we flew, the more grueling the flight became. Wind beat against my every wound, stinging like acid, and agony throbbed in every joint and muscle, but I pushed through. I wanted Ashleigh safely ensconced in my tent as soon as possible.

"I need to return to the palace," she said. She nuzzled her cheek against mine, petting me. Her touch was so gentle, so tender, I caught myself leaning into every stroke.

"You need a healer. One is going to meet us in the tent."

"*You* need a healer. You're injured, and carrying me isn't helping. I'm hurting you."

I wanted to bury my face in the hollow of her neck and breathe in her sweet scent. "I'm going to hurt regardless, Asha. This way, at least, I get to keep the rest of the world at bay."

She went quiet for a moment. "Maybe I can stay with you while the healer works on you, but then I'm going to return to the palace, okay?"

Part with her, when I'd only just gotten her back? That, I couldn't promise.

I let my gaze hold hers for a moment, only a moment. Tone soft, I told her, "I'm sorry Adriel attacked you. I'm sorry he tormented you at the Temple. I never ordered him to do so. Most of all, I'm sorry I didn't take measures to protect you."

"He admitted your mother sent him." Her voice was as soft as mine. "She sent him to hurt me this time, too."

I popped my jaw and nodded, believing her utterly. "Raven will be punished." I should have known this would happen, just as I should have known about the visits to the Temple. Why had I ever thought my mother would have too much pride to send a soldier on her behest? If she could watch her husband attempt to kill her son without intervening, she would harm anyone by proxy.

In both of my previous lives, my mother had despised Leonora. The two went head-to-head and each time the witch won. For round three, Queen Raven had possessed advanced knowledge, thanks to the journals. She'd suspected Ashleigh's true identity and had probably wanted the avian to provoke the girl into using fire magic before rendering a kill.

Though I understood her motives—though I had *lived* her motives—I wouldn't let this go. She had disobeyed my orders. Now her authority as queen would be forever stripped.

We reached the campground a few minutes later. I flew Ashleigh straight to my tent. Avian warriors surrounded it, as usual, and all bowed in deference as I carried my beautiful bundle inside. Few met my gaze, however, and I knew they wondered if I could turn on them as easily as I'd turned on Adriel.

I would explain later. Obey me, and you had nothing to fear.

"Let's get you cleaned up before the healer gets here," I said to my princess, setting her on her feet and ushering her to the pallet.

"Let's get you cleaned up first. I got squeezed. You took a baker's dozen to the face."

I sat, dragging her down with me. She puffed out a breath before relaxing, easing her head against my shoulder.

"You should let me up so I can source any supplies the healer might need," she said.

"Eve will be here shortly to—she'll have a healer with her." Avian didn't have magical powers, so Everly couldn't act as our healer today. Not with Ashleigh in the tent. Thankfully, we had a backup. "He will ensure we mend." Roth could use his voice compulsion, and Ashleigh would never know it.

"I don't need a healer, I really don't," she said, stroking the ring Craven had given Leonora. A nervous tell. What had her worried? "I meant what I said. I need to leave soon. I've been gone from my—palace far too long. Yes, my palace. That isn't weird. That's normal. I definitely need to return there."

For once, I had no desire to rip the ring from its chain. In that moment, I liked that she bore Craven's mark. With a single glance, others would know: hurt her and suffer the Destroyer's wrath.

"I'm not going to punish you, Ashleigh." Not now...not ever again? "I know you aren't Leonora."

She gasped. "You do?"

"You do not bear her memories. Two people with different experiences cannot be the same."

"I...you're right. Of course. This is goodbye, then."

Why did she wish to leave? Had I scared her with my cruelties on the battlefield?

I think the fissure in my chest cracked wider.

"I would like you to stay with me the rest of the night, Asha. Will you?" It was the closest I'd ever come to begging. I needed to be her guard tonight.

She yawned. "I'm worried about my dr— I just want to return to the palace. I like it there. But don't worry, I don't need you to fly me. I'm not tired." Another yawn. "Not even a little. You won't have to hurt yourself further."

Why this insistence? "It's dark outside. I don't want you walking the campgrounds without an escort."

"One of your soldiers can escort me, then."

Before, she'd been terrified of the avian. Now she wished to brave their presence in order to escape me? "Let me rephrase. I don't want you walking the campgrounds without *me* as an escort. I trust no one else with your safety."

Confusion glowed in those emerald eyes. "But—" She thought for several seconds before her expression firmed with determination. "Do you remember the dragon eggs you stole from me?"

I swallowed a groan. Noel and Ophelia still guarded the four eggs on my behalf. "Yes," I said, cautious. I didn't wish to deny the request I knew was coming, but I couldn't comply, either. I couldn't give her back the eggs, allowing her to raise another dragon army. History would surely repeat itself then, past Leonora becoming present Ashleigh, all of the Avian Mountains soon to burn to the ground.

How many times could one kingdom rebuild before it just... stopped?

"Say the dragons were to hatch," she said, plucking at the furs. "Not that it could actually happen or anything, but let's say it could. No, let's say it did, even though it definitely didn't. And won't. Ever. What would you do?"

I could not, would not lie to her, whatever the consequences. There was enough bad blood between us. Hardening my resolve, I told her, "I would slay the dragons for the good of Enchantia. When they rampage... I cannot describe the screams, the odors, the death toll without making you sicken. Survivors will be unable to recover without the aid of magic. Food sources will vanish in a few days' time, leaving those survivors to starve. That's how Leonora was able to kill me twice before. She weakened me with destruction and hunger, then stabbed me in the heart." If not for Noel's warning, I would have already tried to smash the eggs. Not that it would do me any good. Dragon eggs could be as hard as iron.

Tension stole through Ashleigh, bit by bit. "Well," she said with a deadened tone. "I'm ready to return to the palace now. By the way, I've begun remembering some of Leonora's memories. You were right. I'm her, and she's me."

My blood iced over. The transformation had begun, then. Soon, she would be the Leonora of old, Ashleigh no more.

The pressure intensified, my two-week timetable dropping days left and right.

The tent flap lifted. Everly and Roth strode inside, one after the other. The sorceress wore her avian illusion again, and Roth wore the face of a new fae, as we'd planned.

The pair stopped and took in Ashleigh's position on my lap.

Roth arched a brow. Everly grinned.

"Princess Ashleigh," I said, "I'd like you to meet... Roe. A healer."

"Oh, yes. Healer. That's him." Everly hiked her thumb at Roth, then motioned for him to proceed her. "By all means, do your thing, Dr. McHottie."

He hesitated before closing the distance to crouch before us. He was uncomfortable about using his ability with her, like this, but I wanted those bruises gone.

When he reached for me, I shook my head and said, "The girl first."

Blink, blink. He glanced over his shoulder at Everly.

The sorceress shrugged before asking, "Are you sure? You look near death, and she has an owie."

"The girl first," I repeated.

"Don't listen to him," Ashleigh cried. "Obviously, he has *severe* brain damage. The worst. Of course you should heal him first."

"The girl," I insisted, and yes, I was just as surprised as my friend. Maybe I did have some brain damage. But that crack... it had gone deeper, something breaking inside me this time.

I needed Ashleigh's pain gone before I could focus on my own.

I wanted her with me. I didn't want to go another day without her.

I wanted her to *be* with me.

I wanted the promise of what I'd found with her already. Smiles, kindness, and acceptance.

I wanted her so badly I expected my wings to start producing amour at any moment. But I'd felt that way both times before and never had.

So what *could* I have with her?

Ever my friend, Roth took Ashleigh's hands and muttered, "You will heal…right now…let my healing magic flow through you."

A pause. Then, "Ohhh. My throat is tingling."

Her delight caused the corners of my mouth to lift.

Roth repeated the process with me, but my wounds went deeper, and I didn't tingle, I throbbed. The fractures in my bones closed and the swelling drained from my joints. Gashes wove back together. I breathed through it all, comforted when Ashleigh linked our fingers, holding my hand.

Just as the process completed, laughter sounded outside, a new celebration kicking off.

Ashleigh jumped up as if she'd just been biding her time, wrenching from my embrace, severing contact. "Well. Look at you. All better. Now you need your rest. In private. I'll just grab a guard outside and hurry home, like we discussed. Yes, yes." She didn't wait for my response; she barreled out of the tent. Or tried to. The border spell knocked her back.

She whirled on me, eyes flashing. "Why can't I leave?"

"Border spell," I reminded her.

"Let me out."

"Go, then." I waved, shooing her off, granting her the permission she needed to slip past the boundary. I think I was… pouting.

She spun on her heel and raced away, not looking back.

I could only sit there, stunned. I'd just discovered another difference between Ashleigh and Leonora. Leonora had vied for my attention, and I hadn't liked it. Ashleigh continuously ran from me, and I hated this far more.

Roth patted my knee, his eyes glittering with mirth. "You're going to follow her, yes?"

"Yes." I lurched to my feet and shot out of the tent. What I'd do when I caught up to her, though, I didn't know.

17

Hush, hush, baby, don't you cry.
When the truth comes out, the lies will die.

Ashleigh

I didn't bother recruiting an avian guard. Since I had no idea which ones remained loyal to Queen Raven, I knew I would be better off on my own. Besides, Saxon wanted me protected, and I had a dagger, the perfect guard and the best way to protect myself. So, in a way, I had selected a guard, after all, obeying his orders.

My heart galloped at full speed as I ran from the tent, urgency giving my feet wings. Hearing Saxon's plans for any living dragons… I had to get Pagan and Pyre away as swiftly as possible.

I had to hide them.

How many others would fear my babies, hoping to kill them? How many would want them dead?

I hurried around a tree, then another and another, my brow wrinkling. Had even more trees sprouted around the camp?

Someone must be using magic to raise them, and I could think of only one reason—to better hide.

As spectators and combatants returned, overcrowding the walkways between tents, I used the trees to my advantage, masking my presence with shadows. There weren't as many individuals as before, but everyone's emotions were higher. Some people were overly excited by the day's events, while others oozed anger or sadness.

Just get to your babies. If anyone would be strong enough to harm a dragon, it was Saxon. He'd defeated a vampire, a gorgon, a fae, and a giant. A giant. He'd killed Trio right in front of me.

Why had Saxon put my welfare above his own soldier's? Something he'd done in front of other avian warriors, who'd been watching in the stands. And why had he held me afterward as if I were some kind of lifeline he needed to survive?

I knew we were Cinder and the prince, but this seemed too good to be true.

I must be misremembering what happened. Crown Prince Saxon Skylair didn't cherish me…yet. And he shouldn't. Not until I killed Leonora. I *had* to kill the phantom. Not just for revenge, though that would be nice. I didn't want anyone else getting saddled with her.

And then what? Saxon's family would never approve of our relationship, and his people would never respect the Glass Princess. Which was moot. *I* didn't want a relationship with *him*. I couldn't be with someone who plotted the murder of my— what had Noel called them? Oh, yeah. Scale-babies.

Weird noises erupted behind me. I threw a frantic glance over my shoulder. Thick darkness greeted me, broken by thin beams of moonlight and the occasional torch. No one seemed to pay any undue attention to me, but I quickened my pace. Maybe I should have requested a guard, after all.

More noises. A *whoosh, whoosh* making me tense. There was

a grunt, then a thud. I trembled as I threw another glance over my shoulder. Still didn't seem to be in anyone's crosshairs.

Finally I reached the cobblestone path that led to the palace. The iron archway of hanging wisteria perfumed the air. Someone—or several someones—had tied different colored ribbons to the sides, and those ribbons twirled in the breeze. The guards were long gone, of course, taking my unicorn with them. I'd have to walk the path. Alone. In the dark.

Deep breath in, out. I clutched my dagger higher, the ends of my fingers heating as I accessed a tendril of Leonora's magic. Trembling, I motored up, up the mountain.

I hit the halfway mark, still going strong. I would get to my babies, and that was that.

Another thud sounded behind me, and I jerked around— Saxon stood in a beam of moonlight, a large troll at his feet. A large troll who'd been following me without my knowledge? I gulped.

Saxon hadn't changed out of his battle clothes, the garments stained with blood, the sight of him making me weak in the knees. I would never forget how ferocious he'd been on the battlefield, or how tender he'd been with me afterward.

"One day, you'll have to teach me how to defeat an assailant," I said, sheathing my dagger.

"You need to learn to sense one first," he replied.

"Yes, well, that day is not today because…palace," I blurted out. "I'm returning, remember? Anyway, thank you for the assist, goodbye and good night." I turned and hurried on. Hopefully he'd take the hint and return to his tent.

Of course, Saxon flew to my side, landing softly to keep pace with me. "Why did you run from me, Ashleigh?"

"Why does it matter, Saxon?" No reason to deny that's what I'd done.

"Intent always matters."

Yes, I was beginning to think it did.

"Do you truly expect me to teach you how to defeat an opponent?" he asked. "Me? The man you've killed in the past?"

"Well, not when you put it like that," I grumbled.

To my surprise, he flashed a smile, there and gone. "I will teach you, but you'll owe me a boon. One to be determined at a later date."

Wait. He would actually train me? "Why?" I burst out as we marched forward.

"Because no one likes to work for free."

I rolled my eyes. "I mean, why will you help me?"

A prolonged pause, each second more strained than the last. He peered straight ahead, his shoulders back. Finally, with a low voice, he said, "Maybe I hope the war between us will end once and for all."

My heart warmed, slow and steady, as if the sun was dawning under my skin. I wanted to say, *The war* can *end. I'm not Leonora. I'm only possessed by her.* But I didn't. I wanted to protect my dragons more than I wanted a truce with him.

"What about restitution?" I asked. I wanted Leonora to pay it, even if I had to do the hard work.

"You do not have to pay it. That is why the restitution is over and done." He didn't hesitate to offer the pardon. And he spoke with such finality, as if he knew nothing and no one could ever change his mind.

I reeled at the implications. He'd forgiven me for my childhood actions against him? He wished to sever ties with me now instead of later? He desired me as much as I desired him, and he could think of nothing else? *Which one, which one?*

"I *insist* you continue giving me tasks," I told him. "You promised four at the very least, with expert-level difficulty, but so far you've only delivered two novice-level mini-tasks. Do you truly think our war can end if you start our truce with a lie?" I *tsk-tsk*ed, faking disappointment in him.

"Recovering from Adriel's attack counts as the third and fourth tasks."

No way. "What did you have planned for my third task originally?"

He huffed, admitting, "I planned to make you muck a stable. You would shovel manure...with animals bespelled to eliminate each time you came close to finishing."

Ohhh. How perfect. Leonora would hate every second of it. "A never-ending supply of manure?" I laughed, almost gleeful. "Tomorrow, I'm mucking those stalls, and that's that."

He tripped over a rock I couldn't see, then spread and closed his wings in quick succession to right his balance. "Let me see if I understand this correctly. You *want* to be punished in such a way?"

A blue feather floated in front of me, and I caught it with a grin. "Well, yeah. You were right. You were harmed. You deserve recompense."

A weighty pause. "How many memories have you relived?"

"Two." Okay. Time to part with him before I inadvertently admitted something about phantoms. "Well. We should probably—"

"Which two?" he insisted.

He wouldn't leave my side until I told him, I realized. To hurry things along, I said, "The day Leonora and Craven met, and the night he informed her he was kicking her out and wedding someone else, *after* he had been intimate with her."

"You sound offended on her behalf. Did you not see what happened just before that intimacy occurred? Craven walked into the room to speak with her about parting. He hadn't been with her for weeks. He started talking, and she dropped her robe. She...took matters into her own hand."

My cheeks blazed white-hot in a mere blink of time. "No, um, I didn't see that part. And I wasn't defending her actions at any time, in any way. She's a monster. I was just pointing out the fact that Craven was a monster, too, and he bore some responsibility for the war. Now, let's say goodbye and—"

His arm shot out to pull me against him. As I flailed for purchase, startled, he took flight. Realizing he was flying me home, I let my body meld to his. I didn't want him at the palace, but I didn't want him to drop me, either.

"You can't go inside the bedroom with me," I informed him. "I'm tired, and I need my rest." Truth. As Saxon's body heat enveloped me, a wave of fatigue swept me up, up.

No, no. I couldn't rest. If Leonora walked me back to Milo... I suddenly wanted to vomit. I yawned instead.

"You do need rest," Saxon said with a nod. "Your fatigue and strain are palpable."

"So you'll drop me off and go?"

"No."

Deep breath in. "We can talk later. Yes, later sounds good."

"Do you fear me, Asha? Is that what this is about?"

He asked the question so softly, so gently, that I flinched. "I'm not afraid of you." *I'm afraid of what I can do to you. Afraid of what you can do to my dragons. Afraid of what we can do to each other.* "I could be having, uh, female problems." It was an excuse I'd heard other women use upon occasion. For some reason, it never failed to send a man fleeing. "That happens."

As Saxon sputtered, I relaxed, certain I'd headed off disaster. "You can drop me off at the front door," I told him.

His brows knitted together. "Why not our balcony?"

Our balcony? "I believe there's a rule, somewhere, that states a boy should never fight in a tournament for one girl and fly another to her balcony." My tone developed a bite at the end.

His whiskey-colored irises glittered with an emotion I couldn't name. "Can he *kiss* this other girl?"

Kiss? *What?*

Kiss?

He took me straight to the balcony. Because Saxon. I couldn't bring myself to complain. I hadn't wanted to let go of him yet.

I still didn't.

Would he kiss me goodbye?

What am I doing? I couldn't allow myself to discover the answer to that question.

As soon as he set me on my feet, I flattened my hand on his chest to hold him back. "Good night, Saxon."

As calm as rock, he said, "I think I'll stay."

I gave him a stronger push. He didn't budge. "Fine. Stay there all night if you want." I faked a yawn, but a real one quickly supplanted it. "I'll be sleeping inside. Alone."

He clasped my wrist, asking, "What don't you want me to see in the bedroom, Asha?"

"I..." Well, first of all, I wouldn't panic. Second of all, I couldn't bring myself to lie. Through some strange twist of fate, Saxon and I had forged some kind of tentative truce, and I hoped to preserve it. An untruth would be the equivalent of a fireball to the face. "I don't want to tell you."

"All right." He lifted my hand and kissed my knuckles.

Saying goodbye? Oh, thank goodness.

"I'll find out on my own." The ruthless avian released me, walked around my shocked-cold form, and entered the bedchamber.

I couldn't let this happen. Panicked, I raced past him, and scanned the room. I would throw myself in front of... Pagan? Pyre? They were nowhere to be seen. Nor were Noel and Ophelia, who had fixed the furniture before they'd left. Ugh. I was going to have to pay for that.

Had Noel sensed we were on our way and bailed? I'd happily pay double for *that*.

Where were my dragons?

"Hmm." One word from Saxon. No, not even a word. A

sound. And yet, it dripped with disappointment. What had he expected? Naked forest nymphs cavorting about?

"Well, you should probably go," I told him as breezily as I was able. The second he was gone, I would go hunting for my scale-babies.

A commotion erupted outside the door—no, the banging and shaking was coming from *inside* the walls. What the—I floundered as a hidden door I'd never noticed suddenly burst open, the dragons spilling into the room, midwrestle.

The pair spotted me at the same time and popped apart to fly around me, buzzing with excitement. Smoke curled from their nostrils.

I grabbed my dagger and faced off with my adversary. "I won't let you hurt them, Saxon." I would die first.

He didn't spare me a glance as he slowly drew his sword. "How did you retrieve the eggs from Noel and Ophelia?"

"I'll tell you, after you put away the weapon." I backed the babies toward the wall, hoping to lead them to the window. "If you harm the dragons in any way, I will hate you. I will hurt you back. I'll demand reparation, and when I do, I'll make Leonora look like a saint." I was a momma bear, and I'd been woken in my cave.

"You took the eggs from the realm's most powerful witch and oracle. Apple babies." His irises flashed incredulous and fury. "Something only Leonora could do."

I lifted my chin. "I did *not* take the eggs. The girls gave them to me and returned the other two to the earth. The night your family arrived, the eggs hatched and the dragons became my babies forevermore. Our bond is unbreakable."

He exhaled with force as he looked between us. Me. The dragons. Me.

Both Pagan and Pyre sensed danger and squawked, flapping their wings at a greater speed. Thin rivers of molten lava glowed between their scales, brightening as they opened their mouths to blow sparks and plumes of smoke in Saxon's direction.

Valiant effort, my loves.

He coughed, but maintained his battle pose. "We have talked about this, Ashleigh. The first and second Leonora kept dragons, too. She used them to destroy everything and everyone I'd ever loved. Knowing this, you still choose to help history repeat itself?"

"I'm not the one who led the other dragons, and I'm not responsible for the damage done. Leonora is. I might have her memories, but I won't let myself become her. You can doubt me or you can trust me, I don't care. But you can't deny Pagan and Pyre are innocent of any wrongdoing. They are children, and they've never harmed you. Would you punish them for crimes committed by their ancestors?" I petted their scaled heads and added, "These precious darlings haven't had a chance to live. What if they grow up to *aid* our world in some way?"

"They will never aid a world that hates them. One day, they *will* attack."

No. Wrong. "Do we murder living beings for what they might do now?" My voice rose in volume, but I didn't have to worry about being overheard, thanks to Ophelia's spell. "How will we know what they'll do unless we give them a chance, Saxon?"

He stood in silence, his chest rising and falling.

The tips of my fingers began to heat, and oh, oh, oh, but I did like using Leonora's magic. I couldn't deny it. If Saxon attacked, I would have a seriously good chance of defeating him. The power at my fingertips...

One minute bled into another, indecision stamped all over his face. He closed his eyes and breathed. With a heavy exhale, he faced me—and sheathed his weapon.

My fingertips cooled, and I slowly lowered my dagger. "Now, now, girls. All will be well. The warrior isn't going to harm us. Are you, Sax? Say the words aloud so the whole class can hear."

He jolted at the name *Sax*. Then he growled, "I vow I will not harm you—as long as you do not harm me or mine."

I knew how loyal he was. Despite everything, I trusted his word.

"Go on, go meet him," I urged, and the dragons waddled over to give him a good sniffing.

He stood stiff and silent, letting them do it. His tension mounted when Pagan nipped at his feathers, then doubled when Pyre sniffed and licked his boot. But again, he didn't comment.

"We will raise them together," Saxon announced, and nodded. "They will be our dragons. Yours and mine. You will not use them against me again."

"I would never—" I pressed my lips into a thin line. I would never use the dragons against him, but Leonora certainly would. "How can we raise them together? We're going to part in two weeks. Aren't we?" Did he want to stay...together?

He jerked as if I'd elbowed him in the stomach, a violent reaction I didn't understand. "You will continue to live in the palace. I will return to the Avian Mountains, but I will visit often."

I didn't know what I'd hoped he would say, I just knew that wasn't it. A keen sense of irritation sharpened. With a wry tone, I told him, "How nice of you to take over my father's role and plan my life for me." Did I *want* to live in Sevón with my dragons? I didn't know. Did I want to see Saxon, my fated one, every day?

Yes. No thought necessary. Yes, yes, a thousand times yes.

Withering roses.

"You expect to live in the mountains with me?" He shoved the question past clenched teeth. "Only a fool would welcome the Burner of Worlds into their home. My people would revolt."

Ouch. I'd known it, and I even agreed, but the insult still hurt. "I might decide to return to Fleur and only visit on holidays." I would move wherever my dragons were safest. I was a mother now and sacrifices had to be made. I knew the terrain in Fleur, having stared out at it for years from my bedroom window. I knew the seasons and traditions. Sevón was a mystery to me.

If I believed with one hundred percent certainty that Saxon would protect Pagan and Pyre for the whole of his life, though, I would absolutely make Sevón my forever home, despite the risks.

"We'll find a way to make our situation work. Together." He sounded resigned, but also…lighter, as if he'd shed a boulder he'd been dragging around. "So, we're parents now. That's a first for us." He eased onto the edge of the bed.

I hated to ask but… "The children you had with your wives." The families he'd made after parting with Leonora. "If they died, how did your family line continue?"

"At least one avian with Skylair blood has always survived the turmoil, as if magically blessed in some way." He scoured a hand over his face, leaving a glaze of shock behind. "Who else knows about the existence of the dragons?"

"The oracle and the witch, of course." I bet he'd been an amazing father. Protective to the extreme. He would never send his child away for inadvertently hurting someone. "Maybe, um, Milo? Although, if the warlock knew, he would have told my father, who would have demanded answers."

Still and stiff again, he quietly asked, "Why is there a chance Milo knows?"

I couldn't tell him about the nighttime meetings. I just couldn't. Not yet. His willingness to work with the dragons had me rethinking my never-admit-the-truth plan, but I wasn't there yet. Especially since he admitted he believed I was different from Leonora. He'd misunderstood the details, but the concept still applied. "He's powerful, and he could know things," was all I said, and it was the truth without being the full truth.

Saxon didn't relax in the slightest.

When the dragons took flight, their wrestling match revived, the avian scanned the room. "Soon they'll be too big for this space. They'll need a place of their own to create nests."

Nests. Of course.

"Tonight, after everyone has gone to sleep, we'll fly them to the stable I mentioned. The one I planned to have you clean."

"And where is this stable located?"

"The Enchantian Forest."

He couldn't be serious. "No. Not happening." I shook my head for emphasis. "Anyone could stumble upon it and hurt them."

He flicked his tongue over an incisor. "Ophelia used her magic to hide the stable from anyone uninvited. The dragons will be fine. And I will pay for a magical doorway between the secret passage and the stable, allowing us to visit the dragons anytime we wish, without anyone the wiser."

"How do you know the secret passage can hold a magical doorway?" *I* didn't know how big or small it was, or even where it led.

He gave me a little grin, making my heart flutter. "Before your father's invasion, this was my room."

I'd been sleeping in Saxon's bed all this time? The fluttering worsened in the best way. "What if someone finds the secret passage and therefore the doorway?"

"None of your father's people can find the secret passages in this palace, for good reason. King Challen had battle magic. He saw wars coming years in advance and formed strategies to win before the enemy ever even considered striking. One of those times, he paid a royal witch to prevent anyone but his immediate family and a few select others to even see the doors. The same spell was used to hide the stable."

Okay. All right. This was shaping up to be a plan I could support. I knew how well the secret passage had been hidden. I'd been trapped inside this room for six days, and never noticed it.

One last worry kept me from agreeing with his plan. "Why are you being so agreeable, Saxon? What's happened? What's changed?"

He came to me then, stopping just in front of me. "I don't want to be your enemy anymore, Asha. I don't know if we can be friends, considering everything that's happened, but I think I'd like to try."

"You would?" I...couldn't... The fairy tale was unfolding right before my eyes? This was happening?

He gave a brittle laugh. "I'm being as foolish as my past incarnations. I don't know if Craven can ever fully forgive Leonora for what transpired in their lifetime, and I don't know what I'll do if you betray me in mine. But I know I don't want you harmed."

It was. He liked me. I'd charmed him somehow. A slow grin spread, and he scowled at me. My grin only widened.

If he was willing to work with a reincarnated version of Leonora, he might be willing to work with the girl possessed by her spirit. Time would tell. I would wait, and I would watch. If he'd meant what he'd said, if this wasn't some kind of trick, his actions would prove it, and I would disclose the full truth about my circumstances.

And oh, wow. How drastically my life had changed between one minute and the next. This morning I'd been a single mother on the hunt for jobs. This evening, I had a dragon father and a tentative friendship with the avian handpicked by fate.

What part of the fairy tale would come true next?

"Yes," I whispered. "I'd very much like to be your friend, Saxon."

He nodded, satisfied. "Then we'll head to the stable at midnight."

18

*The future both is and isn't fixed,
the past and the present intermixed.*

SAXON

For hours I sat in the backless chair at the desk, riveted by the sight of Ashleigh and the dragons. Anytime she glimpsed them, love shone in her emerald eyes, and it looked as if stars had fallen in a lush meadow. The tenderness, awe, and reverence inherent in her every touch filled me with envy. When she held the dragons, she acted as if she held a priceless treasure. Had anyone ever viewed me in such a way?

Had *I* ever viewed anyone in such a way?

Even though exhaustion clung to Ashleigh, she readily played fetch anytime the dragons brought her a toy—like a hand-carved clock or a priceless antique. The trio was already a family. The kind of family I'd always desired for myself. They were so at ease with each other, secure in the knowledge that one belonged to all, and all belonged to one.

Was this the reason Noel and Ophelia had given two dragon eggs to a reincarnation of Leonora, risking my wrath?

Pagan trotted over to me and sniffed my leg. My first instinct was to jerk away, but I bit my tongue. She flapped her wings and lifted to eye level, staring at me, unnerving me. I'd only ever seen Leonora's dragons after they were fully grown—monstrous beasts bigger than giants. These little dragon pups, though… I hated to admit it, but they were oddly adorable, their scales as smooth as glass.

I maintained eye contact until Pagan decided to fly a circle around me and perch on my shoulder. She kept her gaze straight ahead, as if I wasn't even there. Heat radiated from her, but it wasn't unpleasant.

Would she grow up to wreak destruction across the world? Or, was Ashleigh's love strong enough to change the future, holding history at bay?

The latter was…possible. The princess didn't love me, and yet she'd already changed me; I would be a fool not to bet on her success.

Keeping my movements slow and measured, I reached up to trace my fingers over Pagan's foot—scales, talons. Upon first contact, she tensed, but she didn't try to stop me or fly away. I petted with a bit more pressure. I could feel every individual scale, one stacked next to another.

As time passed, no one came to the door. I grew incensed. Surely King Philipp had heard about Ashleigh's attack at the tournament. Why did he not send a servant to check on her? Why did he not check on her himself?

I'd heard rumors suggesting he was sick. Still. He should care enough about his daughter to check. Instead, he treated her as a nonentity.

I experienced a pang of sympathy. I had to give credit to Princess Dior, though. She came to check on Ashleigh twice, refusing to leave until Ashleigh slipped a note under the door, assuring her all was well.

At last the clock chimed midnight. Not my clock, though.

The toy left in rubble. I'd done enough recognizance to know the king and his staff were asleep now. "It's time," I said.

"I'll pack a bag." Ashleigh yawned and tripped around the room, stuffing things she'd procured before my arrival into a satchel. A bit of food, a canteen of water, a couple of blankets, toiletries, and clean clothes.

She'd wanted to pack earlier, but I'd asked her to wait; that was when I'd thought the king would visit.

I took the bag and hung the strap over my shoulder, then led Ashleigh to the balcony. Moonlight bathed her, the sight stunning, turning her into a dream. A cool breeze drifted past, laden with the fragrance of night blooms.

The dragons joined us.

"Follow my flight path exactly," I said, and I prayed they understood.

As I took Ashleigh into the air, flying her away from the palace, the dragons soared behind us, following.

I breathed a sigh of relief.

"Thank you for giving the babies a chance," she said, wind whipping her hair against me.

"It wasn't the dragons I decided to take a chance on, Asha." I glanced over my shoulder, checking their progress. They must have seen something below and hoped to investigate, because they'd begun to descend.

I put my fingers to my mouth and whistled, gaining their attention, and the duo ascended once again, heeding my request. That simple action inundated me with hope. This arrangement might actually work.

Eventually, we reached the stable, a dilapidated building with rickety wood and a cracked roof ready to cave in at any moment. Or so it appeared. In reality, the structure was brand-new, built with enchanted wood cut from a magical tree; it would never fall.

Before I landed, I told Ashleigh, "I am going to entrust you with a secret. One you must keep." Could I trust her?

"I don't know if you should," she lamented. "What if Leonora tells someone? You said it yourself. She and I are two different people. Sometimes I can't stop her."

It was a risk I had to take. "The stable was built around a mirrored cage. Inside that cage is Princess Farrah, who killed a princess of Azul in order to steal her magical voice. Farrah then compelled me to kill Queen Everly's sister. As punishment, Farrah is forced to relive her crimes again and again as they appear on the glass."

"I'm sorry for your pain," she said, patting my hand.

"What makes you think I hurt?" Her accurate estimation unnerved me. "You've seen me kill many others. Why would any of this bother me?"

"Because you loved Farrah, and she betrayed you. Because you'd judged the victim innocent and undeserving of a death sentence. Because you had no offensive wounds in the garden. Even though I'd harmed you, you never struck back."

Craaack. Another break. For a moment, I struggled to breathe. For the first time since the incident occurred, I felt as if I'd been seen.

I remembered how helpless I'd felt, unable to fight Farrah's compulsion...exactly how Ashleigh must have felt each time she'd awoken and discovered Leonora had taken over.

Why had I never considered her plight? Why had I never offered *her* comfort? Guilt stirred with me, sharpened by regret.

The dragons zoomed past us and darted inside the stable. For now, I set the guilt and regret aside. Ashleigh deserved my best.

I followed the dragons, watching as they searched every stall, frightened the bugs and animals that had taken residence inside them. They claimed the largest stall as their own and promptly fell asleep. Smoke curled from their nostrils.

"The long flight exhausted them," Ashleigh said with a smile.

Fatigued myself, the struggles of the day and my lack of rest catching up to me, I made a pallet beside them. I sat down, spread my wings, and lay back, patting the spot at my right.

"You want me to lie beside you?" Ashleigh asked after a jaw-cracking yawn.

"Or on top of me," I muttered. Teasing tone, serious words. "I'm not picky."

She wrung her hands and rocked from one foot to the other. "Who could have ever guessed I would consider cuddling with an avian?"

"So that's a yes?" I asked, trying to mask my eagerness. I'd been without her for too long, not just these past six days but years and years and years. I needed her back in my arms. "You're considering cuddling?"

"That's a yes." Wringing faster. "I don't want to sleep, though."

I frowned. "You had a terrible day, and you're clearly exhausted."

Faster. "You trusted me with a secret, so I'm going to trust you with one, too. I've been…well, you know Leonora likes to assert her dominance when I'm sleeping and walk me places. Twice I went to bed clean this week and awoke dusty. I don't know what she'll do out here. What if I end up lost?"

I didn't like that she'd been wandering around at night, even as the fire witch. If the wrong person were to stumble upon her…

It was time to reveal another secret. "You won't get lost. I had a tracker spell put on you so that I will be able to find you, wherever you are."

I braced, expecting anger—deserving unfiltered rage.

She surprised me, gifting me with a tinkling laugh before settling beside me. All hint of her unease was gone.

We lay side by side, her body cushioned by one of my wings. "I think that's got to be the sweetest thing anyone has ever done for me. I bet Ophelia was referring to this tracker spell when she mentioned she'd given the spell you'd ordered something extra. Something about me being drawn to magical doorways to watch your friend make out."

I reeled. "You aren't furious with me?" Knowing Ophelia, she'd wanted Ashleigh to see Everly and Roth together so she could tell me about Eve's dalliance with the fae; I softened toward her at that moment, I admitted it.

She placed a hand over her heart. "You cared enough to want to find me."

"I think you're forgetting the part about me wanting to *hurt* you," I reminded her.

"Shhh." Leaning over, she pressed a finger to my lips. "Don't ruin this for me."

I nipped at the finger, and she laughed. "Tonight," I said, "I'll make sure you remain in bed, I swear it."

"This is nice," she whispered, her voice already slurred with exhaustion.

"Better than nice."

She rolled to her side, and I rolled to mine, wrapping my arm around her and breathing in her sweet scent. Mmm. This felt right. She fit me perfectly.

Made for me.

"We should probably seal our new truce with a ki..." The next thing I knew, her breathing evened out, and she went quiet.

I wanted to shout with frustration. *Finish the sentence, Asha.*

Despite that frustration, I felt more contentment than ever before. Ashleigh trusted me to keep her safe. And I would, no matter the cost. Though my eyelids turned heavy, threatening to slide shut, I forced myself to remain awake and on guard the entire night.

I kissed her temple. Inside, both sides of me cried, *Do not betray me this time, Asha. Please.* I doubted I would recover.

★ ★ ★

Sunlight streamed through the stable's wooden slats, dust motes dancing in the cool, crisp air. The dragons had gotten up about an hour ago to explore and play, and they had yet to return. I had Ashleigh all to myself.

I grinned as I stretched. My princess hadn't budged the entire night. I'd kept her in place, as promised. This morning, she slept against me, her petite body warmed by my wings. A blue feathered tangled in her hair.

The contentment I'd felt last night? It did not compare to this…this peace. I was exactly where I was supposed to be, with the one I was supposed to be with. The sensation might be an echo from our past love affairs, but I embraced it, reaching out to trace her cheekbones. Her lips parted with a raspy sigh.

Eyes remaining closed, she breathed, "Mmm. Saxon," before rolling on top of me and fusing her mouth to mine.

The impromptu kiss startled me. I responded, but something niggled at the back of my mind. A sense of familiarity. Yes. That. I'd experienced this kiss a thousand times before—with Leonora.

My blood flash froze.

Ashleigh was not Leonora. They should not kiss the same.

With a curse, I wrenched my face from hers.

She lifted her head and opened her lids, and a curse exploded from me. Her irises were blue.

Leonora had taken over, and I wasn't prepared for it. I leaped to a stand, dumping the fire witch onto the pallet, and wiped my mouth with the back of my hand.

She grinned as she rose to her feet. "You enjoy my newest form. I'm glad."

I wanted Ashleigh back. I wanted Ashleigh back *now*. I could never—*would* never—be able to trust this other part of her. "Why are you here? Why now?"

All want and need, Leonora glided a hand through my wings. "Don't you want me here, lover?"

"I don't," I said, catching her wrist. While Ashleigh exuded excitement, as if she enjoyed the simple act of living, everything she did new and wonderful, Leonora simpered.

One enchanted me. The other repulsed me.

Maybe we didn't have to settle for suppressing this part of Ashleigh with a spell. Ashleigh and Leonora were two halves of the same whole, the edges no longer glued together. One could exist without the other. What if we found a way to erase this part of her?

Never again would memories overtake her, or turn her into Leonora. The magic that saved her heart...would she lose it? Would she die without it, Leonora taking another female from me?

I released her and stepped back, moving out of her range.

She narrowed her eyes. "I'm your fated. I'm the one willing to fight time and space for you. The one you return for. Why do you continue to push me away?"

"I do return for you...to end your reign of terror." As she scowled, I asked, "Are you eager to reignite our war?"

"I have no desire to fight with you again. During our first life, I wanted only to be your wife." Exaggerating the sway of her hips, she shrank the distance between us. "You decided to exile me from the Avian Mountains and wed a princess instead."

"A princess you killed."

She shrugged, as unrepentant as ever. "During our second life, I did everything right. I even created a peaceful home for you, yet you *still* opted to wed another woman."

"Because I knew there was something wrong with our relationship. Then I remembered your crimes against me."

"I only stabbed you because I knew we could start over. If you'll give me a chance, we can finally get this right."

"This," I sneered, "is based on hatred."

Despite paling, she kept her voice modulated. "I can make you happy, Craven. Ashleigh is the one who makes you miserable."

"I am Saxon." The one who wanted Ashleigh. "And you, Leonora, will *never* make me happy." *Must erase the witch.* "Bury the memories of the past. Bring Ashleigh back."

She hissed, "Perhaps I'm here to stay now."

The room spun. *Not yet, not yet.* I wasn't ready.

I would *never* be ready. "If that's true, we have nothing left to say to each other." I would force her to bury the memories, I decided, palming one of the daggers sheathed in my boots. Boots I'd slept in, wanting to be prepared for any threat against my charges. "We might as well get to the killing part of our courtship."

"Is that so?" With an icy grin, she reached into the pocket of her dress, then lifted a dagger to her throat. "Why don't I kill this body now and save you the trouble?"

"No," I roared, dropping my weapon in order to grab her wrist. "Do not harm her."

"Why shouldn't I take her from you, the way you took your love away from me?" Her voice cracked. "Tell me."

"She's a better person than either of us has *ever* been." Those words... I had a sudden and startling realization. With bone-deep certainty, I knew I'd gotten this all wrong. Ashleigh and Leonora weren't two halves of the same whole, one with memories and magic, one without. Ashleigh was not the foundation from which Leonora had been built. She wasn't a clean slate, with a different upbringing; she was a different person entirely. The two females shared no commonalities. One would never have been—or be—the other.

Two females, one completely separate from the other, shared a body.

I didn't know how it was possible; I just knew it had happened.

I'd been so blinded by hatred, so confident I'd found the one responsible for my pain, I'd rationalized obvious tells. Ashleigh hadn't been the one to hurt me. But I'd been the one to hurt her.

Guilt returned with a vengeance, bringing shame along for the ride. More guilt and shame than any one person could ever hope to carry. Ashleigh had deserved none of my wrath, but she'd born all of it.

The house of rage, wrath, and vengeance I'd built inside my mind began to crumble, layer by layer. Guilt flooded in. An acid-tinged rain burning everything it touched. I owed my princess reparation I could never repay, and the knowledge tore up my insides.

I needed to beg for forgiveness I didn't deserve.

A sound of animal pain got trapped inside my head at top volume. I would apologize. I would spend my life making up for what I'd done, and I would find a way to neutralize the witch, or whatever the creature it was that lived inside of her.

Unlike memories, I doubted Leonora could be erased. But we might be able to remove her.

Having accepted the truth, my thoughts aligned, my mind working at a faster clip now. Could Leonora be a goblin, perhaps, able to possess a body for the span of its life rather than a few stolen minutes? Goblins could absolutely be removed; they could also be killed.

If Leonora was a goblin, though, she was the strongest one I'd ever encountered. Half goblin, half witch?

I would ask around, learn what I could and present Ashleigh with the idea. How would she react?

For now, I would make Leonora as miserable as possible, forcing her to fade on her own. "You owe me restitution, witch, and you *will* pay it. You will clean the entire stable. To start." I dragged her into the dirtiest stall. "You will do everything one-handed, so that you aren't able to use your magic to burn the place down."

"Clean? Me? I'll do no such thing." She uttered a shrill laugh that set me on edge. "As your fated queen, however, I'll be happy to supervise our servants."

I spun her around and yanked the ribbon from her hair, then used the satin to tie one of her arms to the back of her gown. "You won't be leaving this stable until you've finished cleaning. For every day you refuse to work, I'll shorten the length of your chains. Yes, you will be chained." She might be powerful, but she wasn't infallible.

"You wouldn't," she gasped out.

I grinned slowly, contentedly. "Watch me. Or, allow Ashleigh to emerge. Let the princess do the cleaning for you." A temptation the selfish creature couldn't resist?

Long, torturous moments passed, her breaths the only sound. "What is it you like about Ashleigh? Her inability to run a short distance without fainting? Her lack of combat skills? No, wait. It must be her lack of magic."

I wanted so badly to yell my defense of the princess, an insult to her an insult to me. *My, my. How quickly things have changed.* Knowing I would only fuel Leonora's stubbornness if I spoke up, I crossed my arms and remained mute.

She puffed a frustrated sigh. "Very well. I'll allow your precious Ashleigh to return—for now—but I'll be back, and we'll settle our differences once and for all." That said, she collapsed, her eyes rolling back into her head.

I flew over to catch her before she hit the ground, then eased her down the rest of the way. As she slept on, I remained crouched at her side, my nerves on edge. What would I see when her lashes parted? Hated blue or adored green?

Seconds passed, each one more agonizing than the last. When a low moan left her and she began to flutter open her lids, I tensed. What color? Please, be green. Please be—green. I exhaled a staggering breath of relief.

"Withering roses," she burst out, jolting into an upright position. With a groan, she massaged her temples. "Leonora locked me in an endless void on the other side of the barrier, and I couldn't fight my way free. But at least I remained somewhat aware this time."

What did she mean, "barrier"? Had she already found a way to suppress the witch, keeping Leonora from taking over any time she wished?

"How do you feel?" I asked, untying the hand that was behind her back. My voice was rough with guilt, the tide I'd managed to hold back while dealing with Leonora surging.

"I'm all right," she replied softly, rubbing her wrists.

I bowed my head.

"What's wrong?" she asked. "What did I do this time?"

"*You* did nothing. You never have. I never should have blamed you for what happened in the past. I never should have punished you. I'm so sorry, Ashleigh." I hated what I'd done. I hated who I'd been. "Tell me what to do to prove my remorse, and I'll do it." I would do anything.

"You don't need to do anything. This situation is insane and complex and twisted. We're both doing the best we can. But I accept your apology," she offered easily. She placed her hand atop mine and squeezed, putting action to words. "To be honest, you aren't the one I blame."

Who was this girl with the broken heart so ready to forgive?

"What did Leonora do this time?" she asked. "For once, I have a vague idea, but I'm kind of hoping I'm wrong."

"She kissed me," I admitted.

"Yeah. That's what I thought." Ashleigh drew a line in the dirt and hay that covered the floor. "That must have been...?"

Disgust flared as I recalled it. "Awful."

"I'm the one who's sorry, then. I should have fought harder to escape."

Escape the endless void she'd mentioned? "Never apologize to me. You owe me nothing." I smoothed a lock of hair behind her ear. "If Leonora subdues you at times, does that mean you are subduing her at all the others? Or does she only surface when she wishes?"

Ashleigh gave her lips a nervous lick before rocking a hand back and forth. "It's half and half. Sometimes I have to fight her to keep her buried, but most often she is dormant."

Ashleigh had strength upon strength upon strength, and always had, much of which I hadn't even known about. "She isn't you." I didn't have a right to ask, but I was going to. The more I knew, the better I could help her. I had to help her. "She's a different entity entirely. And please don't worry that I will use this information to harm you. Your protection is paramount to me, and I'm going to prove it."

Her eyes flared, and she gave a brittle laugh. "Two different entities? Do you comprehend how ridiculous you sound?"

She knew the truth, but she didn't want to admit it to me. She feared my reaction because I'd given her no reason not to. I bowed my head once more, the weight of everything I'd done, everything I'd said settling on my shoulders.

I needed to speak with Noel. The oracle might have insight into the situation and the people involved that I didn't.

The dragons must have sensed their mother's return; they whizzed into the stall, squawking happily. Pagan landed on her right shoulder, Pyre her left and both babies nuzzled her cheek, leaving a streak of soot behind.

In that moment, it felt as if someone had used a mallet on my rib cage, the cracking I'd experienced before just a foretaste. The mallet slammed into my heart next, banging and banging until every inch had been tenderized. The sensation was terrible...wonderful...*perfect*. It was something you forever re-membered because it changed who you were, inside and out.

I'd so badly wanted to be a great king, just once. But how could I lead an army of warriors if I couldn't protect a girl who'd come to mean everything to me?

Ashleigh laughed. Even now, the magical sound soothed me in a thousand different ways. "Hello, my darlings. Did you enjoy your first night outside the bedroom?"

More squawks. Pyre hopped down and tentatively rubbed against me, the scent of fuel and flame wafting from her.

I looked down to watch her but otherwise remained still, not wanting to spook her. After she gave me a few sniffs, she looked up, and our gazes met. The next strike of the mallet landed with more force. The way she looked at me...

It was like staring into an abyss of love.

Children peered at their parents this way, with eyes full of trust and adoration, hope and promise. It made you want to be better, to do better, to move mountains if ever one stood in their way.

My dragons. My family.

Yes. I had created a new family in this life. A family I would not lose.

I will protect what's mine.

Woe to anyone who threatened me or mine.

I gently petted the little fire-breather's snout. "After I feed Ashleigh, I'll clean the stable for you. I'll make it a proper home. Would you like that?"

"*You* are going to clean the stable?" Ashleigh asked, as if shocked to her soul. "Are you trying to punish *yourself*?"

"I am," I confirmed. It wasn't much, but it was a start. And... despite the burn of my guilt, I felt freer than I had in...ever. I felt lighter. "I punished an innocent girl for something she didn't do. So, I will do the work, and you will cheer for my misery."

"No way." She shook her head, dark locks swaying. "I'm helping you."

"There is no reason for you—"

"I'm helping," she insisted.

I exhaled. I didn't want to begin my reparation by arguing with the one I hoped to please. "If you get tired—"

"I'll rest, I promise." She flashed me a grin. "How about we eat breakfast first? Hey," she burst out, frowning. She canted her head to the side and pointed to a spot down the hall. "What's that?"

Because I'd invited her into the stable, she now had access to the spell that surrounded it, allowing her to notice the shimmery outline of the secret door. "Come. I'll show you, then I'll feed you." I took her hand, linking our fingers, and led her down the hall, through the secret door that turned the wall to mist when we came into contact with it. We entered the secret room.

"What *is* this?" She walked around the mirrored cage, studying it, then the large apple tree beside it. Bark as black as night. Leaves as white as snow. Apples as red as blood. "Incredible."

The tree marked the spot Hartly Morrow had died. Everly's sister, and the girl Farrah compelled me to kill. The sight of it flooded me with guilt I'd never been able to eradicate.

"And the glass…it's flawless. There isn't a single crack or seam."

"The mirror contains Farrah."

"This is her prison?" She returned to the cage to trace her finger over the glass, seemingly lost in thought. "Your voice carries a note of affection every time you speak of Farrah. You've forgiven her for her crime against you, haven't you?"

A dangerous topic, considering I'd told both her and her father that I despised the Charmaine siblings. But I was no longer comfortable lying to her like I lied to my enemy. "She's one of my closest friends. A sister of the heart."

"I bet you'll be reunited one day."

From the corner of my eye, I spied movement. With one arm, I thrust Ashleigh behind me. With the other, I withdrew a dagger. Who dared intrude upon us?

Two apparitions appeared in the corner of the room, shimmery outlines of a woman and her daughter, both of whom I recognized.

Though my guilt sharpened, I relaxed my stance.

"What happened?" Ashleigh asked.

"We have visitors." I pointed to Aubrey Morrow, Everly's aunt, and her daughter, Hartly. Both females had dark hair, blue eyes, and golden skin. Today they wore dresses made of ivy and flower petals.

"Um… I'm not seeing anyone," Ashleigh said.

She wasn't? "One is Hartly, an apple baby, like Ophelia. She communes with animals. The other is her mother, Princess Aubrey of Airaria. She ate the apple. Now the two serve as guardians of the forest."

"More apple babies," Ashleigh breathed. "I went from knowing none to learning about three."

I bowed my head to Hartly, then her mother. I'd seen them before, and I'd apologized, but I still felt the urge to announce, "I'm sorry." I hadn't just killed the girl. I'd killed the man she loved.

Warick, the former king of the trolls, had done everything in his power to save her, before I'd gutted him.

I'd tried to make restitution, paying for this stable to protect her tree as well as Farrah's prison. But how could one ever make amends for such a crime?

As many times as I'd seen Hartly, she'd never responded to my apology. She'd only ever smiled at me, as if all were forgiven, no reparation necessary. A concept that baffled my mind. Today, she arched a brow, cast a pointed glance at Ashleigh and wiggled her brows. Then she surprised me further, hiking her thumb to the right.

I followed the direction with my gaze, curious about what I'd find—I had to do a double take. Warick. He was here. Tall, powerfully built, with horns, tusks, and a wealth of scars. He strode to Hartly's side and slung an arm around her waist. She rested her head on his shoulder, radiating contentment, as if to tell me I could finally forgive myself.

I don't know how the spirits had bound the troll's essence to the forest, but I would be forever grateful that they had.

Hartly mouthed something that might have been, *The time nears. Soon the coffin will crack, Farrah's true love returning.* Or maybe she'd said "Truly" instead of "true love." Farrah and Truly had loved each other dearly. If Truly was returning, then the coffin would indeed crack. I would get to see my friend again.

"Why are you trusting me with all this information, Saxon?" Ashleigh asked softly.

"Many reasons." I doubted she'd believe more than a handful of them.

"I know you consider me two different people now, and that's wonderful, I think, maybe, but Leonora is still inside me, still listening. If she were to do something...to tell someone..."

She feared I would blame them both? "Whatever happens, we'll handle it." We'd have to. "You're going to be returning to this stable often, and I don't want you surprised by anything you find. Now you know what should be here and what shouldn't." I nodded a goodbye to the others, then led the princess out of the room, grabbed a blanket and the bag with our supplies, and strode outside.

As we placed the food on the blanket, the dragons flew circles in the sky above, Ophelia's spell keeping them hidden from prying eyes, even up there. I'd paid good gold to ensure no avian could spot the area from the air.

"Among the avian, there's a custom," I said as I smeared strawberry jam on a piece of crusty bread. "When a couple is alone, one feeds the other by hand."

She perked up with interest. "What does this custom signify?"

"That the two bear deep affection for one another." I offered the bread to her, hoping she would understand. That she wanted what I wanted.

She looked at the bread, then me. The bread. Me. Understanding warred with nervousness before my cunning princess leaned over to bite into the bread while I held it.

Satisfaction rumbled inside me, a storm soon to break. She'd understood, and she'd accepted.

When Ashleigh offered me a grape in return, I accepted the fruit with my mouth. As I chewed and swallowed, she smiled down at her lap, beaming with pleasure. Pleasure I had given her with a simple act of affection.

The rumble of satisfaction I'd felt a moment ago? The one that signaled the approach of a storm? The storm hit, contentment raining through me. Winds of peace came rushing in, spinning all around me, walling me in a center of calm. This girl...

She was the rain, and she was the wind.

I basked in the moment...until the dragons landed at the edge of the blanket. Pagan dropped the rat she'd killed, and Pyre roasted it with a thin stream of fire.

I smothered a sound, half groan, half laugh.

While Pyre jumped up and down with eagerness, Pagan picked up the charred body with her teeth and offered it to Ashleigh.

"Oh, sweet goodness," she muttered, flattening a hand on her belly. "That's, um, such a good job, babies. Your hunting and cooking expertise is, um, commendable. But a mother never takes food from her children. She always gives. So, I gift these remains back to you. Please, my darlings, eat up."

Pagan seemed to shrug before jerking back her head to toss the rat into the air and catching it with her mouth.

Ashleigh looked horrified as she clapped, and I fought a grin. I clasped her hands and kissed one of her palms, then the other.

Her breath caught. She peered at me, and I peered at her. Amusement was supplanted by heat. We stared at each other, breathing each other in.

A dragon bumped into her, the moment shattering.

I looked away. "Let's get to work," I suggested.

"Y-yes. Let's."

As we cleaned the stable one stall at a time, I rushed over to carry anything I considered too heavy for her. So, everything. All the while, she sang under her breath, and it wasn't long before I was grinning wide, unable to stop. The girl couldn't hold a tune, but she evinced such joy, I wanted to listen to her forever.

"I think the babies will be happy with their new home," she told me with a satisfied nod.

"I will guard their happiness with my life," I vowed, and everything about her softened.

After the first couple hours of cleaning, Ashleigh grew fatigued, sweat beading on her brow. Never once did she complain.

I took the canteen of water to her, unfastening the lid along the way.

"A little more," I urged as she drank.

When she finished, I splashed some of the drops on my fingers and pressed them to her nape. She closed her eyes, a soft smile hovering at the edge of her mouth.

"Thank you." She met my gaze before rising on her tiptoes to kiss my cheek.

As she bounded off, refreshed, I marveled. For each of my

lives, I'd considered strength to be a test of physical fortitude. It had been an inexcusable mistake on my part. Ashleigh continued to prove herself more mentally and emotionally resilient than anyone I'd ever known. Including myself.

There wasn't a man alive who was worthy of her.

We slipped into comfortable silence as we continued our work. When she hauled a wheelbarrow of old, moldy hay around the corner, disappearing from view, I approached a stalk of ivy growing over the wall to whisper, "I know you can hear me, Everly. Do me a favor and put one of your mirror gateways in the secret passage for my bedroom, and a mirror gateway to the secret passage in the stable. One needs to lead to the other." Best to be clear with these apple babies. "I need this now. Pay the witch to position the mirrors, if you must, and I will reimburse you double." I didn't wish to waste time with negotiations on price. "Remind her I am given the friends and family discount."

"Um, to whom are you talking?"

Well. I turned. Ashleigh stood in the stall door, her brow furrowed.

When she glimpsed the plant, she smiled. "Oh, one of your foliage friends," she said. "Hello, Ivy. I'm Ashleigh."

She thought I was embarrassed to be caught talking to a plant, and hoped to put me at ease, didn't she?

This girl… I grabbed the bag we'd brought, emptied it of everything but our clean clothes, then fit the strap across her chest and drew her against me. "You worked so hard, you earned a reward."

A dirt-smeared hand fluttered to her chest. "A reward? For me?"

My voice deepened as I told her, "Yes. You. So wrap your arms around me."

19

There's nothing sweeter than true love's kiss.
Except a reunion with the one you miss.

Ashleigh

What an amazing day. I'd gone from the lowest of lows, when Leonora had so easily subdued me and stolen my first kiss, to the highest of highs, when Saxon made me the recipient of his deepest affections. He didn't see me as Leonora anymore. Even without knowing I was possessed by a phantom, he saw me as Ashleigh. Just Ashleigh. And now he wanted to give me a gift, as if he hadn't already given me the world?

"I had fun today," I told him, wrapping my arms around him as requested. "I've never cleaned anything with the help of another. I don't need another reward. But I want it, so gimme."

A hungry glint lit his whiskey-dark eyes, sending shivers down my spine. "I have a feeling I'll be giving you anything you ask for."

Mind-bending words. Deliciously husky tone.

More shivers.

He flicked his gaze to my lips, a frisson of heat passing between us. Would he kiss me?

Did I want him to?

More than anything.

But he shook his head, as if he wished to scatter his thoughts, and placed one hand on the back of my head. He pressed the other against my lower back and spread his wings.

A blink, and we were in the air. He flew me over the treetops, calling, "Pagan. Pyre. Follow us."

As we soared through the sky, the dragons gave chase, and an unexpected laugh escaped me. For so long I'd toiled daily, doing my best to find the joy in my circumstances. Had I known this awaited me, I never would have stopped smiling.

"You have an infectious laugh," Saxon said.

I do? "Thank you. And thank you for my gift. I love it."

"Oh, this isn't your gift," he said, nuzzling his cheek against mine. "We've got another ten minutes before we reach our destination."

Ten whole minutes in Saxon's arms? How many presents was I getting today? "Will you tell me about avian society along the way?" My curiosity remained steadfast.

"What would you like to know?"

"Well, why can't a female rule the avian if she's the oldest child? Even Fleuridian law allows this." A fact my father had always lamented. I would have considered the avian more progressive.

He rolled around a cloud, and I laughed again. "A law is a law as long as tradition demands it. The avian are nothing if not traditional, and tradition states an avian ruler must have Skylair blood, the male before the female."

"So Queen Raven can never rule alone because she doesn't have a blood link to the Skylairs. She can only act as regent for you or Tempest?"

"Correct."

"Do you even *want* the avian crown, though?"

"No one else has ever asked me that question," he mused. "I didn't used to. Even though I knew I was Craven, even though I'd led the avian twice before, I thought to give up the crown and change my future. Then my father and brother died, and Craven was to be king once again. That was when I realized you'd have to be…dealt with. I decided I wouldn't abandon my people when they needed me most. I owe them restitution I can never repay. Now I will kill anyone who tries to take the crown from me."

Ohhhh. He'd blamed himself for bringing Leonora into their midst twice before, setting the stage for the near extinction of their kind. He'd feared what she would do this time around.

I could *never* allow the phantom to return to the Avian Mountains.

My determination to end her reached new heights.

"And the bracelets?" I asked gently. "What's the meaning of their tradition?" Would he tell me this time?

He brushed his thumb along my spine. "They serve as a constant reminder that we do not serve ourselves, but each other. At birth, every avian is given three bracelets. The red one represents family. Blood of my blood. The yellow represents a commitment of marriage. The dawning of a new life together. The third is white, to be exchanged for another bracelet on the child's sixteenth birthday, when they choose their own path. We acquire others for significant achievements that aid our people as a whole."

I did a quick, mental count of his bracelets, recalling some were thicker than others. "What does the thickest one represent?"

He pursed his lips, but said, "War. Each time I execute a successful campaign, a new string is added around the metal band."

Whoa! "You've had a lot of successful campaigns."

"Yes," he said, offering no more. "I might not have lived

with the avian, but I had people. There was Roth and Farrah. Vikander, a fae prince, and Reese, a mer who lost his life not too long ago. I fought for them and wear my wars to honor their sacrifices."

What a beautiful picture of friendship, loyalty, and love. "Women who visited the Temple often whispered about a fae named Vikander."

"That's the very one," he said with a sure nod.

"But I didn't even tell you what those whispers suggested he did."

"It doesn't matter. They were speaking of Vikander."

I chuckled, loving this playful side of him. "So what happens if a bracelet falls off or gets stolen?"

"They never fall, and they can't be stolen. They are magically bound to us, growing as we grow, and they must be given freely to be removed."

As we descended, I figured I had time for one more question. "What is *amour*?"

He got real tense, real fast, and I feared I'd overstepped. "It is a special dust the avian produce when they are...very happy."

Was that why the amour had been so important to Leonora? She'd wanted to be the one to make Craven happy? "Why keep the information a secret? Actually, how has this information been kept secret for so long?"

"The avian have always given false histories to the masses, and kept the truth for ourselves. This prevents our enemies from knowing how to fight us properly."

Tricky.

We neared treetops that glowed bright blue, a haze of mist sparkling like diamond dust, but Saxon didn't slow and... I squealed with delight as he twisted and twirled at top speed, somehow avoiding a single strike of a tree branch. Only soft leaves caressed my skin.

He landed on a boulder next to a majestic waterfall. Cool

mist dampened me as the dragons skidded over the water. I twittered happily.

"Such skill," I called to my babies.

Saxon motioned to a crystal-clear pond, where water lilies floated over the surface, perfuming the air. "*This* is your surprise. We're going to swim."

I fluttered a hand over my suddenly racing heart. "Swim?" I'd always wanted to swim. "I'd love to, very much so, but I don't know how."

"Then it will be my pleasure to teach you." He flipped his gaze up, where the dragons circled us. "Go play, but stay close and out of others' view. Squawk if you need us. And no peeking."

They gave him a look, like, *Sure, Dad*, then shot off, disappearing in the trees. The next thing I knew, Saxon had tightened his grip on me and jumped into the pool.

I laughed as cold but refreshing water enveloped me in a single gulp, clothes and all. Had I been alone, I would have been terrified, but with Saxon holding me close, I was exhilarated.

He kicked his powerful legs, propelling us up, up. I was still laughing as we breached the surface. Droplets slipped into my mouth, and the most divine sensation came over me.

My insides tingled as if I'd swallowed a magical peppermint tree. "What's happening?"

"The water is bespelled by the forest's guardian. Anyone who swims is cleaned, inside and out."

Amazing. "Queen Everly did this?"

"You know of Everly?"

"Yes, Sax." I rolled my eyes. "Even I have heard of the new Empress of the Forest."

His features softened when I used the endearment. "That isn't what I meant."

"Well, then—oh! Help me." The weight of my dress was pulling me down, down. "My clothes," I screeched, kicking my legs frantically. I continued to sink, even with Saxon's arms banded around me.

He held me up without sinking an inch himself, and I took comfort in that. "No need to worry, Asha. The clothes are coming off. With your permission, of course."

Wait. "We'll be naked?"

"If you would rather remain dressed—"

"No, no." Excitement and anticipation doused that sudden flare of nervousness as he floated me closer to the shore.

Except for my bath-time experience, I'd never been naked with a boy. But… I wanted to get naked with this one and no other.

"For our safety, we probably *should* disrobe," I said as casually as I could manage. "I mean, if you think we should."

"I do." He lowered his chin, looking every inch a predator. The water had slicked back his hair. Strain had tightened his features, and his pupils had dilated. "For our *safety*."

He sounded like a predator, too, all growly and hot.

For some reason, hearing that tone was like receiving a deluge of pure confidence. A flirting know-how I'd never before displayed and hadn't learned from Leonora. "But, Sax," I purred. "Removing our clothes means *you're* the one getting the reward."

He jerked at *my* tone. "If getting you out of a dress is my reward for cleaning a stable," he said, his eyelids sinking over his eyes, "I'll be cleaning a stable every day for the rest of my life."

He'd just said…he'd just claimed… I think he'd just melted my brain right along with my heart. He wanted to spend every day of his life with me?

He reached a spot where he could stand, then helped me out of the soaking gown with expert precision. He got me out of my shoes, too, tossing everything to the shore…and suddenly I was standing in water that only reached my navel while wearing nothing but a corselet and a pair of panties. Cool air raised goose bumps on my damp skin, but Saxon's gaze kept me warm.

He traced a finger along the chain that held the ring, his blistering expression unchanging. "You never remove this." A statement, not a question. "Your mother gave it to you, you said."

"That's right," I replied, cautious. Every time before, a discussion on this topic had soured his mood.

"What did she tell you about it?" He tugged his shirt over his head, baring his chest, then tossed his boots ashore.

His nipple piercing glinted in the sunlight, mesmerizing me.

He removed his pants, leaving only his undergar—no, he removed that, too.

I wouldn't look down at the water. I wouldn't—

The clear water hid nothing.

I'd looked down, and oh, sweet goodness. I jerked my gaze heavenward, my heart thudding. I'd just glimpsed a male member for the first time, and I didn't know what to think. I probably needed another look—two looks, verging closer to five—ten before I made a decision about it.

In the interest of my education, I performed a second once-over. When I licked my lips, Saxon belted out a laugh. A rusty but charming sound that made me want to laugh, too.

Before I could study the new object of my fascination, my avian fell back into the water, taking me with him to swim us to a deeper part of the pond.

"The ring," he prompted a second time.

Oh, yes. "My mother didn't tell me much about it, to be honest. Only that it belonged with me."

"One day, if you'd like to know more about it, I'll tell you. Now lie back." He eased me into a supine position, keeping one hand underneath me to hold me up.

Long locks of my hair formed dark ribbons in the water around me. "You won't let me go?"

"I swear it. I won't let you go."

As I continued to float, he urged me to try other positions. No matter which way I angled, he remained true to his word, holding me up, unwaveringly patient as I screeched questions.

Like now. "How long does it take to drown?" I demanded as I flailed, water splashing. I had turned stomach down, and if my face went under one more time...

"You're not drowning. I've got you."

I sank a little, swallowing a mouthful of water, and yelped. *"Why are you letting me drown, Saxon?"*

He snickered. "If I allow you to drown, Asha, you can punish me at your leisure."

"How comforting." Eventually, though, I got the hang of everything. "All right. I'm ready. You can release me into the wild. But stay close."

For the first time since we'd entered the water, he eased his hands away. I glided my arms and legs this way and that, just as he'd taught me and...yes! I didn't sink. "I'm doing it, Sax! I'm doing it."

He beamed at me. "I've never been more proud of you, Asha."

I...didn't know what to say or how to act. I'd never made anyone proud before.

I dipped underwater—on purpose—to cool my overheated cheeks. As I came back up, Saxon cupped my nape and eased me closer to his body. In this location, my feet didn't reach the bottom, so I had to tread before him. But that was okay, because he'd taught me how to do that, too.

"Do you have any idea how beautiful you are?" He grazed my cheek, collecting water droplets, his heated gaze searching mine.

"Yes," I replied, very serious. Because I'd always been beautiful to myself. How could I not be? I had come from my mother.

"But thank you for the compliment. I will cherish it every time I catch sight of my reflection."

He grinned at me, sharing his amusement.

"You," I said, unable to look away, "are beautiful, too."

"Thank you. I will cherish the compliment every time I catch sight...of you."

Argh! He was melting my brain again.

With my next inhalation, I picked up a new scent. Mmm. Sweet...rich...intoxicating. What was that? I breathed deep, deeper, hungry for more. My head clouded, even as different parts of me seemed to awaken from a deep sleep. The pulse at the base of my neck throbbed. My every cell buzzed. Flutters teased my belly, while warmth pooled between my legs.

I thought...maybe... "The scent...it's coming from you."

He parted his lips wordlessly, his expression somehow haunted and euphoric at once. "I think it's...the amour."

He'd produced the special dust? I laughed, delighted. "I made you happy."

He met my gaze again, his expression fiercer than I'd ever seen it. My laughter died. His breaths turned raspy. So did mine. We breathed for the other, the space between our mouths diminishing as we both edged closer.

Heart racing, I slid my hands up his chest. A chest he bowed out, seeking firmer contact.

"My wings." He settled his hands on my waist and squeezed. Voice hoarse, he said, "Touch them. Please." The last word emerged as little more than a snarl.

Yes. I would touch. I had to touch. My cheeks flushed as I reached past his shoulders with trembling hands, then fitted my palms over the hard outer ridge of his wings.

A moan left him, and he closed his eyes.

Suddenly I understood why my mother had told me not to ever, ever ask to touch an avian's wings. It was a deeply personal act between two people who trusted each other...desired each other—an act we both desperately craved.

I caressed those exquisite azure feathers, luxuriating in the softness, sharply aware of Saxon's every reaction...and the reactions taking place inside of me. The increase of heat, turning my bones to molten gold. The magnified aches.

"Sax," I breathed.

His eyelids popped open, amber irises aflame. "I want to kiss you. I *need* to kiss you."

Yes! "Kiss me," I commanded him.

And he obeyed.

He pressed his mouth over mine and slid his tongue inside for a quick taste, the connection electrifying me. I melted into him, somehow remaining upright, letting my tongue chase his. *More.*

With a groan, he gave me what I wanted. At first, I didn't know how to return the force of his passion, but he didn't seem to mind and it wasn't long before I got lost in the throes, my body taking over. He kissed me faster and harder, and I instinctively followed his lead. Again, my aches magnified. The pulse at the base of my neck didn't just throb; it galloped. My cells didn't just buzz; they burned. The flutters didn't just dance in my belly; they spread all over.

He tasted like he smelled, all the delicious honeyed whiskey teasing my tongue. A special scent and taste just for me. Because I'd made him happy. A fact I would forever cherish.

When a shadow fell over us, we broke apart, both of us panting. I glanced up to see the dragons swooping past, and I would swear they both blushed before they disappeared in the trees.

I moaned, my cheeks scorched. "They saw us. On the plus side, I think we'll get a little privacy now."

"That's good." His voice dipped. "There are things I want to do to you."

I shivered as Saxon carried me out of the water and laid me

on a moss-covered rock. Cool air nipped at my overheated skin, steam seeming to rise from me.

"Saxon," I whispered, the interruption already forgotten. I wanted more of what he'd given me in the water. Needed it.

He loomed over me, gloriously naked, water dripping from his hair. Flaring his wings, flinging more droplets in every direction, he blocked out the rest of the world. Just then, we were the only two people in existence.

"Touch me," he rasped. "Touch my wings again."

I stroked the feathers, and he returned his mouth to mine with a groan. This kiss was frantic, edged with desperation.

When he settled his heavy weight over me, I thrilled. He covered me like a shield—the most beautiful shield in all the world. He touched me as I touched him. He kneaded me, and he played with me, making me moan, mewl, and beg. But what was I supposed to do for him? How did I make *him* feel this good?

A bomb of fury hit me with such force, I gasped. Leonora didn't like that I was enjoying my time with the avian. "Her" time.

Saxon lifted his head, his brows knitted, his lips kiss-swollen. "Ashleigh?"

The heat drained out of me, leaving me ice-cold. He might be Cinder's fairy-tale prince, but our circumstances hadn't magically changed. I was still possessed by his most hated enemy. I could become her at any moment. And what would happen if—when—Saxon won the tournament? And he would win, no matter what he had to do. He and his people prized strength; he wouldn't return to his kingdom in defeat. So. He would become Dior's betrothed. Dior's.

Not mine.

I was kissing a man who would soon marry someone else.

I wheezed my next breath. While my stepsister believed we could let the winner choose his bride, I knew better. My father rendered the ultimate verdict, and he would select Dior. And maybe he should. Saxon wouldn't have to deal with Leonora anymore. He could be free. He could have his happily-ever-after.

And me? I wouldn't get to enjoy his sweet taste ever again. I wouldn't get to make him happy and smell his intoxicating scent. I wouldn't get to feel his soft skin pressed against mine, or enjoy the softness of his feathers. Dior would.

No, I would spend my days crafting and selling weapons and my nights corralling Leonora. Her fury... One day, she would decide to murder Saxon for a third time, punishing him before they started over. She would murder his wife, too.

My newfound merriment crumbled around me. I had to kill the phantom. I had to kill her soon. Until I did, everyone I loved, liked, or encountered would be in danger. I wouldn't be able to remain at the palace—that option had just gotten swept off the table. I certainly wouldn't want to travel to the Avian Mountains with Saxon and his new bride. I'd have to move far, far away from them.

So where would I go? Unmarried mortal girls weren't allowed to buy homes of their own. I couldn't even rent a room at an inn. My dragons wouldn't fare well in crowds.

Maybe the three of us could move into the stable permanently?

The evil sorceress—Everly—might kick us out, but she'd have to do it face-to-face, giving me the chance to speak with her about Leonora. Could phantoms be syphoned to death, as magic could be?

Was that my only option? Begging a sorceress to remove a phantom?

Would it even harm Leonora? Would she regenerate, as power did? Or would she just jump into someone else, Saxon and Dior still in danger?

"Ashleigh?" Saxon prompted, sounding concerned.

"I—I'm sorry." I turned my head away and blinked back a sudden well of tears. "We need to stop."

At first, he didn't speak. He didn't move, either. Heaving breaths, he peered down at me. "Did I frighten you?"

His go-to question lately. "No," I assured him. I didn't want him thinking he'd done anything wrong. "Nothing like that. I liked what we were doing." So much.

"Did I move too quickly, pressing for more than you wish to give?"

I shook my head. *Don't you dare cry.* "No, not that, either."

"Do you fear what comes after a kiss?" He paused, thoughtful. "Do you *know* what comes after a kiss?"

I licked my lips and offered a slow nod, then gathered my courage to face him again. "We would do what the animals do. A part of you goes…inside me. That, um, part I spotted earlier. The really big one." How was I discussing such an intimate topic even halfway matter-of-factly? "Is that, um, correct?"

Saxon gave a slow nod of his own. A drop of water fell from the ends of his hair and splashed onto my chin. "Yes, that's correct."

"Have you ever…?" *Shut your mouth. End this line of conversation.* I opened my mouth to snatch back the question. "I mean, I know you did in past lives, but what about this one?"

Well. So much for snatching back the question. I'd clarified it and asked for added information.

Again, he nodded. This time, his gaze dropped to my mouth. His attention lingered there, and my flutters returned.

"With who? No, sorry. That's none of my business. I mean, what's it like?" Needing to touch him, I dragged my nails along the center of his chest. "The dryads didn't entertain, um, gentlemen callers."

He radiated stark hunger and looked at me as if I were a last meal. "When done right, it is…consuming. You reach a point where the rest of the world fades and nothing else matters."

I wanted the rest of the world to fade. "Do you have any children in this life?" The thought of miniature Saxons running around made my heart leap.

"No children." He anchored a fist next to each of my temples and motioned to the bracelets that adorned his wrist. "One is imbued with magic to prevent a lover from conceiving." Leaning down, he brushed his cheek against mine, as if he needed to touch me, too. Then, he just stopped, lifting his head. "Come. It's time I returned you to the palace."

Heartbeat. "You don't want to..." Heartbeat. "Be my lover?" Heartbeat, heartbeat, heartbeat.

His eyes blazed. "I do want to, yes. More than I've ever wanted anything. But we won't take that step until you're certain you're ready."

I was disappointed. I was grateful. So much was at stake right now, so much uncertain. "I'm not happy about leaving the dragons in the stable without me."

"I promise you they'll remain unharmed. They'll be shielded by magic. If there is a magical doorway between the secret passage and stable as I requested, you'll be able to visit the babies anytime you wish, without delay."

"How do you afford these magical services, anyway?" Ophelia charged exorbitant prices. "I mean, I know you have the royal avian coffers at your disposal and everything, but that doesn't mean you should spend your people's money on personal things."

"I spend the money I earned collecting bounties for King Challen."

An act of loyalty. *My honorable prince.*

My fated. The boy I wanted.

The man I couldn't have.

Lady Leonora had been Craven's fated one, too. My first incarnation had marked my first possession. Only, Craven hadn't known or accepted our connection because a part of him had sensed the wrongness of the situation. The phantom had tainted their relationship, and he'd parted with her.

The same thing had happened with Tyron and Leonora.

Should *I* be the one who parted with Craven this time?

Different path, different ending, right?

It wasn't like a separation had to be forever. After I won the war with the phantom—I had to win—I could seek out Saxon again. If he was free...

As I sat up, he leaned back. I drew my knees to my chest, and snaked my arms around my legs. Without Saxon's body heat, the cool air quickly chilled my damp skin, and I shivered.

"You're a good prince, Saxon, but you'll be an even better king." I had some thinking to do. I needed to decipher the rest of the fairy tale—was I missing a clue about how to end the stepmother's reign?

"Yes," I finally told my avian, my tone determined. "Let's return me to the palace."

20

Merry, merry, be one, be all.
Soon enough there will be a fall.

SAXON

After we dressed in our clean, dry clothes, I whistled to summon the dragons from the woods. They joined us and followed us into the air. I kept Ashleigh in the safety of my arms.

I would never tire of holding her. My fated.

My mind shied away from the thought, the implications too vast to explore at the moment. *Not ready to go there.*

Usually the princess relaxed against me. This time, she remained quiet, lost in thought. Did she ponder our kiss?

I did. I couldn't get my first taste of her out of my mind. So different from Leonora. The witch kissed like she wanted only to please me. Ashleigh kissed like she wanted to please herself, and my enjoyment was secondary, and I loved it. It meant she'd lost herself in the throes and acted solely on instinct—getting her body what it needed.

I remembered the little mewls of delight she'd uttered, the

sweetness of her lips, the rightness of her scent as it teased and tantalized, and I groaned. Our kiss had teemed with possessiveness and ferocity, unlike anything I'd experienced before. I'd felt as if I was drinking pure, undiluted lust straight from the tap, and nothing less would ever satisfy me again. I'd been consumed by Ashleigh, and happier for it.

When she'd touched my wings of her own volition, I'd nearly burst into flames, my insides nothing but kindling. Frantic need had owned me; I would have eagerly burned. My entire world had suddenly revolved around Ashleigh Charmaine-Anskelisa. True contentment had sparked, making a mockery of everything I'd felt before.

As the heat inside me had worsened, I'd felt the first sting of amour.

Still not ready.

So what had happened there at the end? What had turned her eyes into wounds, making me long to rip out my aching heart and offer it to her?

We reached the stable, and I was pleased to find Everly and Ophelia had created the gateways as requested. Framed like a full-length mirror anchored to the air, the bridge between two separate locations possessed a jellied center that rippled like water.

Ashleigh could return to the palace, as planned, and I could meet with Roth and Everly, as needed. The dragons could play without fear of the unknown. Problem was, I wasn't yet ready to part with my princess. In three lifetimes of pain and misery, she'd given me a glimpse of true peace, and I only craved more.

How could I let her go, even for a moment?

Ever?

She crouched before the dragons, saying, "I must return to the palace, my darlings, but I'd like you to remain at the stable. This is for your safety. The doorway is a no-no unless you're in danger. Do you understand?"

Pagan caught a fly with her tongue. Pyre licked Ashleigh's cheek.

She was the kind of mother I'd always wished I'd had.

"I love you so much." Teary-eyed, she kissed and hugged both dragons, then approached me. Unwilling to meet my gaze, she toyed with the collar of my tunic. "Thank you. For everything."

I experienced one of those pangs only she could conjure. "You owe me no thanks, Asha. Today was a reward for me, as well."

She opened and closed her mouth, eyes glowing with concern, then resolve. "Saxon?"

Concerned myself, I said, "Tell me." Whatever bothered her, I would fix.

"I had fun with you today. The most fun I've had in...ever."

I began to relax.

"But we can't kiss again," she finished.

Denial exploded inside my head. *Addict me, then take away my drug of choice?* "Why?"

"You're part of the tournament, vying for Princess Dior's hand in marriage." She stumbled back a step, then another. "It's not fair to her, and it's not fair to me. Or to you."

Before I had time to reply—what could I say without revealing the truth about Roth and Everly?—she shook her head, as if any response would be moot.

Returning to the spot before me, she rose to her tiptoes and pressed her lips against mine softly. She cupped my cheeks, just as she'd done while we danced. A way I loved, I realized. At first, she held on, saying nothing, as if she were memorizing the feel of me.

"Maybe in our next life, fate will be kinder, eh?" She released me with the saddest smile, then entered the doorway, vanishing from view.

I stood in place for a long while, spreading and curling my

fingers again and again. At last I understood why she'd gone cold during our kiss. The stepsister. A respectful gesture for a girl she'd come to like. But not kiss Ashleigh again? Impossible. And wed Dior? Never. But I couldn't explain my true purpose for entering the tournament.

As I made the return flight to my tent, I considered the other obstacles in our path. I planned to dethrone her father—plans I wouldn't halt. The longer he kept the crown, the faster he destroyed the kingdom. He'd raised taxes twice, offended Violet, Queen of Airaria and Everly's estranged mother, and verged on war with Azul, his own wife's homeland, for offering their beloved Dior as a war prize after using their soldiers to take Roth's kingdom. Selfish Philipp had too much pride and no self-control—a lethal combination.

Would Ashleigh despise me for overseeing her father's downfall? I doubt anyone had missed the longing looks she'd cast him upon her return.

Foreboding pricked the back of my neck, but I shook it off as an ungrounded fear. The king treated her like garbage. He didn't deserve to be part of her life. I thought she'd already begun to accept this truth, just as I had accepted the truth about Ashleigh, my fated, and Leonora, who was not.

I could put off thoughts of the amour no longer.

I'd produced it. It had happened. Ashleigh was my mate, the one I was born to protect and cherish.

The one I'd been waiting for the whole of my lives.

The one I'd hurt again and again.

She'd always been my mate. But the being inside her must have warped the connection. Did that mean Ashleigh was a reincarnate, but the being was not?

A reincarnate, but not a reincarnate.

Could someone be cursed to live for centuries? A ghost, perhaps? One who'd targeted my incarnations and possessed my fated ones?

Could ghosts wield fire magic? Could they be removed and killed?

Protective instincts surged. I needed to save Ashleigh from this being, whatever the cost.

I landed at the campground and strode around a wealth of new trees. I marched past my guards, each of whom congratulated me on yesterday's victory. As I entered my tent, the first thing I noticed was Everly and Roth lying side by side on the pallet. Both were fully clothed. Everly tossed up a grape and caught it with her mouth while Roth continued reading a piece of parchment.

"Well, well," she said when she spotted me. She eased into an upright position and offered me a mocking grin. "Look who finally decided to show up for our morning team meeting."

"I'm ten minutes early." I closed the distance and fell between them, careful not to bend my wings.

"Which means you're fifty minutes late," Roth retorted.

"What time does the test of speed begin?"

"The king had the master of ceremonies blow his horn through the campground an hour before sunrise to summon you. The first to arrive at the coliseum won." He snorted. "I wondered why you allowed Milo to have the victory. Now I know. You weren't here. You were with the princess."

I scrubbed a hand over my face. I'd missed this morning's voluntary test of speed. "What boon did he request of the king?"

"No one knows."

I wasn't going to let myself worry. I had Noel and Ophelia on my side. They would guard my back.

"Oh, goodness. Your lips are so puffy, Saxon." Everly's tone conveyed exaggerated concern. She batted her lashes at me. "Did someone punch you in the mouth?"

Tattletale plants. I cast a scornful gaze to Roth, who regarded me with mirth. "Do you happen to have a muzzle handy?"

My friend snickered. "Why? Are you afraid you can't keep your lips away from Ashleigh without one?"

"Yes!" I lifted my arm to peer at the array of bracelets that adorned my wrist. What would happen if I offered Ashleigh the one reserved for my bride, binding us in holy matrimony? Something *I* wanted more than anything. To wed my fated at last. But how could I even contemplate such a possibility with Leonora in play?

The avian did not part once they were wed. If the being erased Ashleigh as she'd erased my other fated ones, Leonora would become my wife.

Must remove and kill her.

And Ashleigh's heart? What then?

Just as before, the question threw me, those protective urges surging with greater intensity. I hissed a curse. As long as Ashleigh needed magic, I could do nothing permanent to Leonora. As long as Ashleigh carried Leonora, my connection to her jeopardized my people and my future. But...

I couldn't let her go, either. I might be strong, but I would never have enough strength to cut ties with my princess. A fact I accepted. I'd fought hard to get to this realization, and I didn't want to fight it, too. I was already fighting the urge to scoop her up and return to our waterfall; it was an itch in the back...center...and forefront of my mind, and it left me raw and desperate.

We needed to talk, she and I. But first, I needed to figure out my next move. No longer did I plan to have her cursed to an eternal sleep at the end of the tournament. That wasn't even an option.

The tournament had reached its last legs, semifinals this week, finals next week.

Two weeks to go. Fourteen days. An eternity. I wanted to be rid of Philipp now. I wanted Ashleigh to know I had no plans to wed Dior. I wanted Ashleigh at my side as I claimed my new title of king.

Fourteen days. The next seven would feature more bonus battles, along with the two semifinal rounds. I could survive the end of Noel's timeline.

The timeline. The oracle's warning whispered through my mind and nearly stopped my heart. *Let the next three weeks serve as a test. When time is up, there'll be no more. There'll be no going back.*

Had she meant there would be no more time…with Ashleigh? With Leonora?

Sweat beaded on my brow. Fourteen days. A blip, a vapor. I had a mere fourteen days to free Ashleigh from the possible-ghost, without harming her irreparably. Fourteen. Days.

"What do you know of ghosts?" I asked Everly.

"That they whine when you don't find the spirit of their dead boyfriend fast enough. Why?"

"I think Ashleigh is possessed by one." As I spoke, some long buried memory fought its way to the surface. Possessed long term…by a spirit born in fire…possessed by a…phantom? A myth from a child's tale? Unless there was as much misinformation about phantoms as there was about avian, lies purposely fed out to keep the truth from a possible enemy…

Son of a— "What do you know of phantoms?" I asked Roth.

He sat up and stared at me. "No. You can't be thinking… No," he repeated.

"What? What's wrong with phantoms?" Everly threw another grape into her mouth.

"They are spirits, like ghosts, but they can possess someone for the entire span of their life. Some call them invisible dragons and say they wield power over—" His eyes widened. "Fire."

I nodded, certain now. Leonora was a phantom and Ashleigh was possessed. Did Ashleigh know? I thought she might. How deeply I regretted the fact that she didn't feel she could trust me with her secrets. My fault. Only mine.

"So you think Ashleigh is possessed by one of these phantoms?" Everly asked.

"I do." I racked my brain, hoping to remember any other details I'd heard but finding nothing. "Do you recall a single tale that mentions a way to defeat a phantom?"

"I don't," Roth offered grimly. "I'll speak with Noel and Ophelia."

"Remind her that we have fourteen days to save Ashleigh from Leonora," I returned, just as grim.

"All right, enough doom and gloom. Everything could change in a snap, so fourteen days is forever." Everly swiped her hands together, case made. "Let's finish our meeting so you can give yourself a one-armed workout while mooning about your princess, Saxon."

I blinked. Rapidly. Had she just implied...?

Roth burst out laughing. She had. She really had.

She saluted me, yes, mocking me again. "Here's the field report, sir. My plants and vines have been picking up chatter at the palace, just not from the king, who is blocking me with magic. I suspect the warlock has created some kind of shield for him. Through servant gossip, I learned the king plans to invite you and the other semifinalists to dinner tonight. Your mother and sister, too. He has news he wants to drop. Oh, and there will be an extra bonus round tonight, something about being the best negotiator. Also, there's something wrong with him. He's sick and getting sicker. He blames me, because the warlock blames me, claiming I'm an evil sorceress, so it's my nature, blah, blah, blah. The king thinks I'm hiding nearby and draining him in order to weaken him so that Roth can steal the kingdom back. I suspect he's being poisoned."

Roth leaned over to collect a handful of grapes from the bowl next to his girl. "Remember how Noel ensured my death in the tournament so that I could do a job for her? She wanted me to follow Milo…who knocked on Ashleigh's door last night and whispered the phantom's name."

"The warlock is working with Leonora, then. Ashleigh told me she's been taking over at the night." What was the phantom's purpose? I claimed a piece of fruit for myself. "You are no longer a combatant, Roth. You can kill the warlock."

"I thought the same. Alas." Roth gave a mournful sigh. "The oath remains in effect until the tournament's end."

I arched a brow at Everly, all, *Up to slaying a warlock?*

"Because of my bond to this guy—" she elbowed Roth in the stomach "—the oath affects me too. But you should know, you're right on the money about Leonora meeting with Milo. I overheard them speaking at some point."

"What did they discuss?" The words burst from me. "Why am I only just now hearing about this?"

"Because it takes time for certain conversations to filter through all the noise in here." She tapped her temple. "Because I'm still learning. Because I was busy. Geez. It sounded like they are the ones poisoning Philipp, because they want to take the throne and rule the kingdom together. And I gotta admit, I'm glad to hear Ashleigh wasn't the one telling Milo he will be the strongest, most specialest king ever to rule."

So, what was the plan to achieve this goal, then? Milo would kill Philipp, Ashleigh would be crowned queen, and Leonora would bury Ashleigh once and for all? Either she would do it all, hoping to win me back, or she would truly marry Milo.

When we warred, she lived to spite me. And what a punishment it would be. The perfect recompense for me. I had married other women in the past, so, she would marry another man in the present. I would experience her pain and longing for what could not be.

"I will kill Milo in battle, then, rendering him a nonfactor," I vowed. As for Ashleigh… I would see her at dinner.

I better see her at dinner. If Philipp left her in her bedroom, I'd rage.

Learning about the phantom hadn't changed my feelings for her. Had it increased my guilt and shame? Oh, yes. But Ashleigh was a priority now, and if we could rid her of Leonora, I could spend the rest of my life making reparation.

I landed on the palace steps ten minutes early. I couldn't stay away a moment more.

The archway had been decorated with ribbons and flowers. A swarm of pixies flew about, dusting the blooms with their wings. That swarm avoided one area of the foliage, and I narrowed my focus to try and discern why. When the reason peeked out from a cluster of leaves, I snorted.

One of Everly's pet spidorpions crawled up the palace wall to spy on the king, since the sorceress could not hear him through vines.

Sensing movement behind me, I flicked a glance over my shoulder and scowled. My mother and sister had arrived.

"Saxon," they greeted in unison, stiff and formal.

"Crown Prince Saxon," I corrected. I remembered how pompous Philipp had sounded when he'd done this to Ashleigh and strove to match his tone. "Soon to be King Saxon. You will use my title."

Raven stiffened further, but also nodded. "Crown Prince."

Tempest remained quiet, staring ahead and saying nothing else.

Dismissing them, I returned my focus to the palace doors, where two guards were posted. As I stepped forward, they moved aside, allowing me to enter the foyer.

The cool breeze died, the overwarm candlelit air quickly becoming an irritant to my skin. I much preferred the outdoors. Other semifinalists huddled together in the corner. All but Milo. He wasn't here.

The king waited just ahead, with Princess Dior at his side. I searched for Ashleigh, tensing when I couldn't—there. Partially hidden behind Dior.

Ashleigh moved into my line of vision. I should have relaxed at the sight of her, but my every muscle turned to stone. She wore a gown made of little clusters of green avian feathers, the magnificent garment paying proper homage to her curves.

Her hair flowed in rich, sable waves, with only the sides pinned back. A rosy flush painted her luscious skin. Around her eyelids, I detected a subtle line of dragon soot, turning her eyes into a smoky dream.

I'd never seen a more beautiful sight.

As she looked anywhere but my direction, I fought the urge to push my way to her, to crowd her and force her to acknowledge my presence. I approached the king instead, only then noticing the rapidness of his deterioration. Nine days ago, he had been healthy, not a thing wrong with him. Today, he had sallow skin, sunken cheeks, and thinning hair. One of his front teeth had chipped. He had several bruises on his hands.

Everly was right. He was being poisoned, his body wasting away. To remain upright, he leaned on a cane. Since he believed he was being drained by an evil sorceress, he probably wasn't taking precautions, having his food checked by royal tasters.

I derived no satisfaction from his plight, as I once might have, but I could rouse no sympathy for him, either.

"Prince Saxon," he said in greeting. Even his voice lacked substance.

"Your Majesty." Nod. "Princess Dior." Nod. I accepted her offered hand and kissed her knuckles, but my attention remained on Ashleigh, who continued avoiding my gaze.

"Charmed," Dior said as she blushed and curtsied.

"We are honored that the royal avian family has joined us this eve," Philipp said, inclining his head to my relatives. "Queen

Raven, Princess Tempest, I'd like to introduce my daughter Princess Dior." His affection for her was as clear as his disdain for Ashleigh.

The need to defend my princess seethed within me.

Philipp continued, "It is my greatest hope that you can set aside your anger with my other daughter, Princess Ashleigh, and enjoy the festivities. My oracle tells me Prince Saxon has already forgiven the girl."

"Crown Prince." I ruled the skies, and it was time everyone understood that.

I would always rule the skies.

Before we'd begun this journey, Noel warned there would be times she would have to relay our secrets to the king in order to hide her true allegiance. Whenever Philipp asked a direct question, she could not evade. Whenever she provided an answer, she could not lie. Sometimes, her visions happened spontaneously, the details spilling from her unbidden.

Risks we'd decided to take, so I did not blame her for speaking of me to my enemy. I didn't even blame her for giving the eggs to Ashleigh. How could I rail when I appreciated the outcome?

Beaming like a proud papa, Philipp motioned Ashleigh to his side. "Come here, girl."

Proud? I narrowed my eyes. What was his game? Had he learned about Leonora and hoped to use her power?

"I assure you, King Philipp," Raven said, lifting her nose, "I will not forgive—"

"She will," I finished for her. When she opened her mouth to say more, I held up a fisted hand, a command for silence.

She bared her teeth at me, but she went quiet.

Ashleigh floated to her father's side, a vision…a happily-ever-after all on her own, and peered up at the man, confused. "Father? Would you like me to return to my room?"

I jerked at the question.

The king shook his head. "Only for a moment," he said. "I'd like you to fetch the trinkets you had made for me."

Her brow furrowing, she stammered, "Trinkets? I'm sorry, but I'm not sure—"

"The things…the weapons you paid my witch to create for me." He glanced about the room, as if embarrassed for her. "Yes, I know about them. My oracle sees all. Now go and fetch them. As I have no need of such things, you may give them to Queen Raven as a token of your great affections for her and her people."

The corners of her mouth turned down, down, her expression hardening. "Yes, Father. Of course. I shall fetch the *trinkets*."

I planted my heels in the floor as she dashed off. Her father would pay for this.

The minutes without her passed at a snail's pace.

"Your Majesty," I grated, keeping my gaze on the door Ashleigh had exited. "There's no need for Princess Ashleigh to gift my mother with anything. In fact, I won't allow it. It is my mother who owes your daughter reparation for years of abuse."

The queen recoiled at the very thought, but she didn't defend herself, per my order.

Where was—

Ashleigh padded into the room carrying a unique dagger and sword. Two of her best designs. I recognized the grooves for spring-loaded spikes in both. An engraved rose decorated the hilts. Her call sign.

She stopped in front of me to thrust the pieces in my direction, her usually expressive features blank. "For your mother."

I experienced a pang worse than any other. Though I wanted to accept both pieces for myself, I held up my hands, palms out. "You owe the avian nothing, Princess Ashleigh, and you never did. What happened when we were younger wasn't your fault. I was mistaken, and for that, I'm the one who owes *you* restitution."

Slowly the emotionless mask fell away, revealing crushing disappointment. I swallowed, wanting only to hold her close and hold the rest of the world at bay.

With a rough voice, she asked, "So you don't want the weapons, either?"

"I want them badly," I assured her.

"Saxon—Prince Saxon," she amended with a tremble, her gaze sliding to and from her father. "You don't have to be nice to me. I'm sure you can find a better designer."

No longer caring about our audience, I tucked two knuckles underneath her chin and gently urged her eyes to mine. "When have I ever been nice to anyone? And I have *never* come across a better designer or more progressive pieces. But I don't want the weapons given to me—" my mother would not be getting them "—for an apology that isn't owed."

Wonder sparked, burning off some of the disappointment. I almost beat my chest with pride. I'd done that. Me. "I give the pieces in thanks, then," she said softly. "Do you accept?"

"Nothing could stop me." I claimed both of Ashleigh's weapons with the reverence they deserved. After I'd looked them over, admiring every facet of their design, I sheathed them both in their proper places, next to my other weapons. "Thank you, Princess. I will cherish them always." I cupped her fingers, lifted her hand to my lips, and kissed. I turned her palm up to give her a second kiss, flicking my tongue against her throbbing pulse.

A gasp escaped her, one of surprise and excitement, and I reveled in it.

"Ah," the king said, peering beyond us. He brightened. "Our final guest has arrived. The winner of the boon."

315

I pivoted, every muscle in my body tensing as Milo strode into the foyer.

"Has everyone met Milo, my royal warlock?" the king asked. "He is Ashleigh's betrothed."

21

Down, down goes the hourglass sand.
But when will something go as planned?

Ashleigh

I stood in place, utterly shocked, my ability to reason gone. Still, I gave it my best shot.

First, Saxon had entered the palace the way he liked to enter any room—the master of all he surveyed. In that moment, I'd been a live wire of energy, my entire being charged to full power. My prince had only had eyes for me. He'd projected no animosity. Instead, he'd looked almost…tender.

Now, in a split second, I entertained a thousand thoughts all at once. I wondered if we could make a relationship work, after all. I wondered about the evil stepmother's defeat, replaying everything I'd studied today. How her pride had been her downfall, how she'd thought herself better than Cinder, how she'd never viewed the girl as an equal and it had cost her. I considered the difficulties and the rewards of being with Saxon. I replayed my father's summons to his side, how he'd wrapped his arm around me and called me his daughter, I remembered how it had felt as if I were living in a dream. I relived his rejection of my gifts in front of everyone. I heard him tell the boy I'd kissed—the boy I wanted to kiss again—that I would be wedding the warlock. The words continued to echo.

My betrothed?

Betrothed? *Mine?*

The question tolled, a last rite bell, and I shuddered. I had never agreed to marry anyone, much less a boy who'd burned his father's journals just to keep a girl bound to a phantom's whims.

"Her *betrothed*?" Saxon roared.

"For his boon, Milo requested Ashleigh's hand in marriage rather than Princess Dior's," the king explained. "If he wins the tournament, of course."

Though my head spun, I snuck a peek at everyone else to gauge their reaction to this news. Raven evinced satisfaction while Tempest projected relish. Dior looked worried on my behalf. Fury blazed in Saxon's whiskey eyes.

Why had fate picked this prince for me, only to throw unending obstacles in our path? Had our fairy tale twisted so much, we were no longer supposed to be together? Was that it? Were we supposed to prove how hard we'd fight to be together? Or was it something else?

Why did Saxon have to look so beautiful, even now? Why was I falling for him instead of someone—anyone—else? And I *was* falling for him. I couldn't even blame fate. With his loyalty, his sense of humor, and yes, even his kind, caring heart, the avian crown prince was winning me over all on his own.

He had many sides, and I thought I might be attracted to all of them. The carefree boy I'd swam with and cuddled, who'd treated my dragons like family. The warrior who had every right to hate me, but protected me instead. The soldier who'd appreciated my designs, when my own family considered them worthless.

318

The reincarnate who didn't know I hosted a phantom. Or did he, and he just didn't care? He'd already begun to piece things together, and he'd only gotten sweeter.

But he still fought to win Dior—and I would much rather he wed her than die in battle. I was still a danger to Saxon, and now I had to deal with a betrothed? I… I just… I had… I… I couldn't think right now, my emotions too chaotic. My world had just been turned upside down and inside out.

"Father," I rasped. "Majesty."

He stopped me before I could say more. "I will hear your thanks now. Nothing else is acceptable."

Thanks? *Thanks?* I opened my mouth to shout, *I will never wed Milo.* The warlock was Leonora's pawn and my enemy. But it wasn't a negation that flowed from my tongue. "Yes, Father. Thank you. Marrying my favorite warlock will be a dream come true."

What! I would never say… I…

Realization hit, and I went cold. *Leonora.* She'd gained more power over me. Enough to control my speech for a short while.

Please be a short while.

Each time she'd defeated the barrier, she'd only had a few minutes before it reformed.

As much as I wanted to shout *That wasn't me*, I remained silent. The truth would do more harm than good.

Father nodded, looking as satisfied as Raven. Milo cast me a smug grin, as if he had me right where he wanted me. Had he and Leonora planned this when they'd met?

Saxon spit out a vile curse and even reached for his new sword, glaring bloody murder at the warlock. "What of my reparation?"

In his most patronizing tone, my father said, "Only moments ago, you told us you had no need of reparation. Or did I mishear?"

With a growl, the avian prowled closer to the king. My father shrank back. When Saxon attempted to go around me, I moved with him, remaining in front of him to stand between the two.

"No," I said, and oh, thank goodness. I had control of my voice again. I took Saxon's hand and squeezed, and he offered me a curt nod before backing down.

I had to do a double take. All I had to say was "no," and he acquiesced? But that couldn't be right.

My father coughed to cover his moment of fear. "What's done is done."

Another growl from Saxon, but he made no other move toward my father.

The majordomo entered the foyer then and bowed. He wore purple velvet, a uniform usually reserved for the royal servants of Fleur. "Your Majesty. Lords and ladies. Your humble servants request the honor of your presence in the dining room, so that we might serve you a delicious meal."

"Come, come," Father said, sounding relieved. He hobbled in the direction of the dining hall, expecting everyone to follow.

Milo pushed past Saxon, stopped before me, and bowed. "I will escort you, Princess." He offered me his arm, his fierce expression telling me to take it—or else.

In the past, I would have snapped to and accepted. But after scheming to protect my dragons, enduring the wrath of an avian prince, getting choked, and finding out I was possessed by an evil phantom, I found I wasn't intimidated by him any longer. While I needed to speak with Milo about the engagement, about his meetings with Leonora, I wouldn't tolerate threats of any kind.

And why should I? I wasn't just Cinder. I was a mother of dragons, the fated one of Craven, a designer of spectacular weapons, and a slayer of wicked phantoms—slay pending. There was nothing I couldn't do.

"I do not accept," I told him, bristling. "Once you have offered reparation for your behavior today—arranging a marriage without my permission, glaring at me, and speaking to me as if I am your servant—we will chat."

Saxon shouldered Milo aside. "I am her escort," he said, hooking his arm through mine. "Until the tournament's end, Princess Ashleigh Charmaine-Anskelisa belongs to me. A decree her father made the day of her arrival. If he lied to me, if you or anyone else touches her without my express permission, I will consider it a declaration of war." He led me forward.

Oh, my. His intensity…his power. His jealousy? I fanned my overheating cheeks.

To me, he muttered, "I'm proud of you, Asha. You are calm and collected, while I am soon to shatter. How long have you known about the engagement?"

"Two seconds?" Maybe three. "I didn't mean to agree to it, but there was no stopping Leonora."

"That, I know. Your eyes flashed ice blue when you spoke." They had?

"Does she use him or punish me?" he asked.

"Both?" Classic Leonora, always upping the stakes. "But it doesn't matter. You will win the tournament, and I will be released from the engagement. You have to win, Sax."

"I will." He'd never sounded so determined.

And so, the boy I wanted would wed my stepsister, as feared—as hoped—whether he wanted her or not.

I missed my next step, but with Saxon's help I righted quickly. "You are unwell?" he asked.

Yes. I wasn't sure I'd ever be well again. I was going to lose Saxon. I'd known it, but to have it confirmed…

I bit the inside of my cheek. I still hadn't figured out a place to live, but I *had* accepted that my father would never see worth in me, no matter what I did or said.

At the reminder, a damn broke, and years of hurt coursed within me in a rush. Why was I devastated by a truth I should have admitted ages ago? Why had I clung to hope? What had my father ever given me but rejection and toil? Today was the first day he'd ever smiled at me. He'd done it because he'd known what I hadn't. He'd arranged what he considered an advantageous marriage for me. A powerful warlock had chosen his sickly daughter and when we wed—we wouldn't wed—that warlock could aid the kingdom free of charge.

To King Philipp, I was nothing. Less than nothing. A thing to be used for gain.

He didn't deserve my pain.

"Asha? Sweetheart?" Saxon rearranged his arms, slinging one around my lower back to rest his palm on the flare of my hip. He used the other to pin one of my hands to his chest. "Tell me what's going on. If you are worried for Milo's safety—"

"I'm not. I don't like him. He's sneaky and underhanded."

Saxon visibly relaxed. "He's dangerous. Far more so than I realized."

Yes, far more so than *I* had realized, too. Milo knew my secret. The thing I both did and didn't want Saxon to know. Had he guessed or not?

I needed to tell him. Surely I was wrong before. Surely he wouldn't want to use me to kill Leonora.

His family would, though. I tossed a glance over my shoulder. Saxon's family trailed us, both females glaring at me. In that moment, their identities clicked.

Hello, evil stepsisters.

I knew I was right, and glared right back. I wouldn't give them the satisfaction of intimidating me.

Behind the duo, Milo escorted Dior, who looked horrified to be with the boy who'd chosen to wed another.

Undeniable guilt flared. "You should be escorting Dior," I whispered to Saxon. While fate had seemed to strive to keep Saxon and me apart, it seemed to thrust Saxon and Dior together.

"Why?" he asked. "I don't want her."

"That's…" I began to smile, but caught myself. "Terrible. She's a good person and…" The emotional upheaval of the day was beginning to take its toll, this line of conversation suddenly too much for me. I finished with, "You'd be lucky to have her, that's all."

He vibrated with incredulity. "You *want* me to be with her?"

Not even a little. But what I wanted didn't matter. I could only have what I could have.

"Ashleigh?" Saxon prompted.

"I want you happy," I replied, and maybe I could have that.

Gaze softening, he reached out to stroke my ring, hanging between my breasts. "You make me happy."

I gulped. "What does it mean? The ring, I mean."

"Craven gave it to Leonora as a pledge of his eternal love."

After so many other blows today, the information exploded like a bomb inside my head. The ring I'd cherished, the ring I'd derived so much comfort from, had first belonged to the phantom I hated. Not to the original Leonora—me—but the phantom Leonora. Craven had given it to her; and she hadn't even been his fated.

Leonora might not have been what he'd needed, but he'd liked something about her. She'd been something he'd *wanted*. Excitement, perhaps. A challenge. Things I might not have been in the beginning.

I might not have been enough back then.

I might not be enough now. Was that why fate seemed to want Saxon and Dior together?

Growing queasy, I pressed a hand against my belly. Would I ever be enough for *anyone*?

I should fling the ring in the trash and never look back.

My eyes burned, a lone tear sliding down my cheek.

Shadows of guilt and shame whisked through Saxon's irises. "Why has this information upset you?"

I didn't know how to respond to that. "It's been a trying day," I said, and left it at that.

We reached the dining hall, a spacious room with ivory pillars, marble floors, and mirrored walls. A long table occupied the center, displaying a wealth of fine china. Noel and Ophelia were already seated in the center on the left. The oracle grinned and waved, while the witch saluted us with an open bottle of wine. They must have been there awhile because the bottle was half-empty.

My father claimed his seat at the head of the table and frowned. "Must you behave so crassly, witch?"

"Yes, Majesty, I must." Ophelia took a swig straight from the bottle.

Name cards rested on each plate. Dior and I were to sit at the king's right and left, respectively, with Saxon beside my stepsister and Milo beside me.

Eat, next to the warlock? Make conversation with him? My queasiness intensified, what little bravado I'd managed to spackle onto my expression thinning.

Queen Raven was to have the seat at Saxon's other side, followed by his elder sister, Tempest, and one of the combatants. Beside Milo was another combatant, with the final six at the foot of the table.

Saxon pulled out my chair, and I eased down, unsure if my breath hitched due to his incredible intensity or my incredible weakness for him.

With a smooth push, he edged me forward, then leaned down to grip the chair arms, his lips hovering near my ear. For me alone, he whispered, "Just know, Asha. Every time our eyes meet, I'm thinking about kissing you."

Breath escaped me, heat sizzling under the surface of my skin. *He flirts with me so blatantly? Here? Now?* "How can you know for certain that's where your thoughts will be?"

"My thoughts are *always* centered around kissing you." He straightened and walked away then, leaving me reeling.

Milo helped Dior into the chair across from me and strode around the table. As he and Saxon passed each other, the rest of the assembly went quiet, tension thickening the air. But neither boy threw a punch and everyone claimed their seats.

My father clinked a knife against a glass, signaling the servants. "We are having dishes from all of Enchantia. Delicacies from each of the kingdoms, sure to delight. Eat, eat."

Bowls of soup were passed out, different conversations blending together. I stole a glance at Saxon, curious where he'd directed his attention—our gazes met. I shifted in my chair as he slowly lifted his wineglass, took a sip, then licked his lips. Because he was imagining kissing me. Right. This. Second.

I wouldn't moan. I wouldn't crawl atop the table and claim that imaginary kiss for real, if only to subvert reality for a little while.

The amazing scent of crab, butter, and cream saturated the air. My stomach rumbled, and my mouth watered. I'd returned to the stable today and played with the dragons, so I hadn't had a chance to eat.

As I ate, I had to forcibly keep my eyes away from Saxon.

—*Look at Saxon… Look.*—

Leonora whispered temptation in the back of my mind.

I strengthened my resolve to never, ever give the phantom what she wanted. *I can't wait to kill you, Leonora.*

She laughed softly, as if she knew a secret I did not.

I focused on Dior before the top of my head blew off. The poor princess. She did her best to engage Saxon in conversation. Even though I refused to let my attention veer to him, I witnessed him bark his responses at her from the corner of my eye. Eventually she bowed her head and focused on her food, exuding misery.

She'd taken more than one blow today, too. Before, she'd

expressed interest in Milo; today he'd made it clear he didn't want her.

And Saxon was still staring at me.

Oh! I'd let my attention veer. And now I couldn't look away. In his mind, were we standing up or lying down while we kissed? Were we clothed or unclothed?

I dropped my spoon, the silverware clattering. Multiple eyes zoomed to me, and my cheeks blazed.

"You are a vision tonight," Milo told me.

"Thank you," I mumbled, even though I knew he didn't mean it. I wasn't a fool; I knew he only wanted Leonora's power.

I swallowed a spoonful of soup, unable to enjoy its rich flavor. How could I convince this man to end our engagement and give me any details he remembered about the potion's recipe?

"Why do you want to wed me?" I asked. Would he admit the truth?

My boldness surprised him. "You already know the answer. Unlike everyone else, including the avian prince, I comprehend and appreciate who you are and what you can do. We will rule this kingdom together."

"Is that what Leonora promised you? A seat on the throne, at her side?"

"Yes," he replied, unabashed as he enjoyed a bite of soup.

"She's lying to you. She wants Saxon, and no other." A desire we shared.

"You're wrong," he snapped, drawing the notice of others. He slinked down in his seat, his cheeks reddening. Keeping his voice at a lower volume, he said, "She's helping me take my rightful place."

He'd used present tense, not future. *What have you done, Leonora?* "Why do you think a throne is your rightful place?"

"I'm the most powerful warlock in all of Enchantia. Why should bloodline matter?" He smirked, then flicked me a pointed glance and took another bite of soup. "A weak blood-line puts a weak royal on a throne."

I took no insult, not this time. I was too wrung out already. More than that, I knew what I'd survived. And now, I could even add the taming of a fierce avian crown prince to my tally of feats. *Does he still imagine our kiss? Don't look. Don't you dare.*

"What does Leonora expect in return?" I asked.

"She will be my wife, and I will help her conquer the Avian Mountains."

They would destroy two kingdoms. Milo, for the good of himself alone. Leonora, for vengeance. "This isn't going to turn out well for you, warlock. She isn't—"

"Shut up," he hissed. "You don't understand the ways of war."

War, he'd said. Not love. And he was very, very wrong about me. I understood war in ways he never would. My mind had been a war zone since the day of my birth. "You think you're guaranteed to win."

He smirked. "Wrong. I have already won."

"Then I have already lost, and nothing I learn will change that. So tell me. Do you remember your father's recipe? His barrier spell?" Did he and Leonora hope to use them against me?

The smirk deepened. "I remember enough."

Oh, yes. They would use them against me.

For the rest of the six courses, we sat in silence. I accepted that I couldn't convince this boy to betray the phantom. I'd find help another way. I'd played with the idea of visiting the Evil Queen. Everly. So why not do it? Dying was the worst that could happen. But if you were dead anyway…

As servants passed out toffee pudding for dessert, my father gave his glass another clink. The guests grew quiet.

"As you know," he announced, "the tournament is close to its end. A mere ten combatants remain. Tonight, one of you will advance to the final, without having to participate in the semifinals."

Twitters of excitement sprang from all but two of the combatants. Milo lifted his chin, ready to win. Saxon stared at me, making me shiver. What did my father have planned?

"All you have to do," the king continued, "is be the one to convince me to give you this coin, using twenty words or less. A good negotiator can do much with little." He held up a small golden disc, his hand shaking. "We'll start at the foot of the table. Know that if you win, I will expect to receive what is offered."

As selfish as Milo.

The snake-shifter said, "Give me the coin, and I will bring you the head of Roth Charmaine, your greatessst enemy." His forked tongue turned the *s* into a hiss.

"Give me the coin," the goblin piped up next, "and you will have my eternal devotion." A wild pledge for a goblin to make. For the rest of his life, he would be bound to my father's will, his word his literal bond.

Six others shouted their response, one after the other. "I will give you a chest of bigger coins."

"The princess and I will name our firstborn after you."

"I will have my scribe write incredible tales in your honor."

"I will give you my prized Pegasus. A true rarity."

"I will find a fine husband for your youngest daughter, Princess Marabella."

"I will fortify your defenses against any enemy."

Milo's turn arrived. "Give me the coin, and I will bespell you to live forever."

My father perked up at that. Could the warlock do such a thing? Surely not. He would have bespelled *himself* to live forever.

Had he?

Saxon ran his tongue over his teeth. Still peering at me, more intense by the second, he said, "Give me the coin, or lose what you value most." His harsh tone turned the words into a threat. *Give me the coin, or I will take it from you.*

Everyone else had offered gain. Saxon offered loss. I didn't think he referenced the coin, though, and I quaked.

My father pulled at his collar and cleared his throat. "All excellent answers, but I must choose Milo the warlock. Who doesn't wish to live forever?" He tossed the coin Milo's way.

Um... Saxon rolled his eyes, not the least bit worried about this supposed immortality spell, which calmed my nerves about it. Milo must have lied. And it was a good one to tell. When he was proven wrong, King Philipp would be too busy being dead to punish him. But by rose petals and sunshine, this put Milo one step closer to victory.

The warlock held the coin up and bowed his head in thanks. As the others clapped, Saxon made a crude gesture with his hand, and I had to press a hand over my mouth to silence a sudden giggle.

A giggle. Amusement. At a time like this.

But the king wasn't done. "The semifinals will be different from the other battles. The first round won't be physical. In the coming days, each combatant will plan a half-day with Princess Dior. Afterward, she will pick her favorite. The least favorite will be eliminated from the competition."

A thick, heavy silence fell over the room, everyone digesting my father's words. Saxon would be creating a romantic outing with Dior. The girl fate might want him to have. Would he kiss her the way he'd kissed me?

I white-knuckled the arms of my chair.

—*I'll burn the girl alive before I allow her lips near his.*—

A tremor rolled through my limbs. Would I be able to stop the phantom from following through with her threat? The insidious way she'd taken ownership of my mouth earlier... I'd had no warning, and no way to fight her.

329

—He is mine.—

The tips of my fingers heated, and I shot to my feet. I needed to get Leonora away from my stepsister. Now. "P-please excuse me." Just like Cinder, I ran away from a gathering as fast as my feet would carry me, blazing out of the dining hall.

I raced down a hallway and up a winding staircase. I would lock myself in my room. And burn the palace down?

New plan. I would pack a bag, collect my dragons, and head to the forest tonight. We would camp out until Queen Everly made herself known.

The faster I ran, the faster I shed the fragile facsimile of control I'd wielded. All the pain I'd experienced over my father's rejection returned and redoubled, and I choked on a sob.

Footsteps sounded behind me, but I only sobbed harder. Who had given chase? I didn't want to speak with *anyone*. Not even Saxon. Especially not Saxon. I wasn't going to say goodbye. I wouldn't give Leonora an opportunity to interact with him.

—You will remain in this kingdom. Disobey me, and I'll kill someone you love every day that you are gone.—

I whimpered. Would she? Could she? Finally, I flew into my bedroom and shut the door behind me. I'd made it two steps forward when the door swung open behind me.

I spun, my knees knocking as Saxon stormed inside the room, sealed the door shut, and turned the lock.

Leonora quieted without prompting. I felt her curiosity, though, what little remained of our barrier continuing to weaken. She wanted to know what he'd do. So did I.

Holding my gaze, he marched toward me. Too vulnerable already, I couldn't stand my ground. I backed into the wall, but he just kept coming, not stopping until he stood only a breath away.

"Tell me what's wrong." He braced one hand at my temple, then the other, each motion slow and precise. "Why did you leave?"

"It's all too much," I croaked, the truth slipping free. "I'm supposed to marry a stranger. A warlock who doesn't really want me. You're going to romance Dior. Leonora wants Dior dead. What if she attacks, and I can't stop her? I will never win my father's love. I'm a burden to be passed off to the next man. I just…why can't he see my worth? Why can't *anyone*?" I'd asked myself those questions countless times. This was the first time I'd ever voiced them, and they just sounded…wrong.

Saxon lightly pinched my chin to tilt my head back and lift my gaze to his. Those whiskey-rich irises shimmered with pain, as if my hurt had seeped into him. "You shouldn't have to win anyone's love. If it's not freely given, *it* has no worth."

He wasn't wrong. Logically, I knew it. My emotions needed more convincing. "Why couldn't he love me? Just a little? What's so awful about me?" A hot tear streamed down my cheek, and I gave a manic laugh. I'd asked the wrong person that question. Saxon had plenty of reasons to despise me.

"There is *nothing* awful about you," he responded anyway. "You are kind, witty, and strong."

"Strong? Now I know you're lying." I sniffled as I swiped at my damp cheek.

"I've watched you endure trial after trial, yet you always excel. If you fall, you fight to rise again. That is a strength few possess. Your father certainly doesn't have it, and that is why he seeks to belittle you. If he admits the truth, that you are stronger than he is, he'll be forced to acknowledge his own weakness. He would have to admit he finds worth in perception instead of reality. And I know this, because I once did the same."

His words and seeming concern for my well-being left me dizzy with…something. Some wild, frantic emotion I couldn't name. I could only blink up at him, desperate for more of it.

"I meant what I said." He brushed the tip of his nose against mine. "If Milo had touched you, I would have dived over the table and fed him his own teeth. You are mine."

"Yours?" *What is even happening right now?* We were going to admit we had feelings for each other, despite everything else going on?

I flattened trembling hands on his pectorals. He towered over me, his shoulders and wings so wide I couldn't see past him. I didn't want to see past him. I panted my breaths, scenting his amour with every inhalation. I'd made him happy again?

The phantom rose with a vengeance, trying to steal the moment, to claim the amour as her own, but I beat her back. I would not share.

I fought her with such force, she scampered back to her hidey-hole, going quiet.

I'd done it? I'd beaten her back?

I had, I really had. I still had a measure of control. I didn't have to run away to find a new home just yet.

Saxon's heart leaped beneath my palm. "You look happier." His gaze hooded, sliding to my mouth. "Kissable."

My pulse thumped. "You want to?" *Kiss me. Please.* I was high on my victory against Leonora.

"I want…" He smoothed a strand of ivy from my hair, then frowned, cursed, and backed away.

"Saxon?" *What just happened?*

"We need to talk. Alone. There are too many prying ears here." He yanked, pulling a leaf from the vine. "Meet me at the stables tonight at midnight. Let Cinder run *to* her prince this time."

His use of the fairy tale brought an unexpected smile to the surface. "What will we be discussing, exactly?"

"Why don't we start where we left off here?" His gaze dropped to my lips, his entire countenance softening. "And go from there."

22

Can you win against fate?
Or is it already too late?

Ashleigh

To meet with Saxon at midnight or not? I wanted to. Because he would kiss me. I also didn't want to. Because he would kiss me. So I paced throughout my bedroom, thinking. When my gaze snagged on the scuff marks that littered the floor, I paused, curious. This chamber had once belonged to Saxon. Those marks could be from his boots. Had he liked to pace the same trail?

I surveyed the rest of the room with new eyes. A handful of ivy vines had grown over one of the walls, where a mural had been painted. The candles that emitted a delicate perfume of vanilla bean—his favorite scent?—flicking with light, revealing details I'd previously missed. In the mural, a warlord with blue wings led an army of soldiers toward a clearing that teemed with colorful flowers…where a large shadow had begun to fall.

Upon closer inspection, I knew that shadow represented a dragon. The mural itself must represent Craven's war with

Leonora. Did he have it commissioned as a reminder never to love the supposed witch again?

I rubbed my chest to dull a sudden, sharp pang, the mental debate still raging. *I want to see him. But I also don't want to see him. But I do want to see him. But I don't. But I do. I don't. I do. Don't. Do. Don't. Do. Argh!*

Ultimately, the battle was both won and lost with a single thought. Kiss him tonight, and wonder if he kissed Dior tomorrow?

That one stung. Better to keep my distance from Saxon. I was coming to rely on him too much, anyway.

What would happen if I couldn't find a way to kill or even permanently subdue the phantom? I'd been so sure of my success...eventually; then she'd agreed to Milo's proposal on my behalf.

What if I stayed just as I was for the rest of my life? Would Saxon want to be with me?

I could guess the answer, so no, I wouldn't be meeting him tonight.

With a sniffle, I locked and barred my bedroom door with a chair, then perched at the desk to write a quick note for the avian.

I'm sorry, but I think we need some time apart.

A

Because of the tracker spell, he wouldn't worry when I failed to show up at the stable. He would know I remained at the palace.

With the note in hand, I entered the secret passage—a small, dark room with a staircase going up and a staircase going down. The magical doorway to the stable stood between the two staircases. At first glance, it appeared to be a full-length mirror. I walked through the liquid glass, emerging in an empty stall, still dry.

After pinning the note to a wooden beam, I wandered about until I found my dragons sleeping in a stall. Just the sight of them swelled my heart with love. I hadn't meant to wake them, but wake them I did. They bounded up, happy to see me. They must have sensed my sadness, though, because they refused to leave my side.

No help for it. I led my babies through the doorway, returning to the bedroom.

We settled into bed, the two creatures cuddling against me as I read "The Little Cinder Girl." "That's me," I said. "I'm Cinder. Maybe you're the reason I'm as fast as wind, eh? Are you darlings going to give Momma a ride one day?"

Pagan looked at me as if I was a good little human for realizing something that should have been obvious to a rock.

Just how smart were my dragons, anyway? Or any dragon, for that matter. In only a week, my babies had learned to understand a language I'd needed years to master. Well, not master, but utilize somewhat properly. My tutors used to despair during my lessons, when I'd been more interested in daydreaming about "The Little Cinder Girl."

Pyre grinned at me, her big, dark eyes alight with possibilities.

Both of my babies gave my cheeks a lick before settling in more comfortably. They drifted back to sleep, smoke curling from their nostrils, and I yawned, ready for a doze myself.

Nope. Not going to happen. I still refused to sleep. Leonora wouldn't be taking over, and I wouldn't be meeting with Milo. I. Would. Not. And that was that.

I gasped, my eyelids popping open. What. The. *What?* My jaw dropped. I lay in the catacombs of the palace, right outside Milo's closed door. Well, the door I assumed belonged to

Milo, since the markings on it indicated a warlock's chamber and reminded me of the one that belonged to his father.

Scowling, I jumped to my feet. Darkened hallows with stone walls and the occasional torch created a maze all around. Dust hung heavy in the frigid air. A random water droplet splashed on the floor.

I'd had enough of these secret meetings. I banged on the door. "Let me in, Milo. I know you're in there." He must be.

Footsteps. The door swung open, revealing the warlock. He wore a loose tunic and leather pants, his feet bare. His golden locks were disheveled, as if he'd plowed his fingers through the strands—or Leonora had.

I balled my hands. What had she done with him? What had she told him?

He grinned, saying, "You changed your mind." Then the grin fell. "Oh. Ashleigh."

"What are you and Leonora planning? You're eager for more power, and I get it. But why trust her over me, the one who knows *her* secrets?" *Betray her, Milo. Please.*

He slammed the door in my face.

Though I banged and banged and banged, he didn't open up again.

The distinct click-clack of a spidorpion's many legs snagged my attention, and I hissed in a breath. A noise sure to send terror storming through *anyone*. I ran for...the...secret... No! Archways and hallways. Where were the doors? The secret passage?

I skidded to a stop, fighting panic.

A spidorpion dropped from the ceiling and landed a few feet away from me. Fear choked me as I spun to flee—and found another spidorpion behind me.

They'd cornered me.

I was going to die as a nighttime snack.

But...

The second one moved around me, joining the first, who lifted one of his front legs and…pointed? He was telling me where to go? I…that couldn't be right. Unless he wanted to usher me to his nest, where a million of his spidorpion children would feast on my remains for days to come.

Left with no other choice, I followed his preferred direction, walking…running…finally, I came to the door that led to the secret passage.

As soon as I entered my bedroom, I quietly shut the door and leaned against it, trying to catch my breath. The dragons slept on as my mind whirled. Come what may, I couldn't leave Saxon in the dark any longer. I had to tell him the truth about Leonora. He needed to know the phantom was making secret plans with the warlock, so he could mount a defense.

Yes. I nodded. I would do it. I would tell him first thing this morning, before his romantic courtship with Dior. And distract him from his purpose?

I wouldn't be doing either of us any good.

So. I'd tell him after the courtship…and find out what he expected from me in the process. What he wanted.

I paced for hours. By the time sunlight filtered through a crack in the window drapes, I was tired and fried but resolved.

I hadn't changed my mind. I would tell him. I even had a plan. I would go to his tent before the courtship. I would apologize for leaving him a note last night and not facing him then. I would wait for him to return from the courtship. I would tell him the truth. That was the order, the only parts I could control. What happened afterward was up to Saxon.

If he agreed, we could work together to try to end Leonora. And figure out a plan if we failed.

As the dragons slept on, I bathed, brushed my teeth and hair, then dressed in a clean mourning gown. I entered the secret passage once more, taking the same staircase, but stopping in front of each room to peer through little holes, wondering where to exit. Servants were beginning the day's chores. Diamond vases were being dusted. Velvet curtains were beaten with sticks, removing dust and debris. Candles were lit.

Turned out I didn't have to exit through a room. The passage took me right outside. The sun framed the back of the palace, creating a halo effect, casting shades of pink and purple over the cobblestone path that led to the royal stable. A picturesque building with dark wood and copper framing.

I gathered a bridle and headed for a stall, only to smack into Eve.

The beautiful avian gave me a toothy grin. "Your stamina has vastly improved, but your observational skills require more work."

I picked up the bridle I'd dropped upon collision. "Did Saxon send you to follow me?"

"Where are you headed?" she asked, ignoring my question.

I'd take that as a yes. "Saxon's tent." Would I find him angry with me? Hurt? Understanding? Which did I prefer? "Will you transport me?" It would save time.

"Happy to." She leaned a shoulder against a wooden beam, a calculating gleam in her silver eyes. "For a price."

"What do you want?" I asked, and sighed.

"The sword and dagger you gave to Saxon. I want my own."

I pursed my lips. While I loved that my reputation for quality weaponry was already spreading, I didn't want to set a precedent and charge too little for my creations. Yes, I wanted to get to Saxon as quickly as possible, but I was a mother now. I had babies to feed. When I could make a sell, I was going to make a sell. "Though I'm extremely humble about the greatness of my skill—"

"Extremely humble?"

"—I know my work is too valuable to be traded for a ten-minute air ride."

A skittering sound registered, and I had the same reaction

I'd had last night: a hiss of breath as every inch of me tensed. A spidorpion—*the* spidorpion?—crept along the beam Eve was leaning against. "Um… Eve? Don't look now but—"

The fist-size creature hopped onto her shoulder—a shoulder she hiked as if she hadn't a care.

"You're wearing a spidorpion," I bellowed.

"And he's one minute late, the tardy little darling. His name is Phobia, and your look of horror is hurting his feelings." She reached up to pet his head. Pet. His. Head. "What do you want for the weapons?"

To not die as a buffet breakfast? "The ride and a gold coin."

"Deal." The spidorpion raced down her arm. An arm she slowly lifted, palm up. He settled in the crevasse of her fingers, and she brought him to her face for a kiss. As I gaped, she helped him resettle on the beam. Then, she wrapped an arm around my waist and transported me to the inside of Saxon's tent.

Dizziness nearly tipped me over, but I managed to stay upright. "How did you do that? There was no voice magic involved to make me lose track of time. No command telling me to instantly appear where I wanted to be."

"I don't have voice magic. I have energy magic, like Ophelia."

Ohhh. That made sense, and yet there was something about Eve's tone that suggested she was saying more than she was saying. But what?

"Saxon isn't here," she said. "His guards surround the tent, though, and they know they'll be executed if they harm you. You're safe here, and I have duties to attend—apparently I've got to go make a gold coin. Deuces." With another wink, she vanished, leaving me alone.

Where was Saxon? What was he doing? Preparing for the courtship?

Deep breath in, out. It was okay. Everything was okay.

Stupid fate. So dumb.

A commotion erupted outside. A stampede of footsteps. A woman snapped, "The time for change has come. Prince Saxon can no longer be trusted as our sovereign. As a Skylair, I am seizing control from my brother at the tournament's end. Move aside, or consider yourself a traitor to the crown."

"He isn't here, Princess," a male replied. "He—"

"I know he isn't here. Move. Aside."

Shock waves coursed through me, and I tripped backward. Tempest stalked inside the tent a few seconds later, her gaze scanning. She ground to a stop when she spotted me, and grinned as if I'd been expected. Queen Raven entered and stopped behind her daughter, her eyes narrowed to tiny slits. Then both females grinned with relish.

"Well, well, well. The warlock was right," Raven said. "Ashleigh was indeed waiting in the tent this morning."

Heart galloping, I called, "Guards! Guards!" But my shouts did no good, the magical sound barrier preventing my voice from escaping the inside of the tent.

Fear threatened to paralyze me as one female moved in front of me, and the other moved behind me. They walked a circle around me.

"Saxon doesn't want—" I began.

"You don't get to speak his name, girl," the queen hissed. "We know who you are."

Not me. But, if I told them that I was possessed by a phantom, they would certainly kill me to try to kill her. If they believed me at all. "I'm not going to harm your son, or your people."

But Leonora might.

"You're right about that," Raven said, gleeful. "You aren't going to harm any avian. We won't let you."

Tempest yanked my arms behind my back and shackled my wrists with a metal cuff. With a hard shove, she sent me stumbling forward. Both females laughed as I crash-landed on one of my shoulders, pain exploding through the joint.

Tears blurred my vision, but I blinked them back and spat out grains of dirt. My stomach protested as I labored to my feet. "Saxon killed the last avian who dared to attack me."

Tempest purred, "So sure he cares about you? He's currently with your stepsister. The king sent word before sunrise. Saxon is the first to try to win Dior's heart." Another slow grin. "Who says he'll learn what happened to you...or ever find your body?"

They planned to kill me, even without knowing about the phantom?

They lunged. In a blind panic, I kicked my leg to ward off their approach. Tempest went low, avoiding the strike and whisking my remaining leg off the ground at the same time. I toppled, losing my breath on impact. Before I could stand, Raven fisted my hair and yanked me to my knees.

I wrenched back. It did no good. Tempest kicked me in the stomach, what little air I'd regained exploding from my lungs.

As I hunched over, desperate for oxygen, the queen stomped on my ankles, breaking one of the bones. Searing agony consumed me, and I almost vomited. I alternated between panting, gagging, and spitting bile.

Both avian laughed and walked another circle around me.

Dizzy, I tried to stand with only one foot. Almost there...

"Aw. Look at the evil witch," Tempest taunted. "So helpless. You can't even stand. Do you really think you're good enough to sit beside an avian king?"

My only working leg gave out, and I collapsed. I couldn't stand. I'd have to crawl. Inching forward, every movement excruciating...another inch.

"Dior will make a fine mate for him," Raven said, bending down to squeeze my broken ankle until I could contain the vomit no longer. "She isn't the bane of avian existence."

Moving at an incredible speed, Tempest performed a full

spin directly in front of me, flaring and retracting her wings. When she stilled, she grinned at me expectantly.

Sharp stings registered all over my chest and thighs. So sharp they dulled the agony in my ankle. I glanced down, shocked cold. Her wings. The joint hooks. They'd sliced me in multiple places, blood now soaking my clothes.

I shook so hard it felt as if the entire world were trembling. I threw a glance toward the door. I needed help. Someone. Anyone. "Saxon and I called a truce." I slurred the words.

"Saxon isn't going to get what he wants. He's going to get what he needs." Raven glided around me, getting in my face. "Because of you, his father feared what he would do if the boy found you again. Because of you, my son lost his family and his home. Because of you, he's losing his crown. Now, here you are, ripe for a new death. The one you deserve."

The crazed glaze in her eyes... I inhaled, the air suddenly as thick as molasses. She wasn't just planning to kill me. She hoped to make it hurt.

Part of me wanted to shout for Leonora's help.

Pride wouldn't let me. Work with my mother's killer? Never.

The phantom remained silent anyway, though I knew she was aware. I felt her stirring around in my head. But I thought she might...*want* me to die, so that she could jump into someone else.

She wasn't going to die with me, I realized with dawning horror. My worst fear had come true. The phantom was deathless. She would simply float out of my corpse and find someone else to overtake. And Saxon would have no idea she was out there, because I hadn't told him the truth.

"Make no mistake. You are going to die today. The question is, how much fun am I going to have beforehand?" The queen drew back her elbow, then let it fly.

More agony, inside and out. An explosion of it. My eyesight dimmed and blood filled my mouth. I crumpled to the floor.

Punch. Kick. I couldn't raise my hands to protect myself. So much pain…

Unending helplessness…

Raven grabbed a fistful of my hair again. This time, she dragged me out of the tent. Though I was blinded, my eyes swollen shut, I could feel the change in temperature, a cool breeze drilling into my wounds.

Tempest laughed. "How does it feel to know no one will save you? *Everyone* wants you dead."

The next thing I knew, the ground vanished from beneath me. They'd carried me into the sky?

"The Glass Princess will shatter once and for all," Raven said, drawing another laugh from her daughter.

They were going to…drop me. I parted my lips to scream a denial but only a choking noise left me.

Leonora began to laugh and laugh and laugh. She wasn't getting what she'd wanted, but she was getting a rival out of the way and punishing Saxon for his newest betrayal.

Not knowing what else to do, I let my heart shout for the one person I wanted to see most, to tell the truth and save…to say goodbye. "Saxon!"

23

He's late, he's late,
for a very important date!

SAXON

Could this day get any worse?

I held a too-stiff Princess Dior in my arms as I flew her to a private breakfast on a nearby mountaintop. She'd buried her face in the hollow of my neck, too afraid of falling to glance at the magnificent world around us. Mountains stretched as far as the eye could see, each peak dusted with snow and clouds. Other avian were in flight. Birds soared here and there.

There was no way I would be the winner of this competition if I didn't give this my all. I needed to focus, to charm, to help the princess overcome her fears, so that she would enjoy the rest of her time with me. So I wouldn't lose in the semifinals. But my mind continually returned to Ashleigh, who fit me perfectly and adored being in my arms, the wind whipping through her hair. Why did she wish to stay away from me now?

I'd waited in the stable all night, not letting myself fall asleep, just in case she changed her mind. Before sunrise, I'd flown back to my tent, thinking to clean up before I stormed the palace and spoke with her. I'd run into a messenger sent by the king, who'd informed me that my courtship was to come first.

I'd planned to escort Dior to the Avian Mountains and give her a tour of my kingdom. But I hadn't been back since my exile, and she wasn't the one I wanted at my side when I made my first return. So, I'd decided we would dine atop a mountain at the edge of my territory. Simple. Romantic?

My great-grandfather had built a tree house between the tallest trees on the highest peak. My family visited often and kept it well stocked. The tree house was big enough to house two servants in a wing of their own. I'd sent one of my soldiers to tell those servants to clean, prepare a meal, and leave.

Before I'd left to collect the princess, my mother had pulled me aside to say, *Win Dior and forget Ashleigh. Be the king our people need. Be better this go-round and make the right choices, or you will lose everything you've worked so hard to achieve.*

The sting of her words hadn't faded. She'd made it clear: the avian would never accept Ashleigh. They would never see her as an innocent girl possessed by a phantom. They would only ever see her as our greatest enemy. The fire witch responsible for our worst years in history.

If I stayed with Ashleigh, my own men would reject me as leader. Did I *want* to lead without her, though? I'd lived that life already. Twice. I didn't want to do it again.

I wanted the mate fate picked for me. My version of a happily-ever-after.

Could Ashleigh be freed of her intruder?

Could she be saved?

Could I ever give her up?

At the thought, blood pumped to my muscles as my body prepared for war.

What would I do to keep her?

Questions, so many questions. Before I could find any answers, I had to survive this torturous meal. *You have only to charm the girl, remember?*

Dior's teeth chattered, every click of her teeth a sign of failure, and I sighed. The higher we flew, the colder the temperature became—the very reason I'd asked her to wear a heavy coat. Instead, she'd chosen a flimsy scrap of silk. As an avian, I produced more body heat than mortals. I didn't need a coat, so I didn't have one to offer.

As soon as we landed, I hustled her inside the cabin, where a fire already blazed, heating the air.

"Oh, how lovely," she exclaimed.

Yes, it certainly was. Twinkling lights hung from the ceiling, imitating stars. The table—I ground my teeth. The servants must have heard the word *courtship* and assumed I wanted the most intimate setting possible. The "table" consisted of side-by-side pillows with a blanket between them, platters of food spread over the center. No plates. No silverware. We were to feed *each other.*

I helped Dior ease onto a pillow, pretending to be a gentleman, then gave my pillow a discreet nudge to move it several inches away from hers. I should be dining with Ashleigh. Should only ever feed her by hand.

"Uh, whatever I did to make you angry, I'm sorry," Dior cried.

"My apologies," I muttered, shaking my head. "You've done nothing wrong. My mind is…elsewhere."

"I see." Her shoulders rolled in slightly. "You wish you were with someone else, yes?"

I should deny it, but couldn't. Though the only promise Ashleigh and I had made to each other involved the parenting of our dragons, flirting with her sister felt like a betrayal to her.

"You're right," I admitted, *without* issuing an apology. I wasn't sorry, but relieved. Perhaps my honesty would win her over. "Your stepsister has me tied in knots."

"I thought so," she replied with a nod. "And I understand. I do. She's beautiful, and she's smart. But she's betrothed to the warlock now. According to the king, she's too weak to ever produce an heir."

A twitch under my eye as I motioned for Dior to feed herself. She selected her meal from a smorgasbord of fruit, nuts, and different cuts of roasted meat.

The girl had said nothing untrue, but I longed to snap at her for disparaging Ashleigh. "That engagement will end with the next battle. And there are different kinds of strength, just as there are other ways to make a family." Ways I'd learned firsthand when Roth and Farrah had taken me in as a child.

"But don't you hate Ashleigh?" Dior asked, her brow crinkled.

"I feel many things for her, but hate isn't one of them." Not any longer.

"You have no interest in wedding me, then?"

"I do...not." Again, I wouldn't apologize. I didn't owe her my affections, and I couldn't make myself desire her. "I don't tell you this to hurt you. I think you're a lovely girl, and I know you'll make someone very happy one day. But that someone isn't meant to be me."

"I... I understand," she replied, surprising me.

Before I could respond, I experienced a sudden spike of foreboding. For no reason. I frowned and gazed about. Did I sense an impending attack?

The foreboding increased, scraping my nerve endings. I stood to search out the windows. No one approached.

"I cannot be mad at you for being open and honest about your feelings, rather than leaving me to wonder," Dior told me. "In my experience, courage is a rare quality among royals."

"Among anyone."

The princess offered me a wry smile. "By the way, I didn't like saying mean things about Ashleigh, and I know you didn't like hearing them. I just had to be certain you wanted her for the right reasons, not just to punish her."

I jolted. "She told you about the punishments?" What else had she said?

"No, she's very private. But I might have heard a little palace gossip."

I bowed my head, shamed. People were talking about my abysmal treatment of Ashleigh. It was no less than I deserved. I'd blamed her for a terrible act she hadn't actually committed. I'd hurt an innocent. There was no chastisement great enough.

"Ashleigh is a lucky girl, to have such a devoted suitor," Dior said. "There's no way you'll let yourself get killed in the tournament, especially if it means Milo gets to wed her."

"He will never touch her."

"There's got to be a way you can receive the same boon as the warlock and wed Ashleigh instead."

An idea occurred to me, a possible solution to this courtship problem. "Help me survive this portion of the tournament. Vote for me. When I win, I will choose Ashleigh. The king won't be able to stop me." Because he would no longer possess the throne. Would I dare to wed her, though? "Then I will introduce you to my friend Vikander. He's a powerful fae prince and—"

"I know who Vikander is," she rushed out, her cheeks flushing.

Had a bit of a soft spot for the incorrigible fae, hmm? Everyone did.

In a rush, my foreboding reached a shattering crescendo. I felt as if I would bleed out at any moment. My chest was so tight, my lungs couldn't fill properly. I'd never experienced anything like this, as if...as if some kind of spell had just shattered. But, the only spell currently working inside me was—

The tracker spell that linked me to Ashleigh.

I shot to my feet even as I searched for her location inside my head. But…the map wasn't there. Had something happened? "I'm sorry, but we must go. Now. I think there's something very wrong with Ashleigh."

I didn't give Dior a chance to ask questions. I yanked her against me, sprinted out of the tent, and took flight. The ten-minute journey took an eternity. At the palace, I set a pale Dior in front of the entrance and flew off without a word.

Where to go, where to go? Just as I found a shard of the tracker spell buried deep inside my head, gleaning a possible location for Ashleigh, glass shattered above me. The dragons darted across the sky. I gave chase, quickly catching up. They'd sensed their mother's turmoil, as well?

I took the lead. Behind me, the dragons screeched with fear and fury. People would see them, but I was past the point of caring. *Get to Ashleigh.* Nothing else mattered. If I lost her…

Can't lose her.

I couldn't give her up in two weeks. Less than two weeks. I wouldn't. I'd meant what I'd told Dior. I would win this tournament, and I would choose Ashleigh.

We would figure everything else out.

I zoomed past the campgrounds, leading the dragons down the mountains at a steep incline. So close. Searching…searching… Two women crouched over a third.

What am I seeing? That couldn't be…it wasn't… Realization sank in, and there was no denying it. An animalistic sound left from me.

Pagan released a piercing roar; Pyre screeched so loud, sharp pains lanced my brain, and blood leaked from my ears.

We descended in unison. My mother and sister stood beside Ashleigh's broken body. I flapped my wings harder, faster, swooping in.

My beautiful Asha lay partially on her side, her eyes swelled shut, her twisted body motionless. A metal shackle bound her wrists behind her back, and crimson soaked her clothes. Several bones with jagged breaks protruded from her skin.

Mumbling denials, I knocked my mother and sister aside to crouch at Ashleigh's side. Shock. Horror. Too late? Was she… had she…

Tears stung my eyes. She *couldn't* be dead. I needed her here. I needed her alive.

"What did you do to her?" I bellowed with all the rage and pain inside me.

Wailing, the dragons circled us overhead, perhaps unsure if my mother and Tempest had hurt Ashleigh or tried to come to her rescue. Both females peered up at the creatures agog, my presence forgotten.

"But, but…" my mother sputtered.

"How can this be? Dragons are extinct," Tempest gasped out. "The avian dug up their eggs for centuries to ensure they would never again terrorize our world."

"Enemy," I said, pushing the word through gritted teeth.

The dragons opened their mouths to blow streams of fire, creating a circle around Ashleigh and me. My family scrambled backward.

Tempest's shoulder got singed. Raven lost a hank of hair.

Pagan and Pyre landed, each taking a post at Ashleigh's side.

With a trembling hand, I reached out to check for a pulse. A ragged moan left her, blood gurgling from her mouth. Then she blinked open one swollen, bloodshot emerald eye and moaned.

My rage flared anew. "Leonora," I snarled. "You hear me, I know you do. Use your magic to help her heal or…" There was no threat great enough. "I will… I will do what you've always desired."

What would I do to be with Ashleigh? Anything.

"Let her die," my mother commanded from beyond the flames. "Do not make the mistakes of your past."

Blue flooded Ashleigh's eye, some of the swelling in her

face already beginning to fade. Leonora was taking over, healing Ashleigh's body with her power, the battery of her magic. Because with my promise, she'd won our war, and I'd lost it.

I didn't care. Relief nearly bent me over. As gently as possible, I gathered Ashleigh close. In my past lives, I'd told Leonora I craved peace she could never give. She'd sought what she'd thought was my love ever since. Here, now, I knew she'd sought my surrender. Now she had it. But I also had my peace.

Peace wasn't a cessation of turmoil, as I'd once believed. It was utter calm despite it.

Ashleigh was my peace. She was everything I'd never known I'd needed. The reason I'd been reborn.

Once Leonora had healed her enough for flight, I would do as I'd told the phantom. Then I would take Ashleigh to Roth and Everly or Ophelia. I would pay any price to have the phantom contained.

I would keep my end of the bargain. I would wed the one Leonora possessed.

But I owed the phantom no more.

Was Ashleigh back in solitary confinement? Was she in torment, alone and afraid, now that Leonora was at the helm?

My claws lengthened, but I cooed, "I'm here, Asha. I'm here." Could she hear me with Leonora in control? "I'm going to take care of you and make sure nothing like this ever happens again."

"You are worse than a fool," Raven hissed.

The circle of flames was dying, the smoke that curled from the ground growing thinner by the second. When she took a step forward, I clutched Ashleigh closer, every protective instinct I'd ever denied roaring to the surface, becoming a primal drive to kill anyone who threatened the treasure in my arms.

Pagan blew another stream of fire at my mother, ensuring she came no closer.

I clashed eyes with the woman who'd given birth to me.

She'd disobeyed my order because she'd felt she could do so without consequences. Because she believed she could defeat me and put Tempest, the only other Skylair heir, on the throne. I'd heard the whispers this morn. But I was still here, still crown prince, and I would enforce my rules. I would show no mercy, no matter who the offender happened to be.

"Your crimes will not go unpunished," I vowed. Here and now, I had something more important to do.

The bruising faded from Ashleigh's face. A bone in her calf popped into place, her skin weaving closed.

Leonora had kept her end of our bargain.

I removed a bracelet from my wrist—the yellow one reserved for my bride.

Furious protests erupted from my family.

Every life I'd led, every breath I'd taken, had led me here, to this moment. I didn't hesitate. I slid the bracelet over Ashleigh's wrist.

Just like that, it was done and it couldn't be undone. The material was magically bound to her now—at least until she made a decision about our union. If she accepted me, it would remain on her. If not, it would fall off. But the action alone— the sharing of the bracelet—had marked her as my intended queen. In the eyes of all avian, we were now as good as wed. No one could touch her, not even a former queen or a princess.

They might not yet respect me as king, but they would respect our traditions. Was this as foolish as Raven believed? Probably. I'd given Leonora what she'd always wanted. More than that, I'd done it before I'd told Ashleigh that I was working with Roth and Everly, and we had bad things planned for her father. She deserved the truth before I asked her to share the rest of her life with me.

To accept, she had only to verbally agree to be mine.

I would hear Ashleigh's acceptance, not Leonora's. The phantom's agreement meant nothing to me.

I worked my way to my feet, as careful as possible with my precious bundle. "Know this," I announced as my family cursed my actions. "If she dies, *you* die. If anyone helped you do this, they'll die with you. If she lives and you dare to touch her again, if ever you send someone to harm her, I will do more than kill you. I will personally introduce you to the Destroyer." I flared my wings and took flight.

24

When one dream comes true,
find another, one that's new.

Ashleigh

For years—days? hours?—I existed in a world of darkness and pain, trapped in the nightmare in which I'd been dropped, my mind constantly replaying my plummet down a seemingly endless void, my body jerking and cringing in a desperate gambit to escape. Again and again, I learned the void wasn't endless, after all, and hit the ground, every bone in my body breaking.

I remembered Leonora's laughter. How relieved I'd been to feel a slow spread of numbness. I remembered how that relief had evaporated as paralysis set in, stealing my ability to fight back. All the while, my would-be killers had taunted me.

What's taking so long? Die already.

This time, stay dead.

I fought to live, I fought so hard. I couldn't let Leonora win and ruin Saxon's life again. But…what was that noise? Dragon screeches? A male's voice? Yes, yes. A roar of utter devastation. Saxon's roar. Over me?

My heart leaped in my chest. My family had come for me.

Words I didn't have the strength to speak tangled on my tongue as strong arms gently gathered me and lifted me. Saxon.

The phantom purred. —*I have what I've always wanted. It's done. Soon, you'll be gone.*— The more she laughed, the more my thoughts cleared.

She had poured her magic through me, strengthening me and weakening herself.

Voices filtered into my awareness. Saxon was speaking with the healer. The one who'd healed me after Trio's attack.

Saxon: "—do it. Cage her."

Healer: "It's only a temporary fix, and it's going to put her on the offensive when she escapes."

Saxon: "I don't care."

The healer mumbled something I didn't understand, and I heard the phantom scream with rage.

As soon as she quieted, I heard the healer say, "You will sleep and you will heal the rest of the way, Princess Ashleigh." His voice was like a summoning finger, luring me into a darkened room. "Sleep and heal."

A wave of lethargy swept me up, but I fought it. *Can't sleep. Leonora will gain control again and—*

"Sleep."

Yes. Mmm. I would sleep…

Awareness returned gradually. I thought I might be lying on a bed of clouds, Saxon nearby. His husky voice cooed sweet everythings. His incredible scent drugged me. His delicious heat provided a cocoon of tranquility, and the softness of his wings caressed my skin. Part of me clamored to awaken all the way and find out if he was real or imagined. The rest of me demanded I remain in this paradise.

I felt no pain or turmoil. Leonora slept deep inside me, her power recharging. For the first time in what seemed forever,

I couldn't feel the taint of her emotions. There was no Raven or Tempest laughing as I choked on a mouthful of my own blood. *Think I'll stay here forever.*

A calloused fingertip glided between my eyes, down the bridge of my nose, then around my eyes. "Come back to me, Asha. What my family did to you... I'm so sorry. They will pay. They will pay *hard*. Restitution shall be yours. Our dragons have gotten so big. They are the size of horses now. But they still miss their mother." Saxon's deep, smoky voice stroked my ears, and his warm, minty breath fanned my throat as he jumped from one topic to another. "Also, I have a surprise for you. One I know you'll love."

A gift? For me?

"You're safe with me," he said, "but no one else is." The words escaped on a growl. "I'm willing to do bad, bad things for another of your kisses, Asha. Be a darling and wake for me, before *I'm* the one who torches all of Enchantia just to lay the ashes at your feet. Yes. I like this idea. Know that I'm closer to doing it every minute you fail to tell me you are well."

Okay, I *must* be imagining him. Real-life Saxon didn't act as if he couldn't live without me.

"I need you to design and craft more weapons for me. I want an entire suit of armor, too. The final battle of the tournament nears. I should have all the protection I can get, shouldn't I?"

So he could win Dior's hand in marriage? No. But I *did* want him to survive.

Great. Now I could only think about how he would soon face the last—and the strongest—competitors. He might be a savage warlord who'd lived and warred before, but he wasn't infallible. He truly would need every advantage he could get. And my designs *were* extraordinary. Plus, for the right price, Ophelia could make everything Saxon wanted and more.

Wait. Didn't I have a secret to tell him, to save him from

the next incarnation Leonora possessed, if something were to happen to me?

Well. I *couldn't* stay away now. I would do it. I would fight to rejoin the land of the living.

I kicked and paddled through a watery darkness, feeling as if I breached the ocean's surface, only to be met with a crushing wave. Still I kicked, still I paddled and…yes. I gasped, my eyelids popping open. Bright sunlight made my eyes water, and I blinked rapidly.

As my hazy vision cleared, my heart threatened to pound its way out of my chest. Saxon. He hovered over me, his face suddenly all I could see—all I wanted to see. He wore an expression of concern and hope. Lines of tension branched from his bloodshot eyes and bracketed his mouth. A day's worth of scruff decorated his jaw.

"You're alive," he croaked, searching my face. "Are you in pain?"

I wiggled my fingers and toes, rocked my hips, rolled my shoulders. "No," I breathed with wonder, my voice a hoarse rasp. No permanent damage had been done.

He sagged over me and rolled to his back, taking me with him. With one hand on my nape and the other cupping my bottom, he kept me splayed over his body.

"How long have I been sleeping?"

"Seven days."

What!

"The magic needed time to work."

I began to orient, my surroundings crystalizing. We were in the stable, inside a stall, no, inside two stalls that had been joined together to create a bigger space. We rested on a pallet of furs. The dragons slept at our feet—and they were indeed the size of horses. Sweet goodness.

"But the tournament," I said.

"Finalist will be announced tomorrow. Then we'll have six more days of competition before the final battle."

Seven days wasted. Seven days left. I didn't... I couldn't... I frowned. Cool air was kissing a very private area, and I realized I wore a large tunic...and nothing else. Flutters teased my stomach.

"Someone changed me," I said softly, not wanting to wake my babies.

"Your dress was—" His entire body jerked, as if the memory of the bloody garment was too much for him to bear. "You needed clean clothes, so I summoned Ever—the ever tardy Eve. As she bathed and changed you, I was the only other person here, and I swear I kept my back turned. I just couldn't bear to leave your side."

This boy...oh, this boy. Who could have known the heart of a gentleman beat inside the chest of a warlord?

He shuddered, adding, "You aren't allowed to die, Ashleigh."

I hoped he always felt that way, because the time had come to tell him about Leonora; I hadn't changed my mind about that. This amazing, caring boy deserved to hear the truth. So, I would do it. I would give myself a few hours to wake up and center my thoughts, and then I would spill all. Would he believe me when I told him Leonora wouldn't die when I died? That my death wasn't a solution—yet?

"No matter what happens," I said, "I want you to know that I'm grateful for you and everything you've done. Thank you."

"*You* thank *me*?" He rubbed his fingers into his eyes and uttered a bitter laugh. "You owe me nothing, Asha. I owe you everything. I told you this while you were sleeping, but I need to know you've heard it. I'm sorry for what my family did to you, and I swear to you now, they will never hurt you again. They will be punished. Please, tell me you know I didn't want you harmed this way."

His vehemence touched me, somehow healing the wounds

the phantom's magic couldn't reach. Wounds he hadn't even caused. The disdain of my fellow Fleuridians...a friendless existence...years of my father's rejection.

"I know you didn't want me harmed." I reached up to stroke his chest—his warm, strong completely *bare* chest. Silver glinted from a nipple and—hey! One of his bracelets wrapped around my wrist. The yellow one.

How lovely. "You gave me one of your bracelets?"

He held his breath. "I did, yes."

The yellow...what did the yellow mean again? Wait. Yellow meant a commitment of marriage, right? But, that couldn't be right. Could it? My eyes went wide. "Is this your way of...*proposing* to me, Saxon?"

He flushed for some reason. "Yes. But don't tell me if you agree or not. Not yet. All right? Give me a chance to show you how good things can be between us first. We can discuss the...engagement in seven days, before the stroke of midnight. Like the fairy tale. All right?"

Reeling. "I...yes. I mean, yes, I will give you seven days. To consider an engagement. To you. Saxon Skylair. Future king of the avian. Marriage?" I gasped out. I would give anything to marry him, just not while I played host to Leonora.

Maybe an open-ended engagement?

He didn't relax. "I have a gift for you."

"Another one?" Marveling, I said, "Where has my grumpy warlord with a grudge gone?"

He chuckled, the sound of it pure ecstasy to me. "With you, the grumpy warlord is gone *forever.*"

Warm honey seemed to pour over me. "Oh, don't say that. He's fun to play with...and defeat."

Another chuckle, this one rumbling and husky. All that warm honey got hot.

"Have mercy on him. He's not as strong as you are." He

lightly smacked my bottom, and I yelp-laughed. The dragons stirred but didn't wake.

"They must be tired," I remarked.

"This is the first they've slept since we found you." Saxon sat up, taking me with him. He kissed my cheek. "Let's get up, clean up, and I'll show you the gift. I think you'll like it."

He stood and drew me do my feet, but didn't let me go right away. He held on to make sure I remained steady.

After giving my cheek another kiss, he gave me a little push toward the exit, saying, "Head to the next stall."

Confused but excited, I walked over...and drew up short. *Oh. My. Wow.* He'd turned the stall into a luxurious bathing suite. A large tub was already filled, steam curling through the air, rose petals floating over the surface of the water. Along the tub's rim rested the best toiletries money could buy. Things from every kingdom. Minty toothpaste from Sevón, with a toothbrush made from a split twig. Seaweed scrub from Azul. Perfumed oils from Airaria. A lotion from Fleur, made with more rose petals.

I soaked and primped as I'd always wished to do, astounded by the opulence of every product, I cleaned my teeth, plaited my freshly cleaned hair, and donned the clothes he'd left for me—the finest undergarments money could buy and a gorgeous pink gown made of the softest material, with side buttons I could easily latch.

"Saxon?" I called.

Hurried footsteps, as if he'd been waiting for my summons. He blazed into my stall a second later, a dagger drawn.

I stumbled back, hand fluttering over my mouth. Never had I seen a more ferocious expression. "Whoa."

His gaze darted. "Someone threatens you?"

"No, no," I assured him, melting inside. Like me, he'd bathed and dressed. He now wore battle clothes. A white tunic paired with black leather pants and combat boots. "I just wanted you to see the end result."

The tension drained from him, and he sheathed the weapon. The one I'd designed. A smile bloomed. As he roved his gaze over me, his irises heated and his pupils expanded.

Did a hint of possessiveness radiate from him?

"There is no one in this world who compares to you, Asha."

Melting faster. I bit my bottom lip and stepped toward him, a bit shy, a lot eager. Drawn… He stepped toward me, too, closing the remaining distance. My heart galloped, as if I'd been dropped into the middle of a race.

I wanted to kiss him. I wanted to kiss him so bad.

Click, click, click. Uh-oh. A dragon must have awoken.

Sure enough. Pagan barreled into the stall and squawked. As she ran over and rubbed against my leg, Pyre did the same. They were stronger than they realized; if Saxon hadn't wrapped an arm around my waist to hold me up, I would have fallen over.

I laughed. "Daddy wasn't kidding, was he? Look how much you've grown." Soon, they'd be too big for the stable, too, but that was a worry for another day.

Saxon pressed his lips against my temple. "Do you trust me, Asha?"

"Mostly," I hedged.

"Do you trust that I will not harm you?"

After the roar of devastation I'd heard? "I do." This boy had saved me from his family, despite our differences, despite our rocky past. Honestly? I was beginning to think he would never harm me, no matter the circumstances.

Something had changed between us. Something significant, all hint of animosity just…gone.

He rewarded me with a glorious, bone-melting grin that set my cells on fire. Then he wrapped a strip of cloth around my eyes.

Except for an internal spark of excitement, my world went dark. "What's going on?"

"I have another gift for you."

"Another?" I squeaked.

Saxon led me through the stable...and outside? The temperature cooled, the scent of hay replaced by pine.

My heart pounded a frantic beat, my excitement doubling. "Where are we going?"

"Not much farther." He continued leading me forward, being careful with me.

I heard the whoosh of dragons' wings overhead and knew the babies were playing. When he stopped, he moved beside me and untied my blindfold.

Sunlight penetrated my vision, and my eyes burned and watered. I blinked to clear the blur and the landscape came into view, revealing...hmm. What was I looking at? A glittery wall of...what was that? It looked like the portal in my secret passage, just bigger and without a frame. No, not true. Whatever it was, it stretched up, up, creating a dome all around us.

"It's beautiful, and I love it." Or I knew I would love it, whatever it was. "But, um, what is it?" I asked.

"A magical dome, created by Ophelia. Inside these walls, nothing and no one can harm you."

Truly? "That's wonderful."

"Her magic revolves around energy. We will—I mean, we *can*, if you agree—spend the next seven days here. You can finish recovering in peace. I can teach you self-defense and... other things. We can do anything we desire."

Seven days with Saxon and my dragons? No worries or responsibilities? And mmm, mmm, mmm. His voice had deepened there at the end, turning husky with promise. I shivered.

There was still a problem. "What of Dior?"

"I will never wed her, even if I win. I told her so, and she understood," he said. "This, I swear to you."

I almost shouted, *Yes*. Because I wanted this. I wanted to be with him so badly. But he must have had to pay the witch a never-ending fountain of gold for this. I didn't want him emptying his coffers for me. If we got rid of Leonora, I'd be in charge of half that money. I didn't want him wasting it. Especially since I hadn't yet admitted the full truth. "How much did Ophelia charge you?"

"It was her wed—engagement gift to us. Just in case you say yes." He reached out and gently smoothed a lock of hair behind my ear. "Would you like to stay here with me and our dragons, Ashleigh?"

Free magic? I needed no more time to think. "Yes, Sax. I would like to stay here with you and our dragons."

He gave me another bone-melting grin, this one slow and languid. And now I was a puddle of goo. "There's more," he said, and my heart nearly stopped.

More? "More than a beautiful possible-engagement bracelet and magical seven-day vacation together?"

He flinched at "possible-engagement," the muscles in his chest flexing, a reaction I didn't understand. What was I missing? "I know there are obstacles in our path. I know I don't deserve a second—*third* chance with you. I know there's much we must discuss. But I also know this. I want to marry you, whoever you are. Whatever you are. Whatever happened in the past. Whatever will happen in the future."

Head spinning. He needed to stop saying such nice things to me. Because oh, the temptation to say yes…but not with Leonora inside me. I wouldn't change my mind about that. I wouldn't sentence him to a lifetime with the phantom.

When I opened my mouth to respond—what was I going to say?—Saxon pressed a finger against my lips. "You aren't answering my proposal until the stroke of midnight on the seventh day, remember? We will make our pledge—or not—then." He pressed a soft kiss into my cheek. "For now, look over there."

He continued to upend my world with his generosity, and I knew it was his way of making reparation. He didn't owe me anything, but curiosity got the better of me. I slid my gaze to…

Oh, sweet goodness. I couldn't be seeing what I thought I was seeing. "A forge. A real-life forge."

Saxon positioned himself behind me and leaned down to nuzzle his cheek against mine. "Here you'll find everything you need to craft your designs. As long as you wear this—" He reached over me to reveal a pink bracelet pinched between his fingers. "You'll always know what to do. It's a teaching bracelet. When you wear it, magic will quicken your mind with everything you need to know about bringing your designs to life."

So he *had* spent his hard-earned gold on me. "Saxon," I whispered, tears gathering in my eyes. I let him slide the bracelet onto my wrist, next to the other one, and hugged them both to my chest. "You've done too much for me."

"I haven't done nearly enough," he said so softly I almost missed it. He looped his elbow loosely around my neck, clasping my opposite shoulder. It was a possessive, protective hold that pressed my body against his. His wings arced forward, the tips brushing against my calves.

He'd enclosed me with his entire body, becoming my shield against the world.

"How much did you pay Ophelia for the bracelet?" I asked, with a tremor in my voice. "And don't try to tell me it's another gift, because she isn't the giving type."

He sighed, his breath fanning the top of my head. "She took no gold from me. Instead, she demanded something called a get-out-of-jail-free card. She tells me she can now commit any crime against me at some point in the future, and I must forgive her without retaliating or seeking restitution."

"But that's a more expensive price tag than money." What Saxon had done…his thoughtfulness… The fact that he didn't know about Leonora and, and, and—

A sob slipped free, tears pouring down my cheeks.

"What is this?" Saxon turned me and gently collected a tear. Torment etched his features. "This was supposed to make you happy, Asha. I don't break you with cruelty but with kindness? I can—"

"I'm happy," I burst out. "And I'm miserable. This is just so kind of you and you shouldn't have done it, because you don't know the truth. You feel guilty about what Raven and Tempest did to me, and maybe that's why you think you want to have a forever with me— That's it, isn't it? It's a restitution proposal. But, Saxon, you don't owe me anything."

He cupped my cheeks with both of his big, calloused hands. "You are wrong, Asha. I owe you everything. You gave me something I've craved since my first life."

I sniff-sniffed. "I did?"

"You did. You taught me how to find peace. For the first time, I know what I'm fighting for—my own happily-ever-after."

So he'd given me two avian bracelets, my own forge, and now the most romantic words ever uttered, and I'd given him a pack of lies, letting him continue to believe I was a reincarnation of a fire witch.

Another sob left me, and I sagged against him, resting my forehead against the center of his chest. I was the worst person to ever live.

He held me as I cried, tracing his fingertips up and down the ridges of my spine. "What is this about, Asha? The truth you mentioned, the one I do not know? Is it that you have been meeting with Milo in secret? I know you aren't to blame."

"How? How do you know I'm not to blame?"

Rather than answering, he said, "You should know I suspect Milo is poisoning your father and blaming it on Queen Everly, the sorceress. He claims she's draining the king for his magic."

Milo, poisoning my father? "He doesn't have any magic."

Like me? I thought I felt power stirring—power that had nothing to do with Leonora. Buy why would I notice it more now than ever before? "Why would he believe a sorceress drained him?"

"He had a magical infusion at birth. He might not have manifested an ability in adulthood, but he still has the power inside him."

Ohhh. And Milo *did* hope to rule the kingdom. I should have guessed something like this was happening. "The king needs to be told the truth." I didn't like the man, but I didn't want him dead.

"He *has* been told. He refuses to believe it."

Then what more could be done for him? "You were right. I do need to talk to you about the meetings I've had with the warlock, but that wasn't the secret I meant. There's one about... Leonora and me."

He arched a brow. "Do you think my knowledge of this secret will taint our time here?"

"Maybe," I hedged. "Probably."

"I think I know what it is, then," he said, peering deep into my eyes. "But even if there's more, even if I'm off, trust me enough *not* to tell me. Trust me enough not to worry about my reaction when you do confess. Trust me enough to know that this truth won't change how I feel about you, or the future I want with you. Give me this chance to prove myself worthy of you."

Sob. I think I accidentally snotted on his chest, and my cheeks flamed. "I don't deserve your kindness and these wonderful gifts, Saxon." But he did deserve my trust. "I will do it. I will trust you not to break my heart when you learn the truth."

"When I'm holding your heart in my hands, Asha, I swear I will take the greatest care." He offered the words at low volume, but carried great weight. I almost stumbled under the heft of them. "But, sweetheart? There's another gift to be given."

"There's even *more*?" I shouted, lifting my head. "Saxon, it's too much. Whatever it is, it's too much."

"Shall I take it back?"

"Never. Mine! Give it to me."

His shoulders shook as he laughed, and I noticed the amour glistening atop them. I was making him happy.

"I have breakfast waiting in one stall and a combat training zone in another," he said. "I will teach you how to subdue or escape *anyone* who threatens you. Especially the avian. Never again will you be helpless against anyone." As he spoke, he rubbed his hands up and down my sides.

The rhythmic caress lit a fuse underneath my skin. Tingling heat gathered in select places.

Awareness crackled between us. Suddenly I noticed how close we stood to each other...how much of him pressed against me, the hardness that was flush against my softness...how intensely I ached for him, my limbs already trembling.

"Sax?" I rasped.

He searched my face. "Yes, Asha."

"I want...my body wants..." *Everything.* I'd almost died without learning every inch of this boy's body. In seven days, our worlds could change again. Why not celebrate the life we had right now?

Taking a step closer, he backed me into a stable wall. With a husky voice, he proclaimed, "I know what your body wants, and I'm going to give it to you."

25

Is what you want what you need?
To get it, must you plead?

Ashleigh

I had known I was Saxon's fated, the one reborn again and again for the chance to be with him at long last, but the knowledge hadn't meant much to me. I'd been too focused on our failures. I hadn't understood the rightness of our connection.

This...this was everything.

We were worth fighting for.

I had been Craven's obsession and for a time, I'd been Tyron's joy.

The name whispered through my head, a facet of the past opening up to my mind. My memory, not Leonora's. Tyron Skylair, king of the avian, had been ill prepared for Leonora the day she'd strolled into his palace to speak with "the love of her lives." On a rare few occasions, I'd managed to overtake the phantom—because she hadn't killed me in either of my other lives; I'd been confined to the void.

Big surprise. The evil stepmother had lied.

The times I'd managed to break free, I'd sensed great sadness in Tyron, as if he'd lost something precious, but he wasn't sure what that something was. I'd loved to play games with him, to make him laugh. And I had.

He'd kept me around longer than he should have because he'd loved our games, too.

Was I to be Saxon's peace?

Would I also be his torment?

Two hearts, one head. I had the heart of Cinder in my chest. Did I carry Saxon's heart in my hands, the way he carried mine?

Strong of heart.

Could love be the answer to Leonora's hate? At the very least, it gave me hope.

I experienced the first stirrings of...what was that? Bliss? "What of Leonora?" Wait. Equally important... "What of Milo?"

He lowered his clasp to my jaw and ghosted his thumbs over the underside of my cheekbones. "Leonora is currently caged inside your head. It's a temporary fix. When she regains the power she used to heal you, she'll be able to fight her way free. I don't know when that will be. Milo isn't a concern. He won't win the tournament."

I began to shake—oh wow, no. *He* shook, the vibrations rushing through me. Shock. Saxon Skylair, future king of the avian, was shaking because of the Glass Princess.

On the battlefield, his aim had remained steady, no matter the skill or size of his opposition. But here, with me, he'd reached his breaking point?

"It's just you and me right now?" I asked, suddenly breathless.

"It is."

Then I would waste no time. "I want to be with you, Saxon." I offered the words boldly. "I want to do everything with you."

He searched my gaze, his own flaring with hunger. "You are sure?"

I nodded without hesitation. I'd never been more sure about anything.

"Do you crave my kisses, Asha?" he asked.

"More than anything." I wound my arms around his shoulders.

He nipped at my lips. "This *everything* you mentioned?"

"Y-yes?"

"I'm going to give it to you." Without looking away from me, he called, "I'm taking your mother inside. Unless you want to see your parents naked, you'll stay out here."

I laughed as the dragons squawked in horror. But my amusement only lasted a moment. Saxon brought his lips to mine, and I forgot everything else.

We kissed, ravenous, devouring each other. He cupped my bottom and lifted me, and I wrapped my legs around his waist, my dress hem hiking up in the process.

He walked me backward, past the doors, the kiss continuing. The most amazing sensations poured through me. Heat in my veins. Delicious aches here, there, everywhere. Flutters in my belly. Tingles. So many tingles.

He eased me upon the pallet of furs, his weight settling over me. "If I do something you do not like, tell me to stop. If I move too swiftly, tell me to slow down. Your word is my command. Understand?"

I struggled to keep my mind on his speech, my focus remaining on his mouth. I wanted it on me again, his tongue dancing with mine. His minty taste was my drug.

Feeling as if I were in a trance, I nipped at his bottom lip. "I think we're overdressed. I want to see you. Let's wear the same outfit to the party."

"Skin?" His eyes hooded. As he kissed me again, he pulled at my clothes. I pulled at his, too.

Soon, no garments separated us. I'd never revealed my body to a boy. I expected nervousness to flare, maybe a little shyness. As he looked me over, I experienced neither of those things. The most delicious feminine power uncoiled. He didn't just study me. He worshipped me.

The most powerful warrior in all the land wasn't just shaking now. He was quaking before me.

"You are beyond exquisite, and you are all mine." He sifted my ring between his fingers, brushing his thumb over the metal. "I'm glad you have this."

A pang rent my chest. "I'm glad I have *you*."

The look he gave me...my heart *thundered*. He rolled to his back and anchored his hands behind his head. "Study me as long as you wish, Asha. When you finish, I'm going to give you the everything you asked for."

Study him at my leisure? The best gift of all.

I sat up, resting on my haunches between his legs. His knees were bent, caging me in. Light seeped through the wooden slats that made up the walls, illuminating every amazing inch of him. Like, a lot of inches. So many. *Now* nervousness kicked in. No wonder the first time was supposed to hurt.

I forced myself to look away from it, cataloging the rest of him. Muscles galore. Skin dark and smooth. Scars, a testament to his strength. The piercing in one nipple. Tattoos graced his lower abdomen and legs, each one a rose. His own version of the ring? And his wings...those beautiful blue wings. I slid my fingers through the baby-soft down, and he moaned.

Perhaps I was his peace...and his pleasure.

After repositioning, I leaned down to kiss the rose etched on his left thigh, then lifted to kiss the one on his lower abdomen. He groaned, his muscles jerking beneath my lips.

Emboldened, I ran my hands over his chest...his thighs... his calves. Muscles continued to jerk. *So sensitive.* All my aches and tingles grew in intensity, slowly taking me over.

"You are beautiful, Sax. And powerful. And…perfect."

"I'm not perfect." His voice…passion-rough. "Far from it."

"You *are* perfect—for me." I returned my hands to his chest and flicked my finger over the metal bar stabbing through his nipple. A shaft of heat shot straight to my core. Too hot. Not hot enough. I needed…something. "S-Saxon?"

He understood. He rolled me to my back, hovering over me. Then…ohhhhh. The things he did to me.

He kissed his way down my body, his mouth hotter than the forge outside. He touched every inch of me, no spot taboo. He slid two of his fingers *inside* me. I moaned and I writhed, desperate for more and unable to stay still. The wicked things he did with those fingers…the sensations he elicited…rapture, ecstasy. My head fogged, my body hurtling toward some kind of finish line.

Pressure was building…building…my breaths coming faster and far more shallow. My thoughts fragmented, every thought a command. *Want. More. Now.*

"I think you're ready for me, Asha." He growled the words. He positioned himself directly over me, with my legs bracketed outside his hips.

"Please," I begged. *More. Now.* I thrashed my head. I groaned. The pressure needed to splinter. Please, please, please. *Now!*

"Going to make it all better, love." He entered me slowly, and it hurt, just as my mother had claimed, but it also felt *right*. As if we'd waited for this moment our entire lives. As if we were building something strong—unbreakable. Once I'd adjusted to the sensation of being filled, he began to move, as slow as before, arching forward…drawing back. Forward. Back.

He held my gaze, as he liked to do. Forward. Back. Still so agonizingly, blissfully slow. *For…ward.* He draped one of his arms over my head, caging me in fully. I breathed his breaths. He breathed mine. The moment, the man, both were just right, utterly perfect, and it was then that I admitted I'd been madly in love with Saxon Skylair forever, but never more so than now.

We cuddled for hours. Saxon toyed with my hair, and I drew hearts on his chest. Every time I completed a new one, he smiled, and oh, it was a good look for him.

I know Saxon wanted me to wait and trust him, but I was starting to feel guilty. I wanted him to know the truth. And the fact that I did trust him made it so much easier for me to blurt out, "I'm not Leonora's reincarnate. I'm my own reincarnate who's possessed by her spirit. She's a phantom, not a witch, and she's able to jump from body to body, undying. That's what I wanted to tell you before."

He kept playing with a lock of my hair. "I know."

"You know?"

"I figured it out."

And he truly hadn't cared. He hadn't turned on me. "She's possessed me all three lives. This time, she took up residence inside me the day of my birth."

"How did she find you after the first life?"

"Magic, maybe. Instinct? The only reason she didn't overtake me completely this time was because of my mother. Momma knew what Leonora was and took measures against her, paying a warlock for a magical potion and a spell to keep my un-invited guest hidden from me. At the time, I didn't know why Mother forced me to endure the ritual every year. She didn't tell me before I…before she died. Milo is that warlock's son, and he knows Leonora is a phantom, too. He burned his fa-ther's journals so that I couldn't re-create the potion or the spell. Now the barrier has fallen, and there are two of us in here, each vying for control."

A thousand emotions blazed in Saxon's eyes, each one quickly burning up, leaving only remnants behind. Rage: the weapon.

Sorrow, fear, and despair: the wounds. Knowing him, everything he was feeling was self-directed.

Unfortunately, I wasn't done. Stomach protesting, I whispered, "She cannot be killed. When I die, she'll slip free of me and continue on. Equally devastating, I don't know if I can live without her. The more the barrier between us weakened, the stronger I became. But I can't live with her any longer, either. When I fail to stop her from taking over, innocent people usually die."

"Then we will find another way to create the barrier," Saxon said with such force the ground shook, birds taking flight from the stable rafters.

"We can't let her live." What was I doing? Pushing for my death?

"We can if it means you live, as well."

"And risk your life? The lives of your people?"

"We know apple babies. They'll find a way to strengthen your defenses against the phantom. I just wish I'd put the pieces together sooner." He thought for a moment. "Would a magical ability of your own help power your heart?"

"I think I have one. I can feel it, so close to the surface. But as much as I've always wanted to manifest one, I fear it right now. I sometimes have access to Leonora's magic. Do we really want to give her access to mine, making her even more powerful?"

Doomed.

The word echoed in my mind, an insidious beast there to rampage my calm, and I shifted.

"You were twice born into a magical family," Saxon said. "No doubt you have the soul of a witch. Yes, I'd bet you do have a magical ability of your own and Leonora's overshadowed it." He caressed my cheek. "This life has unfolded so differently from the others. It will have a different end, as well. We will make sure of it. We will find a way to subdue her. I'm not losing you again."

I smiled at him, even though I wanted to shout, *Subduing her won't work.* But I was too tired to go there again, a yawn already cracking my jaw. My eyelids were heavy and tried to slide shut, but I forced them open.

"Are you worried you'll sleepwalk?" Saxon asked.

"I call it Leonora-walking now, and I'm pretty much always worried about it."

"Rest easy tonight. I'll be on guard duty." He brought a lock of my hair to his face and rubbed the end over his chin. "Since you aren't going to freely offer the information, I suppose I'll have to ask. What did you think of your first time?"

I almost swallowed my tongue. "We're going to discuss what happened? Out loud?"

Husky chuckle. Melting heart. "Perhaps I require reassurance," he said. "Words this time, rather than piercing screams of pleasure."

Cheeks burning hotter. More than I wanted to bury my face in the hollow of his neck, I wanted to tease the avian right back. So I fluffed my hair. Using my prissiest tone, I told him, "I was magnificent. You were...tolerable. There. Don't you feel so much better now?"

He snort-laughed. "Your screams and moans suggested otherwise, Asha."

Weeds! My cheeks flamed anew. "I'll be quiet next time, okay? Promise!"

"Why? Do you wish to punish *me*?" When my nose scrunched up in confusion, he chuckled again.

He'd liked my odd noises? And had he called me "love"? I wasn't sure because I'd been a little too preoccupied with a world-changing eruption of pleasure at the time. I kept hoping he'd say it again.

"You will admit to my superior skill, or I'm afraid I'll be

forced to punish *you.*" He didn't wait for my response. He got busy tickling me.

I howled with laughter, batting at his hands. "Stop, stop, stop. I'll tell you, I'll tell you."

He paused, both of his brows cocked. "I'm listening."

"You were…adequate. We should practice every single day for the rest of our lives."

I expected laughter and a little more tickling. I got heavy silence.

Saxon stilled with such intensity, he didn't seem to be breathing. "Are you accepting…"

Withering roses. "Not yet," I rushed out. I couldn't tell him I wanted to wait until we'd stopped Leonora for good, but I knew he'd insist, again, that we get happy with subduing her.

"Very well." He started tickling me again, and I could only howl at a higher volume.

"Are you ready to hear about *my* review?" he asked silkily.

"Yes! No!" *Maybe?*

The tickling stopped abruptly. When I sobered, he gifted me with the tenderest smile, sending my pulse into a frenzy.

"You were made for me. You shredded my control, Asha, and gave me more pleasure than I'd even known existed. From now on, nothing separates us. Nothing. Anyone who tries—dies."

26

Love is patient, love is kind.
Hate will stab you from behind.

Ashleigh

O ur stolen days inside the magical dome passed in a blur of happiness. Saxon survived the first, plus several bonus battles in preparation for the final. Yesterday, he'd participated in the second round of semifinals. A dance with Dior. Finalists would be announced tomorrow, the final battle fought.

In between the competitions, we alternated between spending time in bed, combat lessons, studying, playing with the dragons, and bringing my designs to life. The dragons helped, ensuring the fire in the forge never died. So far I'd made Eve's weapons, a practice crossbow, and a sword for Saxon.

Because of all the books I'd studied at the Temple, I knew what to do as well as when and how to do it; I just lacked practical experience. The bracelet helped with that. When I was unsure about the timing of each stage, a thought would whisper through my mind, urging me to stop or continue. And that wasn't even the most amazing thing. The bracelet gave me some kind of magical ability to force two unlikely objects to coexist in harmony. Or I gave it to myself? I'd begun to wonder if it was my magic, manifesting at last. I'd even removed the bracelet once to test my theory, and I'd been able to add rose petals—genuine real rose petals—to a boiling pool of metal, without disintegrating the flowers. Each one graced the hilt of Saxon's sword, creating the outline of a perfect bloom.

I wavered between certainty that I'd done it on my own and certainty that some magical remnants left over from the bracelet were responsible. But if I'd done it on my own, what kind of magic was it, exactly? The ability to meld two objects that didn't belong together was nice and all, but how much good would it do me in a fight? Would it supply enough power to strengthen my heart without Leonora?

I sighed. Crafting weapons with my hands rather than my imagination had proved to be far more laborious than I'd expected. By the end of any session, my muscles would ache, and I would be drenched in buckets of sweat. But I wouldn't be burned. As many times as I'd inadvertently stuck my fingers in the flames, I hadn't blistered. Leonora's fire magic had protected me. But then, I could now access that magic at will, the cage gone, the barrier between us completely eradicated. I was holding her back all on my own.

She'd regained her strength quickly. Every day she'd mounted a new takeover attempt. I'd had to focus on Saxon to keep her at bay, because I refused to lose a second with him.

When we trained, he demonstrated the patience of a saint with me. When we chatted, he hung on my every word, interested in what I had to say. While I worked, he remained nearby, studying the books Noel had tossed through our secret doorway one morning. He'd pored through the pages, searching for information about subduing phantoms. Our one point of contention.

Neither of us had changed our minds. He wanted her caged

repeatedly for the rest of my life. I wanted her gone forever, no cage necessary. In this, I refused to bend.

We didn't waste a lot of time with arguing, though. In our downtime, we skinny-dipped and teased each other about silly things, and I'd never been so happy.

If you could do anything right now, what would you do? I'd asked the first time.

You. The answer is and will always be you.

The boy had enchanted me. Every day he'd presented me with any feathers that had fallen from his wings. "For a new dress," he would say. He relaxed and smiled for longer intervals, and I fell deeper in love with him each time. Not just me, but my past selves. They'd always loved him.

The truth glowed inside me so brightly I wondered how I'd missed it for so long. I loved his intensity. I loved how one's strengths complemented the other's weaknesses. I loved the way he looked at me, and the way he melted for me alone. I loved his protective nature and his unwavering determination to live his best life and lead his people.

I had to kill Leonora so I could be with him always.

Like Saxon, I'd done some studying. I dreamed of being a family. Saxon, Ashleigh, Pagan, and Pyre. The four of us, together forever. I knew of only one way to live my dream: the phantom's death.

The time had come for a little more studying, in fact. Something about a "bodily exchange" and "the expiration of the spirit" had caught my attention during my last read. But, Saxon had just got done worshipping me, body and soul, and I hadn't yet caught my breath.

We were naked. I lay cuddled into his side, resting atop a downy wing. I'd gotten used to sleeping this way, enveloped by his warmth, protected and assured I would be with him when I awoke, and I wasn't sure I'd be able to sleep without him ever again.

Afternoon sunlight streamed through tiny crevices between the wooden beams that made up the ceiling and walls, dust motes dancing. We hadn't bothered sticking to our normal routine today. This was our last day. Tomorrow, we would return to the real world.

He would win the tournament, and we would...what? How would we make this work?

The dragons napped in stalls of their own now. They'd gotten too big to share with us or even each other. Soon, we would have to deal with all of Enchantia knowing about their existence. Raven and Tempest had seen them—not to mention whoever might have noticed them in flight—so rumors would spread. We needed a plan.

I traced a fingertip down the muscle and sinew on Saxon's abdomen. "Are you ready to return to the real world?"

"I'm not sure I'll ever be ready." He kissed my temple, his eyes already at half-mast.

"What are we going to do about the dragons?"

"I can speak to—" He flinched. "I can speak to someone through vines, who passes messages to me."

Understanding dawned. "I thought you were a wee bit odd for chatting with foliage," I admitted. "Why did you flinch, though?"

He didn't try to deny the instinctive reaction. "I have a secret I've been keeping from you. I wish I could tell you, but it's not my secret to tell, and it's something I'm not ready for Leonora to know."

And the secret had to do with the person on the other end of the vine? "I understand why you can't tell me," I said, and I did, but I wanted to shout, *See. This is why the phantom has to die.* As long as I remained possessed, he would never be able to trust me fully.

He gave my temple another kiss. "We can make this work, sweetheart."

I adored when he called me sweetheart, but had he called me "love" that once or not? Would he ever do it again? I knew I made him happy. I'd been sporting a *lot* of amour lately.

"As for the dragons," he continued, "I'm told my mother and sister have said nothing. I'm guessing they don't want to cause a panic, one of the only wise things they have done. I'm also told Noel knew when and where the dragons would be visible, and she had Ophelia cast a spell to ensure no one saw them in the air."

Having a witch and oracle as friends—no, having two apple babies as friends came with more rewards than annoyances.

If apple babies could come up with a way to permanently cage a phantom, couldn't they come up with a way to kill one?

Leonora's displeasure hit me, and I cringed.

"The phantom giving you trouble?" he asked, tenderly brushing a piece of hair from my cheek.

I leaned into his touch, always eager for more. "She knows I want her dead."

He flinched. "She owes you reparation for the years she's stolen from you. Let her magic power your heart."

"I…can't. I hate being dependent on my mother's killer. It offends every part of my being."

He turned into me, draping his arm over my hip to hold me closer. I knew he wanted to distract me from my thoughts. He wanted me to give in, but I wouldn't. "I crave your dowry, love."

Love. He'd done it again, as if it were a declaration. Because it was. He loved me. My heart fluttered, and I forgot my irritation with him. Maybe I'd give in for just an hour or two. Eager to tease him back, I said, "And what dowry is that, hmm?"

A slow grin spread. "You come with an entire kingdom— a new kingdom for me to explore each and every day." He cupped my jaw and stroked his thumb over my mouth. "The bridge to paradise." He cupped my breast next. "The Mountains of Ash."

My breath caught, a giggle and a moan escaping in unison. Tomorrow. I would make my own declaration of love for him tomorrow, my gift to him before we parted.

Where would he visit next?

With languid satisfaction, he ran his fingertips along the center of my stomach and circled my navel. "The Valley of Temptation."

As I writhed underneath his touch, rocking my hips, he shifted me to my back and got between my legs. I peered at his beautiful face, at the dark hair in utter disarray, and gave a breathy moan. "Where else?"

"The Ocean of Nirvana." With a wicked gleam in his eyes, he kissed his way down...

Voices awoke me. I blinked open my eyes and realized night had arrived, our stall full of shadows. A convoy of memories—hours and hours spent in Saxon's arms—rolled through my mind, the queendom of Ashleigh, and my cheeks burned. The things we'd done to each other...

I hadn't known two people could use their mouths in such an intimate way. Hadn't known I would react so wildly. I'd loved how he'd watched me closely, gauging my every reaction to give me more of what drove me to the brink of insanity. My defenses had crumbled, baring more than my body—baring my soul. The glass heart I wanted to place in his hands.

I eased up, clutching a sheet to my naked chest as my hair tumbled around my shoulders. "Saxon?" I said, twisting to peer at—his pillow. Disappointment rocked me. Where had he gone?

Again, muted voices caught my attention. Voices...plural? Was he speaking to someone? Curious, I hurriedly dressed in a new garment Saxon had left for me—a soft blue gown that clung to my curves. It had open-ended pockets, allowing me to reach through them to grip the weapons strapped to my thighs.

Leonora remained blessedly quiet, yet I sensed her seething anger. She felt betrayed by Saxon and remained alert and aware, ready to pounce on me at a moment's notice.

I had to admit, subduing her had become easier and easier, my defenses against her strengthening as I did. The amour might have something to do with that. Or the more bonding magic I wielded. Or all three. Or none. I didn't know, but she was no longer able to assume control as I slept, and that was wonderful. It was.

I still wanted her dead.

Barefoot, I padded outside the stable. I loved the feel of dirt between my toes. As soon as I cleared the stable, the voices got louder. Golden moonlight spilled over the forest, blending with its natural azure glow, the dome down. I'd known it had to happen, yet disappointment flared.

So where was Sax—ah. There. He stood with two others, both of the dragons flanking his sides. And oh, wow. They'd doubled in size *again*.

One of Saxon's companions was a blonde beauty I'd never met, who wore a tunic with writing across the chest. That writing… I narrowed my eyes to sharpen my focus. "Hello, My Name Is Queen of Evil. What's yours?"

The Evil Queen?

The other companion was male and he—my jaw went slack. He was my cousin Roth.

My gaze swung back to the blonde. If Roth was here, and she proudly referred to herself as the Evil Queen, then she must be Everly Morrow. I couldn't make out what the trio was saying, but the three were obviously friendly, not the enemies Saxon had claimed them to be.

Was this the secret he'd kept? "Um, hi guys?" I called as I marched over.

The dragons looked my way. Their expressions plainly said, *We've got this handled, Momma, have no fear.*

Saxon reached out to motion me over, perfectly at ease. "Asha, meet my secrets. You've met King Roth. You also know him as Blaze the fae and the healer fae. My other companion is Everly Morrow. You know her as Eve."

What! The blonde grinned at me. A split second later, an image flashed over her features—another face. Everly, the sorceress I'd once wished to speak with, who supposedly loved Roth, was Eve the avian, a girl I'd liked and admired.

I staggered to a halt at Saxon's side. Well. No wonder he'd kept this secret from me. "Nice to officially meet you," I said, and Roth looked surprised.

Everly patted my shoulder. "I'm glad you finally awoke, sleeping beauty."

"I'm not the sleeping beauty. I'm the cinder girl," I said. The sleeping beauty fairy tale involved blood kisses, vampires and elves, a monster known as a phoenix, and the most evil of magic. I'd stick with my avian prince. "I'm embarrassed I didn't guess who you were. You syphoned your magic from multiple sources, didn't you?"

"Sure did."

Saxon snaked an arm around my waist, kissed my temple, and whispered, "I'm sorry I didn't tell you."

"I know. I understand." Leonora was to blame. I looked to Roth. "Cousin." Nod. "It's nice to see you're alive."

"Is it?" he asked, brows arched.

"I don't know. Give me a little more time to decide."

He grinned.

"I'm glad the truth is finally out." The sorceress hiked her thumb in Roth's direction. "I have a feeling you'll be seeing a lot more of us from now on, Ashleigh."

"You owe me a gold coin," I reminded her.

"Okay, okay." She dug into her pocket and tossed over a coin.

I caught it and put it in my shoe. My first payment. What a thrill.

"I just have one question," I said. "What was the original plan for me?"

Saxon closed his eyes and drew in a deep breath. When next he met my gaze, he evinced pure resolve. "I was going to have you bespelled into an eternal sleep and kill your father."

"The problem with eternal sleep is that it might only affect me, leaving Leonora to roam free. Is Philipp's murder absolutely necessary, though, or could he be locked up for the rest of his life? He has restitution to deliver."

Saxon, Roth, and Everly stared at me as if I'd grown a second head.

"What?" I asked. "I know he's a terrible person and an even worse leader. He usurped Roth's kingdom. He needs Dior to use up her magical ability just to fund daily operations. What will he do when an emergency occurs?"

Saxon caressed my cheek, radiating tenderness. "If possible, we will lock him up."

I couldn't ask for more than that. I didn't like my father, but I didn't want him dead if he could be saved.

Roth took a step toward me. "King Philipp may not have long to live anyway. Not as sick as he is."

Yes. He'd grown sicker over the past week. I'd recommended a food taster at one of the last battles, but he'd waved me away.

The dragons spit darts of ember-laced smoke at him, stopping him. They still weren't sure of him.

I petted Pagan and Pyre in comfort and support, both of them purring. "Are you the ones poisoning him, then?"

"No," Roth and Everly exclaimed in unison.

Then who was?

Twigs snapped as Ophelia and Noel sauntered over, joining our group. They were careful to avoid contact with the dragons. As usual, both girls wore leather tops and pleated skirts, with metal mesh mixed in, looking ready to rumble.

"Oh, good. The gang's all here." Ophelia clapped. "Let's get this party started, then. One, two, three, you're it." She pointed to us, landing on me. With a grin that made me shudder with cold, she waved in my direction.

Suddenly I couldn't move, my body frozen in place from the neck down. "Witch?"

"In case someone hasn't caught up yet," she told us, "the king knows about the ambush you're planning."

"What are—" Everly closed her eyes and dropped, unconscious.

Roth moved to catch her and collapsed beside her.

Saxon tried to push me behind his body, but he froze, too, his wings spread. He bellowed, "Witch."

The dragons screeched and jumped toward me, determined to shield me, before they, too, closed their eyes and toppled.

Fear and fury bombarded me, everything else forgotten. I screamed and fought. "Pagan. Pyre."

"Relax," Noel said. "They're only sleeping. And I'll be staying with them when you leave, making sure they don't torch the whole kingdom in a bid to find and rescue you—yet."

Relax? *Relax?* I struggled harder, giving it everything I had. *Help the dragons*, I beseeched Leonora. Here and now, I had no pride. *Please. Take over and help the dragons.*

Her laugh whisked through my mind. *—Why? I orchestrated this.—*

"What are you doing, witch?" Saxon snarled. A vein throbbed across his brow.

Ophelia sauntered around us, a skip in her step. "I'm doing my job, and thank you for making it so easy. The king has paid me a handsome sum to do a double delivery. Ashleigh will go to his dungeon, and you will go to the coliseum."

The dungeon? "What is he planning to do at the coliseum?" If he harmed Saxon…

"I will kill you for this, Ophelia," Saxon snarled. "Your corpse will feed worms, and your bones will be my trophy."

The witch's grin only widened. "First of all, I dare a worm to touch this. Second, I have a get-out-of-jail-free card, remember, Saxy? You won't be doing anything to me." She patted his cheeks as they drained of color. "But don't worry. I won't rub in my victory more than a little." She turned to me. "You're up first."

"Ophelia—" Saxon bellowed.

"It's time to blow this joint." She clasped my arm. "Sorry not sorry."

I looked at the avian who'd won my heart. He was still staring at me, all the love of the universe seeming to glow in his eyes.

"Ashleigh, I'll—" The forest vanished, cutting him off.

A dim, dank room appeared around me. Noooo. What had Saxon been saying? *I'll find you? I'll love you forever?*

I'll die for you?

Screeching, I spun, ready for battle. But the witch had already done as threatened. Ophelia had already locked me away, transporting me into a cell in the dungeon. I stood behind a wall of bars, the other walls made of dirt and stone, just like the floor. The only piece of furniture was a cot with a paper-thin sheet.

"Hello, Ashleigh." Standing outside the cell, my father hobbled from the shadows. He leaned heavily on a cane. Ophelia and Milo flanked his sides. Behind Milo—I popped my jaw. There stood Dior, staring down at her feet.

Leonora laughed and laughed, just as she'd done the day I was dropped from the sky.

Dior had been working with my father, too? My chest… nothing but a wound, every breath burning as if I'd inhaled flames. Ignoring the others, I cried, "Father? You hate me so much, you'll lock me away like a common criminal?"

"Your. Majesty," he intoned, lifting his chin.

Milo placed a hand on his shoulder, patting him gently before grinning at me. His smug expression said, *Game, set, match.* "In a matter of hours, the sun will rise and the loser of the dance will be announced. The final battle will commence immediately afterward. Thank you for doing your job and keeping the avian distracted as we moved our chess pieces over the war board."

Breath hitched. "How long have you known the truth about Saxon?"

"Since the beginning, thanks to my oracle." He coughed into his hand, spraying droplets of blood. "He will die today, along with his friends Roth and Everly. Finally, I will heal, the sorceress no longer able to syphon the power from me."

"You're being poisoned by Milo. I'm sure of it. He hopes to rule this kingdom with Leonora."

Milo made a chiding sound and rolled his eyes. "And who is this Leonora you speak of?"

Had no one told my father about the phantom?

"My oracle assures me a great evil is responsible for my condition," my father said, "and there is no evil greater than the Evil Queen."

Oh, I could think of plenty greater. My father, for one. Milo. Noel and Ophelia. Raven and Tempest. LEONORA.

"Why am I locked up?" I asked, trying not to panic.

"Because I cannot trust you to do what is right," he said simply.

Me? "What do you plan to do to Saxon?"

"I've made a bargain with his mother. I will arrange for him to be hailed as the strongest in the land, and in return, Tempest will slay him in front of witnesses, proving her right to rule the avian."

Betrayed by his own family.

"This depends on whether or not he survives battle, of course." Milo's grin returned and widened. "There's nothing you can do to stop this, Ashleigh. You should stop fighting the inevitable."

Words he meant in more than one way, no doubt.

My father frowned at the warlock. "Saxon will win. I command it so, and you will lose as you've been told, grateful I have spared your life. Then Tempest will kill her brother and lead the avian army against Roth and Everly, who plan to ambush me at the celebration ball."

"You think the other combatants are going to lose without a fight?" I forced a laugh, when all I wanted to do was cry. "You are a bigger fool than I thought."

Milo glowered at me. "Do you think my magic will allow any ending but the one I seek?"

His smugness had only grown.

"The one *I* seek," my father corrected.

"And Dior?" I motioned to my stepsister. "What of her marriage?"

He dismissed my words. "Dior will wed someone of my choosing—when the time comes. She's far too young right now."

Dior flinched but maintained the mousy pose.

"You mean she needs to stay by your side to continue making gold for you?" I asked.

He narrowed his eyes before telling Ophelia, "Go. Prepare for the day's festivities. There's still much to do. But first, send me back to my room."

A wave from the witch, and he vanished.

My chin trembled. The witch remained behind, alongside Dior. "Dior," I beseeched. She hadn't budged, just rocked from one foot to the other. "Please. If he can do this to me, his flesh-and-blood daughter, he can do this to you one day."

She glanced up, just for a moment, tears wetting her lashes.

"We don't have to do what we're told," I rushed out. "We are strong enough to make our own way. We can marry the one we love, not the one we're commanded to. We can live our wildest dreams. Dior. Please. We're part of the same fairy tale prophecy. We—" That's right. The prophecy. "You can be my fairy godmother right now." Anyone could, I realized. They just had to make the decision to help.

"I'm sorry," she whispered. "I'm told I *must* do this." With a whimper, she hurried down the corridor.

A new protest burst from me. "Ophelia. Good people will die." Gripping and shaking the bars, I told her, "My father is unworthy of your aid." He was unworthy of *me*, and he always had been. I only wished I'd seen the truth sooner.

"Sorry," the witch announced, "but there's only one way to get what I want, and this is it."

"What is it you want, then? Free me, and I'll help you get it. Or let me pay you." I collected the coin from my shoe and tossed it at her.

"A coin?" She scoffed.

With hesitation, I ripped off the ring my mother had given me—the symbol of Craven's eternal love—and pushed my hand through the bars. Anything to help Saxon and my dragons.

—*The ring is mine. Give it away, and I will kill everyone you've ever loved.*—

"Take it," I insisted.

More scoffing. "Why would I want Leonora's castoffs? The ring belongs to you. It was always you, never her." Ophelia held up her hands and stepped back. "I won't let you out, but I *am* willing to show you what transpires with Saxon. Because I'm a giver." After one of her infamous power-waves, mist rose from the floor and covered one wall.

Moving images appeared, as if I were staring through a doorway to another location. Those images formed a complete picture: Saxon and the other nine combatants were lined up shoulder to shoulder in the center of the battlefield as a crowd cheered. I flattened a hand over my stomach to ward off the newest ache.

The screen went black, and I shouted a denial.

"Before the final battle, they're going to recreate each of the dances for the audience. You'll get to enjoy every second from the comfort of your cell. Goodbye, Leonora." Ophelia offered a happy grin. "Tonight you die, once and for all. Tootles." With a pinky wave, she vanished.

27

Plans have gone awry.
A warrior is set to die.

SAXON

I stood in the center of the battlefield with the other combatants. At my left: Milo, the vampire, the fae, and the troll. At my right: the wolfin, two snake-shifters, a mortal, and goblin. There were still ten of us. The one who'd lost the courtship later won a chance to come back.

The sun had risen and fallen. I'd been here, frozen in this exact spot, for hours as a ghostly version of Dior and each of her dance partners whisked through the crowd, one by one. A magical recreation of each dance we'd performed during the second part of the semifinals, followed by endless entertainments.

On the royal dais, the king perched upon his throne, high above the spectators. He wore formal attire—a velvet robe, a red sash, and a bejeweled crown—and he held the royal staff. Dior sat in a small chair at his right, with Noel at his left. They'd arrived not too long ago.

I nearly roared with frustration, rage, and worry. Was Ashleigh trapped in a cell, as promised?

If my Asha bore a single injury…

I will never be able to gain sufficient restitution.

Get to Ashleigh. Just get to Ashleigh. Desperation clawed at me, raced along my nerve endings, and pooled in my cells. But I couldn't move. I remained frozen by Ophelia's magic.

How had I not realized the witch and oracle were plotting against me? *Fool.*

Milo smiled and waved to the audience as his ghostly figure waltzed Dior through the spectators. He told me, "Philipp wants you to win. I want you dead. Guess who's going to get their way? One way or another, you will die today, Saxon Skylair. So will Philipp. I will make myself king, and Leonora will be my queen."

Torches lined the entire stadium, their flickering golden light chasing away shadows. "To kill me, you'll have to survive the coming battle." I would do anything, cross any line, to defeat him and save Ashleigh from a life with a male who would seek her elimination so that he could liberate the phantom.

I needed to see for myself that she was well. She *must* be well.

The witch materialized a few feet away from us and acid corroded over my calm facade. She had her back to us, facing the king.

At her appearance, the crowd erupted into a new round of cheers.

"Where is Ashleigh?" I hissed at her.

"Safe from harm," she said easily, not bothering to turn around. "Why do you care, though? Haven't you figured out the truth yet? She purposely distracted you for her father, keeping you busy while he plotted your downfall."

"You lie." Leonora would do such a thing, but not Ashleigh. Her loyalty ran deep. "She would never purposely hurt me. So try again, witch. Tell me why you're doing this. What is the king paying you?"

She tossed me a banal smile. "I serve the greater good, Saxon. I've *always* served the greater good. Everything I do, I do for Enchantia's continued survival. One day, you'll even thank me. At least, Noel thinks you will. She wasn't one hundred percent. Let's roll the dice and find out, shall we?"

What did any of that even mean? "I will *never* thank you for this."

"Are you sure? You don't want Leonora out of your life once and for all?"

I stiffened. I hated myself, but still I said, "Not if her presence saves Ashleigh."

"And when Leonora has imprisoned Ashleigh in her own mind? What then?"

I threw a curse at her. "That won't happen."

"Are you sure?" When she cast me a glance, I thought I spotted a gleam of satisfaction in her eyes. "Even though I just lost a bet with Noel, I'm happy to tell you that there *is* a way to kill the phantom. And we can do it without hurting Ashleigh... eventually. At first, it's gonna hurt her *real* bad."

Milo blanched. "What are you saying, witch? You would betray me?"

"I would betray anyone," she replied. "Was that not clear? I thought I'd made that clear."

"Tell me," I commanded. I had to know. She'd made the same point Ashleigh had made, every time she'd time to convince me we needed to slay Leonora, no matter the cost.

"Win the battle," she said, "and I'll share the details about how to kill one and keep the other."

Which one of us did she address? "Tell me now."

She pursed her lips. "It might please you to know that Noel polled a bunch of random strangers about our situation, and asked if it was all right to hurt an innocent girl in order to kill an evil phantom. Apparently, polling random strangers is *the* best way to make a decision in the mortal world, so we thought we'd try it here. Most people gave an enthusiastic agreement. We probably should have mentioned your constant complaining about the process, though. They might have changed their minds."

"Enough nonsense. What did you mean by *hurt*?" To kill Leonora, they had to physically harm Ashleigh?

"I mean kill," she replied easily.

Kill... Ashleigh? "No."

"Never," Milo spat at her. "Leonora wants her body."

"What?" Ophelia said to me. "It's not like we can't bring Ashleigh back, probably. Also, I'm disappointed in your lack of trust in me. You shouldn't believe everything you see with your own eyes and hear with your own ears. A little unconditional trust in your witch would have been nice."

My eyelids slitted, my focus on her intensifying. "Are you trying to tell me that you're only pretending to aid the king?"

"Yes, witch. Is that what you're saying?" Milo radiated tension. "Which of us are you truly betraying?"

"Stop being ridiculous, boys. For the lastish time, I'm betraying you both."

No, I didn't think so. Not anymore. Not fully, anyway. There were nuggets of gold in the information she'd so casually offered me. Why bother giving me any help at all if she wasn't on my side?

Part of me actually dared to hope the witch wanted me to win this and save Ashleigh. But would I save her, only to lose her in an attempt to kill the phantom? And if I didn't kill the phantom, would Ashleigh grow to resent me?

Could Ashleigh be brought back from the dead?

Should we risk it, after all?

"By the way," the witch said. "If you hadn't guessed, the king has some real nasty stuff planned for you during the fight."

Didn't matter. Whatever was planned, I would win the coming battle. I wanted the information she possessed.

I wanted Milo dead.

The master of ceremonies announced, "Now that you've seen the dances, tell us—who disappointed you most? We want to know."

They were doing a punishment versus a victory. One of us would lose in the next minute or so.

The crowd erupted, shouting out our species. One word was louder than the others. "Snake."

Ophelia knew which one and twisted slightly to wave her arm in the creature's direction. He paled and shook. Soon, blood began to pour from his eyes, nose, and mouth. His knees buckled, and he collapsed. He didn't rise—he didn't move. The crowd cheered louder.

The witch dusted off her hands to signify a job well done. "Been wanting to do that for a week. Evil man. The worst in every way. He kept a harem of captives."

When the cheers finally died down, the master spoke again. "With our final nine in place, why wait for the last battle?"

More cheers. Ophelia winked at me. "If you're set on keeping Ashleigh, defeat Milo tonight. Otherwise, say goodbye to your love forevermore. You're not going to reincarnate again. Oh, and don't think to abandon the battle to get to Ashleigh. I swear to you now, I won't let you off this battlefield until you win. I've got three pieces of gold riding on your success." She vanished from the field.

Her words kicked me in the lungs. No more reincarnation? No more chances with Ashleigh? Never to see her again if I failed to win? Maybe Ophelia had lied. Maybe not. But I would win this battle. Nothing would stop me.

Aggression plumped my muscles and vibrated in my bones as the magic constraining my feet loosened, allowing me to move at last. I assumed a battle position: one foot in front of the other, knees slightly bent. With a one-two motion, I unsheathed the swords Ashleigh had made me. The one she'd had made for her father, and the one she'd made me specifically. They were lightweight with special features—spikes I could eject by pushing a button on the hilt.

"One will succeed, but all others will fail," the master of ceremonies announced. "Let's find out who's who."

Again the audience cheered. Bloodthirsty lot. What nasty surprises did the king have in store for me?

"Combatants, the time has come to win or lose." He waited until the cheers died before beginning his countdown. "In three...two..." A horn sounded.

We launched into motion, the roar of the audience fading to the background. I wasted no time, swinging my sword and ejecting a handful of spikes in Milo's direction. Three hit their mark, nailing him in the throat, the shoulder, and the stomach. He stumbled back, surprised, dropping his sword.

A few feet away, the vampire fell. The snake-shifter cut off his head, and it rolled across the dirt. That quickly. The fae tripped over his body, and the goblin hacked at him with an ax. The snake moved on to the wolfin, the two tangling together.

I advanced on the warlock, preparing to attack while he was down. Along the way, I bent down, plucked his weapon from the dirt and hurled it at the troll in the midst of a one-on-one battle with the mortal. Success. The troll went down and didn't get back up—because the mortal had used my aid to his advantage and slammed his sword into the male's groin.

The mortal's victory was short-lived, however. The wolfin had killed the final snake and now jumped on his back, reached around, and ripped out his jugular.

Unfortunately, Milo's wounds had already woven back together, his motions under his control once again. His magic... he was a type of healer, then. Good to know. Now I knew I had three ways to end him, with no room for error. Decapitation. A thousand small injuries to drain his power before I delivered a more substantial wound. Or deliver an injury so severe he *couldn't* mend it.

Blink. The goblin stood directly in front of me, his body like mist. Mist that *entered* me. Possessing my body, just as Leonora must possess Ashleigh's. I lost control of my body, and I couldn't wrest it back. Panic closed in.

On one side of me, Milo approached. On the other, the wolfin. Was the warlock working with the others to take me out? *Come on, come on.* I grappled with the goblin internally... *Come on.*

Milo grinned as the wolfin drew back his hand, claws bared. About to strike...

Grappling faster... Yes. My limbs unlocked, the goblin bursting out of me. He solidified as he stumbled, allowing me to grab him by the shoulders and yank him against me. The wolfin's claws raked through *the goblin's* throat.

The goblin careened backward, eyes wide, hands pressing against the wound as blood spurted. He collapsed, his battle over.

Take the others out. Get to Ashleigh.

Milo and the wolfin converged on me. The warlock swung and jabbed at me with his daggers. The wolf swiped those claws faster while snapping his razor-sharp teeth. I avoided many blows, but I took plenty, too, sustaining wound after wound.

The rush of adrenaline dulled the worst of my pain, keeping me steady on my feet. I landed just as many blows as I received, exalting anytime I made Milo bleed.

"Face it, avian," Milo taunted. "You cannot defeat me."

Urgency quickened my motions. Metal clanged against metal as I blocked his next jab. The wolf worked his way behind me, but I couldn't turn with him. I had to block another jab of the warlock's dagger and settle for kicking back my leg, slamming my foot into his groin.

He moaned and hunched over. I went low and spun, swinging a sword at each of the opponents on opposite sides of me. One blade swiped air, Milo jumping back. The other blade slicked through the wolfin's throat, his head flying off his body.

I faced off with Milo, the final obstacle in my path. We circled each other, both of us panting and splattered with blood. My feet dragged a bit; his didn't. He appeared to be receiving energy from an outside source.

"I won't let you have Ashleigh," I spat at him.

"I want nothing to do with her, only Leonora."

"You want control of her power."

"*I want what's mine*," Milo hissed. "I *am* powerful. I should have been born to rule. Leonora sees this."

Tone flat, I told him truthfully, "She's using you."

He swung at me then. I blocked, then drove Milo back pace by pace, swinging, swinging my swords without cease. He managed to block each blow, and with a single sword, no less; he had to move double my speed. Impressive. When I hit him with more spikes from my sword hilt, blood poured from little wounds on his chest. At last he began to tire, his breaths growing more labored.

His battle tells became more obvious to me—a rock back on his heels pointed to an incoming strike, and his gaze darted when he believed I had the advantage, as if he searched for a way out.

On the other hand, his eyes narrowed when he thought he had me cornered—like now. His lids slitted as he jumped up—

In every direction, thick spikes popped out from the dirt.

Two of them pierced my feet, slicing through one end and coming out the other. My back bowed, agony crashing over me. Acid in my veins, weakness in my muscles. Dizzy...

The ground-spikes were poisoned? One of my nasty surprises, then.

As Milo landed roughly twenty feet away from me—successfully avoiding the spikes, as if he had a premade map inside his head—I knew I had two options. Remain nailed to the dirt and allow him to behead me, or yank my feet free and finish the fight.

I roared to the sunlit sky as I yanked my feet free, one after the other. Black dots flashed through my vision...my mind felt as if I'd submerged it in boiling liquid. I flapped my wings to hover over the ground. *Need to focus. Need to see.* My ears twitched as I searched for a flat spot to land. Footsteps. The warlock approached at a clipped pace.

No, I didn't need to see. I was an avian; I'd trained for all facets of war, including fighting blind. I knew to remain aware of changes in temperature...whispers in the wind...vibrations as I landed—*Ignore the pain.* There. A vibration, a shift in the breeze.

I spun, swinging my swords, the tip of one slicking across some part of Milo's body. He grunted and fell back. I swung the swords in a wide arc, the blades traveling in opposite directions. Air. I swiped only air. A terrible pain ripped through one of my wings, the appendage locking in place. The paralysis traveled down one side of me and I dropped, falling on a cluster of spikes. More pain. Thicker black dots and greater weakness.

Though I wobbled, I struggled to my feet. Any advantage I'd gained was gone. *Must survive. Must save Ashleigh.*

Bellowing with fury, the warlock hammered at me with his sword. Again. Again. And again. Metal clinked against metal. "Die already."

I blocked every strike, but I wasn't sure how much longer I could keep going. My body was beginning to fail me, overrun by whatever poison had laced the spikes. My reflexes slowed.

Was I going to perish this eve? Denial screamed inside my head. *You will keep going. You will keep fighting.*

Every breath slashing like a dagger inside my chest, I blocked the next strike with a single sword. Milo grabbed my wrist, stopping me from swinging the second sword. A sword I dropped. Or rather, I appeared to drop. In reality, I'd pressed a second button, and the top layer of the sword thudded to the ground, revealing the dagger than had rested inside its belly.

The warlock loosened his grip on my wrist, thinking me unarmed. I angled my arm to shove the smaller blade in the area of his gut. Warm blood coated my hand. Shuffling footsteps sounded, and I knew he'd stumbled back, widening the distance between us. I sprayed more shards his way, and heard him grunt.

How much time did I have before his magic patched him up, allowing him to regroup?

At last my vision began to clear, light seeping through the darkness as I sweated out more and more poison. Relief cooled me down. And what perfect timing. Milo stood roughly a hundred yards away, pressing a hand to his bleeding belly. With a scowl, he launched into motion, heading straight toward me. He zigzagged closer, avoiding the ground spikes.

A plan formed. A risky one. Big risk, potential for big reward. So I did it. I let him come while pretending to still be blinded, purposely swinging my weapons at nothing. Midway, he launched a small rock toward the left.

Thud. I angled in that direction, following the sound as if he'd fooled me.

Close...

Closer...

Almost within range...

He threw another rock. The newest thud came from the right. Again, I angled the way he wanted. From the corner of my eye, I watched as he drew back his sword, preparing to deliver his final blow.

Almost—

Now. I flapped my broken wings with all my might and jumped. *Ignore the agony.* As he spun with his momentum, cutting oxygen, I tucked in my wings and dropped atop him. He crashed into the dirt, the spikes stabbing through his shoulders, abdomen, and both of his calves. Pinned.

At his cry of anguish, the crowd quieted, no doubt wondering what would happen next.

I stood before Milo, panting, as he struggled to free himself. Blood trickled from his mouth when he attempted to speak. To beg for the mercy he'd been unwilling to show me? To curse my name?

I was good either way. *Do it. Finish this.* Our gazes held as I lifted my blade. He opened his mouth to protest. I swung—

Just before contact, he vanished, leaving a pool of blood in his wake. A roar left me. I turned left, right, waiting for him to reappear…waiting.

"We have a winner," the master of ceremonies announced. "The warlock left the field without blocking his opponent's swing, an act that has disqualified him."

Had Ophelia magically transported the warlock away, denying me my right to protect Ashleigh? Rage burned through me, the only thing keeping me on my feet.

The crowd went wild, many individuals jumping to their feet, waving their arms. Colorful fireworks exploded in the sky, reminding me of the enormity of what had just occurred. I'd done it. I'd won the tournament.

Urgency ripped through me anew, and I took a step forward, ready to run. My knees gave out as if someone had taken a hammer to the back of them. I fell, landing with one knee up and one down. By an act of my will, I maintained a tight hold on my sword, using it as a prop, resting my forehead against the hilt.

The witch still held me on the battlefield. What would I be forced to face next?

The master announced, "The magnificent King Philipp invites one and all to the palace for a ball. We will celebrate the avian's victory with wine, food, and laughter."

New applause rang out, people pouring from the stands, hoping to be the first to drink the king's wine.

Ophelia materialized just in front of me—I recognized her combat boots, emblazoned with gold. She patted the top of my head. "All right, avian. Now that I've helped you again—"

"Helped me?" I roared, my head lifting in a rush.

"Yes. Exactly. You owe me so many favors right now, it's ridiculous. Oh, wait. You don't know all I've done. First, I ensured Ashleigh was safe during your fight. But I told you that already, yes? You're welcome. All the two of you did was complain. I let her watch you, and I'm sure she's all hungry for your sweet, sweet love or whatever. Guaranteed she's going to say yes to your marriage now. And that's just the tip of my scorecard. While my methods are questionable, I do what I must to elicit genuine emotional reactions from others in order to achieve a specific desired end. I always get the job done. So, let's get you to the palace so you can stab Ashleigh."

That was the way she was supposed to die, so she could come back without Leonora? My head shot up. "I will never stab Ashleigh. Not for any reason."

"Oh, really?" She scratched her chin. "Because Noel assured me someone was going to stab the princess, like, tonight. Wait. I see the problem here. No one explained how everything's gonna go down. See, Ashleigh is only just beginning to realize she can bond two things together. But good thing she has because she's got to bond Leonora to her body while severing her own connection to it, essentially becoming the phantom herself. Once we kill the body, its new owner will die. That's Leonora, in case you got lost. Ashleigh will live on, and she can bond with her body anew. Then, we can revive it with magic. At least, we hope we can revive it. The odds are forty-fifty but we're keeping our fingers crossed."

"Your math is off."

"No, the other 10 percent is for my certainty that everyone is going to die."

"I will *never* risk Ashleigh in such a way," I said, not needing any time to think this over.

"What did you imagine we'd do when I mentioned killing her?"

I didn't know, didn't care. My first instincts were right. We'd stick with subduing the phantom. "The cost is too high."

"From the beginning, Noel told you one would live and one would die. What is tonight is what will be tomorrow. There will be no going back. One measly death is a small price to pay for obtaining a happily-ever-after with the woman of your dreams, wouldn't you say?"

"Ashleigh's death is the *only* price I'm unwilling to pay. And I would be the one forced to pay it."

"Are you sure? You know three apple babies, and we're the best chance she's got." She shrugged. "The choice is yours. Just know fate has a deadline for the completion of every fairy-tale prophecy, and we're about to reach yours. You'll lose Ashleigh no matter what then. At least fate is helping us out right now."

"From my vantage point, I don't think fate has ever helped me."

"Then you aren't paying attention."

Could I do this? Could I trust that our fairy tale would end the *right* way at long last?

28

Are you ready to begin?
Who will die and who will win?

Ashleigh

Five minutes earlier

For the past half hour—what had seemed like an eternity—
I'd alternated between worrying about my dragons, watching Saxon fight, in awe of his skill, and squeezing my eyes tightly shut, praying the battle ended with the avian still breathing. A thousand times, I'd tried to pry open the cell door, and a thousand times I'd failed.

I had to get to Saxon. We had to get to the dragons. When it came to the safety of my babies, there wasn't anyone I trusted more than their father. There wasn't anyone I trusted more, period.

"You had an opportunity to become my fairy godmother," I said to Leonora. "You didn't have to remain my evil stepmother. You could have helped me save Saxon and the dragons."

—Why would I save Saxon? He gave me what I wanted only to take it away. So I will let you both die, and I will try again in the next life.—

"Didn't you hear Ophelia? There won't be a next life."

—You can't be sure of that.—

"Ah, yes. Denial. That will make the lies you tell yourself come true," I said. "Why can't you let Saxon go for good and find someone else?"

—Because he's mine, the only thing given to me by fate.—

"He isn't and has never been yours. You just borrowed him from me for a few centuries."

As the crowd cheered, I gaped at the scene now playing on Ophelia's magical screen, my heart about to burst with joy and worry. With the aid of my weapons, Saxon had just won the tournament.

Blood soaked him from head to toe, still leaking from multiple gashes. He looked magnificent. Like the glimpses of Craven I'd had in my memories, coming home from battle wearing so much blood his wings appeared red.

Saxon might have begun as my enemy, but he was now my best friend. He was the first person to see worth in me. The first person to look past my limitations and discover strength. The first person to love all of me. And he did love me. Craven Tyron Saxon Skylair loved me with every fiber of his magnificent being. Just as I loved him. I knew it.

Ophelia appeared before him, and the screen went blank. No! I ran over to beat my fists against the wall, but the screen didn't reappear. Well. I wouldn't remain in this cell, waiting for others to decide my course. I *would* find a way out, and I *would* save Saxon from whatever horrors they'd planned for him.

"Leonora?"

Milo's voice had me whisking around. He stood inside the cell with me, broken and bloody. His knees almost gave out, but he found the strength to remain upright and stumble toward me, arms outstretched. He coughed up blood. "Help me."

I backed up. There was a piece of paper pinned to his shirt, and it read, "A gift for you. Enjoy. —O"

Ophelia had transported him here as a gift for me? But why?

"Help me," Milo repeated, wobbling.

"Help you? The way you helped me?" Fury burned through me. I blinked, nothing more. The next thing I knew, I was standing before him, sinking one of my daggers into the hollow beneath his throat and twisting the blade.

My mouth began to move and form words I didn't want to say. "I guess you can't cast a spell of immortality. You should have listened to the girl. I never would have wed you. I only needed you to relay the information I wanted the king to know, and to weaken him so that Saxon could defeat him when the time came. I can give him what Ashleigh can't. The respect of his people. Your services are no longer needed."

His eyes widened. More blood. As his knees buckled at last, I dropped the weapon and stumbled back, in control once again and horrified with myself. He hit the ground and lay there, going motionless.

I'd just killed someone. A boy. A boy was dead. A boy was dead because of me. He'd been a bad guy, yes. But he'd been weaponless. I'd lost control of my body, yes. But... I should have been able to stop Leonora. She'd overtaken me so easily.

What if she did it again?

Could she, or had the effort cost her much-needed energy?

"You evil hag," I spat.

—*This is only the beginning. I'm going to ruin your life before I end it.*—

I needed to escape this cell. *Now.* If Leonora wanted to be here, I wanted to be anywhere else.

I paced the confines of the cell, sidestepping a single stalk of ivy that had grown through a crack in the floor, before inadvertently bumping into Milo's body and splashing in the pool of his blood. My stomach turned over, concluding the pacing portion of my day.

Think, think. How to save Saxon? How to circumvent Noel's foresight and get to the dragons? How to defeat the phantom once and for all?

What tools did I have at my disposal? The magical bracelet Saxon had given me, a possible ability to bind unlikely objects together in harmony, and the dagger. I could—

Leonora began to sing, loudly and off-key, to distract me. How smug she sounded.

How brilliant she was.

Hours passed, my thoughts too chaotic to align, my body growing more fatigued as I fought her. Midnight loomed. I hadn't eaten at all today, and I felt as if I had a mouth stuffed with cotton. My hands quivered, parts of me as cold as ice, others as hot as fire.

Verging on exhaustion, not knowing what else to do, I closed my eyes and drew in a deep breath, looking inward, past the noise. I imagined a life with Saxon. We would be husband and wife, king and queen, and we would have the dragons at our sides. Love for my family welled up, a sea of tranquility spilling through me. In that sea, reason reigned.

I shook off the phantom's fog of confusion. The first problem that needed addressing—saving Saxon. In the fairy tale, each time the evil stepmother and stepsisters had left Cinder behind, a fairy godmother had aided her. I'd noticed the same trend in my life. I'd acted as my own fairy godmother at times, but I'd also had help from Ophelia and Noel, Dior, Eve—Everly, and even Saxon.

Would I get a fairy godmother this time? Maybe anyone had the ability to be a fairy godmother and become part of the story; they just had to decide to help and follow through.

How could I reach out to let someone, anyone, know that I required aid? Someone, anyone, on my side.

The only one who might be free—big might—was Everly. Had she awakened from Ophelia's sleep spell? Could I awaken her if not? Saxon had always contacted her through a plant, but I had no idea where to find a plant in a…

I spun on my heel, seeking the ivy. Hope turned electric as I jolted into action, falling to my knees before the stalk that had grown through the floor. The tip of the leaf had browned, but the stem still had some green. Would she hear me?

I didn't know how it all worked, but I had to try. "Everly? Everly, I need you to focus on me, all right?" I shouted the words at top volume, just in case. "This is Ashleigh. Listen up. I'm in the dungeon at the palace, and I need your help. Saxon was gravely injured during battle. I don't know what my father is doing to him right now, but I do know he's planning to kill Saxon and Roth at the victory celebration. Please. Help me save the day or whatever." Sweet goodness. Now I was talking like her.

Silence. Waiting…more minutes passing… No movement. No stirring of magic.

Excitement dulled. Hope withered. I bowed my head, a heavy weight settling on my shoulders. Maybe she heard so many voices, speaking so many different things at once, that she had to sift through all the noise to pinpoint an individual voice. Maybe she would hear me…in a few days. Would she be too late? Would I?

Leonora laughed with more of that infuriating glee.

"One escape, coming up."

The familiar voice came from behind me and shut up the phantom. I leaped to my feet, my heart pounding like a war drum. Everly! Despite everything, she'd come for me, just like a true friend. And she was a friend, wasn't she? One of my closest.

She stood outside the bars, a pale-haired, silver-eyed hero in black leather.

"Help me out," I beseeched.

"Here's the deal," she said. "I will help you, and you will help me. We'll save Saxon and take back Roth's crown. Do I have your word?"

"Yes. You want my father? He's yours. You want vengeance against Ophelia and Noel? Maybe I can make them fall in love...with daggers." Could I bond someone's emotions to an object?

I thought I...could. I suspected I'd done it before, the memories buried in my mind with so many others, waiting to spring free as soon as there was room, the phantom gone.

"Ophelia and Noel aren't so bad," Everly said. "They've done what your father ordered to garner his trust. I think. I mean, the witch let me link with her, but she also cast a spell to ensure I couldn't hear anything he said, something she could have pretended to do. But then again, she takes pride in her work, and claiming to perform a spell but not doing so is very, very bad. If a witch can't be trusted, she can't sell her spells."

"The business lesson is nice, honest, but can we pause it so you can get me out of here? And where's Roth?"

She didn't speed into motion. No, she leaned a shoulder against the bars. "He'll be joining the party upstairs at some point, and so will we. He's just taking a route your father cannot predict. Also, Noel told me I won't be able to let you out until you confiscate the key from Milo's neck."

The key my mother had wanted? Did it unlock dungeon cells? I rushed over and crouched at the warlock's side. The leather cord hung from his neck. I trembled as I picked up the bloody dagger I'd dropped earlier and severed the cord to free the key.

What had my mother once said? *I used to have one just like it, and I wish with all my being that I still did, so I could give it to you.*

"Noel had one more message for you," Everly said. "Apparently your mother didn't have a key just like it—she had that exact one. She just used it to pay Milo's father for your barrier spell."

Truly? I gazed down at the iron key with a swirling end, tears welling. "Why would he perform such strong magic for fourteen years in exchange for this?"

"Because it isn't just any key. It can open any lock."

And Momma had wanted me to have it. Because she'd known, deep in her heart, that a day would come when I desperately needed it. "I have the key now, Momma," I whispered. Fate had struck again. How else could a magical key have come full circle, arriving just when I needed it?

Everly stuck her hand through the bars, a silent request for the key. "You want out?"

Yes. Deciding to trust her, I handed over the key.

Everly opened the lock, as hoped; the cell door disconnected and slid out of the way.

Relieved, I raced out of my prison. "Come on." I reclaimed my key and darted down the hall, expecting the sorceress to follow. *Let's get this done.* We would save Saxon. I would accept his proposal and pluck the crown from my father's head. Roth would reclaim his throne, and I would find my dragons.

My father had made a huge mistake today. Before, I would have left the kingdom and never returned, leaving him to his life. Now? He didn't have the strength to stop me. Because yes, I would be making use of Leonora's magic before I killed her, just as she had made use of my body.

I would kill her. I must. My determination had not wavered.

From behind me, Everly latched on to my wrist, jerking me

to a stop before reaching the end of the hallway, where the exit waited. "We need to get you ready for the ball, Cinder baby."

She waved a hand in my direction, a gust of wind hitting me full force. Tingles erupted, lights sparking all around me. My dirty clothes disintegrated in a flash, new garments already forming. But I wasn't wearing a fancy ball gown, as I'd expected. I was wearing the clothes of a warrior. A leather and mesh halter of my own, paired with a pleated leather skirt. I even wore an assortment of weapons—a sword, several daggers and—I gasped. A crossbow with collapsible sides. *My* crossbow. The one I'd designed. During my six days with Saxon, I'd come up with a way to reinforce every movable part. This one was made of gold so clear it appeared to be glass, with a chamber for paper thin gold pieces as long as my index finger, with razor-sharp tips. Upon contact, hooks sprang from those projectiles, embedding in whatever they entered.

Pride infused my spine. Lightweight sheets of golden armor had been strategically placed, interweaving with the leather and mesh. On my feet were a pair of combat boots rather than glass slippers. I. Was. In. Love.

"*The* fashion accessory every warrior princess needs," Everly said, smiling at the boots.

"Agreed. Now let's go." I opened the hidden door and entered the secret passage.

The sorceress followed, saying, "We need to come up with a good catchphrase for you. We're about to kick our way into your father's celebration trap, and a lady should make a proper entrance. Don't worry. I'll help you craft one." She fluffed her fall of pale hair. "They're kind of my specialty."

"I'm not sure I know what a catchphrase is."

"It's a phrase people will associate specifically with you. They'll be talking about it for years to come. As they should."

"What's yours?"

She smiled slowly, wickedly, and purred, "Mirror, mirror on the wall. Who will perish when I call?"

Chills ran down my spine. Okay, yes. I needed a catch-phrase. Because, she was right. This night *would* be remembered for years to come. It was the night a thrice-twisted fairy tale reached its conclusion.

29

Dance the night away.
Keep the misery at bay.

SAXON

Ophelia patted my shoulder, sending a shocking lance of strength through me. "Ready? The ball is soon to begin."

The shaking in my knees lessened. After our conversation, she'd disappeared for a few minutes, leaving me standing in the field, frozen. Whatever she'd done had weakened her.

Though strain tightened her features, she transported me to a spacious chamber with a handful of torches, shelves, and countless jars filled with eyeballs that stared at me. Where was I?

As a clock began to tick down in my mind, midnight closing in, I surveyed the rest of my new surroundings. A bedroom? From the bed frame to the dresser, every piece of furniture was made of solid gold. Gold coins were stacked everywhere, even scattered across the bed in lieu of blankets.

A piece of yellowed parchment materialized atop a pillow, and I limped over to snatch it up.

Dear Saxy,

Clean up. Change clothes. Or not. Up to you. Either way,
I'll be collecting you anytime now for a final showdown
between you and Leonora, with a bonus round between
Roth and Philipp. Don't try to escape. There are no doors.
The only way in and out is magic. If you steal or destroy
anything, I'll know and I WILL collect.

Love,

O

I crumpled the parchment in my fist and tossed it into the
hearth. There might not be doors, but the walls were stone. I
would make a door.

Wait for her to collect me? No. With a snarl, I snatched up
a golden brick and threw it at a wall. My body ached from
the strain, but I still managed to crack a stone. Emboldened, I
picked up another brick and hammered at the wall. The crack
widened. The brick shattered into pieces, leaving gold dust all
over my hands. I grabbed another brick.

I'd made my final decision. We would not be stabbing
Ashleigh tonight.

I'd meant what I'd said. I would take her however I could get
her. She would live. She would suppress the phantom because
she would want a future with me. We would wed.

Whack, whack, whack. *Ignore the pain.* Whack, whack. *Ignore.* Whack. *The.* Whack. *Pain.* Whackwhackwhackwhack.
Sweat poured from me as the crack grew. A hole formed. Not
wide enough to fit through, not yet, but soon.

Panting, I lifted a new brick, unsure how many I'd busted—

The room vanished, a new one taking its place. A curse exploded from me. I'd been whisked into the ballroom. I stood
on a ten-by-ten dais newly built in the center of the room,
facing the empty throne that was on a dais of its own. It was
clear the servants had been decorating for hours. Curly ribbons

hung from the ceiling. Vines and flowers wrapped around pillars, and countless candles glowed with golden light, scenting the air with a rose-infused perfume.

Above the king's throne was a large mirror, which let me see the double doors behind me. One of Everly's mirrors?

I dropped the brick, chipping the wooden platform, and tried to walk forward. Once again, magic anchored my feet in place.

Inhale. Exhale. "Ophelia."

The witch materialized in front of me, her strain less pronounced than before. "Yes, Saxon?" She scanned me from head to toe, noting my blood-and-sweat-soaked clothes, the gold dust seemingly glued to my skin, and pursed her lips. "Decided to attend the final showdown looking like death instead of man candy, did we? Well, okay, then. It's your fairy tale. But I'd stop fighting your confinement, if I were you." She patted my shoulder, just as she'd done before. "You'll be pleased to know the Glass Princess is alive and well and soon to arrive. She accepted her engraved invitation."

Another bolt of energy sped up my naturally swift ability to heal. Torn pieces of flesh began to weave together. I panted through the pain. "Ashleigh isn't like glass. She isn't weak. She's the strongest person I know." At birth, a phantom had possessed her. The equivalent of being dropped into a cauldron of boiling water. She could have hardened, like an egg. She could have softened, like a potato. Instead, she'd changed the water, like a coffee bean.

"Who said anything about being weak? I just paid her the highest compliment." She sauntered off, calling, "Get ready. Here come your guards. Can't you feel the excitement in the air? We're so close to the grand finale."

Footsteps sounded. I peered into the mirror above the throne, seeing the double doors open, ten armed guards marching forward. They climbed the dais to form a half circle behind me. No one said a word. Where was Ashleigh?

More guards marched in next, quickly followed by specta-tors with champagne glasses already in hand. The doors closed behind them, preventing me from checking the hallway for Ashleigh.

I received smiles, waves, and curses for defeating favored combatants. I clenched my teeth through it all. Where. Was. My. Asha?

Conversations blended together, until King Philipp entered the room through a side door and eased upon his throne. As everyone went silent, new tension stole through me, turning my limbs into stone. How smug he appeared. How happy. He even looked as if he'd recovered from his poisoning.

"Welcome, one and all," he called, his voice carrying throughout the room. "Thank you for joining me to celebrate the victory of Crown Prince Saxon Skylair, soon to wed my daughter Princess Dior." He held out his arm, and the princess entered from the same side door, her head bowed, her hands wringing.

Cheers rang out, throwing fuel on the fires of my fury.

I struggled against my confinement, midnight so close.

Suddenly a crash sounded, the double doors at my back swinging open again, flinging two guards across the room. Gasps arose, cheers dying. A hush descended.

Two females entered the room next. Everly Morrow, free of any disguise and—I jolted.

"Ashleigh." Muscles flexed in an effort to get to her. She wore the garments of an avian warrioress, her hair plaited in dark, elaborate knots. Her eyes flashed between brilliant green and vivid blue, and I nearly fell to my knees as dueling tides of relief and dread crashed over me. Ashleigh was indeed alive and well, but Leonora was fighting for control.

"Hello, boys. I mean girls. I mean everyone," Ashleigh an-nounced. She glanced at Everly, who nodded in encourage-ment. "I came here to eat hors d'oeuvres and kick butt, and they're all out of hors d'oeuvres." She awkwardly held out her hands, flames igniting at the ends, and looked at Everly for approval again.

Everly winced but also gave her an encouraging grin.

My chest swelled, breath sawing in and out of my mouth.

The king jumped up, no longer quite so smug. Had he expected a more subtle attack? He shouted, "Traitors to the crown. Attack. Kill the sorceress. Kill them both."

Attendees screamed and rushed for the doors—doors that wouldn't open. We were sealed inside. Thanks to Ophelia?

Protests rang out. My armed guards drew their swords as people stampeded in every direction.

Get to Ashleigh. Must protect her.

Adrenaline burned through me. Fighting…muscles straining…bones threatening to crack… Where had Ashleigh—there. We met gazes through the mirror. Blood pumped through me, thundering in my ears.

The fierce beauty stalked closer, those flames crackling at the ends of her fingers, spreading up, up her arms. Her shoulders. Her neck. Even locks of her hair caught fire, smoke curling from her.

She's mine. Anyone who neared her collapsed before they ever made contact. Body after body dropped, flesh blistering as it melted. The scent of cooked meat and burnt hair created a pungent stench, stinging my nostrils.

Guards tossed weapons at Ashleigh. Even as her clothes remained undamaged by the inferno, all the swords, daggers, spears, and clubs disintegrated before contact was ever made.

I watched her, never glancing away from her reflection, utterly entranced. Such grace. Midway, however, she stumbled, her eyes widening with horror. Though we were still oceans apart, she reached out for me, screaming, "Noooo."

I didn't understand. What—a sharp pain registered in my chest, every beat of my heart causing the torment to intensify.

In the glass, I saw the soldiers on my dais were dead, avian soldiers near the bodies. I saw the back of a winged woman, who stood before me. I jerked my gaze to her face. Tempest. She held a dagger. The dagger she'd pushed through my chest.

Betrayed? Defeated again?

Dying with every heartbeat?

"She worked with King Philipp to do what needed doing." Raven moved behind her, head high. "Half of your army did, too. Face it, son. You were never going to be our king. Twice was enough."

"I'm sorry, brother." A lone tear ran down my sister's cheek. She left the dagger buried deep in my chest. So deep she didn't need to hold it to keep it in place. "When it comes to Leonora, you are weak. You would have been our ruin."

Would have been. As if I were already dead.

I could *feel* myself dying, cold invading my limbs. Pressure in my torso. Quaking in my legs.

For six days, I'd lived with the woman I loved. I'd held her. I'd kissed and pleasured her. I'd talked and laughed with her. I'd played games with her. I'd trained her, and I'd encouraged her as she'd worked on her weapons. I'd known the sweetest peace.

I'd lived for the first and last time.

My dimming gaze returned to the mirror, to Ashleigh. She would be my last sight—I would not end my journey any other way.

She was on her knees, crying, shaking, because she knew what I knew. I couldn't be healed from this. The second the blade was removed, I was dead. Magic wouldn't be able to heal me fast enough. I knew this firsthand.

A moment of communion passed between us, when I projected the things I'd hoped to say to her after she accepted my proposal. *I love you. I'm sorry for every mistake I made with you. You made my life worth living.*

Goodbye, I mouthed.

Ashleigh shouted, "No." She lifted a small crossbow and hammered at the trigger. Tempest jerked, a hiltless golden dagger protruding from the tip of her boot.

In a rage, my sister fought to remove the blade. But it stuck, as if welded to a bone.

At the same time, Raven took a golden dagger to the heel. She couldn't remove it, either, no matter how mightily she tugged.

As they thrashed, Ashleigh threw back her head and screamed to the ceiling. The sound of it... More pain, rage, and sorrow than I'd ever heard. I cringed, warm blood dripping from my ears. From *everyone's* ears. People of every color, creed, and species stopped whatever they were doing to cover their ears.

Glass shattered, raining from champagne glasses and high arching windows. All but the mirror above the throne. In a blind panic, people scrambled to get out of the way. Armed guards attempted to corral the crowd without success.

Strength deserted me. My legs gave out, and I hit my knees. The dais shook, rattling my bones. All around, chaos ruled.

Dimming...

Another commotion broke out. Roth swung from a vine— through the mirror. One of Everly's gateways. His men followed close on his heels.

The second those soldiers were safely ensconced inside the palace, the vines retracted, filling the open spaces to prevent anyone from escaping.

Dimming... I returned my gaze to Asha. She wiped her tears and lumbered to her feet, determination stamped in her expression. Eyes narrowed, she stalked toward me once more, purpose in every step. Almost upon me.

Ashleigh punched my mother in the face with a flaming fist, and a screaming Raven fell. I had no sympathy for her.

Tempest prepared to strike at my princess, but Ashleigh slammed a fist dead center in the girl's sternum, just as I'd taught her. My sister screamed, too, her shirt smoking, the skin beneath it blistering upon contact.

Ashleigh dropped to my side, her flames vanishing. Tears ran down her cheeks as she looked me over. "Oh, Sax."

I lost sight of the rest of the world. Ashleigh was my sun, my every thought revolving around her. "I'm so sorry, Asha. Hurt you. Love you."

"Shh. Shh. Save your strength, my darling."

Blood gurgled from me. Time running out. I used my strength to caress her cheek, leaving a smear of gold dust behind. No, it wasn't gold dust. It was amour, so much stronger than ever before. "You were. Worth. Wait." Worth every trial. Worth...everything. I would have died a thousand more deaths with Leonora, just to have this one life with her.

Her tears came faster. "You're not going to die, Sax. You're going to live, and we're going to kill Leonora together. I'm going to marry you. So fight with everything you've got. I'm going to be doing the same." She reached out with a shaky hand to caress the side of my face, her skin hot but not burning. "This isn't the end for you. This isn't the end for us."

"Die already." Raven bellowed as blood poured from her wounds. She still hadn't removed the dagger from her heel, and it had immobilized her.

Ashleigh didn't look away from me as she raised the crossbow and fired another metal shard into Raven's abdomen.

Chin trembling, she dropped the weapon and reached toward my face once more, only to switch direction midway, aiming for the dagger still embedded in my chest. Except, she drew back once again. "*Be mine.* Never be hers. *I will give you one last chance*—Don't listen to her, Sax—*I will save your life, but first you must pledge*—No. Pledge nothing." She pressed her lips together, going quiet, her eyes flashing between green and blue so quickly I struggled to tell one from the other.

Ashleigh and Leonora were fighting for control. In that moment, I realized the truth. Ashleigh had been right. She never would have been truly happy with Leonora buried inside her. The phantom needed to die.

I tried to speak, to tell her I loved her one last time, how sorry I was that I'd failed us both so many times, but I only made choking sounds. A greater weakness than I'd ever known invaded my muscles...my bones.

"If you do not agree," she continued, eyes blue, then green, blue, green, "Do *not* agree. *I will let you die.* I can save you, just give me a chance. *Then I'll kill the girl.* Me not her." Two women speaking from one mouth elicited pure confusion.

I wasn't at my best, my thoughts as dull as my eyesight; I probably couldn't think my way off a floating log. Deciphering what they'd said was beyond me.

Once again, Ashleigh reached for the dagger—drew back—reached. I was just coherent enough to remember Ashleigh had wanted to touch me before Leonora had begun speaking through her. If Ashleigh wanted to touch me, Ashleigh got to touch me.

With the last remnants of my strength, I bowed my back to the best of my ability, lifting my chest the next time she reached for the dagger... Contact. Her fingers brushed the hilt of my sister's dagger, and the weapon...just...melted, and...and...what was happening? Excruciating.

I threw back my head and roared. I thought the metal might be cooling to form a thin layer of metal where my heart had been cut. Internal armor?

I wheezed every breath, my veins on fire. My vision blurred, clouded by the smoke that curled from my flesh. Sweat trickled from my pores. But...my heartbeat normalized.

I was healing? The metal had truly fused—bonded—to my heart, the two working together? Because of Ashleigh's magic? The ability Ophelia had mentioned?

My princess is stronger than all of us.

Soon, my heartbeat steadied. The smoke thinned, my vision clearing. What I found worried me. Ashleigh's eyes were flashing blue so swiftly, I could barely detect a hint of green anymore.

A roar more ear-piercing than Ashleigh's suddenly cut through the air, and nearly every occupant in the room became paralyzed with terror. Thick tension filled the room, silence descending—until Pagan and Pyre burst through what remained of the windows, entering the palace.

I heard a chorus of gasps and screams as the beasts flew over the masses, blowing targeted streams of fire to form a wall. Raven and Tempest rolled out of the way before the flames could consume them.

I clasped Ashleigh's trembling hand. She'd paled, her skin waxen, the fight with Leonora weakening her.

"She's decided...to kill you and...start over. Won't let her." Eyes flashing faster, Ashleigh wrenched free of my grip and scrambled back. She stumbled to her feet, and I lumbered to mine.

"It's all right, Asha." I reached for her. Noel's forever-ago prediction that all would be settled by midnight filled my head. That what would be, would be. Ashleigh had saved me. What right did I have to condemn her to a life with Leonora? Her happiness meant more to me than my own. What she wanted, I would provide. Always. "We're going to kill the phantom together, love."

She lurched back before I could say more. "Don't come any closer. She's winning." Then she grabbed her crossbow, turned and ran.

"Ashleigh," I shouted.

She didn't look back. One of her boots snagged on a fallen body and slipped free. She kept going, running on broken glass, leaving a trail of crimson in her wake. Too soon, she moved through the flames and vanished into the panicking crowd.

I picked up a fallen sword. As I cracked the bones in my neck, I scanned the room. People running. Bodies motionless on the floor. The avian who had followed my sister and mother fought Roth's men, and they were losing. The king and Dior remained on their thrones. While Dior kept her head down and rocked back and forth, obviously terrified, the furious king twisted this way and that.

He fights for freedom. His stepdaughter had turned his feet into gold. That gold was so translucent, it appeared glass. They must have been heavy because they held him in place as surely as pitch.

Pagan landed next to me and licked my face before her massive, scaled body heaved once, twice, thrice, and she spit out Noel.

Covered in slime, the oracle rolled across the floor. She climbed to her feet, shouting, "I said I wanted a ride *on* you, not *in* you. I had to use up the protective magic Ophelia bottled for me, even though I was saving it for a special occasion." In the midst of her tirade, she spotted me and reared back.

Good. She *should* fear me. They all should.

"Uh, pay no attention to what I just said. I'm *super* protected right now. In other ways. Yes, yes. Other ways. And, um, you don't know it yet, but you need me to save Ashleigh's life. So go kill Leonora before all our hard work is wasted."

Truth or a desperate lie? We would find out. "I will let you live—for now—because Ophelia did aid us. If you are lying, I will make your death a thousand times worse."

"I *can't* lie, remember? And also, I *know* you'll kill me if I manage to lie. Oracle." She tapped her temple.

Someone ran into her, and she stumbled, not quite so invulnerable without her witch friend or the protective magic.

When someone else closed in at a rapid pace, she spun, avoiding contact this time, telling me, "We did what we did to set our only viable shot at victory into motion." *Spin. Spin.* "Think about it. Everything we did and said elicited the necessary emotional responses to get you here, at this moment, with enemies and allies alike piled into one room, making the final battle unavoidable for any of you. You're welcome, by the way."

"Tell me where to find Ashleigh, oracle."

"Oh. That's easy. Just follow the yellow dust road."

30

Misery or happiness, what you seek is what you find.
Always move forward, never look behind.

Ashleigh

Despite my weakness, I continued moving forward, plagued by urgency. I was leaving a trail of gold dust in my wake. The same gold dust that had been all over Saxon's hands was now all over me, falling from my clothes as surely as the blood dripping from my wounds. With my physical weakness, I was losing ownership of my body. Bit by bit, Leonora was taking it from me.

She'd been shoring her strength, waiting.

The time had come to kill her—before she killed me. *But how?*

—*Why don't you use your magic to save yourself?*— Leonora's laughing voice filled my head. —*I know why. Because you can't. Your ability is pathetic.*—

Hardly. I'd used the bonding to help me earlier. When I'd screamed, a force had come over me, melding my voice with currents in the air.

The only thing I knew to do now was leave the palace before Leonora buried me. I just needed a little more time to figure this out. I fell, one of my feet torn to shreds by glass. I crawled. Crawling, crawling. Faster and faster. Putting one hand in front of the other, one knee in front of the other. Moving forward...weakening...

—*Just a matter of time now.*— Laugh.

Pyre landed in front of me, shaking the floor, and picked me up with her mouth, careful not to cut me with her teeth. With a little toss, she maneuvered me onto her back. Then she leaped into the air, blowing fire across the room.

"Good girl." I held tight to one of her horns. *Fast as wind...* "Put me down outside the room, baby, then go protect your father."

—*He doesn't get to break my heart and live.*—

Pyre busted through Everly's vines. Cool, fresh air enveloped me. I breathed deep...except, Ophelia had erected magical doorways outside every exit, and those doorways led right back to the throne room. We *couldn't* leave.

Tears welled, my options withering. I couldn't risk Leonora taking me over in here. "Put me down in that corner," I instructed, guiding Pyre toward a space clear of people.

The dragon landed where I'd requested, and I climbed down as smoothly as I was able. The more ground Leonora gained, the more my head throbbed. Any moment, I expected my temples to explode.

As Pyre flew off to help Saxon as requested, I fell to my knees, my legs unable to support my weight. Deep breath in. Out.

Leonora laughed. —*So close to your defeat.*—

"I would rather die than let you use my body again." I lifted my crossbow and moved the right lever, causing the sides to flatten, revealing a center blade I then pressed to the hollow of my throat.

Was this the end for me? I'd fought to survive all my life, but I wondered if I'd always been building to this moment of sacrifice. Was my destiny to die while the phantom lived on?

How fitting that it should happen with one of my own designs.

Cinder had gotten a happily-ever-after. I wouldn't. And that was okay, I decided, as long as Saxon got his. That would be enough for me. And if this was my last life, that was okay, too. I would be a worthy sacrifice for worthy people. Saxon. Pagan. Pyre. Even Everly, Roth. Maybe even Ophelia and Noel. Definitely Dior. My stepsister might have left me behind in the dungeon, but she must have done it to remain close to my father, so that she could help me during the ball. She'd kept him locked in place the entire time, unable to cause any more damage. I'd seen the results of her magic—she'd done it while staring straight at me, just before I'd made the trek to Saxon.

—*Your death won't change anything. I'll just inhabit another body until you're born again.*— She evinced confidence, but she'd stopped laughing. —*Put the blade down, Ashleigh.*—

Someone raced past me, stepping on my free hand. I hissed in pain, my body rolling in to protect itself. I maintained my grip on the weapon. Other stampeders followed the first, swarming the area. Someone bumped into me, knocking me to the side. I skidded across the floor before crashing into a group of people, who fell on top of me. Others tripped over us. Different screams blended together. A dragon roared.

More footsteps. I squirmed, wiggled, and crawled my way out from under the pile of bodies. My limbs shook. I threw a glance over my shoulder and caught Saxon knocking someone out of the way. He was stomping toward me, on a war path.

No, no, no. He was almost upon me. Crawling again, crawling faster…

Leonora's laughter started up again.

"Everly," he shouted.

Faster… The palace shook, nearly toppling me. Vines shot from the floor, pieces of marble flying about. Those vines latched hold of everyone around me and dragged them to Pagan and Pyre, who were herding the other terrified guests into a corner.

Then, Saxon was beside me. He bound my bloody foot before he scooped me to his chest.

"Put me down. Leonora is—*Hold me, darling. I need you to hold me.*" I forced myself to let go of the blade. The next thing I knew, I'd wrapped my arms around him, clinging to him as he carried me across the room. I felt the phantom readying her fire magic, intending to burn him alive. *Stop, stop.* "Saxon, please. Kill me or let me end myself before she uses me to kill you." New sparks flickered at the ends of my fingers.

The dragons finished their herding mission. Pyre held the majority of guests hostage on one side of the room, while Pagan herded our allies to the opposite side. Roth. Everly. Dior. Ophelia. Noel. As if they sensed my affection for each one.

Raven and Tempest broke free of the masses and sprinted for a door. I knew the magical doorway would lead them right back inside the throne room, but Pagan didn't. She flew over, landed in front of the avian, and blew a stream of fire directly into their faces.

"My eyes," Raven screamed.

"I can't see," Tempest shouted.

Around them, bodies created a sea of death over the floor. Many of them had burned to death when they'd tried to stop me from reaching Saxon. If we'd been in Fleur, they would have been placed in glass coffins and—

Glass. The Glass Princess. Another portion of my prophecy crystalized. I wasn't known as the Glass Princess because I might shatter. I was the Glass Princess because I could put a multitude of people into their graves at any time I wished.

Leonora gained even more ground. Flames spread up my

arms, but I waged war with the phantom to stop them, fighting with every fiber of my being. "Let me go," I pleaded. "Before she burns you."

"Listen to me, love," Saxon said. He picked up my blade. "If you force her to bond with your body and cut your own connection to it, we can kill her by killing your body. You could be raised with magic. That is the hope. Is that what you want?"

We could kill her, after all? By giving her my body? I would just hand it over on a silver platter? But...that went against every self-preservation instinct I possessed. "I want—" Just before I burst into flames, I unleashed my magic, bonding Saxon with the fire.

As we both caught fire, he remained unharmed.

His brow furrowed. "I don't understand. My clothes aren't burning. I feel...powerful."

For a moment, so did I.

—How...?— Even the phantom was baffled, not understanding what I'd done.

"The bonding magic," Ophelia explained with a grin.

"Ashleigh," my father shouted from the throne. He hadn't been herded to one side of the room like everyone else because he couldn't lift his heavy golden shoes. "Ashleigh," he repeated. "Help me. Please."

I spared him the barest glance and called from the flames, "I'd love to help you, Father, but I'm just too...me."

Saxon shuddered with relief as the fire began to die. As those flames were finally extinguished, however, the strength I'd gathered abandoned me completely.

I had a choice to make. Temporarily give Leonora my body, risking her taking over for good?

If I was going to die either way...

I would rather die trying to take the phantom with me.

"Kill...her," I managed to rasp.

Saxon flinched, but nodded. "Pagan," he shouted. "I need my friends."

As my beautiful baby allowed our allies to slip free of the corner and approach us, I got busy, magically stitching Leonora's essence to my body.

—*What are you doing? Stop.*—

"Noel?" Saxon snapped.

"Put her down," the oracle commanded. "Everyone else, form a circle around her and clasp hands. As you heard, Ashleigh has the magical ability to bond two things that do not belong together. That's how she and Saxon lived twice before. The first Ashleigh did not die when the phantom overtook her; she was always in there, working behind the scenes, just as the phantom Leonora did during this life. She figured out her magical ability and fused a piece of her heart to Saxon's. Fate recognized her sacrifice and took care of the reincarnations, giving you other chances to recover what Leonora had stolen, since your hearts are so entwined, but the connection grows thin, unable to thrive in another life. Now, we're going to wait as she gives Leonora her body. Just for a few minutes. Ashleigh, whenever you're ready."

"Let go, love," Saxon cooed. "I've got you."

"Almost...done," I told him. Any second now, I would lock Leonora's connection and cut mine, the pieces now in place. "Need space." I didn't want him anywhere near Leonora.

He kissed my temple. As gently as possible, he laid me on the floor and remained crouched at my side. Roth, Everly, Dior, Noel, and Ophelia formed a circle around me. The entire group clasped hands, as ordered.

—*This isn't going to work. I cannot be killed. I've been inside dying bodies before.*— Despite her words, she sounded nervous.

Flames flickered at the tips of my fingers. Saxon pressed his hands against mine to snuff out the flames, and the bond held. He remained unharmed.

Let the fire rage. Let the flame purify.

"Now," I screamed.

With a final stream of magic, I gave Leonora my body and severed my connection to it. I lost all physical sensation. Suddenly, I was just…floating inside Leonora's mind, watching the world through her eyes.

"I'm sorry, Asha, but there's no other way." Tears ran down Saxon's cheek as he lifted my dagger with a shaky hand.

"Wh-what are you doing?" I heard my voice, but I was not speaking. Leonora was. "Saxon, please don't hurt me. I'm Ashleigh. Your Asha."

He held her down with one hand and pressed the blade to her heart with the other.

"Please," she begged.

His tears fell faster. He stared at her—at me, his heart in his eyes. Our heart. The others offered encouragement, but he grunted and shook his head. "No. I can't. I can't hurt you, even now. I love you, Asha."

No! If Leonora could control my body without a bond, I could hers. And I should have more success, since I was the original owner.

"Don't forget to bond with your body when she's dead," Ophelia called. "We'll do the rest."

"Now, Ashleigh," Noel shouted.

The clock struck midnight—*Ding.*

I managed to smile at him.

Leonora's voice filled my essence, and I knew she was screaming her thoughts at me, the way I'd done to her. "This will not work. This will not work. Don't—"

Ding.

Empowered by my success, I arched my back—sinking the blade into my chest.

31

SAXON

D^{ing.}

Ashleigh—Leonora—screamed, the sound of her pain and anguish almost more than I could bear.

The dragons squawked with fear and fury.

"Heal her," I shouted.

Ding.

"Not yet," Noel snapped.

Leonora peered up at me through her own blue eyes, but she had Ashleigh's face, and I couldn't hate her in this moment.

She parted her lips. Blood gurgled out.

I took her hand and squeezed tight. Could Ashleigh feel me in there?

We waited as Leonora fought the pull of death, her breaths coming faster, shorter. Then...

Her head lolled to the side and her body went lax.

"Now." I sprang out of the way, allowing the others to do their part.

"Roth," Noel snapped. "You're up."

The true and rightful king of Sevón commanded, "Your body will mend itself, Ashleigh Skylair, future queen of the Avian, Queen of Glass."

Ding.

"Come on, love," I said. "Come on. You can do this."

"Ophelia, Everly," the oracle snapped. "Flood her with your best healing magic. Apples, unite!"

The two females knelt on opposite sides of Ashleigh, each one taking her hand. They closed their eyes, focusing on their task.

I remained on my knees, unable to stand. If this failed…

This couldn't fail.

Ding.

The sorceress and the witch fell back, both pale and trembly.

Ding.

"Ashleigh. Love." I scrambled to her side and pressed my lips against hers. Her skin was cold to the touch. "Come back to me. Without you, I have nothing. Without you, I *am* nothing. Come back."

Ashleigh sucked in a mouthful of air, and I stopped breathing, willing to give her mine. Her eyelids popped open, her irises—I roared with denial. Her irises were bright blue. *Leonora's* eyes.

We…we *had* failed. We'd killed my precious Ashleigh. I pulled at hanks of my hair. I would burn this world to the ground.

Ding.

"Saxon," Roth called, pausing my tirade. "Look."

The excitement in his voice shut me up. I shot my gaze down, experiencing a strange tugging in my chest. The blue was fading from her eyes, a beloved shade of emerald taking its place. Finally, there was no blue at all.

Leonora was gone. The phantom was gone!

Ashleigh blinked rapidly. Her brows drew together, and she frowned. "I'm alive?"

"Asha." I gathered her close, easing her into a seated position. "Yes, you're alive. You're alive and you're you. We did it. We killed Leonora."

"She's dead?" With a sob, she threw her arms around me and held on as if she were clinging to a rope in rushing waters. "She is. She's dead. I can't feel her anymore."

Ding.

The final strike, announcing the arrival of midnight. "We finally survived our fairy tale." I held her tighter, so thankful for all we'd won.

When Ashleigh's sobs stopped, she sniffled and offered me a watery grin. "You're happy." She held up a hand covered with my amour.

"Very." I drew back to wipe away the teardrops clinging to her cheeks. "I produce it for you and you alone. My fated queen."

"So it's more than happy dust? And it's all mine, and no one else's?" Her grin widened into the sweetest smile. "I love you so much, and I promise only to sell the dust if our coffers get low. We have dragons to feed."

I snorted. "You are too possessive of your avian to share his dust."

She groaned. "I am, aren't I?"

"I love you so much, too," I said, grinning.

Without Leonora's influence, Ashleigh's eyes sparkled more brightly. Her skin glowed with new health and vitality. Even her hair seemed to possess a greater luster.

"Now that I'm Leonora-free, I'm happy to say I will make you the happiest man in the world and marry you."

About that… I needed to tell her we were married already. And I would. After I'd eased her into it.

"I'm so proud of you. I'm thankful you took a chance on me. I'm humbled that you gave your life for mine so many times, in so many ways."

She pressed her forehead to mine, and I cupped her cheeks. "I'm proud of you, too. You overcame centuries of distrust and hate, allowing your heart to love again. You fought for me, and you showed me I have worth."

"All hail the Glass Queen and avian crown prince!"

The pronouncement came from Ophelia and Noel, who knelt and bowed their heads in our direction. I swept my gaze over the entire room. The vines receded from the doors and windows. As the dragons rushed to Ashleigh to lick her face, guests and guards hurried to escape. Some of the guards, anyway. Others faced Roth and dropped to bended knee, as if awaiting his orders.

"All hail King Roth!"

Ophelia lifted her head and called, "And just like that, all is right in the kingdom. All thanks to a plucky oracle and an exquisite witch."

"Exquisite oracle and plucky witch," Noel corrected. "And all is right in the kingdom…for now. We all know the next fairy tale has already kicked off—no? Just me? I'm the only one who knows?"

The witch winked, then dusted off her hands in a job well done. "Until next time." She blew a kiss and vanished.

Roth stalked to the royal dais and swiped the crown from Philipp's head.

The former king shrank back like the coward he was. "Wh-what are you going to do to me?"

My friend looked to Ashleigh, telling her, "His fate rests in your hands, Queen Skylair."

436

"Why is everyone calling me Queen Skylair? We're only just now engaged," she remarked, a little dazed.

"I guess I'm not going to ease you into this," I said, and cringed. "We're already married. As soon as you voiced your acceptance of me, we were married in the eyes of the avian. But we can have a long postwedding engagement, if you'd like."

She grinned again. "You can't get enough of me. You had to get your bracelet on me so you could keep me forever. You want me with you always."

"I do. I really do."

She gave me a kiss before telling Roth, "Lock my father in the dungeon." Turning her focus to her stepsister, she said, "Your mother has no right to the crown. As Philipp's heir, I'm the new ruler of Fleur. That's law. But I would like to offer the crown to you and give you the right to choose your own destiny. Your mother can serve as your advisor, if you wish." I remembered what she'd said, how the woman expected her to be perfect. "Or you can kick her out. Up to you. The avian require a full-time queen, so I'm going to live there. It's my destiny." Ashleigh turned toward me, expectant. "I'll be a good queen this time, I swear it."

"You'll be a great one," I said, more in love with her in that moment than ever before. Strong of heart? Oh, yes. Fast as wind? When she rode on the back of her dragons, there was no one faster. Unwilling to bend? She'd wanted me, and she'd done everything in her power to help us find each other again. "Though you are now considered my wife, *I* am not fully, technically your husband until you give me a bracelet in return. Which you can do anytime you wish. Whenever you're sure of—"

She ripped off her blacksmithing bracelet and shoved it on my wrist so quickly, I laughed. "I love you," she told me. "I meant what I said. I'd like to live with you and our dragons in the Avian Mountains and rule together. Our soldiers could use some manners. I can make my weapons and armor and help you make more of your amour dust."

"Nothing would make me happier, love." I would start by banishing the soldiers who'd aided my mother. Hurt my precious queen and suffer. Raven and Tempest would be imprisoned.

Ashleigh kissed the tip of my nose, the corner of my mouth, my jawline. "I miss our dome."

I groaned. "So much."

Dior cleared her throat, gaining our attention before we got too intimate. "I accept your offer," she told Ashleigh, "but I'll need other advisors. An entire team. And an army. The gold, I'll be able to handle. I'm the slipper maker, after all." She laughed, a tinkling sound. "Everyone assumed I was Cinder, but I wasn't and wasn't meant to be. All along I was the maker of the slippers."

"I know just the advisor," I said. "As a fae prince, Vikander had to learn how to manage a kingdom at a young age. He can answer any questions you might have." Thus fulfilling the bargain we'd made during our mountaintop breakfast.

Her cheeks reddened, but she nodded eagerly. "Thank you. Yes. I want him—I mean, I need him."

I peered down at my wife, the love of my lives. "My beloved Cinder," I said.

"My honorable-dishonorable prince." She grinned. "The third time, we got it right."

I grinned right back, and suspected I'd be grinning about something for the rest of this life.

I kissed her deeply, then. True love's kiss, one of respect and admiration, desire and promise. We hadn't had the greatest start in life—in any of our lives—but I knew beyond any doubt that we would have the most amazing end.

Her strength infused us both. Weak heart? No. Oh, no. My Asha had the heart of a dragon. She loved fiercely, with a fire of her own burning in her veins. She was a queen who didn't need a king in order to rule her people—but thankfully she wanted one. It was a role I would happily fill for ever, ever after.

EPILOGUE

Soft music played in the background as Saxon—my beloved husband and the new king of the avian—twirled me around the dance floor. Just like our fairy tale, he had eyes only for me. I'd lived in the Avian Mountains for two months now, and I'd honestly never been happier. I knew Saxon felt the same. He smiled and laughed all the time. Plus, he never went to bed without telling me so. I always preened afterward.

Our dragons had moved in with us, of course. This particular palace was perfect for them, offering wide-open spaces for wings, with landing pads on every floor, inside and out. Right now, my babies perched next to our thrones, keeping a sharp eye on everyone who watched us dance.

For the bargain price of getting to live another day, Ophelia and Noel had vowed to never work against us, for any reason. Roth and Everly had moved back into their palace in Sevón, with Everly using her mirrors to go back and forth between the palace and the Enchantian Forest. As a wedding present and housewarming gift, Dior had turned parts of our palace into gold before returning to Fleur. In thanks, my family of four had flown her there. I had ridden Pagan, Dior had ridden Pyre, and Saxon had kept pace between us.

Life without Leonora was incredible. My mind was my own. I didn't have to worry about a takeover attempt in the middle of the night, or losing precious moments with Saxon.

I'd met my real stepmother, a woman just as uptight as advertised, but she had a good heart. I'd really liked her. She'd been relieved to learn her husband resided in the palace dungeon in Sevón, with Raven and Tempest in cells of their own here in the mountains, and she'd begun to relax.

I'd met my second stepsister Marabella, as well. A firecracker with enough spirit to rival Ophelia, Noel, and Everly put together. She liked to talk as much as Dior, but she did it at a much faster pace and just...never...stopped. I loved her. And I was glad the three women would take over Fleur. The kingdom had never been my home. The people didn't know or respect me, but they knew and respected my stepsister. They would thrive with her.

Could I have won their respect? Yes. Never again would I doubt my abilities to do *anything*. Look at everything I'd accomplished so far. And really, I felt as if fate had always wanted me in the Avian Mountains. I belonged here. I adored the height and width of everything. Such grandeur. So much larger than life. I was coming to learn the avian were social creatures who loved color, tradition, and light. Things I hadn't even known I needed.

Some of the avian—most—were still leery of me. Word had spread about who I used to be. But that was all right. In time, I would win everyone over.

"Have I told you today how much I love you?" Saxon nuzzled his cheek against mine.

"Many times, but I'll never tire of hearing it." Each morning he'd presented me with a new gift. A sheet of precious metal. My own personal forge. An entire collection of jewelry.

A wardrobe filled with beautiful clothes, both for battle and balls. A unicorn of my own. Books on the subjects he knew I enjoyed. Feathers, all blue. I swear, I thought he'd plucked himself bald for a week, just so I could make another dress.

In turn, I'd given him an arsenal of weapons and a full suit of armor, all designed and crafted by the one and only Queen Ashleigh Skylair. As I'd savored our time together, I'd realized every life had the potential to be a fairy tale. As for me? I didn't need a happily-ever-after anymore. When I found the joy in every step of my journey, I always had a happily-right-now.

"I love you more than this kingdom. I love you more than anything," he told me.

"Then you almost love me as much as I love you," I teased him, and the corners of his lips twitched.

Our beginning might have been violent and awful, but our right now was amazing. Together, we would only get better.

But now I couldn't help but wonder…whose fairy-tale prophecy would come true next?

★ ★ ★ ★ ★

This twisted tale of Cinderella has reached its end.
But even now, a brand-new story is being penned.
One with adventure, romance, betrayal, and more,
For all of Enchantia will soon erupt in war.